Praise fo

'Deaver is a terrific storyt
a rollercoaster of suspense, violence and mystery'
Daily Telegraph

'The best psychological thriller writer around' *The Times*

'Jeffery Deaver is a master at crafting intricate crimes that are solved through guile, tenacity and sheer creative genius.'
Harlan Coben

'Dazzling' *New York Times*

'The most creative, skilled and intriguing thriller writer in the world . . . [Deaver] has produced a stunning series of bestsellers with unique characterisation, intelligent characters, beguiling plots and double-barrelled and sometimes triple-barrelled solutions' *Sunday Telegraph*

'A master of suspense' *Guardian*

'Brilliant' *The Sunday Times*

Also by Jeffery Deaver

Mistress of Justice
The Lesson of Her Death
Praying for Sleep
A Maiden's Grave
The Devil's Teardrop
The Blue Nowhere
Garden of Beasts
The Bodies Left Behind

THE RUNE SERIES

Death of a Blue Movie Star
Hard News

THE LOCATION SCOUT SERIES

Shallow Graves
Bloody River Blues
Hell's Kitchen

THE LINCOLN RHYME THRILLERS

The Bone Collector
The Coffin Dancer
The Empty Chair
The Stone Monkey
The Vanished Man
The Twelfth Card
The Cold Moon
The Broken Window

THE KATHRYN DANCE THRILLERS

The Sleeping Doll
Roadside Crosses (July 2009)

SHORT STORIES

Twisted
More Twisted

JEFFERY DEAVER

Speaking In Tongues
and
Manhattan Is My Beat

HODDER

Speaking In Tongues first published in the USA in 2000
by Simon & Schuster
Speaking In Tongues first published in Great Britain in 1999
by Hodder & Stoughton
An Hachette UK company

Manhattan Is My Beat first published in the USA in 1989
by Bantam
Manhattan Is My Beat first published in Great Britain in 2000
by Hodder & Stoughton
An Hachette UK company

This Hodder paperback edition 2009

1

A CIP catalogue record for this title is available from the British Library

ISBN 978 0 340 97720 0

Typeset in Plantin Light by Palimpsest Book Production Limited, Grangemouth, Stirlingshire

Printed and bound by Clays Ltd, St Ives plc

Hodder & Stoughton policy is to use papers that are natural, renewable and recyclable products and made from wood grown in sustainable forests. The logging and manufacturing processes are expected to conform to the environmental regulations of the country of origin.

Hodder & Stoughton Ltd
338 Euston Road
London NW1 3BH

www.hodder.co.uk

JEFFERY DEAVER

Speaking in Tongues

HODDER

In the beginning was the Word.
Man acts it out. He is the
act, not the actor.

—Henry Miller

I

THE WHISPERING BEARS

Chapter ONE

Crazy Megan parks the car.

Doesn't want to do this. No way.

Doesn't get out, listens to the rain . . .

The engine ticked to silence as she looked down at her clothes. It was her usual outfit: JNCO jeans. A sleeveless white tee under a dark denim work shirt. Combat boots. Wore this all the time. But she felt uneasy today, in this stuff. Embarrassed, wished she'd worn a skirt at least. The pants were too baggy. The sleeves dangled to the tips of her black-polished fingernails and her socks were orange as tomato soup. Well, what did it matter? The hour'd be over soon.

Maybe he'd concentrate on her good qualities – her wailing blue eyes and blond hair. Oh, and her boobs too. He *was* a man.

Anyway, the clothes covered up the extra seven . . . well, all right, ten pounds that she carried on her tall frame.

Stalling. Crazy Megan doesn't want to be here one bit.

Rubbing her hand over her upper lip, she looked out the rain-spattered window at the lush trees and bushes of suburbia. This April in northern Virginia had been like June or July and ghosts of mist rose from the asphalt. It was so deserted here. She'd never noticed that before.

Crazy Megan whispers, *Just. Say. No. And leave.*

But she couldn't do that. Mega-hassle.

She took off the wooden peace symbol dangling between her breasts and flung it into the back seat. Megan brushed her hair with her fingers, pulled it away from her face. Her ruddy knuckles seemed big as golf balls. A glance in the rear-view mirror. She wiped off the black lipstick, pulled the blond strands into a ponytail, secured the hair with a green rubber band.

Okay, let's do it. Get it over with.

A jog through the rain. She hit the intercom and a moment later the door latch buzzed.

Megan McCall walked into the waiting room where she'd spent every Saturday morning for the last seven weeks. Ever since The Incident. She kept waiting for the place to become familiar. It never did.

She hated this. The sessions were bad enough but waiting really killed her. Dr Hanson *always* kept her waiting. Even if she was on time, even if there were no other patients ahead of her, he always started the session five minutes or so late. It pissed her off but she never said anything about it.

Today, though, she found the new doctor standing in the doorway, smiling at her, lifting an eyebrow in greeting.

'You're Megan?' the man said, offering an easy smile. 'I'm Bill Peters.' He was about her father's age, handsome. Full head of hair. Hanson was bald and looked like a shrink. This guy . . . *Maybe a little George Clooney*, Crazy Megan decides. Her wariness fades slightly.

And he doesn't call himself 'Doctor'. Interesting.

'Hi.'

'Come on in.' He gestured. She stepped into the office.

'How's Dr Hanson?' she asked, sitting in the chair across from his desk. 'Somebody in his family's sick?'

'His mother. An accident. I hear she'll be all right. But he had to go to Leesburg for the week.'

'So you're like a substitute teacher?'

He laughed. 'Something like that.'

'I didn't know shr— therapists took over other patients.'

'Some don't. Dr Hanson likes continuity.' He paused, as if he weren't sure she knew what it meant.

Dr Peters – *Bill* Peters – had called yesterday after school to tell her that Hanson had arranged for him to take over his appointments and, if she wanted, she could make her regular session after all. *No way,* Crazy Megan had whispered at first. But after Megan had talked with Peters for a while she decided she'd give it a try. There was something so comforting about his voice. Besides, baldy Hanson wasn't doing diddly for her. What a loser. All she remembered about the sessions was her lame bitching about school and about being lonely and about Amy and Josh and Brittany, and Hanson nodding and saying she had to be friends with herself. Whatever the hell that meant.

'This'll be repeating some things,' Peters now said, 'but if you don't mind, could we go over some of the basics?'

'I guess.'

He asked, 'It's Megan *Collier*?'

'No, Collier's my father's name. I use my mother's. McCall.' She rocked in the stiff-backed chair, crossing her legs. Her tomato socks showed. She planted her feet squarely on the floor.

'You don't like therapy, do you?' he asked suddenly.

Hanson had never asked that. Wouldn't ask anything so blunt. And, unlike this guy, Hanson didn't look into her eyes when he spoke. Staring right back, she said, 'No, I don't.'

He seemed amused. 'You know why you're here?'

Silent as always, Crazy Megan answers first. *Because I'm fucked up, I'm dysfunctional. I'm a nutcase. I'm psycho. I'm loony. And half the school knows and do you have a fucking* clue *how hard it is to walk through those halls with everybody looking at you and thinking, Shrink bait, shrink bait.* Crazy Megan also mentions what just plain Megan would never in a million years tell him – about the fake computerized picture of Megan in a straitjacket that made the rounds of Jefferson High two weeks ago.

But now Megan merely responded, ''Cause if I didn't come to see a therapist they'd send me to Juvenile.'

When she'd been found, drunk, strolling along the catwalk of the municipal water tower two months ago she'd been committing a crime. The county police got involved and it turned messy. But finally everybody agreed that if she saw a counsellor the commonwealth's attorney wouldn't press charges.

'That's true. But it's not the answer.'

She lifted an eyebrow.

'The answer is that you're here so that you can feel better.'

Oh, please, Crazy Megan begins, rolling her crazy eyes.

And, okay, it was way stupid, his words themselves. But . . . but . . . there was something about the *way* Dr Peters said them that, just for a second, less than a second, Megan believed that he really meant them. This guy's in a different universe from Loser Elbow-Patch Hanson.

He opened his briefcase and took out a yellow pad. A brochure fell out on to the desk. She glanced at it. A picture of San Francisco was on the cover.

'Oh, you're going there?' she asked.

'A conference,' he said, flipping through the brochure. He handed it to her.

'Awesome.'

'I love the city,' he continued. 'I'm a former hippie. Dyed-in-the-wool Deadhead and Jefferson Airplane fan . . . Whole nine yards. 'Course, that was before your time.'

'No way. I'm totally into Janis Joplin and Hendrix.'

'Yeah? You ever been to the Bay area?'

'Not yet. But I'm going someday. Bett doesn't know it. But I am.'

He squinted. 'Hey, you know, there *is* a resemblance – you and Joplin. If you didn't have your hair up it'd be the same as hers.'

Megan wished she hadn't done the cheerleader pert 'n' perky ponytail.

The doctor added, 'You're prettier, of course. And thinner. Can you belt out the blues?'

'Like, I wish . . .'

'But you don't remember hippies.' He chuckled.

'Time out!' she said enthusiastically. 'I've seen *Woodstock*, like, eight times.'

She also wished she'd kept the peace symbol.

'So tell me, did you really try to kill yourself? Cross your heart.'

'And hope to die?' she asked coyly.

He smiled.

She said, 'No.'

'What happened?'

'Okay, what it is is I was drinking a little Southern Comfort. All right, maybe more than a little.'

'Joplin's drink,' he said. 'Too fucking sweet for me.'

Whoa, the *f* word. Cool. She was almost – almost – beginning to like him.

He glanced again at her hair. The fringes on her face. Then back to her eyes. It was like one of Josh's caresses. Somewhere within her she felt a tiny ping – of reassurance and pleasure.

Megan continued her story. 'And somebody I was with said no way they'd climb up to the top and I said I would and I did. That's it.'

'All right, so you got nabbed by the cops on some bullshit charge.'

'That's about it.'

'Not exactly the crime of the century.'

'*I* didn't think so either. But they were so . . . you know.'

'I know,' he said. 'Now tell me about yourself. Your secret history.'

'Well, my parents are divorced. I live with Bett. She has this business? It's really a decorating business is all but she says she's an interior designer 'cause it sounds better. Tate's got this farm in Prince William. He used to be this famous lawyer but now he just does people's wills and sells houses and stuff. He hires people to run the farm for him. Sharecroppers. Sound like slaves, or whatever, but they're just people he hires.'

'And your relationship with the folks? Is the porridge too hot, too cold or just right?'

'Just right.'

He nodded, made a small notation on his pad though he might've been just doodling. Maybe she bored him. Maybe he was writing a grocery list.

Things to buy after my appointment with Crazy Megan.

She told him about growing up, about the deaths of her mother's parents and her father's dad, school, her friends. Her Aunt Susan – her mother's twin sister. 'She's a nice lady, but she's had a rough time. She's been sick all her life. And she really, really wanted kids but couldn't have them.'

'Ah,' he said.

None of it felt important to her and she guessed it was even less important to him.

'What about friends?'

Count 'em on one hand, Crazy Megan says.

Shhhh.

'I hang with the goth crowd mostly,' she told the doctor.

'As in gothic?'

'Yeah. Only . . .' She decided she could tell him the truth.

'What it is is I kinda stay by myself a lot. I meet people but I end up figuring, why bother? There're a lot of losers out there.'

'Oh, yeah.' He laughed. 'That's why my business is so good.'

She blinked in surprise. Then smiled too.

'What's the boyfriend situation?'

'This'll be short,' she said, laughing ruefully. 'I was going with this guy? Joshua? And he was, like, all right. Only he was older. And he was black. I mean, he wasn't a gangsta or anything. His father's a soldier, like an officer in the Pentagon, and his mother's some big executive. I didn't have a problem with the race thing. But Dr Hanson said I was probably involved with him just to make my parents nuts.'

'Were you?'

'I don't know. I kinda liked him. No, I *did* like him.'

'But you broke up?'

'Sure. Dr Hanson said I ought to dump him.'

'He *said* that?'

'Well, not exactly. But I got that impression.'

Crazy Megan thinks Mr Handsome Shrink, Mr *George Clooney* stud, ought to've figured it out. But she explains anyway. *How can a psycho nutcase like me go out with* anybody? *If I hadn't dumped him – which I cried about for two weeks – if I hadn't left, then everybody at his school be on his case. 'He's the one with the loony girl.' And then his folks would find out – they're the nicest people in the universe and totally in love – and they'd be crushed . . . Well, of course I had to leave . . .*

'Nobody else on the horizon?' he asked.

'Nope.' She shook her head.

'Okay, let's talk about the family some more. Your mother.'

'Bett and I get along great.' She hesitated. 'Only it's funny about her – she's into her business but she also believes in all this New Age stuff crap. I'm, like, just chill, okay? That stuff is so bogus. But she doesn't hassle me about it. Doesn't hassle me about anything really. It's great between us. Really great. The only problem is she's engaged to a geek.'

'Do you two talk, your mom and you? Chew the fat, as my grandmother used to say.'

'Sure. . . . I mean, she's busy a lot. But who isn't, right? Yeah, we talk.' She hoped he didn't ask her about what. She'd have to make up something.

'And how 'bout Dad?'

She shrugged. 'He's nice. He takes me to concerts, shopping. We get along great.'

'Great?'

C.M. points out, *Is that the only word you know, bitch?*

'Yeah,' Megan said. 'Only . . .'

'Only what?'

'Well, it's like we don't have a lot to talk *about*. He wants me to go windsurfing with him but I went once and it's a totally superficial way to spend your time. I'd rather read a book or something.'

'You like to read?'

'Yeah, I read a lot.'

'Who're some of your favorite authors?'

'Oh, I don't know.' Her mind went blank.

Crazy Megan isn't much help. *Yep, he's gonna think you're damaged.*

Quiet! Megan ordered. She remembered the last book she'd read. 'You know Márquez? I'm reading *Autumn of the Patriarch*.'

His eyebrow lifted. 'Oh, I loved it.

'No kidding. I—'

Dr Peters added, '*Love in the Time of Cholera*. Best love story ever written. I've read it three times.'

Another ecstatic ping. 'Me too. Well, I only read it once.' The book was sitting on her bedside table.

'Tell me more,' he continued, 'about your father.'

'Um, he's pretty handsome still – I mean for a guy in his forties. And he's in pretty good shape. He dates a lot but he can't seem to settle down with anybody. He says he wants a family.'

'Does he?'

'Yeah. But if he does then why does he date girls named Bambi? . . . Just kidding. But they look like they're Bambis.' They both laughed.

'Tell me about the divorce.'

'I don't really remember them together. They split up when I was three.'

'Why?'

'They got married too young. That's what Bett says. They kind of went different ways. Mom was like real flighty and into that New Age stuff I was telling you about. And Dad was just the opposite.'

'Whose idea was the divorce?'

'I think my dad's.'

He jotted another note then looked up. 'So how mad are you at your parents?'

'I'm not.'

'Really?' he asked, as if he were completely surprised. 'You're sure the porridge isn't too hot?'

'I love 'em. They love me. We get along gre— fine. The porridge is just right. What the fuck is porridge anyway?'

'Don't have a clue,' Peters said quickly. 'Give me an early memory about your mother.'

'What?'

'Quick! Now! *Do it*!' His eyes flashed.

Megan felt a wave of heat crinkle through her face. 'I—'

'Don't hesitate,' he whispered. 'Say what's on your mind!'

She blurted, 'Bett's getting ready for a date, putting on makeup, staring in a mirror and poking at a wrinkle, like she's hoping it'll go away. She always *does* that. Like her face is the most important thing in the world to her. Her looks, you know.'

'And what do you think as you watch her?' His dark eyes were fervent. Her mind froze again. 'No, you're hesitating. *Tell* me!'

'"Slut."'

He nodded. 'Now *that's* great, Megan.'

She felt swollen with pride. Didn't know why. But she did.

'Brilliant. Now give me a memory about your father. Fast!'

'Bears.' She gasped and lifted a hand to her mouth. 'No . . . Wait. Let me think.'

But the doctor pounced. 'Bears? At the zoo?'

'No, never mind.'

'Tell me.'

She was shaking her head, no.

'Tell me, Megan,' he insisted.

'It's not important.'

'Oh, it *is* important,' he said. 'Listen. You're with *me* now, Megan. Forget whatever Hanson's done. I don't operate his way, groping around in the dark. I go deep.'

She looked into his eyes and froze – like a deer in headlights.

'Don't worry,' he said softly. 'Trust me. I'm going to change your life for ever.'

Chapter TWO

'They weren't real bears.'

'Toys?'

'Bears in a story.'

'What's so hard about this?' Dr Peters asked.

'I don't know.'

Crazy Megan gives her a good burst of sarcasm. *Oh, good job, loser. You've blown it now. You* had *to tell him about the book.*

But the other side of her was thinking: Seven weeks of bullshit with Dr Shiny-head Hanson and she hadn't felt a thing but bored. Ten minutes with Dr Peters and she was hooked up to an electric current.

Crazy Megan says, *It's too hard. It hurts too much.*

But Bill couldn't hear her, of course.

'Go on,' he encouraged.

And she went on.

'I was about six, okay? And I was spending the weekend with Tate. He lives in this big house and nobody's around for miles. It's in the middle of his cornfields and it's all quiet and really, really spooky. I was feeling weird, all scared. And I asked him to read me a story. He said he didn't have any children's books. I was really hurt. I started to cry and asked why didn't he have any. He looked all funny and went out to the old barn – where he told me I wasn't ever supposed to go – and he came back with this book. It was called *The Whispering Bears*. Only it turned out it wasn't really a kid's story at all. I found out later it was a book of folk stories from Europe.'

'Do you remember it?'

'Yeah.'

'Tell me.'

'It's stupid.'

'No,' Peters said, leaning forward. 'I'll bet it's anything *but* stupid. Tell me.'

'There was a town by the edge of the woods. And everybody who lived there was happy, you know, like in all fairy stories before the bad shit happens. People walking down the street, singing, going to market, having dinner with their families. Then one day these two big bears walked out of the woods and stood at the edge of town with their heads down and it sounded like they were whispering to each other.

'At first nobody paid any attention then little by little the people stopped what they were doing and tried to hear what the bears were saying. But nobody could. That night the bears went back into the forest. And the townspeople stood around and one woman said she knew what they were whispering about – they were making fun of the people in the village. And then everybody started noticing how everybody else walked funny or talked funny or looked stupid and they all ended up laughing at each other, and everybody got mad and there were all kinds of fights in town.

'Okay, then the next day the bears came out of the forest again and started whispering, blah, blah, blah, you get the picture. Then that night they went back into the woods. And this time some old man said *he* knew what they were talking about. They were gossiping about the people in town. And so everybody figured that everybody else knew all their secrets and so they went home and closed all their windows and doors and they were afraid to go out in public.

'Then – the third day – the bears came out again. And it was the same thing only this time the duke or mayor or somebody said, "*I* know what they're saying! They're making plans to attack the village." And they went to get torches to scare away the bears but they accidentally set a house on fire and the fire spread and the whole town burned down.'

Megan felt a shiver. Her eyes slipped to the top of the desk and she couldn't look up at Dr Peters. She continued, 'Tate only read it to me once but I still remember the last line. It was, "And do you know what the bears were really whispering about? Why, nothing at all. Don't you know? Bears can't talk."'

This is so bogus, Crazy Megan scoffs. *What's he going to think about you now?*

But the doctor calmly asked, 'And the story was upsetting?'

'Yeah.'

'Why?'

'I don't know. Maybe 'cause everybody's lives got ruined for no reason.'

'But there *was* a reason for it.'

Megan shrugged.

He continued, 'The town was destroyed because people projected their own pettiness and jealousy and aggression on some innocents. That's the moral of the story. How people destroy themselves.'

'I guess. But I was just thinking it wasn't much of a kid's story. I guess I wanted *The Lion King* or *A Hundred and One Dalmatians*.' She smiled. But Peters didn't. He looked at her closely. 'What happened after your father finished it?'

Why did he ask that? she wondered. *Why*?

Megan shrugged again. 'That's all. Bett came and picked me up and I went home.'

'This is hard, isn't it, Megan?'

Get a clue.

Quiet!

She looked at Dr Peters. 'Yeah, I guess.'

'Would it be easier to write down your feelings? A lot of my patients do that. There's some paper.'

She took the sheets he nodded toward and rested them on a booklet he pushed forward for her to write on. Reluctantly Megan picked up a pen.

She stared at the paper. 'I don't know what to say.'

'Say what you feel.'

'I don't know how I feel.'

'Yes, you do.' He leaned close. 'I think you're just afraid to admit it.'

'Well—'

'Say whatever comes into your mind. Anything. Say something to your mother first. Write a letter to her. Go!'

Another wave of that scalding heat.

Spotlight on Crazy Megan . . .

He whispered, 'Go deep.'

'I can't think!'

'Pick one thing. Why are you so angry with her?'

'I'm not!'

'Yes, you are!'

She clenched her fist. 'Because . . .'

'Why?'

'I don't know. Because she's . . . She goes out with these young men. It's like she thinks she can cast spells on them.'

'So what?' he challenged her. 'She can date who she wants. She's single. What's *really* pissing you off?'

'I don't know!'

'Yes, you *do!*' he shot back.

'Well, she's just a businesswoman and she's engaged to this dweeb. She's not a fairy princess at all like she'd like to be. She's not a cover girl.'

'But she wears an exotic image? Why does she do that?'

'I guess to make herself happy. She wants to be pretty and young for ever. She thinks this asshole Brad's going to make her happy. But he isn't.'

'She's *greedy*? Is that what you're saying?'

'Yes!' Megan cried. 'That's it! She doesn't care about *me*. The night on the water tower? She was at Brad's and she was supposed to call me. But she didn't.'

'Who? Her fiancé's?'

'Yeah. She went up there, to Baltimore, and she never called. They were *fucking*, I'll bet, and she forgot about me. It was just like when I was little. She'd leave me alone all the time.'

'By yourself?'

'No, with sitters. My uncle mostly.'

'Which uncle?'

'My Aunt Susan's husband. My mom's twin sister. She's been real sick most of her life, I told you. And Bett spent all her time with her in the hospital when I was young. Uncle Harris'd babysit me. He was real nice, but—'

'But you missed your mother?'

'I wanted her to be with *me*. She said it was only for a little while because Aunt Susan was real sick. She said she and Susan were totally close. Nobody was closer to her than her sister.'

He shook his head, seemed horrified. 'She said that to *you*? Her own daughter?'

Megan nodded.

'*You* should have been the person closest to her in the world.'

These words gripped her by the throat. She wiped more tears and struggled for breath. Finally she continued, 'Aunt

Susan'd do anything to have kids but she couldn't. Because of her heart. And here Mom got pregnant with me and Susan felt real bad about that. So Mom spent a lot of time with her.'

'There's no excuse for neglecting children. None. Absolutely none.'

Megan snagged a Kleenex and wiped her face.

'And you didn't let yourself be angry? Why not?'

'Because my mother was doing something good. My aunt's a nice lady. She always calls and asks about me and wants me to come visit her. Only I don't 'cause . . .'

'Because you're angry with her. She took your mother away from you.'

A chill. 'Yeah, I guess she did.'

'Come on, Megan. What else? Why the guilt?'

'Because my aunt needed my mom more back then. When I was little. See . . .'

Crazy Megan interrupts. *Oh, you can't tell him that!*

Yes, I can. I can tell him anything

'See, Uncle Harris killed himself.'

'He did?'

'I felt so bad for my aunt.'

'Forget it!' he snapped.

Megan blinked.

'You're Bett's *daughter*. You should have been the center of her universe. What she did was inexcusable. Say it. Say it!'

'I . . .'

'*Say it!*'

'It was inexcusable!'

'Good. Now write it to her. Every bit of the anger you feel. Get it out.'

The pen rolled from Megan's lap on to the floor. She bent down and picked it up. It weighed a hundred pounds. The tears ran from her nose and eyes and dripped on the paper.

'Tell her,' the doctor said. 'Tell her she's greedy. She turned her back on her daughter and took care of her sister instead.'

'But,' Megan managed to say, 'that's greedy of *me*.'

'Of *course* it's greedy. You were a child, you're supposed to be greedy. Parents are there to fill *your* needs. That's the whole *point* of parents. *Tell* her what you feel.'

Her head swam – from the electricity in the black eyes boring into hers, from her desire, her fear.

From her anger . . .

In ten seconds, it seemed, she'd filled the entire sheet. She dropped the paper on the floor. It floated like a pale leaf. The doctor ignored it.

'Now. Your father.'

Megan froze, shaking her head. 'Next time. Please.'

'No. Now.'

Her stomach muscles were hard as board. 'Well, I'm mad 'cause why doesn't he want to *see* me? He didn't even fight the custody agreement. I see him every two or three months.'

'Tell him.'

'I—'

'Tell him!'

She wrote. Forgetting grammar, spelling, she poured her thoughts out. When the sheet was half full her pen braked to a halt.

'What else is it, Megan? What aren't you telling me?'

'Nothing.'

'Oh, what do I hear?' he said. 'The passion's slipping. Something's wrong. You're holding back. Whispering bears. Something about that story. What?'

'I don't know.'

'Go into the place where it hurts the most. We go deep, remember. That's how I operate. I'm Super-Shrink.'

Crazy Megan can't take it any more. She just wants to curl up into a little crazy ball and disappear.

The doctor moved closer, pulling his chair beside her. Their knees touched. 'Come on. What is it?'

'No. I don't know what it is . . .'

'You want to tell me. You *need* to tell me.' He dropped to his knees, gripped her by the shoulders. 'Touch the most painful part. Touch it! Your father's read you the story. He comes to the last line. "Bears can't talk." He puts the book away. Then what happens?'

She sat forward, shivering, and stared at the floor. 'I go upstairs to pack.'

'Your mother's coming to pick you up.'

Eyes squinting closed painfully. 'She's here. I hear the car in the driveway.'

'She walks inside. You're upstairs and your parents are downstairs. They're talking?'

'Yeah. They're saying things I can't hear at first then I get closer. I sneak down to the landing.'

'You can hear them?'

'Yes.'

'What do they say?'

'I don't know. Stuff.'

'What do they *say*?' The doctor's voice filled the room. 'Tell me!'

'They were talking about a funeral.'

'Funeral? Whose?'

'I don't know. But there was something bad about it. Something really bad.'

'There's something else, isn't there, Megan? They say something else.'

'No!' she said desperately. 'Just the funeral.'

'Megan, tell me.'

'I . . .'

'Go on. Touch the place it hurts.'

'Tate said . . .' Megan felt faint. She struggled to control the tears. 'He called me . . . They were talking about me. And my daddy said . . .' She took deep gulps of air, which turned to fire in her lungs and throat. The doctor blinked in surprise as she screamed, 'My daddy shouted, "It would all've been different without *her*, without that damn inconvenient child up there. She ruined everything!"'

Megan lowered her head to her knees and wept. The doctor put his arm around her shoulders. She felt his hand stroke her head.

'And how did you feel when you heard him say that?' He brushed away the stream of her tears.

'I don't know. . . . I cried.'

'Did you want to run away?'

'I guess I did.'

'You wanted to show him, didn't you? If that's what he thinks of me I'll pay him back. I'll leave. That's what you thought, isn't it?'

Another nod.

'You wanted to go someplace where people weren't greedy, where people loved you, where people had children's books for you, where they read and talked to you.'

She sobbed into the wad of Kleenex he offered her.

'Tell him, Megan. Write it down. Get it out so you can look at it.'

She wrote until the tears grew so bad she couldn't see the page. Then she collapsed against the doctor's chest, sobbing.

'Good, Megan,' he announced. 'Very good.'

She gripped him tighter than she'd ever gripped a lover, pressing her head against his neck. For a moment neither of them moved. She was frozen here, embracing him fiercely, desperately. He stiffened and for a moment she believed that he was feeling the same sorrow she was. Megan started to back away so that she could see his kind face and his black eyes but he continued to hold her tightly, so hard that a sudden pain swept through her arm.

A surge of alarming warmth spread through her body. It was almost arousing.

Then they separated. Her smile faded as she saw in his face an odd look.

Of dreadful triumph. His eyes were cold, his smile cruel. He was suddenly a different person.

'What?' she asked. 'What's wrong?'

He said nothing.

She started to repeat herself but the words wouldn't come. Her tongue had grown heavy in her swollen mouth. It fell against her dry teeth. Her vision was crinkling. She tried once again to say something but couldn't.

She watched him stand and open a canvas bag that was resting on the floor behind his desk. He put away a hypodermic syringe. He was pulling on latex gloves.

'What're you? . . .' she began, then noticed on her arm, where the pain radiated, a small dot of blood.

'No!' She begged him again to tell her what he was doing but the words vanished in comic mumbling. She tried to scream.

A whisper.

He walked to her and crouched, cradling her head, which sagged toward the couch.

Crazy Megan is beyond crazy. She loves him, she's terrified of him, she wants to kill him.

'Go to sleep,' he said in a voice kinder than her father's ever sounded. 'Go to sleep.'

Finally, from the drug, or from the fear, the room went black and she slumped into his arms.

Chapter THREE

One hundred and thirty years ago the Dead Reb had wandered through this field.

Maybe shuffling along the very path this tall, lean man now walked in the hot April rain.

Tate Collier looked over his shoulder and imagined that he saw the legendary ghost staring at him from a cluster of brush fifty yards away. Then he laughed to himself and, crunching through rain-wet corn husks and stalks – the waste from last year's harvest – he continued through the field, inspecting hairline fractures in an irrigation pipe that promised far more water than it had been delivering lately. It'd have to be replaced within the next week, he concluded, and wondered how much the work would cost.

Loping along awkwardly, somewhat stooped, Tate was in a Brooks Brothers pinstripe beneath a yellow sou'wester and outrageous galoshes, having come here straight from his strip mall law office in Fairfax, where he'd just spent an hour explaining to Mattie Howe that suing the Prince William *Advocate* for libel because the paper had accurately reported her drunk-driving arrest was a lawsuit doomed to failure. He'd booted her out good-naturedly and sped back to his two-hundred-acre farm.

He brushed at his unruly black hair, plastered around his face by the rain, and glanced at his watch. A half-hour until Bett and Megan arrived. Again, the uneasy twist of his stomach at the thought.

He glanced once more over his shoulder – toward where he'd seen the wisp of the ghostly soldier gazing at him from the cluster of vines and kudzu and loblolly. Tate returned to the damaged pipe, recalling what his grandfather – born Charles William Collier but known throughout northern Virginia as the Judge – had told him about the Dead Reb.

A young private in the bold experiment of the Confederacy took a musket ball between the eyes at the First Battle of Bull Run. By all laws of mercy and physiology he should have fallen dead by the picket line. But he'd simply dropped his musket, stood up and wandered southeast until he came to the huge woods that bordered the dusty town of Manassas. There he lived for six months, growing dark as a slave, sucking eggs and robbing cradles (the human victuals were legend only, the Judge appended in a verbal footnote). The Dead Reb was personally responsible for the cessation of all foot traffic after dusk through the Centreville woods that fall – until he was found, stark naked and dead indeed, sitting upright in what was the middle of Jackson's Corner, now a prime part of Tate Collier's farm.

Well, no ghosts here now, Tate reflected, only a hundred feet of pipe to be replaced . . .

Straightening up now, he wiped his watch crystal.

Twenty minutes till they were due.

Look, he told himself, relax.

Through the misty rain Tate could see, a mile away, the house he'd built eighteen years ago. It was a miniature Tara, complete with two Doric columns, and was white as a cloud, built in a style that he called John Deere Gothic. This was Tate's only real indulgence in life, paid for with some inheritance and the hope of money that a young prosecutor knows will be showered upon him for his brilliance and flair, despite the fact that a commonwealth's attorney's meager salary is a matter of public record. The six-bedroom house still groaned beneath a hearty mortgage.

When the Judge deeded over the fertile Piedmont land to Tate twenty years ago – skipping Tate's father for reasons never articulated though known to one and all of the Collier clan – the young man decided impulsively he wanted a family home (the Judge's residence wasn't on the farmland itself but was eight miles away in Fairfax). Tate kept a two-acre parcel fallow for one season and built on it the next. The house sat between the two barns – one new, one the original – in the middle of a rough grassy field, punctuated with patches of black-eyed Susans, hop clover and bluestem, a stand of bitternut hickory trees, a beautiful American beech, and eastern white pines.

The eerily balmy wind grabbed his rain slicker and shook hard. He closed two buckles of the coat and happened to be gazing toward the house when he saw a downstairs light go out.

So Megan had arrived. It had to be the girl; Bett didn't have keys to the house. No hope of cancellation now. Well, if you live three miles from a Civil War battlefield, you have to appreciate the persistence of the past.

He glanced once more at the fractured pipe and started toward the house, heavy boots slogging through the untilled fields.

Like the Dead Reb.

No, he reflected, nothing so dramatic. More like the introspective man of forty-four years that he'd become.

An enthymeme is an important rhetorical device used in formal debate.

It's a type of syllogism ('All cats see in the dark. Midnight is a cat. Therefore Midnight sees in the dark'), though the enthymeme is abbreviated. It leaves out one line of logic ('All cats see in the dark; therefore Midnight sees in the dark.'). Experienced debaters and trial lawyers like Tate Collier rely on this device frequently in their debates and courtroom arguments but it works only when there's a common understanding between the advocate and his audience. Everybody's got to understand that the animal in question is a cat; they have to supply the missing information in order for the logic to hold up.

Tate reflected now that he, his ex-wife and Megan had virtually none of this common understanding. The mind of Betty Susan McCall would be as alien to him as his was to her. Except for his ex-wife's startling reappearance seven weeks ago – with the news about Megan's drunken climb up the water tower – he hadn't seen her for nearly two years and their phone conversations were limited to practical issues about the girl and the few residual financial threads between people divorced fifteen years.

And as for Megan – how can anyone know a seventeen-year-old girl? Her mind was a moving target. Her only report on the therapy sessions was: 'Dad, therapy's for, like, losers. Okay?' And the Walkman headset went back on. He didn't expect her to be any more informative – or articulate – today.

As he approached the house he now noticed that *all* of the house lights had been shut off. But when he stepped out of the field he saw that neither Megan's nor Bett's car was in the drive.

He unlocked the door and walked into the house, which echoed with emptiness. He noticed Megan's house keys on the entryway table and dropped his own beside them, looking up the dim hallway. The only light in the cavernous space was from behind him, the bony light from outside, filtering through the entryway.

What's that noise?

He cocked his head. A wet sound, sticky, came from somewhere on the first floor. Repetitive, accompanied by a faint, hungry gasping.

The chill of fear stirred at his neck.

'Megan?'

The noise stopped momentarily. Then, with a guttural snap of breath, it resumed again. There was a desperation about the sound. Tate's stomach began to churn and his skin prickled with sweat.

And that smell . . . Something pungent and ripe.

Blood! he believed. Like the smell of hot rust. Blood and flesh.

'Megan!' he called again. Alarmed now, he walked further into the house.

The noise stopped though the smell was stronger, almost nauseating.

Tate thought of weapons. He had a pistol but it was locked away in the barn and there was no time to get it. He stepped forcefully into the den, seized a letter opener from the desk, flipped on the light.

And laughed out loud.

His two-year-old Dalmatian, her back to him, was flopped down on the floor, chewing intently. Tate set the opener on the bar and approached the dog. His smile faded. What *is* that? Tate squinted.

Suddenly, with a wild, raging snarl, the dog spun and lunged at him. He gasped in shock and leapt back, cracking his elbow on the corner of a table. Just as quickly the dog turned away from him, back to its trophy.

Tate circled the animal then stopped. Between the dog's bloody paws was a bone from which streamed bits of flesh. Tate stepped forward. The dog's head swivelled ominously. The animal's eyes gleamed with jealous hatred. A fierce growl rolled from her sleek throat and the black lips pulled back, revealing bloody teeth.

Jesus . . .

What *is* it? Tate wondered, queasy. Had the dog grabbed some animal that had gotten into the house? It was so badly mauled he couldn't tell what it had been.

'No,' Tate commanded. But the dog continued to defend its prize; a raspy growl rose from her throat.

'Come!'

The dog dropped her head and continued to chew, keeping her malevolent eyes turned sideways toward Tate. The crack of bone was loud.

'Come!'

No response.

Tate lost his temper and stepped around the dog, reaching for its collar. The animal leapt up in a frenzy, snapping at him, baring sharp teeth. Tate pulled back just in time to save his fingers.

He could see the bloody object. A beef knuckle bone. The kennel-owner from whom he'd bought the Dalmatian told him that bones were dangerous treats; he never bought them. He assumed Megan must have been shopping on her way here and picked one up. She sometimes brought chewsticks or rubber toys for the animal.

Tate made a strategic retreat, slipped into the hallway. He'd wait until the animal fell asleep tonight then throw the damn thing out.

He walked to the basement stairs, which led down to the recreation room Tate had built for the family parties and reunions he'd planned on hosting – people clustered around the pool table, lounging on the bar, drinking blender daiquiris and eating barbecued chicken. The parties and reunions never happened but Megan often disappeared down to the dark catacombs when she spent weekends here.

He descended the stairs and made a circuit of the small rooms. Nothing. He paused and cocked his head. From upstairs came the sound of the dog's growl once more. Urgent and ominous.

'Megan, is that you?' his baritone voice echoed powerfully.

He was angry. Megan and Bett were already twenty minutes late. Here he'd gone to the trouble of inviting them over, doing his fatherly duty, and this was what he got in return. . . .

The growling stopped abruptly. Tate listened for footsteps on the ground floor but heard nothing. He climbed the stairs and stepped out into the drizzle once more.

He made his way to the old barn, stepped inside and called Megan's name. No response. He looked around the spooky place in frustration, straightened a stack of old copies of *Wallace's Farmer*, which had fallen over, and glanced at the wall – at a greasy framed plaque containing a saying from Seaman Knapp, the turn-of-the-century civil servant who'd organized the country's agricultural extension services program. Tate's grandfather had copied the epigram, for inspirational purposes, in the same elegant, meticulous lettering with which he filled in the farm's ledgers and wrote legal memos for his secretary to type.

What a man hears, he may doubt. What he sees, he may possibly doubt. But what he does, he cannot doubt.

There you have it, Tate thought, stepping outside once again.

'Megan?' he called.

Then his eye fell on the old picnic bench and he thought of the funeral.

No, he told himself. Don't go thinking about *that*. The funeral was a thousand years ago. It's a memory deader than the Dead Reb and something you'll hate yourself for bringing up.

But of course think about it he did. Pictured it, felt it,

tasted the memory. The funeral. The picnic bench, Japanese lanterns, Bett and three-year-old Megan . . .

A cluster of week-old Halloween candy lying in grass, a hot November day long ago. . . .

Until Bett had shown up at his door nearly two months ago with the news of Megan and the water tower he hadn't thought of that day for years.

What he does, he cannot doubt. . . .

The rain began in earnest once again and he hurried back to the house, climbed to the second floor.

'Megan?'

She wasn't there either.

He walked downstairs again. Reached for the phone.

He jumped a mile when, outside, a car door slammed.

Dr Peters – well, Dr Aaron Matthews – sped away from Tate Collier's farm in Megan's Ford Tempo. His hands shook and his breath came fast.

Two close calls.

He didn't know why Collier had returned home this morning. He *always* kept Saturday hours at his office. Or had every Saturday for the last three months. Ten to four. Clockwork. But not today. When Matthews had driven to Collier's farm – with Megan in the trunk, no less – he'd found, to his shock, that the lawyer had returned. Fortunately he was heading out into the fields. When he was out of sight Matthews had parked in a cul-de-sac of brush beside Collier's driveway, fifty feet from the house, had snuck into the large colonial structure using Megan's keys. He'd tossed the Dalmatian a bone to keep it busy while he did what he'd come for.

He'd managed to escape to the Tempo just as Collier was returning. But as he started to pull out of the bushes into the long driveway Megan's mother's Volvo had streaked past. He braked quickly and she hadn't seen her daughter's car.

Nearly seen a second time! What was going on? Matthews had wondered. Why was *she* here? They couldn't have known what had happened to Megan. Not yet.

Still, it unnerved him. It was bad luck. And although he was a Harvard-trained psychotherapist and did not, professionally, accept the existence of luck, sometimes it took little more than a shadow of superstition like this to drop him into the cauldron of a Mood. Matthews was bipolar – the diagnosis that used to be called manic depression. In order for him to carry out the kidnapping he'd gone off his meds; he couldn't afford the dulling effects of the high doses of Prozac and Wellbutrin he'd been taking. Fortunately, once the medication had evaporated from his bloodstream he found himself in a manic phase and he'd easily been able to spend eighteen hours a day stalking the girl and working on his plan. But as the weeks had worn on he'd begun to worry that he was headed for a fall. And he knew from the past that it took very little to push him over the edge.

But the near miss with Collier and his wife faded now and he remained as buoyant as a happy child. He sped to I-66 and headed east – to the Vienna, Virginia, Metro lot, the huge station for commuters, fifteen miles west of D.C. It was Saturday morning but the lot was filled with the cars of people who'd taken the train downtown to visit the monuments and museums and galleries.

Matthews drove Megan's car to the spot where his gray Mercedes was parked then climbed out and looked around. He saw only one other occupied car – a white sedan, idling several rows away. He couldn't see the driver clearly but the man or woman didn't seem to be looking his way. Matthews quickly bundled Megan out of the Tempo's trunk and slipped her into the trunk of the Mercedes.

He looked down at the girl, curled fetally, unconscious, bound up with rope. She was very pale. He pressed a hand to her chest to make sure that she was still breathing regularly. He was concerned about her; Matthews was no longer licensed in Virginia and couldn't write prescriptions so to knock the girl out he'd stockpiled phenobarb from a veterinarian, claiming that one of his Rottweilers was having seizures. He'd mixed the drug with distilled water but couldn't be sure of the concentration. She was deeply asleep but it seemed that her respiration was fine and when he took her pulse her heart rate was acceptable.

Between the front seats of the Tempo he left the well-thumbed Amtrak timetable that Megan had used as a lap desk to write the letters to her parents and that now bore her fingerprints. He'd circled all the Saturday trains to New York. He'd been very careful – wearing gloves when he'd handled the timetable and the writing paper he'd stolen from Megan's room in Bett McCall's house. He'd spent hours in her room – when the mother was working and Megan was in school. It was there that he'd gotten important insights into her personality: the three Joplin posters, the black light, the Márquez book, notes she'd gotten from classmates laced with words like 'fuck' and 'shit'. (Matthews had written a paper for the APA *Journal* on how adolescents unconsciously raise and lower emotional barriers to their therapist according to the doctors' use of grammar and language; he'd observed, during the session that morning, how the expletives he'd used had opened her psyche like keys.)

He'd been careful to leave no evidence of his break-in at Bett McCall's. Or in Leesburg – where Dr Hanson's mother lived. That had been the biggest problem of his plan: getting Hanson out of the way for the week – without doing something as obvious, though appealing, as running him over with a car. He'd done some research on the therapist and learned that his mother lived in the small town northwest of D.C., Washington, and that she was frail. On Wednesday night

Matthews had loosened the top step leading from her back porch to the small yard behind her house. Then he'd called, pretending to be a neighbor, and asked her to check on an injured dog in the back yard. She'd been disoriented and reluctant to go outside after dark but after five minutes he'd convinced her. She'd fallen straight down the stairs onto the sidewalk. The tumble looked serious and for a moment Matthews wondered if Hanson would have to cancel his appointments because of a funeral. But he waited until the paramedics arrived and noted that she'd merely broken bones.

Now, feeling confident, Matthews switched cars – parking Megan's in the space his Mercedes had occupied – and then sped out of the parking lot.

He took his soul's pulse and found his mood intact. There was no paralysis, no anger, no sorrow dishing up the fishy delusions that had plagued him since he was young. The only hint of neurosis was understandable: Matthews found himself talking with Megan, repeating what he'd told her in the session and what she'd said to him. *Go deep . . .*

Finally, he turned the Mercedes on to the entrance ramp to I-66 and, doing exactly fifty-eight miles an hour, headed toward the distant mountains. Megan's new home.

Chapter FOUR

The woman walked inside the house of which she'd been mistress for three years and paused in the gothic, arched hallway as if she'd never before seen the place.

'Bett,' Tate said.

She continued inside slowly, offering her ex-husband a formal smile. She paused again at the den door. The Dalmatian looked up, snarling.

'Oh, my, Tate . . .'

'Megan gave her a bone. She's a little protective about it. Let's go in here.'

He closed the den door and they walked into the living room.

'Did you talk to her?' he asked.

'Megan? No. Where is she? I didn't see her car.'

'She's been here. But she left. I don't know why.'

'She leave a note?'

'No. But her house keys're here.'

'Oh. Well.' Bett fell silent.

Tate crossed his arms and rocked on the carpet for a moment. He walked to the window, looked at the barn through the rain. Returned.

‘Coffee?’ he asked.

‘No, thank you.’

Bett sat on the couch, crossed her thin legs, clad in tight black jeans. She wore a black silky blouse and a complicated silver necklace of purple and black stones. She sat in silence for a few moments then rose and examined the elaborate fireplace Tate’d had built several years ago. She caressed the mortar and with a pale-pink fingernail picked at the stone. Her eyes squinted as she sighted down the mantelpiece. ‘Nice,’ she said. ‘Fieldstone’s expensive.’

She sat down again.

Tate examined her from across the room. With her long, pre-Raphaelite face and tangle of witchy red hair, Betty Susan McCall was exotic. Something Virginia rarely offered – an enigmatic Celtic beauty. The South is full of temptresses and lusty cowgirls and it has matriarchs galore but few sorceresses. Bett was a northern Virginia businesswoman now but beneath that façade Tate believed that she remained the enigmatic young woman he’d first seen singing a folk song in a smoky apartment on the outskirts of Charlottesville twenty-three years ago. She’d sung a whaling song *a capella* in a reedy, breathless voice.

It had, however, been many years since any woman had ensnared him that way and he now found himself feeling very wary. A dozen memories from the days when they were getting divorced surfaced murkily.

He wondered how he could keep his distance from her throughout this untidy family business.

Bett’s eyes had disposed of the fireplace and the furniture in the living room and were checking out the wallpaper and molding. His eyes dogged after hers and he concluded that she found the place unhomely and stark. It needed more upholstered things, more pillows, more flowers, new curtains, livelier paint. He felt embarrassed.

After several minutes Bett said, 'Well, if her car's gone she probably just went out to get something.'

'That's probably it.'

Two hours later, no messages on either of their phones, Tate called the police.

The first thing Tate noticed was the way Konnie glanced at Bett.

With approval.

As if the lawyer had finally gotten his act together; no more dumb blondes for him. And it was damn well about time. This woman was in her early forties, very pretty. Smooth skin. She had quick eyes and seemed smart. Detective Dimitri Konstantinatis of the Fairfax County Police had commented once, 'Tate, why're all the women you date half your age and, lemme guess, a third your intelligence? If that. Why's that, Counselor?'

Konnie strode into the living room and stuck his hand out toward her. He shook the startled woman's vigorously as Tate introduced them. 'Bett, my ex-wife, this is Konnie. Konnie's an old friend from my prosecuting days.'

'Howdy.' Oh, the cop's disappointed face said, the ex. Giving *her* up was one bad mistake, mister. The detective glanced at Tate. 'So, Counselor, your daughter's up 'n' late for lunch, that right?'

'Been over two hours.'

'You're fretting too much, Tate.' He poked a finger at him and said to Bett, 'This fella? Was the sissiest prosecutor in the commonwealth. We had to walk him to his car at night.'

'At least I could *find* my car,' Tate shot back. One of the reasons Konnie loved Tate was that the lawyer joked about Konnie's drinking; he was now in recovery and hadn't had a drink in four years and not a single soul in the world except Tate Collier would dare poke fun at him about it. But what every other soul in the world didn't know was that what the cop respected most was balls.

Bett smiled uneasily.

Tate and Konnie had worked together frequently when Tate was a commonwealth's attorney. The somber detective had been taciturn and distant for the first six months of their professional relationship, never sharing a single personal fact. Then at midnight of the day a serial rapist-murderer they'd jointly convicted was 'paroled horizontal', as the death row parlance went, Konnie had drunkenly embraced Tate and said that the execution made them blood brothers. 'We're bonded.'

'Bonded? What kind of pinko, Robert Bly crap is that?' an equally drunken Tate had roared.

They'd been tight friends ever since.

Another knock on the front door.

'Maybe that's her,' Bett said eagerly. But when Tate opened it a crew-cut man in a cheap, slope-shouldered gray suit walked inside. He stood very straight and looked Tate in the eye. 'Mr Collier. I'm Detective Ted Beauridge. Fairfax County Police. I'm with Juvenile.'

Tate led him inside and introduced Beauridge to Bett while Konnie clicked the TV's channel selector. He seemed fascinated to find a TV that had no remote control.

Beauridge was polite and efficient but clearly he didn't want to be here. Konnie was the sole reason Megan's disappearance was getting any attention at all. When Tate had called, Konnie'd told him that it was too early for a missing person's report; twenty-four hours' disappearance was required unless the individual was under fifteen, mentally handicapped or endangered. Still, Konnie had somehow accidentally forgotten to get his supervisor's okay and had run a tag check on Megan's car with other agencies for auto accidents. And he'd put in a request for Jane Doe admissions at all the area hospitals.

Tate ushered them into the living room. Bett asked, 'Would

you like some coffee or . . . ?' Her voice faded and she laughed in embarrassment, looking at Tate, undoubtedly remembering that this had not been her house for a long, long time.

'Nothing, thanks, ma'am,' Beauridge said for them both.

In the time it had taken Konnie to arrive, Bett had called some friends of Megan's. She'd spent the night at Amy Walker's. Bett had called her first but no one had answered. She left a message on the Walkers' voice mail, then called some of her other friends. Brittany, Kelly and Donna hadn't seen Megan or heard from her today. They didn't know if she had plans except maybe showing up at the mall later. 'To, you know, like, hang out.'

Konnie asked Tate and Bett about the girl's Saturday routine.

'She normally has a therapy session Saturday morning,' Bett explained. 'At nine. But the doctor had to cancel today. His mother was sick or something.'

'Could she just've forgotten about coming here for lunch?'

'When we talked yesterday I reminded her about it.'

'Was she good about keeping appointments?' Beauridge asked.

Tate didn't know. She'd always shown up on time when he took her shopping or to dinner at the Ritz in Tysons. He told them this. Bett said that she was 'semi-good about being prompt'. But she didn't think the girl would miss this lunch. 'The three of us being together and all,' she added with a faint cryptic laugh.

'What about boyfriends?' Konnie asked.

'She didn't—' Tate began.

Then halted at Bett's glance. And he realized he didn't have a clue whether Megan had a boyfriend or not.

Bett continued, 'She did but they broke up last month.'

'*She* the one broke it off?'

'Yes.'

'So is he trouble, you think? This kid?' Konnie tugged at a jowl.

'I don't think so. He seemed very nice. Easy-going.'

So did Ted Bundy, Tate thought.

'What's his name?'

'Joshua LeFevre. He's a senior at George Mason.'

'He's in senior in *college*?' Tate asked.

'Well, yes,' she said.

'Bett, she's only seventeen. I mean—'

'Tate,' Bett said again. 'He was a nice boy. His mother's some executive at EDS, his father's stationed at the Pentagon. And Josh's a championship athlete. He's also head of the Black Students' Association.'

'The *what*?'

'Tate!'

'Well, I'm just surprised. I mean, it doesn't *matter*.'

Bett rolled her eyes.

'It doesn't,' Tate said defensively. 'I'm just—'

'—surprised,' Konnie offered wryly. 'Mr ACLU speaks.'

'You know his number?' Beauridge asked.

Bett didn't but she got it from directory assistance and called. She apparently got one of his roommates. Joshua was out. She left a message for him to call when he returned.

'So. She's been here and gone. No sign of a struggle?' Konnie looked around the front hall.

'None.'

'What about the alarms?'

'I had them off.'

'There a panic button she could hit if somebody was inside waiting for her?'

'Yep. And she knows about it.'

Bett offered, 'She left the house keys here. She has her car keys with her.'

'Could somebody,' Konnie speculated, 'have stole her purse maybe, got the keys and broken in?'

Tate considered this. 'Maybe. But her license has Bett's

address on it. How would a burglar know about this place? Maybe she had something with my address but I don't know what. Besides, nothing's missing that I could see.'

'Don't see much worth stealing,' Konnie said, looking at the paltry entertainment equipment. 'You know, Counselor, they got TVs nowadays bigger'n cereal boxes.'

Tate grunted.

'Okay,' Konnie said, 'how 'bout you show me her room?'

As Tate led him upstairs Beauridge's smooth drawl rolled, 'Sure you got nothing to worry about, Mrs Collier—'

'It's McCall.'

Upstairs, Tate let Konnie into Megan's room then wandered into his own. He'd missed something earlier when he'd made the rounds up here: his dresser drawer was open. He looked inside, frowned, then glanced across the hall as the detective surveyed the girl's room. 'Something funny,' Tate called.

'Hold that thought,' Konnie answered. With surprisingly lithe movements for such a big man he dropped to his knees and went through what must have been the standard teenage hiding places: under desk drawers, beneath dressers, waste baskets, between mattresses, up under box springs, in curtains, pillows and comforters. 'Ah, whatta we got here?' Konnie straightened up and examined two sheets of paper.

He pointed to Megan's open dresser drawers and the closet. 'These're almost empty, these drawers. They normally got clothes in them?'

Tate hesitated, concern on his face. 'Yes, they're usually full.'

'Could you see if there's any luggage missing.'

'Luggage? No . . . Wait. Her old backpack's gone.' Tate considered this for a moment. Why would she take that? he wondered. Looking at the papers, Tate asked the detective, 'What'd you find?'

'Easy, Counselor,' Konnie said, folding up the sheets. 'Let's go downstairs.'

Chapter FIVE

What would Sidney Poitier do?

Joshua LeFevre shifted his muscular, trapezoidal body in the skimpy seat of his Toyota and pressed down harder on the gas pedal. The tiny engine complained but slowly edged the car closer to the Mercedes.

Come on, Megan, what the hell're you up to?

He squinted again and leaned forward as if moving eight inches closer to the Merce were going to let him see more clearly through his confusion. He assumed the man, not Megan, was driving though he couldn't be sure. This gave him a sliver of comfort – for some reason the thought of this guy tossing Megan the keys to his big doctor's car and saying 'You drive, honey' riled the young man beyond words. Made him furious.

He nudged the car faster.

Sidney Poitier . . . What would you do?

LeFevre had seen *In the Heat of the Night* when he'd been ten. (On video, of course – when the film had originally come out, in the sixties, the man who would be his father was doing basic training pushups in Fort Dix and his to-be mother was listening to Smokey Robinson and Diana Ross while she worked on her 4.0 average at St Albans.) The film had affected him deeply. The Poitier character, Detective Tibbs, ended up stuck in the small Southern town, butting horns with good-old-boy sheriff Rod Steiger. Moving slow, solving a local murder, step by step. . . . Not getting flustered, not getting pissed off in the face of all the crap everybody in town was giving him.

Sure, the movie didn't have real guts, it was *Hollywood's* idea of race relations, more softball than gritty, but even at age ten Joshua LeFevre understood the film wasn't really about black and white – it was about being a man and being persistent and not taking no when you believed yes.

It choked him up, that flick – the way those movies that give us our role models always do, whether it's the first time we see them or the hundredth.

Oh yes, Joshua Nathan LeFevre – an honors English major at George Mason University, a tall young man with his father's perfect physique and military bearing and with his mother's brains – had a sentimental side to him thick as a mountain. (The week students in his nineteenth-century lit seminar were picking apart a Henry James novel like crows, LeFevre had slunk back to his apartment with a very different book hidden in a brown paper bag. He'd locked his door and read the entire novel in one sitting, crying unashamedly when he came to the last page of *The Bridges of Madison County.*)

Sentimental, a romantic. And, accordingly, Sidney Poitier – rather than Wesley Snipes – appealed to him.

So, what would *Mister* Tibbs do now?

Okay, he was saying to himself, let's analyze it. Step by step. Here's a girl's got a bad home life. None of that talk-show abuse, no, but it's clearly a case of Daddy don't care and Momma don't care. So she drinks more than she ought and hangs with a bad crowd – until she meets LeFevre. And seems to get her act together though she falls off the normal wagon every once in a while. And then one night she climbs up to the top of a water tower (and why didn't she call me, dammit, instead of guzzling Comfort with Donna and Brittany, capital L losers, the Easy Sisters?). And once she's up there, the highest structure in Fairfax, she does a little dance on the scaffolding and the cops and fire department come to get her down.

And she goes to see this shrink . . .

Who tells her she's got to break up with him.

And so she does.

Why? LeFevre had asked her a few weeks ago, as they sat in his car, parked in front of her house on what turned out to be their very last date. *'Why?'*

It's not the differences . . . Meaning the age, meaning the race. It was . . . what the hell was it? He replayed Megan's little speech.

'It's just that I'm not ready for the same kind of relationship you want.'

And what kind is that? I don't remember proposing.

'Oh, Josh, honey, don't cry . . . I need to see things, do things. I feel, I don't know, all tied down or something . . . Living with Bett's like living with a roommate. You know, her date for Saturday's the biggest deal in the world. All she worries about is her skin getting old.'

Old skin? I like your mom. She's pretty, smart, off-beat. I don't get it. What's her skin got to do with breaking up? LeFevre had been very confused as he sat in the car beside the woman he loved.

'Oh, honey, I just need to get away. I want to travel, see things. You know.'

Travel? Where was *this* coming from? I've got a trust fund, Mom and Dad're loaded. I've lived in Jeddah, Cyprus, London and Germany. I speak three languages. I can show you more of the world than the Cunard Line.

'Okay What it is is this therapist. Dr Hanson? See, he

thinks it's not a good idea for me to be in a relationship with you right now.'

Then, we'll back off a bit. See each other once a week or so. How's that?

'No, you don't *understand*,' Megan had said brutally, pulling away from him as he tried to take the Southern Comfort bottle out of her hand. And she'd climbed out of the passenger seat and run into her house. LeFevre now leaned over and sniffed the headrest to see if he could smell her perfume. Heartbreakingly, he couldn't.

He pushed the accelerator harder, edging up on the gray Mercedes.

'No, you don't understand.'

No, he hadn't.

Joshua LeFevre had waited a tormented three weeks, then – this morning – woke up on autopilot. He hadn't been able to take the suffocating frustration any more. He'd driven to Hanson's office around the time Megan's appointment would be over. He'd parked up the street, waiting for her to come out. Josh LeFevre could bench-press two hundred and twenty pounds, he could bicycle over a hundred and fifty miles a day. But he wasn't going for intimidation. Oh, no. He was going to Poitier the man, not Snipes him.

Why, he was going to ask the doctor, did you talk her into breaking up with me? Isn't that unethical? Let's talk about it together. The three of us. He had a dozen arguments all prepared. He believed he could talk his way back into her heart.

'No, you don't understand.'

But *now* he did.

God, I'm an idiot.

The doctor had her break up because he wanted to fuck her.

No psychobabble here. No inner child. Nope. The shrink

wanted to play the two-backed beast with LeFevre's girlfriend. Simple as a shot in the head.

From where he'd been parked near the office he hadn't been able to see clearly but, suddenly, before the appointment was supposed to be over, Megan's Tempo was pulling out of the lot – with the shrink himself driving, it seemed, and heading north.

He'd followed the car to Manassas – to Megan's dad's farm – where LeFevre'd waited for about twenty minutes. Then, just when he'd been about to pull into the long drive the car had sped out again, and they'd driven to the Vienna Metro parking lot. They'd switched cars – taking his shrinkmobile – and headed west on 66.

What was it all about? Had she picked up some clothes from her father's? Was she going away for the weekend?

LeFevre was crazed. He had to do *something*.

But what would Sidney Poitier do? The script had changed.

Wait till they got to the doctor's house? The inn they were going to? Confront them there?

No, that didn't seem right.

Oh, hell, he should just go home. . . . Forget this crap. Be a man.

His foot eased up on the gas. . . . Good idea, get off at the next exit. Quit acting like a lovesick loser. It's embarrassing. Go home. Read your Melville. You've got a presentation due a week from Monday . . .

The Mercedes pulled ahead.

Oh, yeah, he thought, I'm going to deconstruct motifs in some fucking story about a big-ass whale while my girlfriend's in bed whispering soft words into her therapist's ear?

He jammed his foot to the floor.

Would Poitier do this?

You bet.

And so LeFevre kept his sweating hands on the wheel of

the car, straining forward, and sped after the woman whom he loved and, he believed somewhere in a portion of his sloppy heart, who loved him still.

'She's run away?' Bett whispered.

The four of them were in the living room, like strangers at a cocktail party, knees pointed at one another, sitting upright and waiting to become comfortable. Konnie continued, 'But y'all should consider that good news. The profile is most runaways come back on their own within a month.'

Bett stared out the window at the misty darkness. 'A month,' she announced, as if answering a trivia question. 'No, no. She wouldn't leave. Not without saying anything.'

Konnie glanced at Beauridge. Tate caught the look.

'I'm afraid she did say something.' Konnie handed Bett and Tate what he'd found upstairs. 'Letters to both of you. Under her pillow.'

'Why there?' Bett asked. 'That doesn't make any sense.'

'So you wouldn't find 'em right away,' Konnie explained. 'Give her a head start. I've seen it before.'

Beauridge asked, 'Is that her handwriting?'

Konnie added, 'There's a buddy of mine, FBI document examiner, Parker Kincaid. Lives in Fairfax. We could give him a call.'

But Bett said it was definitely Megan's writing.

'"Bett,"' she read aloud, then looked up. 'She called me Bett. Why would she do that?' She started again and read in a breathless, ghostly voice, '"Bett – I don't care if it hurts you to say this . . . I don't care how *much* it hurts . . ."'

She looked helplessly at her ex-husband then read to herself. She finished, sat back in the couch, and seemed to shrink to the size of a child herself. She whispered, 'She say she hates me. She hates all the time I spent with my sister. I . . .' Mystified, hurt, she shook her head and fell silent.

Tate looked down at his note. It was stained. With tears? With rain? He read:

Tate:

The only way to say it – I hate you for what you've done to me! You don't listen to me. You talk, talk and talk and Bett calls you the silver-tongued devil and you are but you never listen to me. To what I want. To who I am. You bribe me, you pay me off, and hope I'll go away. I should of run away when I was six like I wanted to. And never come back.

I've wanted to do that all along. I still want to. Get away from you. It's what you want anyway, isn't it? To get rid of your inconvenient child?

His mouth was open, his lips and tongue dry, stinging from the air that whipped in and out of his lungs. He found he was staring at Bett.

'Tate. You okay?' Konnie said.

'Could I see that again, Mrs McCall?' Beauridge asked.

She handed the stiff sheet over.

'You're sure that's her writing paper?'

Bett nodded. 'I gave it to her for Christmas.'

In a low voice Bett answered questions no one had asked. 'My sister was very sick. I left Megan in other people's care a lot. I didn't know she felt so abandoned . . . She never said anything.'

Tate noted Megan's careless handwriting. In several places the tip of the pen had ripped through the paper. In anger, he assumed.

Konnie asked Tate what he'd found in his own room.

It took him a minute to focus on the question. 'She took four hundred dollars from my bedside drawer.'

Bett blurted, 'Nonsense. She wouldn't take . . .'

'It's gone,' Tate said. 'She's the only one who's been here.'

'What about credit cards?' Konnie asked.

'She's on my Visa and MasterCard,' Bett said. 'She'd have them with her.'

'That's good,' Konnie offered. 'It's an easy way to trace runaways. What it is we'll set up a real-time link with the credit card companies. We'll know within ten minutes where she's charged something.'

Beauridge said, 'We'll put her on the runaway wire. She's picked up anywhere, for anything, on the Eastern Seaboard they'll let us know. Let me have a picture, will you?'

Tate realized that they were looking at him.

'Sure,' he said quickly, and began searching the room. He looked through the bookshelves, end-table drawers. He couldn't find any photos.

Beauridge watched Tate uncertainly; Tate guessed that the young officer's wallet and wall were peppered with snapshots of his own youngsters. Konnie himself, Tate remembered from some years ago, kept a picture of his ex-wife and kids in his wallet, tucked away behind his social security card. The lawyer rummaged in the living room and disappeared into the den. He returned some moments later with a snapshot – a photo of Tate and Megan at Virginia Beach two years ago. She stared unsmilingly at the camera. It was the only picture he could find.

'Pretty girl,' Beauridge said.

'Tate,' Konnie said, 'I'll stay on it. But there isn't a lot we can do.'

'Whatever, Konnie. You know it'll be appreciated.'

'Bye, Mrs Coll— McCall.'

But Bett was looking out the window and said nothing.

The white Toyota was staying right behind him. He wondered if it was the same auto he'd seen in the Vienna Metro lot when he was switching cars. He wished he'd paid more attention.

Aaron Matthews believed in coincidence even less than he believed in superstition. There were no accidents, no flukes. We are completely responsible for our behavior and its consequences even if we can't figure out what's motivating us to act.

The car behind him now was not a coincidence.

There was a motive, there was a design.

Matthews couldn't understand it yet. He didn't know how concerned to be. But he *was* concerned.

Maybe he'd cut the driver off and the man was mad. Road Rage.

Maybe it was someone who'd seen him heft a large bundle into the trunk of the Mercedes and was following out of curiosity.

Maybe it was the police.

He slowed to fifty.

The white car did too.

Sped up.

The car stayed with him.

Have to think about this. Have to do something.

Matthews slid into the right lane and continued through the mist toward the mountains in the west. He looked back as often as he looked forward.

As any good therapist will advise his patients to do.

Chapter SIX

The rain had stopped but the atmosphere was thick as hot blood.

In her stylish shoes with the wide, high heels, Bett McCall came to Tate's shoulder. Neither speaking, they stood on the back porch, looking over the back sixty.

The Collier spread was more conservative than most Piedmont farms: five fields rotating between soy one year and corn and rye the next.

'Listen to me, Tate,' the Judge would say.

The boy always did.

'What's a legume?'

'A pea.'

'Only a pea?'

'Well, beans too, I think.'

'Peas, beans, clover, alfalfa, vetches . . . they're all legumes. They help the soil. You plant year after year of cereals, what happens?'

'Don't know, sir.'

'Your soil goes to hell in a hand basket.'

'Why's that, Judge?'

The man had taught the boy never to be afraid to ask questions.

'Because legumes take nitrogen from the air. Cereals take it from the soil.'

'Oh.'

'We'll plant Mammoth Brown and Yellow for silage and Virginia soy too. Wilson and Haerlandts are good for seed and hay. How do you prepare the land?'

'Like you're planting corn,' the boy had responded. 'Sow them broadcast with a wheat drill.'

Out of the blue the Judge might glance at his grandson and ask, 'Do you cuss, Tate?'

'No, sir.'

'Here. Read this.' The man thrust into Tate's hand a withered old bulletin from the Virginia Department of Agriculture and Immigration. A circled chapter bemoaned the rise of young farmers' profanity. *Even some of our girls have taken to this deplorable habit.*

'I'll keep that in mind, Judge,' Tate had said, remembering without guilt how he'd sworn a blue streak at Junior Foote just last Thursday.

Gazing at his fields, the Judge had continued, 'But if you *do* find it necessary to let loose just make sure there're no womenfolk around. Almost time for supper. Let's get on home.'

Tate stayed at his grandparents' house in Fairfax as often as at his parents'. Tate's father was a kind, completely quiet man, best suited to a life as, say, a court reporter – a career he'd never dared pursue, of course, given the risk that he'd be assigned to transcribe one of his father's trials. The Judge had agonized over whether or not to leave the farm to his only son and had concluded the man just didn't have the mettle to handle a spread of this sort. So he deeded it over to Tate while the other kin got money. (Ironically, as Tate learned during one of the few frank conversations he'd ever had with his father, the man had been dreading the day that the Judge would hand over the farm to him. His main concern seemed to be that running the farm would interfere with his passion of collecting Lionel electric trains.) Tate's timid, ever-tired mother suited her husband perfectly and Tate could remember not a single word of dissension, or passion, between the two. Little conversation either.

Which is why, given his druthers, young Tate would hitch or beg a ride to his grandparents' house and spend as much time as he could with them.

As the Judge presided at the head of the groaning board table on Sunday afternoons Tate's grandmother might offer in a whisper, 'The only day to plant beans is Good Friday.'

'That's a superstition, Grams,' young Tate had said to her, a woman so benign that she took any conversation directed toward her, even in disagreement, as a compliment. 'You can plant soy all the way through June.'

'No, young man. Now listen to me.' She'd looked toward the head of the table, to make sure her husband wasn't listening. 'If you laugh loud while planting corn it's trouble. I mean, serious trouble. And it's good to plant potatoes and onions in the dark of the moon and you better plant beans and corn in the light.'

'That doesn't make any sense, Grams.'

'Does,' she'd responded. 'Root crops grow below ground so you plant them in the dark of the moon. Cereals are above ground so you plant in the light.'

Tate admitted there was a certain logic there.

This was one of three or four simultaneous discussions going on around the dinner table – aunts and uncles and cousins, as well as the inevitable guest or two that the Judge would invite from the ranks of the bench and bar in Prince William and Fairfax counties. One crisp, clear Sunday, young Tate shared an iced tea with one guest who'd arrived early while the Judge was *en route* from the farm. The slim, soft-spoken visitor showed a great interest in Tate's ant farm; it wasn't until a dozen years later that Tate realized the visitor was Supreme Court Justice William Brennan and that he'd probably taken a break from penning his opinion in a decision – maybe a landmark like *Roe v. Wade* – to come to Judge Collier's farm for roast beef, yams and collard greens.

'And,' Grams would continue, scanning the table for the sin of empty serving bowls, 'it's also bad luck to slaughter hogs in the dark of the moon.'

'Sure is for the hogs,' Tate had offered.

The dinner would continue until four or five in the afternoon, Tate sitting and listening to legal war stories and planning and zoning battles and local gossip thick as Grams's mashed potatos.

Now, because his ex-wife stood beside him, gazing out over the acres his grandfather had so lovingly and uncompromisingly nurtured, Tate was keenly aware that those Norman Rockwell times, which he'd hoped to duplicate in his own life, had never materialized.

The vestige of a familial South for Tate hadn't survived long into his adulthood. He, Bett and Megan were no longer a family. Among the multitude of pretty and smart and well-rounded women he'd dated Tate Collier hadn't found a single chance for family.

And so, as concerned as he now was about Megan, the return of these two into his life was fraught with pain.

It brought practical problems too. He was preparing for the biggest case he'd had in years. A corporation was petitioning Prince William County for permission to construct an historical theme park near the Bull Run Battlefield. Liberty Park was going to take on King's Dominion. Tate was representing a group of residents who didn't want the development in their back yard even though the county had granted tentative approval. Last week Tate had won a temporary injunction halting the development for ninety days, which the developer immediately challenged. Next week, on Thursday, the Supreme Court in Richmond would hear the argument and rule whether or not to let the injunction stand. If it did, the delay alone might be enough to put the kibosh on the whole deal.

Overnight Tate Collier had become the most popular – and unpopular – person in Prince William County, depending on whether you opposed or supported the project. The developer of the park and the lenders funding it wanted him to curl up and blow away, of course. But there were hundreds of local businessmen, craftsmen, suppliers and residents who also stood to gain by the park's approval and the ensuing migration of tourists. One editorial, lauding the project, called Tate 'the devil's advocate'. A phrase that certainly resonated in this fervent outpost of the Christian South.

Liberty Park's developer, Jack Sharpe, was one of the richest men in northern Virginia. He came from old money and could trace his Prince William ancestry back to pre-Civil War days. When Tate had brought the action for the injunction Sharpe had hired a well-known local firm to defend. Tate had chopped Sharpe's lawyers into little pieces – hardly even sporting – and the developer had fired them. For the argument in Richmond he'd gone straight to Washington, D.C., to hire a law firm that included two former attorneys general, one former vice-president, and, possibly, a future president.

Tate and Ruth, his secretary/assistant/paralegal, had been working nonstop on the argument and papers for a week, and would continue to do so until, probably, midnight of the day before the argument.

So Bett's reappearance in his life – and Megan's disappearance from it – might have some serious professional repercussions.

Queasy, he thought again of that day when he and Bett had fought so bitterly – fifteen years ago. He thought of the note Megan had written.

That inconvenient child up there . . .

Why had fate brought them back into his life? Why now?

But however he wished otherwise, they *were* back. And there was nothing he could do about it.

Finally Tate asked his ex-wife, 'Think we should call my mother?'

'No,' Bett said. 'Let's give it a few days. I don't want to upset her unnecessarily.'

'What about your sister?'

'Definitely not her.'

'Why not?' Tate wondered aloud. He knew Susan cared very much for Megan. More than most aunts would for a niece. In fact she'd always seemed almost jealous that Bett had a daughter and she didn't.

'Because we don't have any answers yet,' Bett responded. Then, after a few moments, she sighed. 'This isn't like her.' She glanced at the letter in her hand. Then shoved it deep into her purse.

Tate studied his wife's face. Tate Collier had inherited several talents from the Judge. The main gift was, of course, a way with words, and the other, far rarer, was the ability to see the future in someone's face. Now he looked into his ex-wife's remarkable violet eyes, saw them narrow, alight on his and move on, and he knew exactly what was going through her mind. Debate is not just about words, debate is about intuition too. The advocate who can see exactly where his adversary is headed will always have an advantage, whatever rhetorical flourishes the opponent has in his repertoire.

He didn't like what he now saw.

Bett stepped determinedly off the porch and into the back yard, toward the west barn, where her car was parked. He followed and paused on the shaggy lawn, which was badly in need of a mowing. He stared intently at the white streak of the energetic Dalmatian, which had finally forsaken the bone and was zipping through the grass like a greyhound.

Tate glanced at the old barn, alien and yet very familiar. Then his eyes fell on the picnic bench that he and Bett had bought at one of the furniture stores along Route 28. They'd used it only once – for the gathering after the funeral fifteen years ago. He remembered the events with perfect clarity now. It seemed like last week.

He saw Bett looking at the bench too. Wondered what she was thinking.

That had been an unseasonably warm November – just as odd as this April's oppressive heat. He pictured Bett standing on the bench to unhook a Japanese lantern from the dogwood after the last of the guests had left or gone to bed.

Today, Tate paused beside the tree, which was in its expansive, pink bloom.

'Are you busy now?' she asked. 'Your practice?'

'Lot of little things. Only one big case.' He nodded at the house where a paralyzing stack of documents for the Liberty Park argument rested. When they were married the house had been lousy with red-backed legal briefs, forty or fifty pages long. *The Supreme Court of the Commonwealth of Virginia.* Many of them were for death penalty cases Tate was prosecuting. Although he'd been the Fairfax County commonwealth's attorney Tate had often argued down in Richmond on behalf of other counties. 'Have voice, will travel,' his staff had joked. His specialty had become special circumstance murder cases – the euphemism for capital punishment cases.

Bett didn't approve; she was opposed to the death penalty.

Death, Tate reflected, always seemed to lurk behind their relationship. Her sister Susan's continual battle with serious heart disease, and the suicide of Susan's husband, Harris. Then the death of Bett's parents and Tate's father and grandfather, all in the tragically short period of three years.

Tate kicked at piles of corn stalks.

'It's a feeling.' Bett's hands lifted and dropped to her sides. 'Do you understand what I mean?'

No. He didn't. Tate was dogged and smart, but feelings? No, sir. Didn't trust them for a minute. He saw how they got the people he'd prosecuted into deep, deep trouble. When they'd been married Bett lived on feelings. Intuition, sensations, impressions. And sometimes, it seemed, messages from the stars. Drove him crazy.

'Keep going,' he said.

She shrugged. 'I don't believe this.' She tapped her purse. Meaning the letter, he supposed.

'Why do you think that?'

'I was remembering something.'

'Hmm?' he offered noncommittally.

'I found a bag under Megan's bed at home. When I was cleaning last week. There was a soap dish in it.'

He noticed the tears. He wanted to step close. Tried to remember the last time he'd held her. Not just bussed cheeks but actually put his arms around her, felt her narrow shoulder blade beneath his large hands. No memory came to mind.

'It was a joke between us. I never had a dish in my bathroom. The soap got all yucky, Megan said. So she bought this Victorian soap dish. It was for my birthday. Next week. There was a card too. I mean, she wouldn't buy me a present and a card and then do this.'

Wouldn't she? Tate wondered. Why not? When the pressure builds up the volcano blows – whatever the season, whoever's picnicking on the slopes, trysters or churchgoers. Any lawyer who's done domestic relations work will testify to that.

'You think someone *made* her do this? Or that it's a prank?' Tate asked.

'I don't know. She might've been drinking again. I checked

the bottles at home and they didn't look emptier but . . . I don't know.'

'That's not much to go on,' her ex-husband said.

Suddenly she turned to him and spoke. 'It's not a hundred percent thing we've got, Megan and me. There're problems. Of course there are. But our relationship deserves more than that damn letter. More than her running out. . . .' She crossed her arms, gazed into the fields again. She repeated, 'Something's wrong.'

'But what? Exactly? What do you think?'

'I don't *know.*'

'Well, what should we do?'

'I want to go look for her,' Bett said determinedly. 'I want to find her.'

Which is exactly what he'd seen in her purple eyes. What he'd known was coming.

Yet now that he thought about it he was surprised. This didn't sound like Bett McCall at all. Bett the dreamer, Bett the tarot card consulter. Passive, she'd always floated where the breezes took her. Forrest Gump's feather . . . The least likely person imaginable to be a mother. Children needed guidance, direction, models. That wasn't Bett McCall. When he'd heard from Megan that Bett had become engaged last Christmas Tate was surprised only that it had taken her so long to accept what must have been her dozenth proposal since they'd divorced. When they'd been married she'd been charming and flighty and wholly ungrounded, relying on him to provide the foundation she needed. He'd assumed that once they'd split up she'd find someone again quickly.

He wondered if he was standing next to a different Betty Susan McCall than the one he'd been married to (and wondered too if *she* was thinking the same about him).

'Bett,' he said to reassure her, and himself, 'she's fine. She's a mature young woman. She vented some steam and's going out on her own for a few days. I did it myself when I was about her age. Remember?' He doubted that she did but, surprising him, she said, 'You made it all the way to Baltimore.'

'And I called the Judge and he came to get me. A two-day runaway. Look, Megan's had a lot to deal with. I think the soap dish is the key.'

'The dish?'

'You're right – nobody'd buy a present and a card and then not give them to you. She'll be back for your birthday. And know what else?'

'What?'

'There's a positive side to this. She's brought up some things that we can talk about. That *ought* to be talked about.' He too nodded – toward the house, where *his* letter rested like a bloody knife.

Logic. Who could argue with it?

But Bett wasn't convinced.

'There's something else I have to tell you.' She chewed on her narrow lower lip as he'd remembered her doing whenever she'd been troubled. She gripped the porch banister and lowered her head.

Tate Collier, intercollegiate debate champion, national moot court winner, and expert forensic orator, recognized the body language of a confession when he saw one.

'Go ahead,' he said.

'The night before the water tower thing – I was . . . out.'

'Out?'

She sighed. 'I mean, I didn't get home. I was at Brad's in Baltimore. I didn't plan on it; I just fell asleep. Megan was really upset I hadn't called.'

'You apologized?'

'Of course.'

'Well, it was one of those things. An accident. She'd know that.'

Bett shook her head, dismissingly. 'I think maybe that's what started her drinking before she climbed up the tower. And she doesn't like Brad much.'

The girl had described Bett's fiancé as a dweeb who parted his hair too carefully, probably wore sweaters with reindeer on them and spent too much time in front of the TV. Tate didn't share these observations with Bett now.

'Always takes a little while to get used to step-parents. I see it all the time in my practice.'

'I held off going over to his place for a while after that. But last night I went there again. I asked her if she minded and she said she didn't. I dropped her at Amy's on my way to Baltimore.'

'So, there.' Tate smiled and caught her eye as she glanced his way.

'What?'

He lifted his palms. 'The worst is it's a little payback. She's over at somebody's house, going to let us sweat a bit.'

So, no need to worry.

You go your way and I'll go mine.

'That may be,' she said, 'but I'll never forgive myself if something happened to her.'

Tate's phone buzzed. He answered it.

'Counselor,' Konnie's gruff voice barked.

'Konnie, what's up?'

'Got good news.'

'You found her?'

Bett's head swivelled.

The detective said, 'She's on her way to New York.'

'How do you know?' Tate asked.

'I put out a DMV notice and a patrol found her car at the Vienna Metro station. On the front seat was an Amtrak schedule. She'd circled Saturday trains to Penn Station. Manhattan. You know anybody up there'd she'd go to visit?'

Tate told this to Bett, who took the news cautiously. He asked about where she might be going.

She shook her head. 'I don't think she knows a soul up there.'

Tate relayed the answer to Konnie.

'Okay, well, at least you know where she's going. I'll call NYPD and have somebody meet the trains and ask around the station. I'll send 'em her picture.'

'Okay. Thanks, Konnie.' He hung up. Looked at his ex-wife. 'Well,' he said. 'That's that.'

But the violet eyes were disagreeing.

'What, Bett?' he asked.

'I'm sorry, Tate. I just don't buy it.'

'What?'

'Her going off to New York.'

'But *why*? You haven't told me anything specific.'

Her palms slapped her hips. 'Well, I don't *have* anything specific. You want evidence, you want proof. I don't have any.' She sighed. 'I'm not like you.'

'Like me?'

'I can't *convince* you. I don't have a way with words. So I'm not even going to try.'

He started to say something more, to cinch his argument. But something she'd said stopped him. He recalled what the Judge had told him after Tate had finished an argument before the Supreme Court in Richmond in a death penalty case, which he later won. His grandfather had been in the audience, proud as a pup that his offspring was handling the case. Later, over whiskies at the ornate Jefferson hotel in Richmond, the somber old man had said, 'Tate, that was wonderful, absolutely wonderful. They'll rule for you. I saw it in their eyes.'

I did too, he'd thought, wondering what else the Judge had in mind. The old man's eyes were dim.

'But I want you to understand something.'

'Okay,' the young man said.

'You've got it in you to be the most manipulative person on earth.'

'What's that?'

'If you were greedy you could be a Rockefeller. If you were evil you could be a Hitler. You can talk your way into somebody's heart and get them to do whatever you want. Judge or jury, you've got that skill. Words, Tate. Words. You can't see them but they're the most dangerous weapons on earth. Remember that. Be careful, son.'

'Sure, sir,' Tate had said, paying no attention to the old man's advice, wondering if the court's decision would be unanimous. It was.

What he does, he cannot doubt.

Bett gazed at him and in a soft voice – sympathetic, almost pitying – she said, 'Tate, don't worry about it. It's not your problem. You go back to your practice. I can handle it.'

She fished in her purse, pulled out her car keys.

He watched her walk away. Then called, 'Come on in here. Please.' She hesitated then followed as he wandered into the barn, the original one – built in the 1920s. It was a grimy place, filled with as much junk as farm tools. He'd played here as a boy, had a ream of memories: horses' tails twitching with muscular jerks on hot summer afternoons, sparks flying as the Judge edged an axe on the old grinding wheel. He'd tried his first cigarette here. And learned much about the world from the moldy stacks of *National Geographic*'s. He also got his first glimpse of naked women – in the *Playboys* the sharecroppers had stashed here.

He slipped off his suit jacket, hanging it up on a pink, padded coat hanger. What was it doing here? he wondered. A former girlfriend, he believed, had left it after they'd taken a trip to the Caribbean.

Bett stood near him, holding on to a beam that powder-post beetles had riddled.

Tate rummaged through a box. Bett watched, remained silent.

He didn't find what he was looking for in one box and turned to another. He glanced up at her then continued to rummage. He finally found the old beat-up leather jacket. He pulled it on, took off his tie and unbuttoned the top button of his dress shirt.

Then he righted a battered old cobbler's bench, dropped down on to it and took off his Oxford wingtips and then his socks. He massaged his feet.

His eyes fell again on the picnic bench, visible just outside the door. Thinking again of the night of the funeral. Megan in bed. Bett, unhooking the Japanese lantern, the November night still oddly balmy. She seemed to float like a ghost in the dim air above the bench. He'd come up next to her. Startled her by saying, 'I have something to tell you.'

Now he shoved that hard memory away and pulled on work socks and his comfortable boots.

She looked at him in confusion, shook her head. 'What're you doing?'

'You did it after all,' he said with a faint laugh.

'What?'

'You convinced me.' He laced the boots up tight. 'I think you're right. Something happened to her. And we're going to find out what. You and me.'

II

THE INCONVENIENT CHILD

Chapter SEVEN

The rain had started up again.

They were inside now, sitting at the old dining-room table, dark oak and pitted with wormholes.

Tate poured wine, offered it to Bett.

She took the glass, cradled it between both hands the way he remembered her doing when they'd been married. In their first year of marriage, because he was a poor young prosecutor and Bett hadn't yet found her career they couldn't afford to go out to dinner often. But at least once a week they'd try to have lunch at a nice restaurant. They always ordered wine.

She sipped from the glass, set it on the table and watched the sheets of rain roll across the brown fields.

'What do we do, Tate?' she asked. 'Where do we start?'

Prosecutors know as much about police investigations as cops do. But those gears in Tate's mind hadn't been used for a long time. He shrugged. 'I don't know . . . Let's start with her therapist. Maybe she said something about running away, about where she'd go. What's his name?' Tate felt he should have remembered.

'Hanson,' Bett said. She looked up the number in her book

and dialed it. 'It's his service,' she whispered to Tate. 'What's your cell number?'

She gave the doctor's answering service both of their mobile numbers and asked him to return the call. She said it was urgent.

'Try that friend again,' Tate suggested. 'Amy. Where she spent the night.' He tried to picture Amy. He'd met her once. He'd counted nine earrings in the girl's left ear but only eight in her right. He'd wondered if the disparity had been intentional or if she'd merely miscounted.

He thought again about her boyfriend. Well, she *was* seventeen. Why shouldn't she go out? But with a college *senior*? Tate's prosecutorial mind thought back to the Virginia provisions on statutory rape.

Bett shifted and cocked the phone closer to her ear. Apparently someone was now home.

'Amy? It's Megan's mother. Honey, we're trying to find her. She didn't show up for lunch. You know where she went this morning after she left you and your mom's?'

Bett nodded as she listened and then asked if Megan had been upset about anything. Her face was grim.

Tate was half listening but mostly he was studying Bett. The tangles of auburn hair, the striking face, the prominent neck bones, the complexion of a woman who looked ten years younger than her age. He tried to remember the last time he'd seen her. Maybe it was Megan's sweet sixteen party. An odd evening . . . For a fleeting moment as he stood beside the girl and her mother, delivering what everyone declared to be a brilliant toast, he'd had a sense of them as a family. He and Bett had shared a momentary smile. Which faded fast, and they'd stepped out of the spotlight and returned to their separate lives. When he'd seen her after that, Tate couldn't remember.

He thought: She's less pretty now but more beautiful. More

confident, more assured, her sunset-sky eyes were narrowed and not flitting around – coy and ethereal – the way they'd habitually done fifteen years ago.

Maybe it's maturity, Tate reflected. And he wondered again what her impression of *him* might be.

Bett put her hand over the receiver and said, 'Amy said Megan left about nine-thirty this morning and wouldn't tell her where she was going. She said she was secretive about it. She left her bookbag there. I thought it might have something in it that'd give us a clue where she went. I said we'd be by to pick it up later.'

'Good.'

Bett listened to Amy again. She frowned in concern. 'Tate . . . She said that Megan told her somebody'd been following her.'

'Following? Who?'

'She doesn't know.'

Okay, hard evidence. The latent prosecutor in Tate Collier awakened a bit more. 'Let me talk to her.'

Tate took the phone. 'Amy? This is Megan's father.'

A pause. 'Um, hi. Is Megan, like, okay?'

'We hope so. We just want to find out where she is. What's this about somebody following her?'

'She was, like, pretty freaked. I mean, her and me, we were sitting around watching this movie, I don't know, on Wednesday, I guess, and it was about a stalker and she goes, "I don't want to watch this." And I'm like, "Why not?" And she's like, "There's this car with some older guy in it and I think he's been following me around." And I go, "No way." But she's like, "Yeah, really."'

'Where?' Tate asked.

'Around the school, I think,' Amy said.

'Any description?'

'Of the guy?'

'Or the car.'

'Naw. She didn't tell me. But I'm like, "Right, somebody following you . . ." And she's like, "I'm not bullsh—I'm not fooling." And she goes, "It was there yesterday. By the field."'

'What field?'

'The sports field behind the school,' Amy answered.

'That was this last Tuesday?'

'Um, yeah.'

'Did you believe her?'

'I guess. She looked pretty freaked. And she says she told some people about it.'

'Who?'

'I don't know. Some guys. She didn't tell me who. Oh, and she told Mr Eckhard too. He's an English teacher at the middle school but he coaches volleyball after school and on the weekends. And he said if he saw it he'd go talk to the driver. And I'm like, "Wow. This is totally fuck—totally weird."'

'His name's Eckhard?'

'Something like that. I don't know how to spell it. But if you want to, like, talk to him there's usually volleyball practice on Saturday afternoon, only I don't know when. Volleyball's for losers, you know.'

'Yeah, I know,' Tate said. It had been the only sport he'd played in college.

'You think something, like, happened to her? That's way lame.'

'We'd just feel a little better knowing where she is. Listen, Amy, we'll be around to pick up her bookbag in the next couple of hours. If you hear from her give us a call.'

'I will.'

'Promise?' he asked firmly.

'Yeah, like, I promise.'

As soon as Tate pushed the End button on Bett's phone it

buzzed again. He glanced at her and she nodded for him to answer it. He pushed Receive.

'Hello?'

'Um, is this Megan's father?' a man's voice asked.

'That's right.'

'Mr McCall . . .'

'Actually it's Collier.'

'That's right. Sure. Sorry. This is Dr Hanson.'

'Doctor, thanks for calling. . . . I have to tell you, it looks like Megan's run away.'

There was a pause. 'Really?'

Tate tried to read the tone. He heard concern and surprise.

'We got some . . . well, some pretty angry letters from her. Her mother and I both did. And then she vanished. Is there any way we can see you?'

'I'm in Leesburg now. My mother's had an accident.'

'I'm sorry to hear that. But if Bett and I drove up could you spare a half-hour?'

'Well . . .'

'It's important, Doctor. We're really pretty concerned about her.'

'I suppose so. All right.' He gave them directions to the hospital.

Tate looked at his watch. It was noon. 'We'll be there in an hour or so.'

'Actually,' Hanson said slowly, 'I think we *should* talk. There *were* some things she told me that you ought to know.'

'What?' Tate asked.

'I want to think about them a little more. There are some confidentiality issues . . . But it's funny – I'd expect any number of things from Megan, but running away? No, that seems odd to me.'

Tate thanked him. It was only after hanging up that he felt a disturbing twist in his belly. What were the any number of things Megan was capable of? And were they any worse than her running away?

His precious cargo was in the trunk. But while Aaron Matthews would have liked to meditate on Megan McCall and on what lay ahead for both of them he instead was growing increasingly anxious.

The fucking white car.

He was cruising down Route 66. He'd planned to stop at the house he'd rented last year in Prince William County – only two or three miles from Tate Collier's farm – and pick up some things he wanted to take with him to the mountains.

But he couldn't risk leading anyone to his house and this car was just not going away.

It was raining again, a gray drizzle. In the mist and rain, he couldn't see the driver clearly though he was now certain he was young and black.

And because he followed Matthews so carelessly and obviously he sure wasn't a cop.

But who?

Then Matthews remembered: Megan had a black boyfriend. Josh or Joshua, wasn't it? The boy that Dr Hanson had suggested she leave – if Megan had been telling the truth about that bit of advice, which he suspected she might not have been.

Who was this guy?

As a scientist of the mind Matthews believed in logic. The only time people acted illogically was when they were having seizures, he believed. We might not be able to *perceive* the logic they operated by. It might be illogical to rational observers but that was only because they were not being empathetic. *Once we climb into the minds of our patients,* he wrote in his well-received essay on delusional behavior in bipolars, *once we understand their fears and desires – their own internal system of logic – then we can begin to understand their motives, the reasons behind their actions, and we can help them change . . .*

What was this young man thinking?

Maybe Megan had planned to meet him at the office after the appointment. Maybe he'd just happened to see her car, being driven by a man he didn't recognize, and followed it.

Or maybe – this accorded with Matthews's perceptions on the frightening pathology of love – he'd been waiting at the office to confront the doctor about the break-up. Maybe even attack him.

Thanks for that, Hanson, he thought acerbically. Should have broken *your* hip, not Mom's . . . Rage shook him for a moment. Then he calmed.

Did the boy have a car phone? Had he called the police and reported the Mercedes's license number? It was a stolen plate but it didn't belong to a gray Mercedes and that would be reason enough for the cops to pull him over and look in the trunk.

But no, of course, he hadn't called the cops. They'd be after him by now if he had.

But what if he'd called her *parents*? What did Tate Collier know? Matthews brooded. What was the man thinking? What was he planning to *do*?

Matthews sped on until he came to a rest stop then he pulled suddenly into the long driveway, weaving slowly through the trailer tractors and four-by-fours filled with vacationers. He noticed that the white Toyota had made a panicked exit and was pulling into the rest stop after him. Fortunately the rain was heavy again. Which gave Matthews the excuse to hold an obscuring *Washington Post* over his head as he ran to the shelter.

Chapter EIGHT

They were trotting through the rain to Tate's black Lexus when his cell phone buzzed.

As they dropped into the front seats he answered. 'Hello?'

'Tate Collier, please.' A man's voice.

'Speaking.'

'Mr Collier, I'm special agent William McComb, with the FBI's Child Exploitation and Kidnapping Unit. We've just received an inter-agency notice about your daughter.'

'I'm glad you called.'

'I'm sorry about your girl,' the agent said, speaking in the chunky monotone Tate knew so well from working with the feds. 'Unfortunately, I have to say, sir, based on the facts we've got, there's not a lot we can do. But you made some friends here when you were a commonwealth's attorney and so we're going to open a file and put her name out on our network. There'll be a lot more eyes looking for her.'

'Anything you can do will really be appreciated. My wife and I are pretty upset.'

'I can imagine,' the agent said, registering a splinter of emotion. 'Could you give me some basics about her and the disappearance?'

Tate ran through the physical details, Bett helping on the specifics. Blonde, blue eyes, five six, a hundred twenty-eight pounds, age seventeen. Then about the letters. Tate asked, 'You heard about her car?'

'Um, no, sir.'

'The Fairfax County police found it at Vienna Metro. It looks like she went to Manhattan.'

'Really? No, I didn't hear that. Well, we'll tell our office in New York about it . . . But do I hear something in your voice, sir? Are you thinking that maybe she *didn't* run away? Are you thinking there was some foul play?'

Tate had to smile. He'd never thought of himself – especially his speech – as transparent. 'As a matter of fact, we've been having some doubts.'

'Interesting.' McComb said in a wooden monotone. 'What specific elements lead you to believe that?'

'A few things. Megan's mother and I are on our way to Leesburg right now to talk to her therapist. See what he can tell us.'

'He's in Leesburg?'

'His mother's in St Mary's hospital. She had an accident.'

'And you think he might be able to tell you something?'

'He said he wanted to talk to us. I don't know what he's got in mind.'

'Any other thoughts?'

'Well, Megan told her girlfriend that there was a car following her over the past few weeks.'

'Car, hm? They get any description?'

'Her girlfriend didn't. But we think a teacher did. Eckhard's his name. Something like that. He's supposed to be at the school later, coaching volleyball. But I'd guess that's only if the rain breaks up.'

'And what's her friend's name?'

He gave the agent Amy Walker's name. 'We're going to talk to her too. And pick up Megan's bookbag from her. We're hoping it might have something in it that'll give us a clue where she's gone.'

'I see. Does Megan have any siblings?'

'No.'

'Is there anyone else who's had much contact with the girl?'

'Well, my wife's fiancé.'

Silence for a moment. 'Oh, you're divorced.'

'That's right. Forgot to mention it.'

'You have his name and number?' McComb asked.

Tate asked Bett, who gave him the information. Into the phone he said, 'His name's Brad Markham. He lives in Baltimore.' Tate gave him Brad's phone number as well.

'Do you think he was in any way involved?' the agent asked Tate.

'I've never met him, but, no, I'm sure not.'

'Okay. You working with anyone particular at the Fairfax County Police?'

'Konnie . . . That'd be Dimitri Konstantinatis.'

'Out of which office?'

'Fair Oaks.'

'Very good, sir. . . . You know, nearly all runaways return on their own. And most of the ones that don't, get picked up and *sent* back home. A little counseling, some family therapy, and things generally work out just fine.'

'Thanks for your thoughts. Appreciate it.'

'Oh, one thing, Mr Collier. I guess you know about the law. About how it could be, let's say, troublesome for you to take matters into your own hands here.'

'I do.'

'Bad for everybody.'

'Understood.'

'Okay. Then enough said.'

'Appreciate *that* too. I'm just going to be asking a few questions.'

'Good luck to both of you.'

They hung up and he told Bett what the agent had said. Her face was troubled.

'What is it?' He felt an urge to append a 'honey' but nipped that one fast.

'Just that it seems so much more serious with the FBI involved.'

How foolish people are, how trusting, how their defenses crumble like sand when they believe they're talking to a friend. And oh how they want to believe that you *are* a friend . . .

Why, no wild animal in the world would be as trusting as a human being. It's amazing we're not extinct.

Aaron Matthews, no longer the stony-voiced FBI agent, protector of the weak, hung up the phone after speaking with Tate Collier. He almost felt guilty – it had been so easy to draw information out of the man.

And what information it was! Oh, Matthews was angry. His mood teetered precariously. All his preparation – such care, such finesse, everything set up to send Collier and his wife into a fit of paralysis and dismay and sit home, brooding about their lost daughter . . . and what were they doing but playing amateur detectives?

Their talking to Hanson could be a real problem. Megan might have said something about loving her parents and never even considering running away. Or, even worse, they might become suspicious of Matthews's whole plan and have the police go through Hanson's office. He'd been careful there but hadn't worn gloves all the time. There were fingerprints – and the window latch in the bathroom where Matthews had snuck in was still broken.

Then there was Amy Walker, Megan's friend. With a

bookbag that *probably* didn't have anything compromising but might – maybe a diary or those notes teenage girls are always passing around in school. And this Eckhard, the teacher and coach.

Reports of a car following her . . .

Much of Matthews's reconnaissance had been conducted around the school. If the teacher *had* walked up to the car he might easily have gotten the license number of the Mercedes or even a look at Matthews himself. Mentioned it to school security. And he hadn't changed the license plates to the stolen ones until yesterday. And even if Eckhard didn't *think* he'd seen much, there were probably some prickly little facts locked away in his subconscious; Matthews had done much hypnosis work and knew how many memories and observations were retained in the cobwebby recesses of the mind.

Why the hell was Collier doing this? Why hadn't the letters fooled him? The lawyer was supposed to be *logical*, he was supposed to be *cold*. Why didn't he believe the bald facts in front of him?

A Mood began to settle on Matthews but he struggled to throw it off.

No, I have no time for this now!

(He thought of how many patients he'd wanted to grab by the lapels: Oh, quit your fucking complaining and do something about it! You don't like her, leave. *She* left *you*? Find somebody else. You're a drunk, stop drinking.)

He returned to the phone and called three Walkers in Fairfax before he got the household that included a teenage Amy.

He spoke with her mother.

'Yes, Amy's my daughter. Who's this?'

'I'm William McComb, with the County. I've gotten a call from Child Protective Services.'

'My God, what's wrong?'

'Nothing to be alarmed at, Mrs Walker. This doesn't involve your daughter. We're investigating a case involving Megan McCall.'

'Oh, no! Is Megan all right? She spent the night here!'

'That's what we understand. It seems she's missing and we've been looking into some allegations about her father.'

There was a moment's pause as if she was here trying to remember, who he was.

'Tate Collier,' Matthews said.

'Oh, right. I don't know him. You think he's involved? You think he did something?'

'We're just looking into a few things now. But I'd appreciate it if you'd tell your daughter she shouldn't have any contact with him.'

'Why would she have any contact with him?' the edgy voice asked. How easily she'd cry, Matthews predicted.

'We don't know. We don't think there'd be any reason for him to hurt or touch her—'

'Oh, God. You don't *think*?'

'We just want to make sure Amy stays safe until we get to the bottom of what happened to Megan.'

'"Happened to Megan"? *Please* tell me what's going on.'

'I can't really say more now. Tell me, where's your daughter now?'

'Upstairs.'

'Would you mind if I spoke to her?'

'No, of course not.'

A moment later a girl's lazy voice: 'Hello?'

'Hi, Amy. This is Mr McComb. I'm with the County. How are you?'

'Okay, I guess. Like, is Megan okay?'

'I'm sure she's fine. Tell me, has Megan's father talked to you recently?'

'Um,' the girl began.

'You answer,' the mother said sternly from the extension.

'Yeah, like, he said she's run away and asked me about it. He was going to come by and get her bookbag.'

'Is there anything in there that might suggest where she's gone?'

'I dunno. I don't think so. Just books and shi—stuff.'

The mother: 'You were going to let him in here? And not tell me?'

The girl snapped, 'Mom, just, like, cut it out, okay? It's Megan's dad.'

Matthews said, 'Amy, don't talk to him. And whatever you do, don't go anywhere with him.'

'I—'

'If he suggests going away, getting into his car, going into his barn . . .'

'God, his *barn*?' her mother gasped. Yep, Matthews could hear soft weeping.

He continued, 'Amy, if he offers you something to drink . . .'

Another gasp.

Oh, my, this was fun. Matthews continued calmly, ' . . . just tell him no. If he comes over don't answer the door. Make sure it's locked.'

'Like, why?'

'You don't ask, young lady. You do what the man says.'

'Mom, like, come on . . . What about her bookbag?'

'You just hold on to it until you hear from me or someone at Child Protective Services. Okay?'

'I guess.'

'Should we call the police?' Mrs Walker asked.

'No, it's not a criminal charge yet.'

'Oh, God,' said Amy's mother, the woman of the limited epithets. 'Amy, tell me. Did Megan's father ever touch you? Now, tell the truth.'

'Who? Megan's father? Jeez, Mom. You're such a loser. I never even met him.'

'Mrs Walker?'

'Yes. I'm here.' Her voice cracked.

'I really don't want to alarm you unnecessarily.'

'No, no. We appreciate your calling. What's your number, Mr McComb?'

'I'm going to be in the field for a while. Let me call you later, when I'm back at the office.'

'All right.'

Matthews felt a cheerful little twinge as he heard her crying. Though Amy's silence on the other extension was louder.

He couldn't resist. 'Mrs Walker?'

'Yes?'

'Do you have a gun?'

A choked sob. 'No, we don't. I don't. I've never . . . I wouldn't know how to use one. I guess I could go to Sports Authority. I mean—'

'That's all right,' Matthews said soothingly. 'I'm sure it's not going to come to anything like that.'

'What if Megan's mother, like, calls?' the girl asked.

'Yes,' Mrs Walker echoed, 'what if her mother calls?'

A concerned pause. 'I'd be careful. We're investigating her too. . . . It was a very troubled household, it seems.'

'God,' Mrs Walker muttered.

Matthews hung up.

What a mess this could become. It had seemed so simple in theory. And was so complicated now. Just like the art of psychiatry itself.

Well, there were other things to do. But first things first. He had to get Megan to her new home – with his son Peter – deep in the mountains.

Matthews returned to the Mercedes. He pulled back onto the highway, noting that the white car was still sticking with him like a lamprey to a fish.

Chapter NINE

Amy wasn't home.

Oh, brother. Tate sighed. Looked through a window, saw nothing. Walked back to the front door. Pressed the bell again.

Standing on the concrete stoop of the split-level in suburban Burke, Tate kept his hand on the doorbell for a full minute but neither the girl nor her mother came to the door.

Where'd she gone? Bett had said that they'd stop by soon. Why hadn't Amy stayed? Or at least put the bookbag out on the door stoop?

Was this adolescent friendships nowadays?

'Maybe the bell's broken,' Bett called from the car.

But Tate pounded on the door with his open palm. There was no response. 'Amy!'

'Go round back,' Bett suggested.

Tate pushed through a scratchy holly bush and rapped on the back door.

Still no answer. He decided to slip inside and find the bag; a missing teenager took precedence over a technical charge of trespass (thinking: I could make a good argument for an implied license to enter the premises. Interesting legal concept). But as he reached for the doorknob he believed he heard a click. When he tried to open the latch he found the door was locked.

He peered through the window and thought he saw some motion. But he couldn't be sure.

Tate returned to the car.

'Not there.' He sighed. 'We'll call later.'

'Leesburg?' Bett asked.

'Let's try that teacher first. Eckhard.'

It was only a five-minute drive to the school. The rain had stopped and youngsters were gathering on the schoolyard – boys for baseball, girls for volleyball, both for soccer. Hackeysacks, Frisbees, skateboards. After speaking with several parents and students they learned that Robert Eckhard, the volleyball coach, had put together a practice for three that afternoon. It was now a quarter to two.

Tate flopped down into the passenger seat of the Lexus. He stretched. 'This police work. I don't see how Konnie does it.'

Bett kicked her shoes off and massaged her feet. 'Wish I'd worn boots, like you.' Then she glanced toward the school. 'Look,' she said.

When they'd been married Bett assumed that he knew exactly what she was thinking or talking about. A gesture of her finger, an eyebrow raised like a witch casting a spell – he'd follow her glance and have not a clue as to her meaning. Today, though, he turned his head toward where she was looking and saw the two blue-uniformed security guards, standing in one of the back doorways of the school.

'Good idea,' he said. And they drove around to the door.

By the time they got there the guards had gone inside. Bett and Tate parked and walked inside the school

The halls had that smell of all high schools – sweat, lab gas, disinfectant, paste.

Tate laughed to himself at the instinctive uneasiness he

felt being here. Classwork had come easily to him but he'd spent his time and effort on Debate Club in high school and the teachers were forever booting him into detention hall for skipped classes or missing homework. That he would pause at the door on the way out of home room and resonantly quote Cicero or John Calhoun to his teacher didn't help his academic record any, of course.

The security offices in Megan's school were small cubicles of carpeted partitions near the gym.

One guard, a crew-cut boy with half-mast eyelids, wearing a perfectly pressed uniform, listened unemotionally to Tate's story. He adjusted his glistening black billy club.

'Don't know your daughter.' He turned, called out, 'Henry, you know a Megan McCall?'

'Nope,' said his partner, who resembled him to an eerie degree. He stepped into the school proper and disappeared.

'What we're concerned about is this car. A man seemed to be following her.'

'A car. Following her.' The young man was skeptical.

Bett took over. 'Around the schoolyard. This past week.'

Tate: 'We were wondering if anybody might've reported it.'

The man's face eased into that put-upon look security guards are very good at. Maybe they're resentful that they're not full-fledged cops and could carry guns. And use them.

'Are the police involved?' the man asked.

'Somewhat.'

'Hm.' Trying to figure that one out.

'What happens if somebody sees something unusual? Is there any procedure for that?'

'The Bust-er Book,' the guard said.

Bett asked, 'The . . . uh?'

'Bust-er. He's a dog. I mean, a cartoon dog. But it's like "Bust" as in get busted. Then a dash, then E-R. If the kids see something weird they come tell us and we write it down in the Bust-er Book and then there's a record of it, for the police. If anything, you know, happens.'

Tate recalled what Amy'd said. 'It was on Tuesday. Out in the parking lot by the sports field. Could you take a look?'

'Oh, we can't let you see it,' the guard said.

'I'm sorry?'

'Parents don't have, you know, access to it. Only the administration and police. That's the rule.'

'That's it right there?'

The guard turned around and glanced at the blue binder with the words 'Bust-er' on the spine and a cartoon effigy of a dog wearing a Sherlock Holmes deerstalker hat. 'Yessir.'

'If you don't mind . . . See, our daughter's missing. As I was saying.'

'Just have the police give us a call.'

'Well, she's not officially a missing person.'

'Then I guess you don't really need to look at the book.' The guard's lean face crinkled. His still eyes looked Tate up and down and his muscular hand caressed his ebony billy club. He was everything Tate hated about northern Virginia. Snide and sullen. This young man would see nothing wrong with a tap on the wife's chin or a belt on his kids' butts to keep them in line. He was master of the house; everyone else did as told. Dinner on the table at five even if I'm out late drinking, and we're all going to church, and, sure, there are some all-right Negroes but that's as far as I'm going . . . And what're these fucking Orientals doing all over the place here?

A bastard mix of Southern hate and Northern ignorance.

Tate looked at Bett. Her eyebrows were raised as if she were asking: what was the problem? After all, he *was* the silver-tongued devil. He could talk anybody into anything. (Resolved: the Watergate break-in was justifiable as a means to a valid end. Lifelong Democrat, grandson of a lifelong Democrat, Tate had leapt to take that irreverent position. For the pure joy of going up against overwhelming odds. He'd won, to the Judge's shock and permanent amusement.)

'Officer,' Tate began, thinking of the rhetorical tricks in his arsenal, the logic, the skills at persuasion. Ratiocination. He paused, then walked to the door and motioned the guard to follow.

The lean man walked slowly enough to let Tate know that nobody on earth was going to make him do a single thing he didn't want to do.

Tate paused at the front door and looked out over the schoolyard. 'What do you see there?'

The guard hesitated uncertainly. He'd be thinking, what kinda question's that? I see trees, I see cars, I see fences, I see clouds.

Tate waited just the right amount of time and said, 'I see a lot of young people.'

'Um.' Well, what the hell else're you gonna see on a schoolyard? *Course* there're kids.

'And those young people rely on us adults for everything. They rely on us for food, for shelter, for schooling, and you know what else?'

Video games, running shoes, Legos? How'm I supposed to know? What's this Bozo up to?

'They rely on us for their safety. That's what you're doing here, right? It's the reason they hired a big, strong guy like you. A man who's got balls, who's not afraid to mix it up with somebody.'

'I dunno. I guess.'

'Well, my daughter's relying on me for her safety. She needs me to find out where she is. Maybe she's in trouble, maybe she isn't. Hey, let's take an example: you see some tough big kids talking to a little kid. Maybe they're just brothers, fooling around. Or maybe they're trying to sell him some pot or steal his lunch money. You'd go and find out, right?'

'I would. Sure.'

'That's all I'm doing with my daughter. Trying to find out if she's okay. And going through that book would sure be a big help.'

The guard nodded.

'Well?' Tate asked expectantly.

'Nosir. Rules is rules. Can't be done.'

Tate sighed. He glanced at Bett, who said icily, 'Let's go, Tate. Nothing more to be accomplished here.'

As they walked to the car, the guard called, 'Sir?'

Tate turned.

'That was a good try, though. I almost bought it.' With a sneering grin, he picked up a magazine on customized pickup trucks and sat down.

Tate and Bett continued to the car then climbed in and drove out of the lot.

Neither of them could contain the laughter for long. They both roared. Bett gasped and said, 'That was the biggest load of hogwash I ever heard. "It's the reason they hired a big, strong guy like you."'

Wiping tears from his eyes, Tate controlled his laughing. 'But I kept his attention. That was some pretty good double teaming.'

Bett reached under her blouse and pulled out twenty or thirty sheets of notebook paper. 'I figured I better leave the notebook itself.' She muttered, 'The Bust-er Book? The *Bust-er* Book? Do people really take that stuff seriously?'

Tate drove about three blocks and pulled over to the curb.

'Okay,' she said, 'Tuesday . . . Tuesday.' Flipping through the pages. 'If the stormtrooper back there's the one who keeps the book he's got handwriting like a sissy. Okay, Tuesday . . .' She nodded then read: '"Two students reported a gray car, no school parking permit, parked on Sideburn Road. Single driver. Drove off without picking up student."'

'A gray car. Not much to go on. Anything else?'

'Not then. But Amy said Megan'd been thinking she'd been followed for a while.' Bett flipped back through the pages. Her perfect eyebrow rose in a delicate arc. 'Listen. A week ago. "M. McCall (Green Team)—" That's her class section at school. "—reported gray car appeared to be following her. Security Guard Gibson took report. Did not personally witness incident. Checked but no car seen. Subject did not know tag or make of vehicle." He spelled vehicle wrong,' Bett added. Then looked at her ex-husband. 'Why didn't she tell me about it, Tate? Why?'

Tate had no answer. He asked, 'Any description of the driver?'

'None, no.'

'What kind of car did her boyfriend drive?'

'White . . . I think a Toyota.'

'He could've borrowed one to follow her,' Tate mused.

'Could have, sure.'

More questions than answers.

Tate stared at the turbulent clouds overhead. The sun tried to break through but a line of thick gray rolled over the sky heading eastward. 'Let's go to Leesburg,' he said.

Chapter TEN

Joshua LeFevre glanced down at the odometer. He'd driven another twenty miles along I-66 in his battered old Toyota since the last time he'd checked. Which put him about seventy miles from Fairfax.

Mr Tibbs, the unflappable police detective within him, had figured out where Megan and her therapist lover were going. To the doctor's mountain place. It was now chic for professionals to have vacation homes in the Blue Ridge or in West Virginia, where you could buy a mountaintop for a song.

The rain had stopped and he cranked the sunroof open, listening to the wind hissing through the Yakima bike rack.

It was early afternoon when he broke through the Shenandoahs and saw the hazy Blue Ridge in front of him. Not evocative gunmetal today, the literature major in him thought – the hills were tinted with the green frost of spring growth. Nice place for picnics, he thought, recalling that he and Megan had talked about a bike tour along Skyline Drive later in the spring.

He was lost in this reverie when the Mercedes got away from him.

Never would have happened to Sidney Poitier.

Damn . . .

The Merce had pulled out to pass a semi and he'd followed. But as soon as the big gray car had cleared the cab of the truck the doctor had skidded hard to the right and pulled on to the exit ramp as the truck driver laid on his air horn and braked.

LeFevre's Toyota was caught in the left lane and he couldn't swerve back in time to make the exit.

His head swivelled around and he saw the roof of the Mercedes sink below the level of the highway as it slowed along the ramp.

LeFevre slammed his fists on the wheel. Tantrums were definitely not Poitier's style but he couldn't help it. He thought about making an illegal U over the median but here he was a black kid with knobby dreads driving through the crucible of the Confederacy; the fewer laws he broke, the better.

The next exit was a mile down the highway and by the time he'd followed the Möbius strip of ramps and returned to the exit the Mercedes had taken there was no sign of the big car – only an intersection of three different country roads, any one of which they might have taken.

And, now that he thought about it, the doctor might just have stopped for gas and gotten back on to the interstate, continuing west.

He closed his eyes in frustration and pressed back hard into the headrest.

What the hell'm I doing here?

The stuff love makes you do, he thought.

Hate it, hate it, hate it . . .

LeFevre pulled into the gas station, filled up at the self-service island then walked up to the skinny, sullen attendant with long hair sprouting from under a Valvoline giveaway cap, which was as greasy as the hair. Smiled at him.

'How you doing?' Sidney Poitier asked very politely.

'Okayyourself?' the man muttered.

'Not bad. Not bad.'

The man stared at LeFevre's hair, which was not exactly modeled on Mr Poitier's, circa 1967, but was much closer to a Menace II Society fan's.

'Helpya?'

It occurred to LeFevre that even Officer Tibbs, in suit, tie and polished Oxfords, wouldn't get very far around here asking which way a seventy-thousand-dollar automobile had just gone.

Not without some incentive.

LeFevre opened his wallet and extracted five twenties. Looked down at them.

So did the attendant. 'That's cash.'

'Yes, it is.'

'You charged your gas. I seen you.'

'I did.'

'Well, whatsitfor?'

'It's for you,' LeFevre said in his most carefully crafted Queen's English.

'Uh-huh. Uh-huh. Why's it for me?' The man seemed to sneer.

'I have a little problem.'

The stubbly face asked, Who cares?

'I was driving down sixty-six and this Mercedes cut me off, ran me off the road. Nearly killed me.' (This had happened to Sidney Poitier in *In the Heat of the Night*. More or less.) 'Did it on purpose. The driver, I mean.'

'Don't say.' The man yawned.

'Front end's all screwed up now. And see the bodywork I need?'

Thank goodness, LeFevre thought, he'd never fixed the damage after he'd scraped the side of the car on a barricade when he'd dropped his mother off at Nieman Marcus in Tysons last month.

But the attendant looked at the car without a splinter of interest.

'So you want me to lookit the front end?'

'No, I want the license number of that Mercedes. He came by here five, ten minutes ago.'

This had seemed like a good way to break the ice – asking for the license number. It made things official – as if the police were going to get involved. LeFevre believed this trick was definitely something that Sidney Poitier would do.

'Why'd he run you off the road?' the man asked abruptly.

Which brought LeFevre up cold.

'Um, I don't know.' LeFevre shrugged. Then he asked, 'You know which car I mean?' He remained respectful but decided not to be too polite. Sidney Poitier had glared at Rod Steiger quite a bit.

'Maybe.'

'So he stopped here for gas.'

'Nope.' The scrawny guy looked at the money. Then he shook his head; his slick grin gave LeFevre an unpleasant glimpse of some very bad teeth. 'Fuck. You're shittin' me. You don't want that tag number.'

'Um, I—'

'What you want is to find out where that sumvabitch lives. Am I right?'

'Well . . .'

'An' I'll tell you why you want that.'

'Why?'

''Cause he was drivin' his big old Mercedes and he thunk t'himself, why, here's a black man only he was thinking the N word, driving a little shit Jap car and I can cut him off 'cause he don't mean shit to me.' A faint laugh. 'And you don't want no tag number for State Farm insurance or the poe-leece. Fuck. You wanna find him and you wanna beat the shiny crap outta him.'

So, end of story. Well, it was a nice try. LeFevre was about to put the money away and return to his car – before the man called some real-life Rod Steigers – when the attendant said, 'Now, that frosts me, what he done. Truly does.'

'I'm sorry?' LeFevre asked.

'I mean, I got friends're black. Couple of 'em. And we have a good time together and one of them's wife cooks for me and my girlfriend nearly every week.'

'Well, that right?'

'Fuck, yeah, that's right.' The twenties were suddenly in the man's stained fingers. 'I say, more power to you. Find him and wail on him all you want.'

'How's that?' LeFevre blinked.

'I know that sumvabitch.'

'The man in the Mercedes?'

'Yeah.'

'Dr Hanson, right?'

'I don't know his name. But I seen him off and on for a spell. He comes and goes. Never stops here but I seen him. Pisses me off royal, people like him. Moving everybody down the mountain.'

'What do you mean, "moving down the mountain?"' Sidney Poitier asked politely, smiling now and giving the man plenty of thinking room.

'Any sumvabitch in a Mercedes going into them hills's a real-estate weasel. See, what happened was when folk settled here they moved to the top of the Ridge. Naturally, where else? But they couldn't keep the land, most of 'em. Money troubles, you know. Taxes. So they kept selling to the government for the Park or to rich folks wanted a weekend place, and families kept moving down the mountain. Now, most everybody's in the valley – most of the honest folk, I mean. Pretty soon there won't be no mountains left 'cept for the rich pricks and the government. 'S what my dad says. Makes sense to me.'

'Where's his place?'

The skinny young man nodded toward one narrow road.

'Up that one there. I don't know where exactly his house is. Only place I know of up there's the hospital. That's what I figure he's turning into condos or something.'

'What hospital?'

'Loony bin. Closed a few years back.'

'How far is it?'

'Five miles, give'r take. At the end of Palmer Road yonder.' He pointed. 'Now, you ain't going to kill him, are you? I'd have some problems with that.'

'No. I really do just want to talk.'

'Uh-huh. Uh-huh.' The man squinted then grinned his bad-tooth grin again. 'You know, you remind me of that actor.'

'I do?'

'Yeah. He's a good one. Don't exactly look like him but you sound like him and sort of hold yourself like him. What's his name? What's his name?'

LeFevre, grinning himself, answered his question.

The man blinked and shook his head. 'Who the hell's Sidney Poitier?'

LeFevre said, 'Maybe he was before your time.'

'What's that guy's name? I can picture him . . . Kicked the shit out of some ninjas in this movie with Sean Connery. Wait! Snipes . . . Wesley Snipes. That's it. That man can *act*.'

LeFevre walked to the edge of the tarmac. The smell of gasoline mixed with the scent of spring growth and clayish earth. Palmer Road vanished into a dark shaft of pine and hemlock, winding up into the mountains.

The young attendant stuffed a strand of slick hair up under his hat. 'He may have a trailer up there. Lotta developers have those Winnebagos or like that. Or maybe he's staying in the hospital itself. Shit, I wouldn't do that for any money. Hear stories about it. People sometimes get attacked. By wild dogs or something.'

Or something?

'Find bloody bones sometimes. And not much else left.'

LeFevre's anger was turning to concern. Megan, what've you gotten yourself into? 'I just follow that road?'

'Right. Five miles, I'd guess. Keeps to the high ground. Then circles back on itself like a snake.'

'A snake,' LeFevre said, absently staring into the murky forest. Thinking of the quote from Dante's *Divine Comedy: Halfway through life's journey I came to myself in a dark woods, where the straight way was lost.* Recalling the story too: How Beatrice took Virgil on a trip to hell.

'Listen,' the attendant said, startling him, 'you stop on your way back, okay? Let me know what happens.'

LeFevre nodded and shook the man's oily hand. He climbed into his car and sped along Palmer Road. In an instant, civilization vanished behind him and the world became black bark, shadows and the waving arms of tattered boughs.

The things we do for love, LeFevre thought. The things we do for love.

Aaron Matthews pulled the Mercedes into a grove of trees beside the asphalt and climbed out, looking back over Palmer Road.

No sign of the white car.

He was sure he'd tricked the boyfriend just fine when he'd sped off the highway beside the truck. The kid was probably in West Virginia by now and even if he managed to figure out which exit they'd taken and backtracked he'd have no way of knowing which way Matthews had gone into the maze of back roads here. Although Matthews had been coming to the deserted hospital for the past year, ever since he'd brought his son here, he'd made a point of never stopping for gas or food at the service station or grocery store at the foot of the exit ramp off Route 66. He was sure the local hicks knew nothing about him.

He climbed back in the car and continued on to the Blue Ridge Mental Health Facility.

Just past the cleft where the road passed between two steep vine-covered hills, the ground opened into the shallow bowl of a valley. Through a picket line of scabby trees a sprawl of low, decrepit buildings was visible.

BRMHF had been the last destination for the hard-core crazies in the commonwealth of Virginia. Schizophrenics, uncontrollable bipolars, borderline personalities, delusionals. Security was high – the patients (i.e., inmates) were locked down at night in restraint (padded) quarters (cells). The eight-foot chain-link fence enclosing the ten-acre grounds was 'designed to provide comforting security to patients and nearby residents alike' (translation: it sported a live current of 500 volts).

The hospital had served its purpose well, until two years ago, when it had been closed down by the state, and the patients were shipped to other facilities and halfway houses.

Matthews was intimately familiar with the place; the patients here had found him a confidant, confessor, judge . . . a virtual father over the course of his four-year tenure. When he thought of home he thought first of this hospital and second the Colonial house in Arlington, Virginia, he'd lived in with Margaret and their son, Peter.

Matthews braked the car to a halt and examined the place carefully for signs of intruders though a break-in would have been very unlikely. The current to the fence had been shut off long ago but the grounds were patrolled by five knob-headed Rottweilers, as raw and brutal as dogs could be, teeth sharp as obsidian; they hunted in packs and one or twice a week killed one of the deer that often strolled through the gate when it was open.

He listened carefully again – no sound of approaching cars – and unlocked the two tempered steel locks securing the gate. He drove inside and parked.

Then he lifted Megan from the trunk and carried her inside, pushing through a door with his shoulder. He'd reversed the locks on the doors – you could simply push in from the outside but couldn't get back out without a key, in effect turning a hospital into a prison.

He stepped into the lobby.

Asylums smell far more visceral than do regular hospitals because even though their province is the mind, the byproduct of that type of pathology is piss, shit, sweat, blood. This was still true of the Blue Ridge Hospital; the air stank of bodily functions and decay.

Through these murky halls Matthews carried his prize in his arms. Feeling every ounce of her weight – though it wasn't the weight of a burden; it was the weight of treasure. Gold or platinum, solid and perfect in his arms.

Matthews carried Megan into the room he'd fixed up for her. He laid her on the bed and undressed her. First the blouse and the bra. Then jeans and panties and socks. His eyes coursed up and down her body. Yet he touched her only once – to make sure her pulse was regular.

Taking her clothes, he left the room, locked her door with a heavy padlock. He thought about stopping to see his son but the boy was in a different part of the hospital and Matthews had no time for that now. He left the building, got into his car and started through the gate. He'd gotten only ten feet before he heard the thump-thump-thump of the flat tire.

Oh, not now! His mood suddenly darkened. And he fought to keep the blackness at bay. He thought of Megan. It buoyed him just enough. Matthews climbed out and walked to the rear of the car.

He took one look at the slash mark in the Michelin and

flung the door open, trying to get to the pistol in his glove compartment.

Too late.

'Don't move.' The young man held the rusty machete, left over from the grounds-keeping Matthews had done when he'd brought his son, Peter, here. He gripped the long knife awkwardly but with enough manic determination to make Matthews freeze and raise his hands. The boy's muscles were huge.

He blurted, 'I'll give you my wallet. And there's—'

'I want to know what's going on.'

The young man's voice was astonishing. What a beautiful patois. Carolinian and Caribbean and some succulent English, which tempered the two. This man could fuck any woman he wanted simply by telling her she was beautiful.

'Don't hurt me,' Matthews said desperately.

A flicker of uncertainty in the brown eyes.

'What've you done with Megan?'

Matthews frowned. 'Who *are* you?'

Ah, young man, asked the silent therapist within Matthews, you're not a fighter at all, are you? You're a bit out of your element . . . And why do you feel so guilty, why do you feel so unsure?

The pistol was in the glove compartment only feet away. But his assailant was riding on pure nerves. With his strength it wouldn't take much for the boy to injure Matthews seriously, without even trying. And besides, while he *believed* he wasn't dangerous, Matthews had learned that premature diagnoses can be very risky.

He smiled and lowered his hands. He nodded knowingly. 'Wait, wait. You're not . . . You must be Joshua.'

The boy's face squirreled up into a frown. 'You know me?'

'Sure, I know you,' Matthews said smoothly. 'I was *hoping* we'd get a chance to talk.'

Chapter ELEVEN

'You startled me,' said the soothing voice of Aaron Matthews. 'I didn't mean to react the way I did.'

He glanced at the tire, laughed. 'But then again you did attack my Mercedes with a machete.'

With his voice trembling (love that voice, *love* it), the boy said, 'I thought you'd just brought her here on a date. To show her some of your property or something. Then I saw you carry her inside. What the hell's going on? Tell me!'

'Wait. Carry who inside?' Matthews frowned.

Show her some of your property?

'Megan. I *saw* you two.'

So he's thinking real estate development. Matthews shook his head, glanced toward the hospital. 'You mean just a few minutes ago? Well, I carried in some bags of cleaning supplies. And a tarp. I bought this place and I'm turning it into condos.'

A minuscule lessening of his suspicion. Not believing your own eyes, are you? How often we don't. And you don't do well with embarrassment, do you? A gift from the African-American executive mum, by chance? The one with practiced elocution and the Chanel scarf over the shoulder of the suit she bought at Tysons Galleria?

Matthews noted, however, that the boy continued to hold the rusty blade firmly in his hand. 'Where is she? What were you doing with her car?'

'Joshua,' Matthews said patiently, 'I just dropped Megan off at my weekend place up the road.' He pointed into the woods. 'A couple miles from here. She wanted to get a head start on making lunch.'

'Why'd you switch cars at Metro?'

'Megan's got a friend. Amy.' He paused.

Joshua said, 'I know Amy.'

'Amy's borrowing her car. We left it at the Metro for her and took the Mercedes.'

The boy frowned. 'I didn't think Amy had a license.'

Matthews laughed. 'Oh? She didn't share that with us. I wondered why she didn't want to borrow her mother's.'

'Good, Matthews told himself, giving his performance high marks.

'But wait . . . I didn't see Megan in your car when I was behind you.'

'You were following us?'

'Yes, I was following you. How did you think I found you?'

'I assumed that Megan told you about me. And that we come up here sometimes.'

Joshua blinked.

Matthews studied the young man for a moment then tilted his head and said with sympathy, 'Look, Joshua, don't do this to yourself.'

'Do what?'

Oh, the desperation Matthews could see in the olive eyes was so sweet. He nearly shivered with pleasure. He whispered, 'You should forget about her.'

'But I love her!'

'Forget about her. For your own good.'

So, Matthews had been right. The man had probably arrived

at Hanson's office toward the end of the session, planning to confront Megan – and presumably the doctor too – about Hanson's advice on breaking up. A little obsessive, are we?

Or just too much testosterone in the blood.

If it weren't for romance we poor psychiatrists would have nothing to do. As Freud said, more or less, Love's a bitch, ain't it?

'You talked her into breaking up with me so you could see her!' Joshua said.

'Megan said that? Well, it's not true. That's completely unethical and I'd never do it.'

Joshua blinked at the vehemence in Matthews's voice. The therapist had deduced that the boy would be a rule-and-regulation victim. Thanks to Dad, of course – the soldier.

The therapist continued, 'She *decided* to break up with you on her own, Joshua. And *then* we started going out.'

'That's not what she said. She said you told her to break up with me.'

'No, Joshua. That's not the way it was at all.'

'But she *told* me!'

'Well, we can't blame her for not being completely honest all the time, now, can we?'

'Blame her?'

'See, Megan has trouble taking responsibility for certain things. Not unusual, not a serious problem. We all suffer from it to varying degrees. It's hard for her to express her inner feelings. Given her parents. . . . You know Tate and Bett?'

Hearing the names, the familiarity in Matthews's voice, the boy's defenses slipped a bit more. But he was still dangerous. Too confused, too much in love, riding on too much emotion. Matthews decided he couldn't win the boy's confidence; he'd have to go in a different direction. 'I've met her mother, not her father.'

'Well, believe me, they're to thank for a lot of her

problems. Her lying, for instance. And she'd lose her temper sometimes, wouldn't she?'

'A couple of times. But who doesn't?'

The question told Matthews that the boy was buying the argument. He laughed. 'Joshua, put that thing down and go home. Forget about Megan. This is only going to mean heartache for you.'

'I *love* her.' He was nearly in tears.

By now Matthews had pegged the boy the way a geologist recognizes quartz. An underachiever terrified of his parents, of course. Military dad. Supermother. Who were probably – to use Megan's tired adjective – *great* people. And so Joshua wouldn't let himself be angry with them.

Though the anger was there. It had to be. But where?

Let's find out . . .

'Joshua, you don't understand. You—'

'Then tell me.'

'It's not appropriate—'

Joshua persisted. 'Tell me! What is going on?'

Matthews's eyes went wide, as if he were losing his temper. He said, 'All right! You want to know the truth?'

'Yes!'

Matthews started to speak then, shook his head as if he were struggling to control himself. 'No, no, you don't.'

'Yes I do!' The boy stepped forward, menacingly.

'All right. But don't blame me. The truth is Megan didn't *like* you.'

The young man's face froze into a glossy ebony mask. 'That's not true!'

Matthews's mouth grew tight. 'She told me that the first night we slept together.'

Joshua gasped. 'You're lying.'

'You don't think we're lovers?' Matthews asked viciously, as befit a man no longer fearful but angry.

'No, I don't.'

'Well, then how do I know about that birthmark just below her left nipple?'

Joshua couldn't hold Matthews's cold eyes and he looked down at the moss covering a fallen tree. His hands were shaking.

'What do we think of her pubic hair? Yellow as the hair on her head. And what does she like in bed? She likes men to go down on her all night long. And she loves to get fucked in the ass.'

But not by you apparently. Matthews noted the young man's shocked face.

'Stop it!'

But he continued, 'Our first session she asked me how she could get rid of you.'

'No.'

'Yes!' Matthews spat out, 'You know what she called you? The white nigger.'

The eyes glazed over in pain as the scalpel of his words incised the young man's soul.

'She'd *never* say that.'

'You were the big minority experiment. She wanted a black man to fuck. But not too black. And she thought you were a good compromise. About as white as they come. But then she decided she'd got herself a clunker. She told me she had to drink a half-bottle of Southern Comfort just so she could kiss you!'

'No!'

'She and Amy'd stay up all night making fun of you. Megan does a great impression of you. She's got you down cold.'

'Go to hell!'

'Joshua, you asked for this!' Matthews shouted. '*You* pushed me, so you're going to hear the truth whether you want it or not. She wanted your pathetic face out of her life. White nigger. You were a toy. She told me again this morning. When we were fucking on the desk in my office.'

It was enough.

The boy erupted. And, while it might have driven someone else to act ruthlessly and efficiently, it drove Joshua manically forward toward Matthews. He dropped the machete and flailed away with his fists. *'She never said that!'* he cried. 'She never said that she never said that she never said that—'

Matthews fell to the ground, covering his head with his left arm. And when he rose a moment later he was holding the machete, which he swung directly into Joshua's throat.

The boy's mournful litany ended in a gurgling scream. Matthews leapt back, away from the boy's swinging fist, and slashed his arm deeply. Then his leg. Joshua fell on to his back, cradling the gash in his throat.

Matthews drew back and plunged the rusty blade into the young man's abdomen. But with astonishing strength Joshua pushed Matthews off, twisted away, and rose to his knees, choking. The blood flowed between the fingers clutching his torn neck. Matthews struck him several times more but Joshua was crawling fast, like an animal, through the gate toward the hospital. Pathetically trying to escape the terrible blade. Matthews didn't bother to pursue him. Joshua got thirty feet into the field surrounding the hospital before collapsing in a stand of Queen Anne's lace, which turned a deep purple under the spray of his blood.

Matthews slowly walked toward him. Then stopped. He heard snarling, growing closer. He backed quickly away from the quivering body.

The Rottweilers charged forward hungrily. Matthews stepped through the gate and swung it closed as the dogs swarmed in a single muscular pack over the body, which had looked so strong and impervious a moment ago and was now just ragged meat.

Matthews leaned against the bars of the gate, enraptured, watching the young man die. Joshua fought – he tried to rise and struggled to hit the dogs. But it was useless. The big male Rottie closed his enormous jaws on the back of Joshua's neck and began to shake. After a moment the body went limp.

The animals dragged him into the ravine for the feast. His body vanished under the mass of snarling, bloody mouths.

Matthews quickly changed the Mercedes's tire and climbed into the car then sped down the rough road. He'd bury what remained of the boy's corpse later. He didn't have time now. Too many things to do. He was thinking that this was just like when he was a practicing therapist. Busy days, busy days. There were people to see, people to talk to.

I'm here to change your life for ever.

Who is he? *Who?*

Megan McCall floated on a dark ocean, that one question the only thing in her thoughts. She opened her eyes and gripped the thin, filthy mattress she lay on. The room swayed and bobbed.

She was dizzy and nauseated. Her mouth painfully dry, her eyes swollen half closed. She rolled onto her back and examined the small room. There were flaking cushions mounted on all the walls, bars on the windows.

A padded cell.

And the whole place stank so bad she thought she might puke.

She sat up briefly, trying to find a light. There was none. The overhead lamp had been removed and the room was dark. Maybe she—

Suddenly roaring filled her ears. Her vision dissolved into black grains and she collapsed back on the bed, passed out. Sometime later she opened her eyes again, managed to sit up then waited until the dizziness passed and stumbled into the tiny bathroom. The drugs he'd given her . . . still in her system. She'd have to take it slow.

Megan sat down on the toilet, spread her legs and finally worked up the courage to examine herself. No tenderness or pain. No come. He might have groped but he hadn't raped her. She sighed in relief then urinated and washed her hands and face in the basin. She drank a dozen handfuls of icy water. As she stood – careful, careful! Take your time – she caught sight of herself in the metal mirror bolted to the wall. She gasped. Pale and haggard, blond hair knotted and filthy. Eyes red and puffy. She was angry at how frightened she looked and stepped away from the mirror quickly.

She looked for her clothes. Nothing. She couldn't find anything to wrap herself in. No sheets or curtains. This started a crying fit. She huddled in a ball and sobbed.

Wondering how long she'd been unconscious. A week, a day? She wasn't hungry so she guessed it was still Saturday. Maybe Sunday at the latest.

Was anyone looking for her?

Did anyone know she was missing?

Her parents, of course. She'd missed the lunch. Which she'd been going to blow off anyway. Thank God she hadn't called Bett and told her she wasn't coming, the way she'd planned. If that had happened they *still* wouldn't miss her.

And Amy . . .

Should have told her where I was going.

But Crazy Megan was embarrassed. Crazy Megan didn't want anybody to know she's seeing a shrink. Fuck. She should've gone to Juvie after all. Ten days in detention and it'd be over with. But no, she picked the nut doctor.

Who *is* he? she screamed to herself. Was he the man in that car that'd been following her? She'd started to believe that was her imagination.

Standing by the bed, Megan looked out the barred window

into a huge field of tall grass and brush. Some trees, many of them cut down and left to rot.

She gasped suddenly as a huge dog trotted past the window and stopped, staring up at her. A bit of bloody flesh dangled from its mouth, red, like a scrap of steak. Its eyes were spooky – too human – and it seemed to recognize her. Then suddenly the dog tensed, wheeled and vanished.

She examined the window. The iron bars were thick and the space between them was far too small for her to get through.

Frustrated, she pounded her palms against the wall.

Who *is* he?

Megan strode to the door, gripped and pulled it hard. It was, of course, locked tight. The tears returned suddenly; they fell on her breasts and her nipples contracted painfully from the sobbing and the dank cold of the dismal room.

Who *is* he?

Why did they make her go to see him?

What'd I do to deserve this? Nothing! I didn't do a thing!

If her mother was going to fuck nerds in Baltimore then for Christ's sake why didn't she call me? Just a three-minute phone call. Sorry honey I'm going to be late call Domino's and use the charge card have Amy over and all right even Brittany too but no boys . . .

If her father was going to spend his life chasing bimbettes why couldn't he at least spend more than one weekend a month with her?

This was *their* fault! Her parents!

I hate you so much! I fucking *hate* you. I—

A sound.

What was it?

A scuttling . . .

It came from the ceiling. Looking up, she saw a number of dark clusters where the wall met the ceiling. She moved closer. Spiders! Huge black ones. And a hundred hundred tiny dots of infants flowed down the wall like black water.

Megan shivered, overwhelmed with disgust, her skin crawling at the sight. She raced toward the door, slamming into it with all her weight, and collapsed on to the splintery floor. She crawled along it, pushing at the baseboards, trying to find a weak spot. Nothing.

She curled up in a ball on the cold floor. Cried for five minutes.

What's that? Crazy Megan asks her alter ego.

This stopped the tears.

Squick, squick.

That sound again. In the ceiling and the walls.

Squirrels, she decided. Then stood and walked to the wall. It was cinder block. How could there be animals in the walls if they were made out of stone?

Then she glanced into the bathroom and squinted. *Those* walls were just plasterboard. And there was a rectangular plate about twelve by eighteen inches mounted on the wall beside the toilet. It had been painted over a dozen times. What did it lead to?

She walked inside, crouched down and ran her finger across the edge of the metal. In the corners she felt three indentations and one screw head. If she could break through the paint she could pull the plate up and bend the metal till it snapped.

But the enamel was thick, like glue, and with her short nails she couldn't get a grip on the edge. She thought of Brittany, with the killer claws, a regular at a local Vietnamese manicure parlor. That was what she needed – slut nails . . .

She searched the bedroom once more but couldn't find anything to use as a tool. Sighing, she returned to the bathroom, lay on the floor and slugged the metal plate. It resounded hollowly, tantalizing with the promise of an empty passageway on the other side. But it didn't move a millimeter. *Keep going*, Crazy Megan says.

Megan slammed her fist into it again and again, until her knuckles began to bruise and swell. She turned around and kicked with her heel. As the center pushed in slightly, a hairline crack formed around the edge and she kicked harder. Her foot felt as if it were going to shatter.

Go! C.M. encourages. *Go for it!*

Megan spun round and tried to grab the side of the plate with her short nails again. They just weren't long enough to get a purchase in the crack and she howled in frustration then lunged forward, bared her teeth and shoved her face against the wall, trying to dig her incisors into the crack.

Her gum tore open on the rough paint and plaster. Her jaw exploded with pain and she tasted blood. Then suddenly, with a snap, her front tooth slipped into the crack and pulled the plate away from the wall a fraction of an inch. Megan leaned away, pressed her hands to her face to ease the pain and spit blood. Then she grabbed the plate and yanked so furiously it gave way at once, ripping the remaining screw from the wall. She fell backwards.

'Jesus,' Crazy Megan says respectfully. *Good job*.

With a gasp of joy she sat up, seeing faint light through the hole. She shoved her head into the opening, looking into another room. The plate had apparently covered an old heating vent. There was a thin grille on the other side about a foot away. She kicked and it fell clattering to the floor. She froze. Quiet! she reminded herself. He could be near by.

Then she started into the opening, head first. Her shoulders were broad but she managed to ease them through. She had to reach down, cramping her arm, and cradle her breasts to keep her nipples from scraping on the sharp bottom edge of the hole. One inch at a time she forced her way through the vent. As she eased through she examined the other room.

There were bars on these windows too. But the door was standing open several inches. She could see a dim corridor beyond the doorway.

Another foot, then one more.

Until her hips. They stopped her cold.

Those fucking hips, Crazy Megan mutters. *Hate 'em, hate 'em, hate 'em. You just couldn't lose those ten pounds, could you?*

I don't need any of your crap now, okay? Megan thinks to her alter ego.

The vent on the other side of the wall was slightly smaller than the one in her room. Megan tried wriggling, tightening her muscles, licking her fingers and swabbing her sides with spit but she still remained frozen, exactly halfway into each room, her butt dead center in the wall.

No way, she thought to herself. I'm not getting stuck here! A terrible burst of claustrophobia passed through her. She fought it down, wriggled slightly and moved forward an inch or two before she froze again.

Then she heard the noise. *Squick, squick.*

The scuttling of clawed feet in the wall above. Accompanied by a high-pitch twitter.

Oh, my God, no. The squirrels.

Her heart began to pound.

Squick, squick.

Right above where she was stuck. Two of them, it sounded like. Then more, gathering where the wall met the ceiling.

But . . . what if they weren't squirrels?

Oh, fuck, they're rats! Crazy Megan blurts.

Megan began to sob. The noise of their little feet started coming down the wall. She stifled a scream as something – a bit of insulation or wood – fell on to her skin.

Squick. Squick squick squick. Walking along the ceiling, several of them gathering above her, curious. Maybe hungry.

Hundreds of terrible creatures moving toward her stuck body – cautiously but unstoppably.

More rats. *Squick.*

Twitters and scuttling, growing closer still. There seemed to be a dozen now, two dozen. She pictured needle-sharp yellow teeth. Tiny red tongues.

Closer and closer. Curious. Attracted to her smell. There'd been no toilet paper; she hadn't wiped herself after urinating. And she'd just finished her period a day ago. They'd smell the blood. They'd head right for it.

More scuttling.

Oh . . .

She closed her eyes and sobbed in terror. It seemed that the whole wall was alive with them. Dozens, hundreds of rats converging on her. Closer, closer. *Squick squick squick squick-squicksquick* . . .

Megan slapped her palms against the wall and pushed with all her strength, kicking her feet madly. Then, uttering a dentist's-drill squeal, one rat dropped squarely on to her ass. She gasped and felt her heart stutter in terror. She slapped the wall, wriggling furiously. The startled animal climbed off and she felt the snaky tail slip in between her legs as he moved back up the wall.

'Oh,' she choked. 'No . . .'

As she pounded the wall beside her and scrabbled her feet on the bathroom floor, another animal tentatively reached out with a claw and then stepped on to the small of her back. Then she felt four paws. They gripped softly and began to move. A damp whiskered nose tapped on her as the creature sniffed along her skin.

Her arms cramping, she shoved hard. Her foot caught the edge of the toilet in the bathroom behind her and she pushed herself forward two or three inches. It was just enough. She was able to wriggle her hips free. The rat leapt off her and

Megan burst into the adjoining room. She crawled frantically into the far corner, as four rats escaped from the wall and vanished through the open door.

She sobbed, gasping for breath, brushing her palms over her skin frantically to make sure none of them clung to her. After five minutes she'd calmed. Slowly she stepped back to the vent and listened. *Squick squick squick*. . . . More scuttling, more twitters. She slammed the grille against the vent opening. The rest of the rats vanished up the wall. An angry hiss sounded from the hole.

God . . .

She found some stacks of newspapers, removed the grille, wadded up the papers and stuffed them inside the wall to keep the creatures trapped inside.

She collapsed back on the floor, trying to push away the horrible memory of the probing little paws, filthy and damp.

Looking into the dim corridor, cold and yellow, windows barred, filthy, she happened to glance up at a sign on the wall.

PATIENTS SHALL BE DE-LOUSED ONCE A WEEK.

The sign – a simple sign – brought the hopelessness home to her.

Don't worry about it, Crazy Megan tries to reassure.

But her alter ego wasn't listening. Megan shivered in fear and disgust and curled up, clutching her knees. Hating this place. Hating her life, her pointless life . . . Her stupid, superficial friends. Her sick obsession with Janis, the Grateful Dead and all the rest of the cheerful, lying fake-ass past.

Hating the man who'd done this to her, whoever he was.

But most of all hating her parents.

Hating them beyond words.

Chapter TWELVE

The forty-minute drive to Leesburg took Tate and Bett past a few mansions, some redneck bungalows, some new developments with names like Windstone and The Oaks. Cars on blocks, vegetable stands selling – at this time of year – jars of put-up preserves and relishes.

But mostly they passed farmland.

Looking out over just-planted land like this, some people see future homes or shopping malls or townhouses and some see rows of money to be plucked from the ground at harvest time. And some perhaps simply drive past seeing nothing but where their particular journey is taking them.

But Tate Collier saw in these fields what he felt in his own land – a quiet salvation, something he did yet not of his doing, something that would let him survive, if not prosper, graciously: the silence of rooted growth. And if at times that process betrayed him – hail, drought, tumbling markets – Tate could still sleep content in the assurance that there was no malice in the earth's heart. And that, the former criminal prosecutor within him figured, was no small thing.

So even though Tate claimed, as any true advocate would, that it made no nevermind to him whether he was representing the plaintiffs or defendants in the Liberty Park case, his heart was in fact with the people who wanted to protect the farmland from the concrete and concession stands and traffic.

He felt this even more now, seeing these rolling hills. And he felt too guilt and a pang of impatience that he was distracted from his preparations for the hearing. But a look at Bett's troubled face put this discomfort aside. There'd be time to hone his argument. Right now there were other priorities.

They passed the Oatlands farm and as they did the sun came out. And he sped on toward Leesburg, into old Virginia. Confederate Virginia.

There weren't many towns like this in the northern part of the state; many people in Richmond and Charlottesville didn't really consider most of Northern Virginia to be in the commonwealth at all. Tate and Bett drove through the city limits and slowed to the posted thirty miles per hour. Examining the trim yards, the white clapboard houses, the incongruous biker bar in the middle of downtown, the plentiful churches. They followed the directions Tate had been given to the hospital where Dr Hanson was visiting his mother.

'Can he tell us much?' Bett wondered. 'Legally, I mean.'

She'd be thinking, he guessed, of the patient-doctor privilege, which allowed a doctor to keep silent on the conversations between a patient and his physician. Years ago, when they'd been married, Tate had explained this and other nuances of the law to her. But she often grew offended at these arcane rules. 'You mean if you don't read him his rights, the arrest is no good? Even if he *did* it?' she'd ask, perplexed. Or: 'Excuse me, but why should a mother go to jail if she's shoplifting food for her hungry child? I don't get it.'

He expected that same indignation now when he explained that Hanson didn't *have* to say anything to them. But Bett just nodded, accepting the rules. She smiled coyly and said, 'Then I guess you'll have to be extra persuasive.'

They turned the corner and the white-frame hospital loomed ahead of them.

'Well, busy day,' Bett said, assessing the front of the hospital as she flipped up the car's mirror after refreshing her lipstick. There were three police cars parked in front of the main entrance. The red and white lights atop one of them flashed with urgent brilliance.

'Car wreck?' Bett suggested. Route 15, which led into town, was posted fifty-five but everybody drove it at seventy or eighty.

They parked and walked inside.

Something was wrong, Tate noted. Something serious had happened. Several nurses and orderlies stood in the lobby, looking down a corridor. Their faces were troubled. A receptionist leaned over the main desk, gazing down the same corridor.

'What is it?' Bett whispered.

'Not a clue,' he answered.

'Look, there he is,' somebody said.

'God,' someone else muttered.

Two policemen were leading a tall, balding man down the corridor toward the main entrance. His hands were cuffed behind him. His face was red. He'd been crying. As he passed, Tate heard him say, 'I didn't do it. I *wouldn't* do it! I wasn't even *there!*'

Several of the nurses shook their heads, eying him with cold expressions on their faces.

'I didn't do it!' he shouted.

A moment later he was in a squad car. It made a U-turn in the driveway and sped off.

Tate asked the receptionist, 'What's that all about?'

The white-haired woman shook her head, eyes wide, cheeks pale. 'We nearly had our first assisted suicide.' She was very shaken. 'I don't believe it.'

'What happened?'

'We have a patient – an elderly woman with a broken hip. And it looks like he—' She nodded toward where the police car had been. '—comes in and talks to her for a while and next thing we know she's got a syringe in her hands and's trying to kill herself. Can you imagine? Can you just *imagine?*'

'But they saved her?' Tate asked.

'The Lord was watching over her.'

Bett blinked and glanced at the woman.

She continued, 'A nurse just happened by. My goodness. Can you imagine?'

Bett shook her head. Tate recalled that she felt the same about suicide as she did about the death penalty. He thought briefly of her sister's husband's death. Harris. He'd used a shotgun to kill himself. Like Hemingway. Harris had been an artist – a bad one, in Tate's estimation – and he'd shot himself in his studio, his dark blood covering a canvas that he'd been working on for months.

Absently he asked the receptionist, 'That man. Who is he? Somebody like Kevorkian?'

'Who *is* he?' the woman blurted. 'Why, he was her *son!*'

Tate and Bett looked at each other in shock. She said in a whisper, 'Oh, no. It couldn't be.'

Tate asked the woman, 'The patient? Was her name Hanson?'

'Yes, that's the name.' Shaking her head. 'Her own son tried to talk her into killing herself! And I heard he was a therapist too. A doctor! Can you *imagine?*'

Tate and Bett sat in the hospital cafeteria, brooding silence between them. They'd ordered coffee that neither wanted. They were waiting for a call from Konnie Konstantinatis. They'd spoken only ten minutes ago but it seemed like hours.

Tate's phone buzzed. He answered it before it could chirp again.

''Lo.'

'Okay, Counselor, made some calls. But this is all unofficial. There's still no case. *Got* it? Are you *comfortable* with that?'

'Got it, Konnie. Go ahead.'

The detective explained that he had called the Leesburg police and spoken to a detective there.

'Here's what happened. This old lady, Greta Hanson, fell and broke her hip last week. Fell down her back stairs. Serious but not too serious. She's eighty. You know how it is.'

'Right.'

'Okay, today she's tanked up on painkillers, really out of it, and she hears her son. *Your* Dr Hanson. Hears him telling her – well, she *thinks* he's telling her – it looks like the end of the road, they found cancer, she only has a few months left. Yadda, yadda, yadda. The pain's gonna be terrible. Tells her it's best to just finish herself off, it's what everybody wants. Leaves her a syringe of Nembutal. She says she'll do it. She sticks herself but a nurse finds her in time. Anyway, she tells 'em what happened and the administrator calls the cops. They find the son in the gift shop buying a box of candy. Supposedly for her. They collar him. He denies it all. Of course. What else is he going to say? So. End of story.'

'And this all happens fifteen minutes before Bett and I are going to talk to him about Megan? It's no coincidence, Konnie. Come on.'

Silence from Fairfax.

'Konnie. You hear me?'

'I'm telling you the facts, Counselor. I don't comment otherwise.'

'She's sure it was her son who talked to her?'

'She said.'

'Anyway, we can talk to him?'

'Nope. Not till the arraignment on Monday. And he's probably not gonna be in any mood to talk to you even then.'

'All right. Answer me one question. Can you look up what kind of car he drives?'

'Who? Hanson? Yeah, hold on.'

Tate heard typing as he filled in Bett on what Konnie'd said.

'Oh, my,' she said, hand rising to her mouth.

A moment later the detective came back on the line. 'Two cars. A Mazda 929 and a Ford Explorer. Both this year's models.'

'What colors?'

'Mazda's green. The Explorer's black.'

'It was somebody else, Konnie. Somebody was following Megan.'

'Tate, she took the train to New York. She's going to see the Statue of Liberty and hang out in Greenwich Village and do whatever kids do in New York and—'

'You know the Bust-er Book?'

'What the hell is a buster book?' the detective grumbled.

'Kids at Jefferson High are supposed to write down anybody who comes up and offers 'em drugs, candy, maybe flashes 'em, you know.'

'Oh, that shit. Right.'

'A friend of Megan's said there'd been a car following her. In the Bust-er Book, some kids reported a gray car parked near the school in the afternoon. And Megan herself reported it last week.'

'Gray car?'

'Right.'

A sigh. 'Tate, lemme ask you. Just how many kids go to that school of hers?'

'I'm not saying it's a *good* lead, Konnie—'

'And just how many parents in gray cars pick 'em up?'

'—but it *is* a lead.'

'Tag number? Make, model, year?'

Tate sighed. 'Nothing.'

'Look, Counselor, get me at least one of the above and we'll talk. . . . So, what're you thinking, somebody snatched her? The Amtrak schedule is bogus?'

'I don't know. It's just fishy.'

'It's not a case, Tate. That's the watchword for today. Look, I better go.'

'One last question, Konnie. *Does* she have cancer? Hanson's mother?'

The detective hesitated. 'No. At least it's not what they're treating for.'

'So somebody talked her into believing she's dying. Talked her into trying to kill herself.'

'Yeah. And that somebody was her son. He could have a hundred motives. Gotta go, Counselor.'

Click.

He relayed to Bett the rest of his conversation with Konnie.

'Megan was seeing a therapist who tried to kill his mother? God.'

'I don't know, Bett,' he said. 'You saw his face. Did he look guilty?'

'He looked caught,' she said.

Tate nodded in concession. He glanced at his watch. It was 2.30. 'Let's get back to Fairfax and find that teacher. Eckhard.'

Crazy Megan finally gets a chance to talk.

Listen up, girl. Listen here, kiddo. Biz-nitch, you listening? Good. You need me. You're not sneaking cigarettes in Fair Oaks mall parking lot. You're not flirting with a George Mason junior to get him to buy you a pint of Comfort or Turkey. You're not sitting in Amy's room, snarfing wine, hating it and saying it's great while you're like: 'Sure, I come every time Josh and I fuck. I mean, it's like so easy. It is for everybody, isn't it? I mean . . .'

Leave me alone, Megan thought.

But C.M. won't have any of this *attitude*. She snaps, *You hate the world. Okay. What you want—*

'A family is what I want,' Megan responded. 'That's all I wanted.'

Oh. Well, that's precious, her crazy side offers, nice and sarcastic. *Who the fuck doesn't? You want Mommy and Daddy to wave their magic wand and get you out of here? Uh-huh. Uh-huh. Well, ain't going to happen, girl. So get off your fat ass and get out.*

I can't move, Megan thought.

Up, girl. Up. Look, he—

And who *is* he?

Crazy Megan is in good form today. *What difference does it make? He's the bogy-man, he's Jason, he's Leatherface, he's Freddy Krueger, he's your father—*

All right, stop it. You're like so . . . tedious.

But C.M.'s wound up now. *He's everything bad, he's your mother giving Brad a blow job, he's the barn at your father's farm, he's an inconvenient child, he's a whispering bear—*

'Stop it, stop it, stop it!' Megan screamed out loud.

But nothing stops Crazy Megan when she gets going. *It doesn't matter what he is. Don't you get it? He thinks you're locked up tight in your little padded cell. But you're not. You're out. And you may not have much time. So get your shit together and get the hell out of here.*

I don't have any clothes, Megan pointed out.

That's the girl I love. Oooo. The sarcasm is thick as Noxema. *Sit back and find excuses. Let's see: You're pissed 'cause Mom's off to Baltimore to fuck Mr Rogers and do you say anything about it? No. It rags you that Dad fits you in around his dates with girls who've got inflatable boobs but do you bitch about it?*

Do you call him on it? No. You go off and get drunk. You have another cigarette. What other distractions can we come up with? Nail polish, CDs, Victoria's Secret Taco Bell the mall the multiplex a boy's fat dick gossip . . .

I hate you, Megan thought. I really, really hate you. Go away, go back where you came from.

I am where I came from, Crazy Megan responds. *You may have some time to fuck around like this, whining, and you may not. Now, you're buck naked and you don't like it. Well, if that's an issue, go find some clothes. And, no, there's no Contempo Casual around here. Of course I personally would say, Fuck the clothes, find a door and run like hell. But that's up to you.*

Megan rolled to her feet.

She stepped into the corridor.

Cold, painful. Her feet stung from the kicking. She started walking. Looking around, she saw it was a rambling place, one story, and built of concrete blocks. With the padded cell, she figured it was a mental hospital but she couldn't imagine treating patients here. It was way depressing. No one could have gotten better here. All the windows had thick bars on them.

She found a door leading outside and pushed it. It was locked tight. The same with two others. She looked outside for a car, didn't see one in the lot. At least she was alone. Dr Peters must have left.

Keep going, Crazy Megan insists.

'But—'

Keep. Going.

She did.

The place was huge, wing after wing, dozens of corridors, gloomy wards, private rooms, two-bed rooms. But all the doors leading outside were sealed tight and all the windows were barred. Every damn one of them. Two large interior doorways had been bricked off sloppily with cinder blocks and

Sakrete – maybe because they led to less restricted wings that didn't have barred windows and doors. Dozens of the large concrete blocks that hadn't been needed lay scattered on the floor. She picked up one and slammed it into a barred window. It didn't even bend the metal rods.

For several hours she made a circuit of the hospital, moving quietly. She was careful; in the dim light she could make out footprints, hundreds of them. She couldn't tell if they'd been left by Dr Peters alone or by him and someone else but she was all too aware that she might not be alone.

By the time she'd made it back to her cell she hadn't found a single door or window that looked promising.

Shit. No way out.

Okay, Crazy Megan offers, chipper as ever. *At least find something you can use to nail his ass with.*

What do you mean?

A weapon, bitch. What do you think?

Megan remembered seeing a kitchen and returned there.

She started going through drawers and cupboards. But there wasn't anything she could use. There were no metal knives or forks, not even dinner knives, only hundreds of packages of plastic utensils. No glasses or ceramic cups. Everything was paper or Styrofoam.

She pulled open a door. It was a pantry full of food. She started to close the door but stopped, looked inside again.

There was enough food for a family to live on for a year. Cherios, condensed milk, Diet Pepsi, Doritos, Lays potato chips, tuna, Hostess cupcakes, Cup-a-soup, Chef Boy-R-Dee . . .

What's funny here?

Jesus. Crazy Megan catches on first.

Megan's hand rose to her mouth and she started to cry.

Jesus, Crazy Megan repeats.

These were exactly the same brands that Megan liked. This

was what her mother's cupboards were stocked with. On other shelves were her shampoo, conditioner and soap.

Even the type of tampon that Megan used.

He'd been in her house, he knew what she liked.

He'd bought this all for her!

Don't lose it, babes, don't . . .

But Megan ignored her crazy side and gave in to the crying.

Thinking: if a family of four could live on this for a year, just think how long it would last her by herself.

Twenty minutes later Megan rose from the floor, wiped her face and continued her search. It didn't take her long to find the source of the footprints.

In a far wing of the hospital were two rooms that had been 'homified', as Bett would say when she'd dress up a cold-looking house to make it warmer and more comfortable. One room was an office, filled with thousands of books and files and papers. An armchair and lamp and desk. The other room was a bedroom. It smelled stale, turned her stomach. She looked inside. The bed was unmade and the sheets were stained. Off-white splotches.

Guys're so disgusting, Crazy Megan offers.

Megan agreed; who could argue with that?

This meant that someone else probably lived here – someone young, (she supposed older guys jerked off too but tried to imagine, say, her father doing it and couldn't).

Way gross thought. From C.M.

Then she saw the closet.

Oh, please! She mentally crossed her fingers as she pulled the door open.

Yes! It was filled with clothes. She pulled on some jeans, which were tight around her hips and too long. She rolled the cuffs up. She found a work shirt – which was tight around her boobs. Didn't matter. She felt a hundred per cent better.

There were no shoes but she found a pair of thick, black socks. For some reason, covering her feet gave her more confidence than covering the rest of her body.

She looked through the closet for a knife or gun but found nothing. She returned to the other room. Rummaged through the desk. Nothing to use as a weapon, except a Bic pen. She took it anyway. Then she poked through the rest of the room, focusing at first on the bookshelves.

Some books were about psychiatry but most were fantasy novels and science fiction. Some were pretty weird. Stacks of comic books too. Japanese, a lot of them. Megan flipped through several. Totally icky – girls being raped by monsters and gargoyles and aliens. R- and X-rated. She shivered in disgust.

The name inside the books and on the front of the comic books was *Pete Matthews.* Sometimes he'd written *Peter M.* It was written very carefully, in big block letters. As if he were a young kid.

Megan looked through the files, most of them filled with psychological mumbo-jumbo she couldn't understand. There were also stacks of the American Psychiatric Association *Journal*. Articles were marked with yellow Post-Its. She noticed they'd been written by a doctor named Aaron Matthews. The boy's father? she wondered. His bio gave long lists of credentials. Dozens of awards and honorary degrees. One newspaper clipping called him the 'Einstein of therapists. He can dissect a psychosis from listening to patient's words for three or four minutes. A master diagnostician.'

In between two file folders was another clipping. Megan lifted it to the light. It showed Dr Peters and a young man in his late teens. But wait . . . The name wasn't Peters. The caption said only, 'Dr Aaron Matthews leaves the funeral home after the memorial service for his wife. He is accompanied by his son, Peter.'

Matthews . . . the one who wrote those articles. So he must have been a doctor here. That's how he knew about the hospital.

Megan studied the picture again, feeling crawly and scared. The son was . . . well, just plain weird. He was a tall boy, lanky, with long arms and huge hands. He had thick floppy hair that looked dirty and his forehead jutted over his dark eye sockets. He had a sick smile on his face.

Leaving his mother's funeral and he's *smiling*?

So the other resident here was the son. Maybe Peters well Matthews . . . kept the boy locked up here, a prisoner too.

Her eyes fell to an official-looking report. She read the top page.

EMERGENCY INTAKE EVALUATION

Patient Peter A. Matthews presents with symptoms typical of an antisocial and paranoid personality. He is not schizophrenic, under DSM-III criteria, but he has, or claims to have, delusions. More likely these are merely fantasies, which in his case are so overpowering that he chooses not to recognize the borderline between his role playing and reality. These fantasies are generally of a sado-erotic nature, with him playing a non-human entity – stalking and raping females. During our sessions Peter would sometimes portray these entities – right down to odd mannerisms and garbled language. He was often 'in character', and quite consistent in his portrayals of these creatures. However, there was no evidence of fugue states or multiple personalities. He changed personas at his convenience, to achieve the greatest stimulation from his fantasies.

Peter is extremely dangerous. He must be hospitalized in a secure facility until the determination is made for a course of treatment. Recommend immediate psychopharmacological intervention.

Stalking . . . rape.

Megan put the report back on the desk. She found a notebook. Peter's name was written on this too. She read through it. In elaborate passages Peter described himself as a spaceman or an alien stalking women, tying them up, raping them. She dropped the book. There were dozens of others.

Tears again.

Then another thought: Her cell! This Dr Matthews, her kidnapper, had locked her up not only to keep her from getting out but to keep his son from getting *in*. He was—

A creak, a faint squeal. A door closed softly in a far part of the hospital.

Megan shivered in terror.

Move it, girl! Crazy Megan cries, in a silent voice as panicked as uncrazy Megan's. *It's him, it's the kid.*

She grabbed a pile of things to take with her – several of the magazines, file folders about the hospital, letters. Anything that might help her figure out who this Matthews was. Why he'd taken her. How she might get out.

Footsteps . . .

He's coming. He's coming here . . . Move it. Now!

Holding the files and clippings under her arm, Megan fled out the door. She ran down the corridors, getting lost once, pausing often to listen for footsteps. He seemed to be circling her.

Finally she found her way and raced into the room that adjoined hers, the 'ratroom' she thought of it. She rubbed the grate along the edges of the hole in the wall to widen it. She started through and, whimpering, clawed her way forward. Five inches, six, a foot, two feet. Finally she grabbed the toilet in her room and wrenched herself through the hole. She replaced the grate on the far side of the wall and then slammed the metal plate into place in her bathroom.

She ran to the door and pressed her ear against it. The footsteps grew closer and closer. But Peter didn't stop at her door. He kept moving. Maybe he didn't know she was here.

Megan sat on the icy floor with her hands pressing furiously against the plate until they cramped.

Listen, C.M. starts to say. *Maybe you can—*

Shut up, Megan thought furiously.

And for once Crazy Megan does what she's told.

Chapter THIRTEEN

The eyes.

The eyes tell it all.

When Aaron Matthews was practicing psychotherapy he learned to read the eyes. They told him so much more than words. Words are tools and weapons and camouflage and shields.

But the eyes tell you the truth.

An hour ago, in Leesburg, he'd looked into the glassy, groggy eyes of a drugged Greta Hanson and knew she was a woman with no reserves of strength. And so he'd leaned close, become her son and spun a tale guaranteed to send her to the very angels that she was babbling on and on about. It's quite a challenge to talk someone into killing herself.

He doubted she'd die from the dosage of Nembutal he'd given her and he doubted that she could find a vein anyway. Besides, it was important for her to remain alive – to blame her son for the Kevorkian number. Poor Doc Hanson. Now either in jail or on the run. In any case, he'd be no help as a witness to Tate Collier and his wife.

Now, as he strolled along the sidewalk near Jefferson High school, Aaron Matthews was looking at another set of eyes.

Robert Eckhard's. Matthews was concluding that the man might or might not have been a good English teacher but he didn't doubt that Eckhard was one hell of a girl's volleyball coach. The diminutive, tweedy man sat with a book on his lap outside the sports field between the grade and high schools.

Wearing a baseball cap and thick-framed reading glasses he'd bought at Safeway – he remembered that Eckhard might have seen him near the school in the Mercedes – Matthews walked slowly past. He studied his subject carefully. The teacher was a middle-aged man, in Dockers and a loose tan shirt. Matthews took all these observations and filed them away but what was helpful were the eyes; they told him everything he needed to know about Mr Eckhard.

Continuing down the sidewalk, Matthews walked into a drug-store and made several purchases. He slipped into the restroom of the store and five minutes later returned to the schoolyard. He sat down on the bench next to Eckhard's and rested the *Washington Post* in his lap. He gazed out at the young girls playing informal games of soccer or jump-rope in the schoolyard.

Once, then twice, Eckhard glanced at him.

The second time Matthews happened to turn his way and saw the teacher look back with a hint of curiosity in his tell-all eyes.

Matthews's face went still with shock. He waited a judicious moment then stood quickly and walked past Eckhard. But as he did, the disposable camera fell from the folds of his newspaper. He stepped forward suddenly to pick it up but accidentally kicked the yellow-and-black box. It went skidding along the sidewalk and hit Eckhard's foot.

Matthews froze. The teacher, his eyes on Matthews's, smiled again. He reached down and picked up the camera, looked at it. Turned it over.

'I—' Matthews began, horrified.

'It's okay,' Eckhard said.

'Okay?' Matthews's voice faltered. He looked up and down the sidewalk, faint ill-ease in his face.

'I mean, the camera's okay,' Eckhard said, rattling it. 'It doesn't seem to be broken.'

Matthews began speaking breathlessly, over-explaining, as this script required. 'See, what it was, I was going to D.C. later today. I was going to the zoo. Take some pictures of the animals.'

'The zoo.' Eckhard examined the camera.

Matthews again looked up and down the sidewalk.

'You like photography?' the teacher asked.

After a moment, Matthews said, 'Yes, I do. A hobby.' Smiled awkwardly, summoning a blush. 'Everybody should have a hobby. That's what my father said.' He fell silent.

'It's my hobby too.'

'Really?'

'Been doing it for about fifteen years,' Eckhard said.

'Me too. Little less, I guess.'

'You live around here?' the teacher asked.

'Fairfax.'

'Long time?'

'A couple of years.'

Silence grew between them. Eckhard still held the camera. Matthews crossed his arms, rocked on his feet. Looking out over the schoolyard. Finally he asked, 'You do your own developing and printing?'

'Of course,' Eckhard said.

Of course. The expected answer. Matthews's eyes narrowed and he appeared to relax. 'Harder with color,' he offered. 'But they don't make the throwaways in black and white.'

'I'm getting a digital camera,' Eckhard said. 'I can just feed the pictures into my computer at home.'

'I've heard about those. They're expensive, aren't they?'

'They are . . . But you know hobbies. If they're important to you you're willing to spend the money.'

'That's my philosophy,' Matthews admitted. He sat down next to Eckhard. They looked out on the playing field, at a cluster of girls around ten or eleven. Eckhard looked through the eyepiece of the camera. 'Lens isn't telephoto.'

'No,' Matthews said. Then after a moment: 'She's cute. That brunette there.'

'Angela.'

'You know her?'

'I'm a teacher at the high school. I'm also a grade school counselor.'

Matthews's eyes flashed enviously. 'Teacher? I work for an insurance company. Actuarial work. Boring. But summers I volunteer at Camp Henry. Maryland. You know it?'

Eckhard shook his head. 'I also coach girls' sports.'

'That's a good job too.' Matthews clicked his tongue.

'Sure is.' Eckhard looked out over the field. 'I know most of these girls.'

'You do portraits?'

'Some.'

'You ever photograph her?'

But Eckhard wouldn't answer. 'So, you take pictures just around the area here?'

Matthews said, 'Here, California. Europe some. I was in Amsterdam a little while ago.'

'Amsterdam. I was there a few years ago. Not as interesting as it used to be.'

'That's what I found.'

'Bangkok's nice, though,' Eckhard volunteered.

'I'm planning on going next year,' Matthews said in a whisper.

'Oh, you have to,' Eckhard encouraged, kneading the yellow box of the camera in his hands. 'It's quite a place.'

Matthews could practically see the synapses firing in Eckhard's mind, wondering furiously if Matthews was a cop with the Child Welfare unit of the Fairfax County Police or an FBI agent. Matthews had treated several pedophiles during his days as a practicing therapist. He recognized the classic characteristics in Eckhard. He was intelligent – an organized offender – and he'd know all about the laws of child molestation and pornography. He could probably just keep the testosterone under control to avoid actually molesting a child but photographing them and collecting child porn was a compulsion that ruled his life.

Matthews offered another conspiratorial smile then glanced at a young girl bending down to pick up a ball. Gave a faint sigh. Eckhard followed his gaze and nodded.

The girl stood up. Eckhard said, 'Nancy. She's nine. Fifth grade.'

'Pretty. You wouldn't happen to have any pictures of her, would you?'

'I do.' Eckhard paused. 'In a nice skirt and blouse, I seem to recall.'

Matthews wrinkled his nose. Shrugged.

He wondered if the man would take the bait.

Snap.

Eckhard whispered, 'Well, not the blouse in all of them.'

Matthews exhaled hard. 'You wouldn't happen to have any with you?'

'No. You have any of yours?'

Matthews said, 'I keep all of mine on my computer.'

One of Matthews's patients had seven thousand images of child pornography on computer. He'd collected them while serving time for a molestation charge. The computer they resided on was the warden's at Hammond Falls State Penitentiary in Maryland. The prisoner had written an encryption program to keep the files secret. The FBI cracked it anyway and, despite his willingness to go through therapy, the offense earned him another ten years in prison.

Matthews said, 'I don't have too many in my collection. Only about four thousand.'

Eckhard's eyes turned to Matthews and they were vacuums. He whispered a long, envious 'Well . . .'

Matthews added, 'I've got some videos too. But only about a hundred of them.'

'A *hundred?*'

Eckhard shifted on the bench. Matthews knew the teacher was lost. Completely. He'd be thinking: At worst, it's entrapment. At worst, I can talk my way out of it. At worst, I'll flee the country and move to Thailand . . . As a therapist Matthews was continually astonished at how easily people won completely unwinnable arguments with themselves.

Still, you land a fish with as much care as you hook it.

'You seem worried . . .' Matthews started. 'And I have to say, I don't know you, and I'm a little nervous myself. But I've just got a feeling about you. Maybe we could help each other out . . . Let me show you a couple of samples of what I've got.'

The eyes flickered with lust.

Always the eyes.

'That'd be fine. That'd be good. Please.' Eckhard cleared his excited throat.

Oh, you pathetic thing . . .

'I could give you a computer disk,' Matthews suggested.

'Sure. That'd be great.'

'I only live about three blocks from here. Let me run up to my house and get some samples.'

'Good.'

'Oh,' Matthews said, pausing. A frown. 'I only have girls.'

'Yes, yes. That's fine.' Breathless. A bead of spit rested in the corner of the mouth.

'Age?' Matthews asked, like a clerk inquiring about a customer's shirt size.

Eckhard's eyes moved slowly to a ten-year-old girl skipping rope.

Matthews nodded. 'I've got some good ones I think you'll like.'

Desperately Eckhard said, 'Can you go now?'

'Sure. Be right back.'

'I'll be here.'

Matthews started up the street.

He turned back and saw the teacher, a stupid smile on his face, grinning from ear to ear, looking out over the field of his sad desire, rubbing his thumb over the disposable camera.

In the drug-store once again, Matthews walked up to the pay-phone and called 911.

When dispatch answered, he said urgently, 'Oh, you need somebody down to Markus Avenue right away! The sports field behind Jefferson School.' He described Eckhard and said, 'He took a little girl into the alley and pulled his, you know, penis out. Then took some pictures. And I heard him ask her to his house. He said he's got lots of pictures of little girls like her on his computer. Pictures of little girls, you know . . . doing it. Oh, it's disgusting. Hurry up! I'm going back and watch him to make sure he doesn't get away.'

He hung up.

Matthews didn't know if snapshots of a fully dressed little girl in a schoolyard next to frames of a man's erect dick (Matthews's own penis, taken in the drug-store restroom twenty minutes ago) were an offense anywhere but once the cops got a search warrant for the man's house Eckhard would be out of commission – and a completely unreliable witness about gray Mercedes or anything else – for a long, long time.

By the time he was back on the street, walking toward his car, Matthews heard the sirens.

Fairfax County took children's well-being very seriously, it seemed.

Tate and Bett arrived at the schoolyard, taking care to avoid the main building, just in case the clean-cut young fascist of a security guard had happened to glance inside the Bust-er Book after Tate and Bett had left and found twenty or so pages missing.

But volleyball practice had been cancelled for today, it seemed. Nobody quite knew why.

In fact the yard was almost deserted, despite the clear skies.

They found two students and asked if they'd seen Eckhard. They said they hadn't. One teenage girl said, 'We were coming here for the practice.'

'Volleyball?'

'Right. And what it was was somebody said it's been canceled and we should all go home. Stay away from here. Totally weird.'

'And you haven't seen Mr Eckhard?'

'Somebody said he had to go someplace. But they didn't tell us where. I don't know. He was here earlier. I don't get it. He's *always* here. I mean, always.'

'Do you know where he lives?'

'Fairfax, someplace. I think.'

'What's his first name?'

'Robert.'

Tate called directory assistance and got his number. He left a message. He had a thought. He asked his ex-wife, 'Where did she hang out?'

'Hang out?' Bett asked absently. He saw her looking into her purse, eyes on the letter containing her daughter's searing words.

'Yeah, with her friends. After school.'

'Just around. You know.'

'But where? We'll go there, ask if anybody's seen her.'

There was a long hesitation. Finally she said, 'I'm not sure.'

'You're not?' Tate asked, surprised. 'You don't know where she goes?'

'No,' Bett answered testily. 'Not all the time. She's a seventeen-year-old girl with a driver's license.'

'Oh. So you don't know where she'd spend her afternoons.'

'Not always, no.' She glanced at him angrily. 'It is not like she hangs out in southeast D.C., Tate.'

'I just—'

'Megan's a responsible girl. She knows where to go and where not to go. I trust her.'

They walked in silence back to the car. Bett grabbed her phone again and her address book. She began making calls – to Megan's friends, he gathered. At least she had *their* numbers; still, it irked him that she didn't seem to know basic information like this – important information – about the girl.

When they arrived at the car she folded up the phone. 'Her favorite place was called the Coffee Shop. Up near Route Fifty.' Bett sounded victorious. 'Like Starbuck's. All right? Happy?'

She dropped into the seat and crossed her arms. They drove in silence north along the parkway.

Chapter FOURTEEN

Braking to five miles an hour, Tate surveyed the crowded parking lot.

He found a space between a chopped Harley-Davidson and a pickup bumper-stickered with the Reb stars 'n' bars. He navigated the glistening Lexus into this narrow spot.

They surveyed the cycles, the tough, young men and women, all in denim, defiantly holding open bottles, the tattoos, the boots. At the other end of the parking lot was a very different crowd, younger – boys with long hair, girls with crew cuts, layers of baggy clothes, plenty of piercing. Bleary eyes.

Welcome to the Coffee Shop.

'Here?' Bett asked. 'She came *here*?'

Starbuck's, Tate thought. I don't think so.

She glanced at the notes she'd jotted. 'Off Fifty near Walney. This's it. Oh, my.'

Tate glanced at his ex-wife. Her horrified expression didn't diminish his anger. How could she have let Megan come to a place like this? Didn't she check up on her? Most of the parents he knew gave their children pagers. Why hadn't Bett gotten one for her? Or a cell phone?

Her own daughter, for Christ's sake . . .

Tate pushed the door open and started to get out.

Bett popped her seatbelt but he said abruptly, 'Wait here.'

He walked up to the closest cluster – the bikers; they seemed less comatose than the slacker gang at the other end of the lot.

He began asking them about Megan. But no one had heard of her. He was vastly relieved. Maybe it was a misunderstanding. Maybe her friend meant a generic coffee shop someplace.

At the far end of the lot he waded into a grungy sea of plaid shirts, Doc Marten boots, JNCO jeans and bellbottom Levi's. The girls wore tight tank tops over bras in contrasting colors. Their hair was long, parted in the middle, like Megan's. Peace symbols bounced on breasts and there was a lot of tie-dyed couture. The images reminded Tate of his own coming-of-age era, the early '70s.

'Megan? Sure, like I know her,' said a slim girl, smoking a cigarette she was too young to buy.

'Have you seen her lately?'

'She's here a lotta nights. But not in the last week, you know. Like, who're you?'

'I'm her father. She's missing.'

'Wow. That sucks.'

'How'd she get in? She was seventeen.'

'Uhm. I don't know.'

Meaning: a fake ID.

He asked, 'Do you know if anybody's been asking about her? Or been following her?'

'I dunno. But her and me, we weren't, like, real close. Hey, ask him. Sammy! Hey, Sammy.' To Tate she added, 'They'd hang out some.'

A large boy glanced their way, eyed Tate uneasily. He set a paper cup behind a garbage can and walked up to him. He was about the lawyer's height, with a pimply face, and wore a baseball cap backwards. He carried a pager and a cellphone. He eyed Tate cautiously.

'I'm looking for Megan McCall. You know her?'

'Sure.'

'Have you seen her lately?'

'She was here this week.'

'She comes here a lot?' Tate asked.

'Yeah, she, like, hangs here. Her and Donna and Amy. You know.'

'How about her boyfriend?'

'That guy from Mason?' Sammy asked. 'The one she broke up with? Naw, this wasn't his scene. I only saw 'em together once, I think.'

'Was somebody – some man in a gray car – asking about her, following her around?'

Sammy gave a faint laugh. 'Yeah, there was. Last week, Megan and me, we were here and she was like, "What's he want? Him again." And I'm like, you want me to go fuck him up?' And she goes, "Sure." And she goes inside. And I go up to the car but the asshole takes off.'

'Did you get a look at him?'

'Not too close. White guy. Your age, maybe a little older.'

'You get the plate number?'

'No. Didn't even see what state. But it was a Mercedes. I don't know what model. All those fucking numbers. American cars have names. But German cars, just fucking numbers.'

'And you don't have any idea who he was?'

'Well, yeah, I figured. But, you know, Megan doesn't like to talk about it. So I let it go.'

Tate shook his head. 'Talk about what?'

'You know.'

'No, I *don't* know,' Tate said. 'What?'

'Well, just . . .' Sammy lifted his hands. 'What she used to do. I figured he was looking for some more action and had tracked her down here.'

'Action? I don't understand. What are you saying?'

'I figured he and Megan had . . . get it? And he wanted some more.'

'What are you talking about?' Tate persisted.

'What d'you think I'm talking about?' The kid was confused. 'He fucked Megan and liked what he got.'

'Are you saying she had a boyfriend in his forties?'

'Boyfriend?' Sammy laughed. 'No, man. I'm saying she had a *customer*. I don't know how the hell old he was.'

'What?'

'Sure, she—'

The boy probably had twenty or thirty pounds on Tate but farm work keeps you strong and in two seconds Sammy was flat on his back, the wind knocked out of him. Both hands were raised, protecting his face from Tate's lifted fist.

'What the fuck're you saying?' he raged.

Sammy shouting back, 'No, man, no! I didn't do anything. Hey . . .'

'Are you saying she had sex for money?'

'No, I'm not saying nothing! I'm not saying a fucking thing!'

The girl's voice was close to his ear, the blonde he'd first spoken to. 'It's, like, not a big deal. It was a couple years ago.'

'Couple years ago? She's only seventeen *now*, for Christ's sake.' Tate lowered his hand. He stood up, brushed the dust off. He looked at the people in front of the bar. The huge, bearded bouncer was amused. His jurisdiction didn't extend outside the front door, it seemed. Bett was half out of the car, looking at her ex-husband with alarm. He motioned her to stay where she was.

Sammy said, 'Fuck, man, what'd you do that for? I didn't fuck her. She gave it up a while ago. You asked me what I thought and I told you. I figured the guy liked what he had and wanted more. Jesus.'

The girl said, 'Sorry, mister. She had a thing for older men. They were willing to pay. But it was okay, you know.'

'Okay?' Tate asked, numb.

'Sure. She always used rubbers.'

Tate stared at her for a moment then walked back to the car.

Sammy stood up, picked up his beeper, which had fallen off his belt in the struggle. 'Fuck you, man. *Fuck* you! Who're you anyway?'

Turning back, Tate said, 'I'm her father.'

'Father?' the boy asked, frowning.

'Yeah. Her father.'

Sammy looked at the girl, who shrugged. The boy said, 'Megan said she didn't have a father.'

Tate stared at him.

'She said he was a lawyer or something but he ran off and left her when she was six. She hasn't heard from him since.'

In the car Tate asked angrily, 'You didn't know she went there?'

'I told you I didn't. You think I'd *let* her go to a place like that?'

'I just think you might want to know where she was. From time to time.'

'You "just think". You know when people say that?'

'What are you—?' he began.

'They say that when they mean, you damn well *ought* to know where she was.'

'I didn't mean that at all,' Tate snapped.

Though of course he had.

He sped out on to the highway, tires squealing, gravel flying from beneath the tires. Putting the Coffee Shop far behind them.

She finally asked, 'What was that all about?'

He didn't answer.

'Tate? What were you fighting with that boy about?'

'You don't want to know,' he said darkly.

'Tell me!'

He hesitated but then he had to say it. 'He said he thought the guy in the gray car might've been a customer.'

'Customer? At the Coffee Shop?'

'Of Megan's.'

'What? Oh, God. You don't mean—?'

'That's exactly what I mean. That's what the boy said. And that girl too.'

'Vile. You're disgusting . . .'

'Me? *I'm* just telling you what he said.'

Tears coming down her face. 'She wouldn't. There's no way. I believe that in my heart. It's impossible.'

'*They* didn't seem to think it was impossible. They seemed to think she did it pretty often.'

'Tate! How can you say that?'

'And he said it was a couple years ago. When she was *fifteen*.'

'She didn't. I'm certain.'

A wave of fury consumed him. His hands cramped on the steering wheel. 'How could you not know? What were you so busy doing that you didn't notice any condoms in your daughter's purse? Didn't you check who called her? Didn't you notice when she got home? Maybe at midnight? At one? Two?'

'Stop it!' Bett cried. 'Don't attack me. It's not true! It's a misunderstanding. We'll find her and she'll explain it.'

'They seemed to think—'

She screamed, 'It's a lie! It's just gossip. That's all it is! Gossip. Or they're talking about somebody else. Not Megan.'

'Yes, Megan. And you should have—'

'Oh, you're blaming me? It isn't my fault! You know, you *might* have been more involved with her life.'

'Me?' he snapped.

'Okay – sure, your happy family didn't turn out the way you wanted. Well, I'm sorry about that, Tate. But you could have checked on her once in a while.'

'I did. I paid support every month—'

'Oh, for Christ's sake, I don't mean money. You know how often she'd ask me, Why doesn't daddy like me? And I'd say, He does, he's just busy with all his cases. And I'd say, It's hard to be a real daddy when he and Mommy are divorced. And I'd say—'

'I spent Easters with her. And the Fourth of July.'

'Yeah, and you should've heard the debriefings on *those* joyous holidays.' Bett laughed coldly.

'What do you mean? She never complained.'

'You have to *know* somebody before you complain to them. You have to care about them.'

'I took her shopping,' he said. 'I always asked her about school. I—'

'You could've done more. We might've made some accommodation. Might've been a little more of a family.'

'Like hell,' he spat out.

'People've done it. In worse situations.'

'What was I supposed to do? Take up your slack?'

'This isn't about me,' she snapped.

'I think it is. You're her mother. You want somebody else to fix what you've done? Or haven't done?'

'I've done the best I could!' Bett sobbed. 'By myself.'

'But it wasn't you yourself. It was you and the boyfriends.'

'Oh, I was supposed to be celibate?'

'No, but you were supposed to be a mother first. You should've noticed that she had problems.'

Tate couldn't help but think of Bett's sister Susan. The woman had desperately wanted children, while Bett had always been indifferent to the idea. After her husband Harris's death Susan had moved in with a man very briefly – he was abusive and, from what Tate heard, half crazy. But he was a single man – divorced or widowed – with a child. And Susan put up with a lot of crap from him just to have the young boy around; she desperately wanted someone to mother. After they'd broken up, the lover had stalked her for a while but even at the worst moments Susan still seemed to regret the loss of the child in her life. Tate now wished Bett had shown some of that desire for Megan.

'I saw she was unhappy,' Bett said. 'But who the hell isn't? What was I supposed to do? Wave a magic wand?'

His anger wouldn't release the death grip it had on his heart. 'Hell, that's probably exactly your idea of mothering. Sure. Or cast a spell, look up something in the I Ching. Read her tarot.'

'Oh, stop it! I gave up all that shit years ago . . . I tried to be a good mother. I tried.'

'Did you?' he was astonished to find himself saying. 'You sure you weren't out looking for your King Arthur? Easier than changing diapers or helping her with homework or making sure when she was home after school. Making sure she wasn't fucking—'

'I tried . . . I tried . . .' Bett was sobbing, shaking.

Tate realized the car was nudging eighty. He slowed. A deep breath. Another.

Long, long silence. His eyes too welled up with tears. 'Listen, I'm sorry.'

'I tried. I wanted . . . I wanted . . .'

'Bett, please. I'm sorry.'

'I wanted a family too, you know,' she whispered, wiping her face on the sleeve of her blouse. 'I saw the Judge and his wife and you and the rest of the Colliers. I didn't talk about it the way you did but I wanted a family too. But then something happened . . . Everybody died. My mom and dad and your father . . . And you were always in court and you were so distant all the time. So wrapped up in the cases. I was sure you didn't love me . . .'

'I lost my temper. I don't . . . You're right. Those kids back there . . . it was probably just gossip. I'm sure it was.'

But his words were flaccid. And of course they came far too late. The damage had been done. He wondered if they'd separate now and never speak to each other again. He supposed that would happen. He supposed that it would *have* to.

And oddly, he realized how much the idea upset him. No, it terrified him; he had no idea why.

A long moment passed.

Bett spoke first. He was surprised to hear her say, in a calm, reasoned voice, 'Maybe it's true, Tate – what you heard about her. Maybe it is. But you know, people change. They can. They really can.'

They continued on in silence. Bett closed her eyes and leaned her head back on the headrest.

What a man hears, he may doubt.

What he sees, he may possibly doubt.

'Bett? I am sorry.'

What he does . . .

'Bett?'

But she didn't answer.

Chapter FIFTEEN

She decided she was safest here, in her cell.

If the father – Aaron Matthews – had wanted to kill her he could have done so easily. He didn't have to sock her away here, he didn't have to buy all the food. No, no, she had this funny sense that though he kidnapped her he didn't want to hurt her.

But the son . . . *He* was the threat. She needed protection from him. She'd stay here locked in Crazy Megan's padded cell until she figured out how to escape.

She opened one of the files she'd taken from Peter's room. In the dim light she scanned the pages, trying to find something that might help her. Maybe the place was near a town. Were there photos or brochures of the hospital and grounds? Maybe she could find a map. If she started a fire, people might see the smoke. Or maybe she'd find ventilation shafts or emergency exits. She remembered a padlocked door marked 'Basement' down one of the corridors near by. If she could break the lock on the door, were there exits down there she might get through? She flipped through the documents, looking for a picture or photo of the hospital – trying to find basement windows or doors she might climb out of.

Damn, that's smart, says an impressed Crazy Megan.

Shhhh . . .

Megan happened to glance at the papers on the top of the pile.

. . . patient Victoria Skelling, 37, paranoid schizophrenic, was found dead in her room at 0620 hours, April 23. COD was asphyxia, from inhalation of mattress fibers. County Police (see annexed report) investigated and declared the death suicide. It appeared patient Skelling gnawed through the canvas ducking of her mattress and pulled out wads of stuffing. She inhaled approximately ten ounces of this material down her throat. The patient had been on Thorazine and Haldol, delusions were minimal. Orderlies described her in 'good spirits' for much of the morning of her death but after spending the day on the grounds with a group of other patients her mood turned darker. She was complaining that the rats were coming to get her. They were going to chew her breasts off (earlier delusions and certain dreams centered around poisoned breast milk and suckling). She calmed again at dinner time and spent the evening in the TV room. She was extremely upset when she went to bed and orderlies considered using restraints. She was given an extra dose of Haldol and locked into her room at 2200 hours. She said, 'It's time to take care of the rats. They win, they win.' She was found the next morning dead. . . .

Gross.

She flipped through more pages.

. . . Patient Matthews (No. 97–4335) was the last person to see her alive and he reported that she seemed 'all spooky'.

So the boy had been hospitalized here. And after the hospital was closed his father brought him back. Why, she couldn't guess. Maybe he felt at home here. Maybe his father broke him out of another hospital to have him nearby.

She flipped through another report – someone else had committed suicide.

. . . The body of Patient Garber (No. 78–7547) was found behind the main building. The police and coroner had determined that he had swallowed a garden hose and turned the water on full force. The pressure from the water ruptured his stomach and several feet of intestine. He died from internal hemorrhaging and shock. Although several patients were near by when this happened (Matthews (No. 97–4335) and Ketter (No. 91–3212), they could offer no further information. The death was ruled suicide by the medical examiner.

Megan read through several other files. They were all similar – reports of patients killing themselves. One victim was found in the library. He'd apparently spent hours tearing apart books and magazines, looking for a sheet of paper sturdy enough to cut the artery in his neck. He finally succeeded.

She shivered at the thought.

Someone else had leapt out of a tree and broken his neck. He didn't die but was paralyzed for life. When asked about why he'd done it he said, *'He'd been talking to "some patients" and he realized how pointless life was, how he was never going to get better. Death would bring some peace.'*

There were six deaths altogether, the last one about a year ago.

Yet another report stated, *'Patient Matthews was the last person to see victim alive.'* The administrator wondered if he'd been involved and the boy had been interviewed and evaluated but no charges were brought.

Reading more, she found that not long after the last suicide a reporter from the Washington *Times* heard of the deaths and filed an investigative report. The state board of examiners looked into the matter and closed the hospital.

But of course, Megan understood, the deaths weren't suicides at all. How could they have missed it? Peter had killed the other patients and somehow covered up the evidence.

She flipped through the rest of the files and clippings.

Nothing she found told her anything helpful. She shoved them under the bed. What can I do? There has to—

Then she heard the footsteps.

Faint at first.

Oh, no . . . Peter was coming up the hall.

Well, he might not know she was here. And if he did, he might not know she was in this room.

But there was a new padlock on it. He'd see that.

Closer, closer. Very soft now, as if trying not to make any noise.

She heard his breathing and remembered the picture of the eerie-looking boy – his twisted mouth, the tip of his pale tongue in the corner of his lips. She remembered the stained sheets and wondered if he was walking around, looking for her, masturbating . . .

Megan shivered violently. Started to cry. She eased up to the door, put her head against it, listened.

No sounds from the other side.

Had he—?

A fierce pounding on the door. The recoil knocked her to her knees.

Another crash.

A whispered voice. 'Megan . . .' And in that faint word she heard lust and desperation and hunger. 'Megan . . .'

He knows I'm here . . .

Peter was rattling the lock. A few loud slams of a brick or baseball bat on the padlock.

No, please . . . Why'd Matthews left her alone with him? As much as she hated him, Megan prayed he'd return.

'Megannnnnnn?' It now sounded as if he was laughing.

A sudden crash, into the door itself. Then another. And another. Suddenly a rusty metal rod – like the spears in some of his horrible comic books – cracked the wood and poked through a few inches. Just as Peter pulled the metal back out, Megan leapt into the bathroom, plastered herself against the wall. She heard his breath on the door and she knew he was looking through the hole he'd made.

'Megan . . .'

But from that angle he couldn't see that there was a bathroom; the door was to the side.

For an eternity she listened to his lecherous breathing. Finally he walked off.

She started back into the room. But stopped.

Had he really gone? she wondered.

She decided she couldn't go into the room until dark. Peter might be waiting outside and he'd see her. And if she plugged up the hole he'd know she was there.

She sat on the toilet, lowered her head to her hands and cried.

Come on, girl. Get up.

I can't. No, I can't. I'm scared.

Of course you're scared, Crazy Megan chides. *But what's that got to do with anything? Lookit that. Lookit the bathroom window.*

Megan looked at the bathroom window.

No, it's nuts to think about it.

You know what you've got to do.

I can't do it, Megan thought. I just can't.

Yeah? What choice've you got?

Megan stood and walked to the window, reached through the bars and touched the filthy glass.

I can't.

Yes, you can!

She realized that her crazy side – the angry side, the side that she kept locked up thanks to Southern Comfort and to pot and to fucking old men – that side was dead right. She didn't have any choice at all.

Megan crawled into the room, praying that Peter wasn't outside the door, looking through the peephole he'd made. She reached under the bed, sure she'd come up with a handful of rat. But no, she found only the manila file folder she'd been looking for. She returned to the bathroom and eased up to the window, pressed the folder against the glass. She drew back her fist and slugged the pane. The punch was hard but the glass held. She hit it again and this time a long crack spread from the top to the bottom of the window. Finally, another slug and the glass shattered. She pulled her fist back just in time as the sharp shards fell to the windowsill.

She picked a triangular piece of glass about eight inches long, narrow as a knife. Taking her cue from patient Victoria Skelling's sad end, Megan, using her teeth, ripped a strip off one of the pads on the wall. She wound this around the base of the splinter to make a handle.

Good, C.M. says with approval. Proud of her other self.

No, better than good: *Great*. Fuck you, Dr Matthews. I feel *great*! It reminded her of how she'd felt when she'd written those letters to her parents in Dr Hanson's office. It was scary, it hurt, but it was completely honest.

Good.

Crazy Megan wonders, *So what's next?*

'Fuck him up,' Megan responded out loud. 'Then get his keys and book on out of here.'

Atta girl, C.M. offers. *But what about the dogs?*

They've got claws, *I've* got claws. Megan dramatically held up the knife.

Crazy Megan is impressed as hell.

'There's a van.'

'A van?' Bett asked.

'Following us,' Tate continued, as they drove past the Ski Chalet in Chantilly.

Bett started to turn.

'No, don't,' he said.

She froze. Looked at her hands, fingers tipped in faint purple polish. 'Are you sure?'

'Pretty sure. A white van.'

Tate made a slow circle through the shopping center then exited on Route 50 and sped east. He pulled into Greenbriar strip mall, stopped at the Starbuck's and climbed out. He bought two teas, topped with foamed milk, and returned to the car.

They sipped them for a moment and when a red Ford Explorer cut between his Lexus and the van he hit the gas and took off past the bookstore, streaking onto Majestic Lane and just catching the tail end of the light that put him back on Route 50, heading west this time.

When he settled into the right lane he noticed the white van was still with him.

'How'd he do that?' Tate wondered aloud.

'He's still there?'

'Yep. Hell, he's good.'

They continued west, passing under Route 28, which was the dividing line between civilization here and the farmland that led eventually to the mountains.

'What're we going to do?'

But Tate didn't answer, hardly even heard the question. He was looking at a large sign that said 'Future home of Liberty Land . . .'

He laughed out loud.

This was one of those odd things, noticing the sign at the same time the van was following them. A high-grade coincidence, he would have said. Bett – well, the old Bett – would of course have attributed it to the stars or the spirits or past lives or something. Didn't matter. He'd made the connection. At last he had a solid lead.

'What?' she cried, alarmed, responding more to his outrageous U-turn, skidding 180 degrees over the grassy median, than to the harsh laugh coming from his throat.

'I just figured something out. We're going to my place for a minute. I have to get something.'

'Oh. What?'

'A gun.'

Bett's head turned toward him then away. 'You're serious, aren't you?'

'Oh, yep. Very serious.'

Some years ago, when Tate had been prosecuting the improbable case of the murder of a Jamaican drug dealer at a Wendy's restaurant in suburban Burke, Konnie Konstantinatis had poked his head into Tate's office.

'Time you got yourself a piece.'

'Of what?'

'Ha. You'll wanta revolver 'cause all you do is point 'n' shoot. You're not a boy to mess with clips and safeties and stuff like that.'

'What's a clip?'

Tate had been joking, of course – every commonwealth's attorney in Virginia was well versed in the lore of firearms – but the fact was he really didn't know guns well. The Judge didn't hold with weapons, didn't see any need for them and believed the countryside would be much more populated without them.

But Konnie wouldn't take no for an answer, and within a week Tate found himself the owner of a very unglamorous Smith & Wesson .38 special, sporting six chambers, only five loaded, the one under the hammer being forever empty, as Konnie always preached.

This gun was locked away where it'd been for the past three or four years – in a trunk in Tate's barn. He sped up his driveway and leapt out, observing that with his manic driving he'd lost the white van without intending to. He ran into the barn, found the key on his chain and after much jiggling managed to open the trunk. The gun, still coated with oil as he'd left it, was in a zip-lock bag. He took it out, wiped it clean and slipped it into his pocket.

In the car Bett asked him timidly, 'You have it?' The way a college girl might ask her boyfriend if he'd brought a condom on a date.

He nodded.

'Is it loaded?'

'Oh.' He'd forgotten to look. He took it out and fiddled with the gun until he remembered how to open it. Five silver eyes of bullets stared back from the cylinder.

'Yep.'

He clicked it shut and put the heavy gun in his pocket.

'It's not going to just go off, is it? I mean by itself?'

'No.' He noticed Bett staring at him. 'What?' he asked, starting the engine of the Lexus.

'You're . . . you look scary.'

He laughed. 'I feel scary. Let's go.'

Manassas, Virginia, is this:

Big-wheeled trucks, sullen pick-a-fight teenagers (the description fitting both the boys and the girls), cars on the street and cars on blocks, Confederate stars 'n' bars, strip malls, PCP labs tucked away in the woods, concrete postwar bungalows, quiet mothers and skinny fathers struggling, struggling, struggling. It's domestic fights. It's women sobbing at Garth's concerts and teens puking at Aerosmith's.

And a little of it, very little, is Grant Avenue.

This is Doctors' and Lawyers' Row. Little Taras, civil war mansions complete with columns and detached barns for garages, surrounded by expansive landscaped yards. It was to the biggest of these houses – a rambling white colonial on four acres – that Tate Collier now drove.

'Who lives here?' Bett asked, cautiously eying the house.

'The man who knows where Megan is.'

'Call Konnie.'

'No time,' he muttered and he rolled up the drive, past the two Mercedes – neither of them gray, he noticed – and skidded to a stop about five feet from the front door, nearly knocking a limestone lion off its perch beside the walk.

'Tate!'

But he ignored her and leapt from the car.

'Wait here.'

The anger swelled inside him even more powerfully, boiling, and he found himself pounding fiercely on the door with his left hand, his right gripped around the handle of the pistol.

A large man opened the door. He was in his thirties, muscular, wearing chinos and an Izod shirt.

'I want to see him,' Tate growled.

'Who are you?'

'I want to see Sharpe and I want to see him now.'

Pull the gun now? Or wait for a more dramatic moment?

'Mr Sharpe's busy right at the—'

Tate lifted the gun out of his pocket. He displayed it, more than brandished it, to the assistant or bodyguard, or whatever he was. The man lifted his hands and backed up, alarm on his face. 'Jesus Christ!'

'Where is he?'

'Hold on there, mister, I don't know who you are or what you're doing here but—'

'Jimmy, what's going on?' a voice called from the top of the stairs.

'Got a problem here, Mr Sharpe.'

'Tate Collier come a-calling,' Jack Sharpe sang out. He glanced at the gun as if Tate were holding a butterfly net. 'Collier, whatcha got yourself there?' He laughed. Cautious, some. But it was still a laugh.

'Was he driving the white van?' Tate pointed the gun at the man in the chinos, who lifted his hands. 'Careful, sir. Please!'

'It's okay, Jimmy,' Sharpe called. 'Just let him be. He'll calm down. What van, Collier?'

'You know what van,' Tate said, turning back to Sharpe. 'Was he the asshole driving?'

'Why'n't you put that thing away so's nobody gets hurt. And we'll talk . . . No, Jimmy, it's okay, really.'

'I can shoot him if you want, Mr Sharpe.'

Tate glanced back and found himself looking into the muzzle of a very large pistol, chrome-plated, held steadily in Jimmy's hand. It was an automatic, he noticed – with clips and safeties and all the rest of that *stuff*.

'No, don't do that,' Sharpe said. 'He's not going to shoot anybody. Collier, put it away. It might be better for everybody.'

Jimmy shrugged, kept the gun pointed at Tate's head.

Tate put his own pistol back into his pocket with shaking hands.

'Come on upstairs.'

'Should I come too, Mr Sharpe?'

'No, I don't think we'll needya, Jimmy. Will we, Collier?'

'I don't think so,' Tate said. 'No.'

'Come on up.'

Tate, breathless, after the adrenalin rush, climbed the stairs. He followed Jack Sharpe into a sunlit den. He glanced back and saw that Jimmy was still holding the shiny pistol pointed vaguely in Tate's direction.

Sharpe – wearing navy blue polyester slacks and a red golfing shirt – was now all business. No longer jokey.

'What the fuck's this all about, Collier?'

'Where's my daughter?'

'Your daughter? How should I know?'

'Who's driving the white van?'

'I assume you're saying that somebody's been following you.'

'Yeah, somebody's been following me.' When Tate had seen the Liberty Park sign he'd remembered that his clients in that case had complained to him last week that private eyes had been following them. Tate'd told them not to worry – it was standard practice in big cases, (though he added that they shouldn't do anything they wouldn't want committed to videotape). 'Same as somebody's been following my clients. And probably my wife—'

'Thought you were divorced,' Sharpe interrupted.

'How'd you know that?'

'Seem to remember something.'

'So if you were following us—'

'*Me?*' Sharpe tried for innocence. It didn't take.

'—you've been following my daughter too. Who just happened to disappear today.'

Sharpe slowly lifted a putter from a bag of golf clubs sitting in the corner of his study, addressed one of the dozen balls lying on the floor and sent it across the room. It missed the cup.

'I hire lawyers to fight my battles for me. As *you* well know, having decorated the walls of the courtroom with their hides recently. That's *all* I hire.'

Tate asked, 'No security consultants?'

'Ha, security consultants. That's good. Yeah, that's good. Well, no, Collier. There ain't no private eyes and no see-curity consultants. Not on my part at any rate. Now, what's this shit about your daughter?'

'She's missing and I think you're behind it.'

Another putt. He missed the cup again.

'Me? Why? Oh, I get it. To take you outta the running next Thursday down in Richmond, right?'

'Makes sense to me.'

'Well, it don't make sense to me. I don't need to do that. You know I fired those half-assed shysters you reamed at the trial. I got the big boys involved now. You've seen the briefs. Lambert, Stone & Burns. They're gonna run right over you. Don't flatter yourself. They'll burn you up like Atlanta.'

'Liberty Park, Sharpe. Tell me. How much'll you lose if it doesn't get built?'

'The park? It don't go through? I don't lose a penny.' Then he smiled. 'But the amount I won't *make* is to the tune of eighteen million. Say, ain't it unethical for you to be here without my lawyer being present?'

Tate said, 'Where is she? Tell me.'

'I don't know what you're talking about.'

'Come on, John. You think I don't know about defendants harassing clients and lawyers so they'll drop cases?'

Sharpe ran his hand through his white hair. He sat down, beneath a picture of himself on the eighteenth tee of the Bull Run Country Club, a place that proudly had not a single member who wasn't white and Protestant. Male too – though that went without saying.

'Collier, I don't kidnap people.'

'But how about some of those little roosters that work for you? I wouldn't put it past a couple or three of them. That project manager of yours. Wilkins? He was in Lorton for eighteen months.'

'Passing bad paper, Collier, not kidnapping girls.'

'Who knows who they might've hired? Some psycho who *does* kidnap girls. And maybe likes it.'

'Nobody hired nobody,' Sharpe said, though Tate could see in his eyes that he was considering the possibility that one of his thugs had snatched Megan. But five seconds on the defensive was too much for Jack Sharpe. 'Running outta patience here, Collier. And whatta I know, I'm just a country boy – but if I'm not mistaken, isn't that slander or libel or some such you're spouting?'

'So file suit, John. But tell me where she is.'

'You're barking up the wrong tree, Collier. You're gonna have to look elsewhere. You're not thinking clear. You know Prince William as good as your grandfather did before you. If you do a deal like Liberty Park you play hardball. That's the way business works in these parts. But for Christ's sake, this ain't southeast D.C. I'm not gonna hurt a seventeen-year-old girl. Now it's time for you to leave. I got work to do.'

He sank the next putt into a small cup, which spit the ball back to him.

Tate, chin quivering with rage, stared back at the much calmer face of his opponent.

From the doorway, Jimmy asked calmly, 'You want me to help him outside?'

Sharpe said, 'Naw. Just show him to the door. Hey, so long, Counselor. See you in Richmond next Thursday. I intend to be in the front row. Hope you're rested and comfy. They're going to rub every inch of your skin off. It's gonna be pretty to watch.'

Chapter SIXTEEN

Rhetoric, Plato wrote, is the universal art of winning the mind by argument.

Tate Collier, at eleven years of age, listened to the Judge recite that definition as the old man rasped a match to light his fragrant pipe and decided that one day he would 'do rhetoric'.

Whatever that meant.

He had to wait three years for the chance but finally, as a high school freshman, he argued (what else?) his way into debate club, even though it was open only to upperclassmen.

Tournament debating started in colonial America with the Spy Club at Harvard in the early 1700s and opened up to women a hundred years later with the Young Ladies Association at Oberlin, though hundreds of less formal societies, lyceums and bees had always been popular throughout the colonies. By the time Tate was in school intercollegiate debate had become a practiced institution.

He argued in hundreds of National Debate Tournament bouts as well as the alternative-format – Cross Examination Debate Association – tournaments. He was a member of the forensic honorary fraternities – Delta Sigma Rho, Phi Rho Pi and Pi Kappa Delta – and was now as active in the American Forensics Association as he was in the American Bar Association.

In college – when it was fashionable to be anti-military, anti-frat, anti-ROTC – Tate shunned bellbottoms and tie-dye for suits with narrow ties and white shirts. There, he honed his technique, his logic, his reasoning. *If . . . then . . .* Major premise, minor premise, conclusion. Combating straw men, circular logic, *ad hominem* tactics by the opponents. He fought debaters from Georgetown and George Washington, from Duke and North Carolina and Penn and Johns Hopkins, and he beat them all.

With this talent (and, of course, with the Judge for a grandfather) law school was inevitable. At UVA he'd been the state moot court champion his senior year at the Federal Bar Moot Court open in the District. Now he frequently taught well-attended appellate advocate continuing-ed courses and his American Trial Lawyer's tape was a bestseller in the ABA catalog.

When he'd been a senior at UVA and the champion debater on campus the Judge had traveled down to Charlottesville to see him. As predicted, he'd won the debate (it was the infamous pro-Watergate contest). The Judge told him that he'd heard someone in the audience say, 'How's that Collier boy do it? He looks like a farmboy but when he starts to talk he's somebody else. It's like he's speaking in tongues.'

No, there was no one Tate Collier would not match words with. Yet the incident with Sharpe had left him unnerved. He'd let emotions dictate what he'd said. What was happening to him? He was losing his touch.

'I blew it,' he muttered. And told Bett what had happened.

'Did he have anything to do with it?'

'I think he did, yeah. He was slick, too slick. He was expecting me. But he was also surprised about something.'

'What?'

'I think something happened he hadn't planned on. It's true. I don't think his boys would kidnap Megan themselves. But they may've hired somebody to do it. Oh, and he knew we were divorced and that Megan was seventeen. Why'd he know that?'

'Are you going to tell Konnie?'

'Oh, sure. But people like Sharpe are good. They don't leave loose ends. You follow the trails and they vanish.'

She picked up the pistol, which he'd set on the dashboard. She slipped it in the glove compartment distastefully. 'Aren't we a pair, Tate? Guns, private eyes.'

He said, 'Bett, I'm sorry. About before.'

She shook her head. 'No,' she offered definitively.

They drove in silence for several moments.

She sighed then asked reflectively, 'Do you like your life?'

He glanced at her. Responded: 'Sure.'

'Just sure?'

'How much more can you be than sure?'

'You can be convincing,' she said.

'What's life,' he asked, 'but ups and downs?'

'You ever get lonely?'

Ah. Sometimes the girls would stay the night, sometimes they'd leave. Sometimes they decided to return to their husbands or lovers or leave him for other men, sometimes they'd talk about getting divorced and sometimes they were single, unattached and waiting for a ring. Sometimes they'd introduce Tate to their parents or their cautious-eyed children or, if they had none, talk about how much they wanted some. A boy first, they'd invariably say, and then a girl. Two probably. Maybe three.

They all faded from his life and, yes, most nights he was lonely.

'I keep pretty busy,' he said. 'You?'

She said quickly, 'I'm busy too. Everybody needs interior design.'

'Sure,' he agreed. 'Things working out well with Brad?'

'Oh, Brad's a dear. He's a real gentleman. You don't see many of them. You were one. I mean, you still are.' She laughed. 'You know, I keep expecting to see you on TV,' she said. 'Prosecuting serial killers or terrorists or something. Channel Nine loved you. You gave great interviews.'

'Those were the days.'

'Why'd you quit practice?'

He kept his hands at ten to two on the wheel and his eyes straight ahead.

'Tate?' she repeated.

'Prosecuting's a young man's game,' he said. Thinking he was the epitome of credibility.

But Bett said, 'That's *an* answer. But not *the* answer.'

'I didn't quit practice.'

'You know what I mean. You were the best CA in the state. Remember those rumors that you'd get that job at the Supreme Court?'

Solicitor General – the lawyer who represented the government in cases before the Nine Supremes. The most important forensic orator in the country. Tate's grandfather had always hoped his grandson might get that job. And Tate himself had for years had his sights on that job.

'I wanted to spend more time on the farm.'

'Bullshit.' Well, this was *definitely* a new Bett McCall. The ethereal angel had come to earth with muddy cheeks. 'Why won't you tell me?'

'Okay. I lost my taste for blood,' he explained. 'I prosecuted a capital case. I won. And I wished I hadn't.'

Bett had been deeply ashamed that while they were married Tate had sent six men to die in the commonwealth's death chamber in Jarrett, Virginia. This had always seemed ironic to him, for she believed in the immortality of souls and Tate did not.

'He was innocent?' she asked.

'No, no. It was more complicated than that. He killed the victim. There was no question about that. But he was probably guilty of manslaughter at best. Criminally negligent homicide, most likely. The defense offered a plea – probation and counseling. I rejected it and went for lethal injection. The jury gave him life imprisonment. The first week he was in prison, he was killed by other inmates. Actually . . .' His voice caught. 'He was tortured and then he died.'

'God, Tate.'

What a man hears, he may doubt . . .

'I talked him to death, Bett. I conjured the jurors. I had the *gift* on my side. Not the law. And he's dead when he shouldn't be. If he'd been out of prison, had some help he'd be alive now and probably a fine person.'

But what he does, he cannot doubt.

He waited for her disgust or anger.

But she said only, 'I'm sorry.' He looked at her and saw not pity or remorse but simple regret at his pain. 'They fired you? The CA's office?'

'Oh, no. No. I just quit.'

'I never heard about it.'

'Small case. Not really newsworthy. The story died on the Metro page.'

Staring at the road, Tate confessed, 'You know something?'

He felt Bett's head turn toward him.

He continued, 'I wanted to tell you about what happened. When I heard that he'd died I reached for the phone to call you – before anybody else. Even before Konnie. I hadn't seen you in over a year. Two years maybe. But you were the one I wanted to tell.'

'I wish you had.'

He chuckled. 'But you hated me taking capital cases.'

There was a long pause. She said, 'Seems to me you've served enough time over that one. Most everybody gets a parole hearing, don't they?' As Tate signaled to make the turn for Bett's exit she said, 'Could we just drive a bit? I don't feel like going home.'

His hand wavered over the signal stem. He clicked it off.

Chapter SEVENTEEN

Tate piloted his Lexus back through Centreville, which some of the redder of the rednecks around these parts disparagingly called New Calcutta and New Seoul – because of the immigrants settling here. He made a long loop around Route 29 and turned down a deserted country road.

The sun was low now but the heat seemed worse. The sour, sickly aroma of rotting leaves from last year's autumn was in the air.

'Tate,' Bett asked slowly, 'what if nothing happened?'

'Nothing happened?'

'What if nobody kidnapped her. What if she really did run off? On her own. Because she hates us.'

He glanced at her.

She continued, 'If we find her—'

'*When* we find her,' he corrected.

'What if she's so mad at us that she won't come home?'

'We'll convince her to,' he told her.

'Could you do it, do you think? Talk her into coming back home?'

Can I? he wondered.

There's a transcendent moment in debate when your

opponent has the overwhelming weight of logic and facts on his side and yet still you can win. By leading him in a certain direction you get him to build his entire argument on what appears to be an irrefutable foundation, the logic of which is flawless. But which you nonetheless destroy at the same time as you accept the perfection of his argument.

It's a moment, Tate tells his classes, just like in fencing, when the red target of a heart is touched with the button of the foil. Not flailing away, no chops or heavy strokes, but a simple, deadly tap the opponent never sees coming.

All cats see in the dark.

Midnight is a cat.

Therefore Midnight can see in the dark.

Irrefutable. The purest of logic.

Unless . . . Midnight is blind.

But what kind of argument could he make to convince Megan to return home?

He thought about the letters she'd written and he didn't have any thoughts at all; he saw only her perfect anger.

'We'll get her back,' he told Bett. 'I'll do that. Don't worry.'

Bett pulled down the makeup mirror in the sunvisor to apply lipstick. Tate was suddenly taken back to the night they met – at that party in Charlottesville. He'd driven her home afterwards and had spent a passionate half-hour in the front seat of a car removing every trace of her pink Revlon.

Five weeks later he'd suggested they move in together.

A two-year romance on campus. He'd graduated from law school the year Bett got her undergraduate degree. They left idyllic Charlottesville for the District of Columbia and his clerkship at Federal district court; Bett got a job managing a new age bookstore. They lived the bland, easy life that Washington offered a young couple just starting out. Tate's consolation was his job and Bett's that she finally was close to her twin sister, who lived in Baltimore and had been too ill to travel to Charlottesville.

Married in May.

His antebellum plantation built the next spring.

Megan born two years later.

And three years after that, he and Bett were divorced.

When he looked back on their relationship his perfect memory was no longer so perfect. What he recalled seemed to be merely sharp peaks of an island rising from a huge undersea mountain range. The wispy, ethereal woman he'd seen at the party, singing a sailor's mournful song of farewell. Walks in the country. Driving through the Blue Ridge into the Massanutten Mountains. Making love in a forest near the Luray Caverns. Tate had always enjoyed being out of doors – the cornfields and back-yard barbecues. But Bett's interest in the outside arose only at dusk. 'When the line between the worlds is at its thinnest,' she'd told him once, sitting on the porch of an inn deep in the Appalachians.

'What worlds?' he asked.

'Shhh, listen,' she'd said, enchanting him even while he knew it was an illusion. Which was, he supposed, irrefutable proof of her ability to cast a spell.

Betty Sue McCall, devoted to her twin sister, with whom she had some mystical link that unnerved even rationalist Tate, reedy folk singer, collector of the unexplained, the arcane, the invisible . . . Tate had never figured out if her sublime mystique magnified their love falsely or obscured it or indeed if it was the essence of their love.

Magic . . .

In the end, of course, it didn't matter, for they separated completely, moved far away from each other emotionally. She became for him what she'd been when he was first captivated by her: the dark woman of his imagination.

Today she prodded her face in the mirror, rubbed at some

invisible blemish as he remembered her doing many times. She'd always been terribly vain.

She flipped the mirror back.

'Pull over, Tate.'

He glanced at her. No, it was not an imperfection she'd been examining; she'd been crying again and seemed dismayed at her ruddy eyes.

'What is it?'

'Just pull over.'

He did, into the Parks Service entrance to the Bull Run Battlefield.

Bett climbed from the car and walked up the gentle slope. Tate followed and when they were on level ground they stopped and simultaneously gazed at the tumultuous clouds overhead.

'What is it, Bett?' He watched her stare at the night sky. 'Looking for an angel to help you decide something?'

Suddenly he was worried that she'd take offense at this though he hadn't meant it sardonically.

But she only smiled and lowered her eyes from the sky. 'I was never into that angel stuff. Too Hallmark card, you know. But I wouldn't mind a spirit or two.'

'Well,' he said, 'this'd be the place. General Jackson came charging out of those trees right over there and stopped the Union boys cold in their tracks. Right here's where he earned himself the name Stonewall.' The low sun glistened off the Union cannons' black barrels in the distance.

Suddenly Bett turned, took his hands and pulled him to her. 'Hold me. Please.'

He put his arms around her – for the first time in years. They stood this way for a long moment. Then found a bench and sat. He kept his arm around her. She took his other hand. And Tate wished suddenly, painfully, that Megan were here with them. The three of them together and all the hard events of the past dead and buried, like the poor, broken bodies of the troops who'd died bloody on this very spot.

Wind in the trees, billowing clouds overhead.

Suddenly a streak of yellow flashed past them.

'Oh, what's that?' Bett said. 'Look.'

He glanced at the bird that alighted near them.

'That'd be, let me see, a common yellowthroat. Nests on the ground and feeds in the tree canopy.'

Her laugh scared it away. 'You know all these *facts*. Where do you learn them?'

A girlfriend, age twenty-three, had been a birdwatcher.

'I read a lot,' he said.

More silence.

'What are you thinking?' she wondered after a moment.

A question women seem to ask whenever they find themselves in close contact with a man.

'Unfinished business?' he suggested. 'You and me?'

She considered this. 'I used to think things were finished between us. But then I started to look at it like doing your will before you get on a plane.'

'How's that?'

'If you crash, well, maybe all the loose ends're tied up but wouldn't you still rather hang around for a little while longer?'

'There's a metaphor for you.' He laughed.

She spent a moment examining the sky again. 'When you argued before the Supreme Court five or six years ago. That big civil rights case. And the *Post* did that write-up on you. I told everybody you were my ex-husband. I was proud of you.'

'Really?' He was surprised.

'You know what occurred to me then, reading about you? It seemed that when we were married you were my voice. I didn't have one of my own.'

'You were quiet, that's true,' he said.

'That's what happened to us, I think. Part of it anyway. I had to find mine.'

'And when you went looking . . . so long. No half-measures for you. No compromises. No bargaining.'

The old Bett would have frozen or dipped into her enigmatic silence at these critical words. But she merely nodded in agreement. 'That was me, all right. I was so rigid. I had all the right answers. If something wasn't just perfect I was gone. Jobs, classes . . . husband. Oh, Tate, I'm not proud of it. But I felt so young. When you have a child, things do change. You become more . . .'

'Enduring?'

'That's it. Yes. You always know the right word.'

He said, 'I never had any idea what you were thinking about back then.'

Bett's thoughts might have been on what to make for dinner. On King Arthur. On a footnote in a term paper. She might have been thinking of a recent tarot card reading.

She might even have been thinking about him.

'I was always afraid to say anything around you, Tate. I always felt tongue tied. Like I had nothing to say that interested you.'

'I don't love you for you oratorical abilities.' He paused, struck by the tense of the verb. 'I mean, that's not what attracted me to you.'

Then reflected: Oh, she's so right – what she'd said earlier. . . . We humans have this terrible curse; we alone among the animals believe in the possibility of change – in ourselves and those we love. It can kill us and maybe, just maybe, it can save our doomed hearts. The problem is we never know until it's too late which.

'You know when I missed you the most?' she said finally. 'Not on holidays or picnics. But when I was in Belize—'

'What?' Tate asked suddenly.

She waved lethargically at a yellow jacket. 'You know, you and I always talked about going there.'

They'd read a book about the Mayan language and the linguists who trooped through the jungles in Belize on the Yucatan to examine the ruins and decipher the Indian code. The area had fascinated them both and they planned a trip. But they'd never made the journey. At first they couldn't afford it. Tate had just graduated from law school and started working as a judge's clerk for less money than a good legal secretary could make. Then long, long hours in the Commonwealth's Attorney's office. Then there was the first of the Supreme Court arguments that took months of his life. After that, when they had the money saved up, Bett's sister had a serious relapse and nearly died; Bett couldn't leave home. Then Megan came along. And three years after that they were divorced.

'When did you go?' he asked.

'Three years ago. January. Didn't Megan tell you?'

'No.'

'I went with Bill. The lobbyist?'

Tate shook his head. 'Have a good time?'

'Oh, yeah,' she said haltingly. 'Very nice. It was hotter than Hades. Really hot.'

'But you like the heat,' he remembered. 'Did you see the ruins?'

'Well, Bill wasn't into ruins so much. We did see one. We took a day trip. I . . . Well, I was going to say – I wished you'd been with me.'

'Two years ago February,' Tate said.

'What?'

'I was there too.'

'No! Are you serious?' She laughed hard. 'Who'd *you* go with?'

Her face grew wry when it took him a moment to remember the name of his companion.

'Cathy.'

He *believed* it was Cathy.

'Did *you* get to the ruins?'

'Well, we didn't exactly. It was more of a sailboarding trip. I don't believe it. . . . Damn, how 'bout that. We finally got down there. We talked about that vacation for years.'

'Our pilgrimage.'

'Great place,' he said, wondering how dubious his voice sounded. 'Our hotel had a really good restaurant.'

'It was fun,' she said enthusiastically. 'And pretty.'

'Very pretty,' he confirmed. The trip had been agonizingly dull.

Her face was turned toward a distant line of trees. She was thinking probably of Megan now and the Yucatan was far from her thoughts.

'Let me take you home,' he said. 'There's nothing more we can do tonight. We should get some rest. I'll call Konnie, tell him about Sharpe.'

She nodded.

They drove to Fairfax and he pulled up in front of her house. She sat in the front seat in silence for a while.

'You want to come in?' she asked suddenly.

His answer was balanced on the head of a pin and for a long moment he didn't have a clue which way it was going to tilt.

Tate pulled her to him, hugged her, smelled the scent of Opium perfume in her hair. He said, 'Better not.'

Chapter EIGHTEEN

Crazy Megan reveals her true self.

She isn't crazy at all and never has been. What C.M. is is furious.

He's going down, she mutters. *This asshole Peter is going down hard.*

Megan McCall was angry too but she was much less optimistic than her counterpart as she moved cautiously through the corridors of the hospital, clutching three boxes of plastic utensils under her arm and her glass knife in the other.

Though she was feeling better physically, having eaten half a box of her favorite cereal – Raisin Bran – and drunk two Pepsis.

Listening.

There!

She heard a shuffle, a few steps of Peter's feet. Maybe a whisper of breath.

Another shuffle. A voice.

Her name?

Yes, no?

She couldn't tell.

This could be it! Got a good grip on the knife?

Be quiet! Megan thought.

Megan shivered and felt a burst of nausea from the fear. Wished she hadn't eaten so fast. If I puke that'll be it . . .

She inhaled slowly.

Then there was silence and she continued on.

A clunk near by. More footsteps. These were nearby.

She'd almost turned right down the corridor where he'd been standing.

Megan gasped and closed her eyes, remaining completely still, huddling behind an orange fiberglass chair.

She pressed into the wall and began mentally working her way through Janis Joplin's *Greatest Hits* album line by line. She cried noiselessly throughout 'Me and Bobby McGee', then grew defiant once more when she mind-sang 'Down on Me'.

His footsteps wandered away, back toward his room, and she continued on. Ten endless minutes later she made it to the end of the corridor she'd decided to use for her trap.

She needed a dead end – she had to be sure of the direction he'd come at her from. Crazy Megan points out, though, that it also means she'll have no escape route if the trap doesn't work.

'Who's the pussy now?' Megan asked.

Like, excuse me, C.M. snaps in response. *Just letting you know.*

She rubbed her hand over the wall.

Sheetrock.

Megan had recalled one time she'd been at her father's house. A few years ago. He'd been dating a woman with three children. As usual he'd been thinking about marrying her – he *always* did that, it was *so* weird – and'd gone so far as to actually hire a contractor to divide the downstairs bedroom into two smaller ones for her young twins. He got halfway through the project and they'd broken up; the construction went unfinished but Megan recalled watching the contractors easily slice through the Sheetrock with small saws. The material had seemed as insubstantial as cardboard.

She took a plastic dinner knife from the box. It was like a toy tool. And for a moment the hopelessness of her plan overwhelmed her. But then she started to cut. Yes! In five minutes she'd sliced a good-sized slit into the wall. The blades were sharper than she'd expected.

For about fifteen minutes the cutting went well. Then, almost all at once, the serrated edge of the knife wore smooth and dull. She tossed it aside and took a new one. Started cutting again.

She lowered her head to the plasterboard and inhaled its stony-moist smell. It brought back a memory of Joshua. She'd helped him move into his cheap apartment near George Mason. The workmen were fixing holes in the walls with plasterboard and this smell reminded her of his studio. Tears flooded into her eyes.

What're you doing? an impatient Crazy Megan asks.

I miss him.

Shut up and saw. Time for that later.

Cutting, cutting . . . Blisters formed on the palm of her right hand. She ignored them and kept up the hypnotic motion. Resting her head against the Sheetrock, smelling mold and wet plaster. Hand moving back and forth by itself. Thoughts tumbling . . .

Thinking about her parents.

Thinking about bears . . .

No, bears can't talk. But that didn't mean you couldn't learn something from them.

She thought of the *Whispering Bears* story, the illustration in the book of the two big animals watching the town burn to the ground. Megan thought about the point of the story. She liked her version better than Dr Matthews's; the moral to her was: people fuck up.

But it didn't have to be that way. Somebody in the village could have said right up front, 'Bears can't talk. Forget about 'em.' Then the story would have ended: 'And they lived happily ever after.'

Working with her left hand now, which was growing a crop of its own blisters. Her knees were on fire and her forehead too, which she'd pressed into the wall for leverage. Her back also was in agony. But Megan McCall felt curiously buoyant. Food and caffeine inside her, the simple satisfaction of cutting through the wall, the fact that she was doing *something* to get out of this shithole.

Thinking about what she'd do *when* she got out.

Dr Matthews had tricked her – to get her to write those letters. But the awesome thing was that what she'd written had been true. Oh, she *was* pissed at her parents. And those bad feelings had been bottled up in her forever, it seemed. But now they were out. They weren't gone, no, but they were buzzing around her head, getting smaller, like a blown-up balloon you let go of. And she had a thought: The anger goes away; the love doesn't. Not if it's real. And she thought maybe, just maybe – with Tate and Bett – the love might be real. And once she understood that she could recall other memories.

Thinking of the time she and her father went to Pentagon City on a spur-of-the-moment shopping spree and he'd let her drive the Lexus back home, saying only, 'The speedometer stops at one-forty and you pay any tickets yourself.' They'd opened the sunroof and laughed all the way home.

Or the time she and her mother went to some boring New Age lecture. After fifteen minutes Bett had whispered, 'Let's blow this joint.' They'd snuck out the back door of the school, found a snow saucer in the playground and huddled together on it, whooping all the way to the bottom of the hill. Then they'd raced each other to Starbuck's for hot chocolate and brownies.

And even her sweet sixteen party, the only time in – how long? – five, six years she'd seen her parents together. For a moment they'd stood close to each other, near the buffet table, while her father gave this awesome speech about her. She'd cried like crazy. For a few minutes they seemed like a perfectly normal family.

If I get home, she now thought . . . No, *when* I get home, I'll talk to them. I'll sit down with them. Oh, I'll give 'em fucking hell. I'll do what I should've done a long time ago.

The anger goes away; the love doesn't . . .

A blister burst. Oh, that hurt. Oh, Jesus. She closed her eyes and slipped her hand under her arm and pressed hard. The sting subsided and she continued to cut.

After a half-hour Megan had cut a six-by-three-foot hole in the Sheetrock. She worked the piece out and rested it against the wall. Lay against the wall for a few minutes, catching her breath. She was sweating furiously.

The hole was ragged and there was plaster dust all over the floor. But the window at this end of the corridor was small and covered with grease and dirt; very little light made it through. She doubted that Peter Matthews would ever see the trap until it was too late.

She walked back to where his father had bricked up the entrance to the administration area of the hospital and, quietly, started carting cinder blocks back to the trap, struggling under their weight. When she'd lugged eight bricks back to the corridor she began stacking them in the hole she'd cut, balancing them on top of one another, slightly off center.

Megan then used her glass knife and sliced strips off the tail of her shirt. She knotted them into a ten-foot length of rope and tied one end to the stack of blocks. Finally she placed the piece of Sheetrock back in the opening and examined her work. She'd lead Peter back here and when he walked past the trap she'd pull the rope. A hundred pounds of concrete would crash down on top of him. She'd leap on him with the knife and stab him – she decided she couldn't kill him. But she'd slash for his hands and feet – to make sure he couldn't attack or chase her. Then she'd demand the keys and run like hell.

Megan walked softly down to the main corridor and looked back. Couldn't see anything except the tail of rope.

Now, she just needed some bait.

'Guess that's gonna be us, right?' she asked, speaking out loud, though in a whisper.

Who else? Crazy Megan answers.

Bett McCall poured herself a glass of Chardonnay and kicked her shoes off.

She was so accustomed to the dull thud of the bass and drums leaching through the floor from Megan's room upstairs that the absence of the sound of Stone Temple Pilots or Oasis brought her to tears.

It's so *frustrating*, she thought. People can deal with almost anything if they can *talk* about it. You argue, you make up. You discover differences and you slowly separate into different lives. Or you find you can talk and talk and talk and learn that you're soul mates. But if the person you love is gone – if you *can't* talk – then you have less than nothing. It's the worst kind of pain.

The house hummed and tapped silently. A motor somewhere clicked, the computer in the next room hummed a pitch slightly higher than the refrigerator's.

The sounds of alone.

Maybe she'd take a bath. No, that would remind her of the soap dish. Maybe—

The phone rang. Heart racing, she leapt for it. Praying that it was Megan. Please . . . Please . . . Let it be her. I want to hear her voice so badly.

Or at least Tate.

But it was neither. Disappointed at first, she listened to the caller, nodding, growing more and more interested in what she heard. 'All right,' she said. 'Sure . . . No, a half-hour would be fine . . . Thank you. Really, thank you.'

After she hung up she dropped heavily into the couch and sipped her wine.

Wonderful, she thought, feeling greatly relieved after just talking to him for three minutes. Megan's other therapist – a colleague of Dr Hanson's, a doctor named Bill Peters – was coming over to speak to her about the girl. He didn't have my specific news but just wanted to talk to her about her daughter's disappearance.

She was curious only about one thing. Why did he want to see her alone? Without Tate there?

III

THE DEVIL'S ADVOCATE

Chapter NINETEEN

'When you called,' Bett confessed, 'I was a little uneasy.'

'Of course,' he said, walking into the room. Dr Peters seemed confident, comfortable with himself. He had a handsome face. His eyes latched on to Bett's and radiated sympathy. 'What a terrible, terrible time for you.'

'It's a nightmare.'

'I'm so sorry.' He was a tall man but walked slightly stooped. His arms hung at his side. A benign smile on his face. Bett McCall, short and slight, was continually aware of the power of body stature and posture. Though she was a foot shorter and much lighter, she felt – from his withdrawing stance alone – that he was one of the least imposing men she'd ever met.

He looked approvingly at the house. 'Megan said you were a talented interior designer. I didn't know quite *how* talented, though.'

Talented?

Bett felt a double burst of pleasure. That he liked her painstaking effort to make her house nice. But, much more, that Megan had actually complimented her to a stranger.

Then the memory of the letter came back and her mood

darkened. She asked, 'Have you heard about Dr Hanson? That terrible thing with his mother?'

Dr Peters' face clouded. 'It's got to be a mix-up. I've known him for years.' He glanced at a crystal ball on her bookshelf. 'He's been an advocate for assisted suicide and I think he *did* talk about it with his mother. But I heard she wasn't all that sick. I'm sure it'll get cleared up.'

'Doctor . . .'

'Oh, call me Bill. Please.'

'Is he a good therapist?'

Peters examined a framed tapestry from France, mounted above the couch.

Why was he hesitating to answer?

'He's very good, yes,' Dr Peters said after a moment. 'In certain areas. What was your impression of him?'

'Well,' she said, 'we've never met.'

'You haven't?' He seemed surprised. 'He hasn't talked to you about Megan?'

'No. Should he have?'

'Well, maybe with his mother's accident . . . he's had a lot on his mind.'

'But that just happened this week,' Bett pointed out. 'Megan's been seeing him for nearly two months.'

In his face she could see that he couldn't really defend his friend. 'Well, frankly, I think he *should* have talked to you. I would have. But he and I have very different styles. Mrs McCall—'

'Bett, please.'

'Betty?'

'Betty Sue,' she smiled, and then blushed. Hoped he couldn't see it, thankful for the dimmed lighting. 'All right . . . Deep, dark secret. It's *Beatrice* Susan McCall. My sister—'

'Your twin. Megan told me.'

'That's right. She's Susan Beatrice. We were named dyslexically. I can't tell you how many years we plotted revenge against Mom and Dad for *that* little trick.'

He laughed. 'Say, could I trouble you for a glass of water?'

'Of course.'

She noticed that he examined her briefly – the tight black jeans and black blouse. Wild earrings dangled; crescent moons and shooting stars. She started toward the kitchen. 'Come on in here. Would you rather have a soda? Or wine?'

'No, thanks . . . Oh, look.' He picked up a bottle of Mietz Merlot, which Brad had bought for them last week and they hadn't gotten around to drinking. He glanced at the eighteen-dollar price tag. 'Funny, I just bought a case of this. It's a wonderful wine. Eighteen's a great price. I paid twenty-one a bottle – and that was supposed to be a discount.'

'You know the brand? Brad said it's real hard to find.'

'It is.'

She said, 'Let's open it.'

'You're sure?'

'Yep.' Bett was happy to impress him. She opened and poured the wine. They touched glasses.

'Do you live in the area?' she asked.

'In Fairfax. Near the courthouse. It's a nice place. Only . . . there're a lot of law offices around there and I get these lawyers coming and going at all hours. Drives me crazy sometimes.'

She gave a brief laugh. He lifted an eyebrow. She'd been thinking of all the nights Tate had spent in that very neighborhood, interviewing prisoners and police and getting home at ten or eleven. 'Tate—'

'Your ex.'

'Right. I'm afraid he's one of them. Working late, I mean.'

'Oh, that's right. Megan told me he was an attorney. But he doesn't live in Fairfax, does he? Didn't she tell me he's got a farm somewhere?'

'Prince William. But his office is here.'

Dr Peters smiled and examined the collection of refrigerator magnets that she and Megan collected. It pinched her heart to see them. And she had to look away before the tears started.

He asked her some questions about the interior design business in Virginia. It turned out his mother had been a decorator.

'Where?' she asked.

'Boston.'

'No kidding! That's where the McCalls are from.' She pointed to some pictures of her family in front of Old Ironsides and in their front yard, the Prudential building towering over the skyline in the background.

'Sure,' he said. 'I thought I detected a bit of accent. I'm driving the cah to the pahty . . .'

She laughed.

'You miss it?' he asked.

'No. We moved here when I was ten. The South definitely appeals to me more than New England.'

'To the extent this is the South,' he offered.

'That's true.'

He took her glass and refilled it. He handed it back and leaned against the island, glanced at the expensive, stainless-steel utensils. 'I love to cook,' he said. 'It's a hobby of mine.'

'Me too. It's relaxing to open some wine, come out to the kitchen and start slicing and dicing.'

He lifted the heavy Sabatier butcher knife and tested the edge carefully with his thumb. Nodded. 'Sharp knives are—'

'—safer than dull ones,' she said. 'My mother taught me that.'

'Mine too,' he said, weighing the knife in his hand for a moment. Then he set it on the table. 'Should we go back in the other room?'

'Sure.'

He nodded toward the door. She preceded him into the living room.

She sat on the couch and he walked over to the bookshelves, looked at the crystals and several boxes of tarot cards.

He chided, 'Didn't you know you're supposed to keep your tarot cards wrapped in silk?'

'You *know* about that?' She laughed.

'Sure do.'

'I was really into the occult a long time ago.' She smiled and realized that she was relaxing for the first time all day. 'I was kind of crazy when I was young.'

'You look embarrassed. You shouldn't be. I think our spiritual side's as important as our physical and our psychic sides. I use a lot of holistic remedies. They have both organic and psychosomatic effects.'

'I try to use them whenever I can,' Bett said.

'If my patients need *something* I'd rather it was St John's wort instead of Prozac.'

He was a *doctor* who felt this way? How often had she explained these things to doctors, or to friends, or to *Tate*, only to be met with a politely wary gaze – at best.

Dr Peters continued. 'It makes a lot of sense to me. Take tarot cards . . . do they predict the future? Well, in a way they do. They make us look at who we are, where we fit in with the godhead or the Oversoul—'

'Oh, you know Emerson?' she asked, pointing to a book of his essays.

Dr Peters walked to it and pulled the volume off the shelf. He flipped through it.

'I've been reading him since college. . . . No, a tarot card reading makes us look at where we fit in with that force, what our relationships are like, makes us question where we're going. That *has* to affect our future.'

'That's true,' she said, feeling warm and comfortable. More wine. 'That's what I've always felt. Most people don't get it.

They just make fun of the Madame Zostra's fortune-telling stuff. It's not fair. My ex . . .'

But she decided to let the thought die. And Peters didn't push her to finish.

The doctor was looking at her bookshelf, head cocked sideways. Pointing out volumes. 'Ah, Joseph Campbell. That's very good. Sure, sure . . . You know Jung?'

'Sort of, not really.'

'About the archetypes? There are certain persistent myths we see surfacing in people's lives. The Arthurian legend – you know it?'

Know it? she thought, laughing to herself. I lived it.

'T.H. White, Camelot, the whole thing.' She pointed out an old copy of *The Once and Future King*.

'What a book that is,' he said. 'Oh, and *The Mists of Avalon—*' nodding at the book.

'The best,' she said enthusiastically. Remembering how Tate didn't have time for any of it. She found the old angers and resentments churning up again. Here was a man who understood her. It was so refreshing . . .

Dr Peters tapped his glass to hers and they sipped. Her glass was nearly empty. Yet she didn't feel drunk, she felt elated. He sat down close to her.

'Um, Bett . . . I don't know how much Megan told you about me.'

'Nothing, really. But then she didn't want to talk about her therapy sessions. That's what we were going to do today. Meet her for lunch and find out how it was going.'

He nodded. He was really quite a handsome man, well proportioned. Interior designer Bett McCall thought: Proportions are everything.

'Dr Hanson saw her more frequently than I did. But I wanted to come over tonight and just talk to you about her a little. Try to reassure you.'

Oh, I'll take that. Anything you want to give me in the reassurance department, I'll take.

'Have you heard anything from her?' he asked.

'Not a word. But there are some funny things going on.'

'What sort of things?'

'We think maybe somebody was following her. My husband . . . my ex-husband thinks it might have to do with a case he's working on. He thinks the man he's suing is trying to distract him or something. I don't know.'

'Any . . . what would they say on *NYPD Blue?* Any concrete leads?'

'Not really. But Tate was going to call a friend of his at the police.'

'Oh, is that the detective who called me? He asked me a few questions about Megan. Um, What's his name again?'

'Konstantinatis.'

'Right. Well,' he continued, pouring more wine, 'I think you should know what I told him.'

'What's that?'

'That I don't think she's in any danger.'

'Oh, did she say something to you about running away?' Bett asked quickly. 'You'd tell me if she did.'

'Ordinarily that'd be confidential. But . . . yes, I would tell you. And she didn't say anything specific about it though she was always talking about going to a big city like San Francisco or New York.'

'They found an Amtrak timetable in her car. She'd marked trains to New York.'

He nodded, as if a mystery had been explained. 'I'd guess that's what happened. No, I'd say I'm *positive* that's what happened. I really doubt there are stalkers or bogy-men out to get her.'

'Why're you so sure?'

He didn't answer her. Instead he said, 'I think we need

more wine. I'll get it.' Dr Peters vanished into the kitchen, calling, 'Okay?'

'Sure.'

He returned a moment later, sat down and poured. After a moment he asked, 'How does your husband feel about his daughter?'

'Tate's . . .' She groped for words.

He supplied one. 'Indifferent?'

'Yes. He's never been very involved with Megan.'

'I understand that. But why?'

She now looked at the crystal ball. In it was captured the orange glow from a wall lamp. She stared at the distorted trapezoid of light. 'Tate wanted to be his grandfather. He was a famous lawyer and judge in the area. He had a big family. Well, Tate wanted a farm wife.' She lifted her hands and slapped her thighs. 'He got me instead. Big disappointment.'

'No, that's not you. I can see that. That was very unfair to you to expect that.'

'To me?' she asked. 'Unfair?'

'Of course,' he offered as if it were obvious. 'Your husband had a distorted view of the past and tried to project that on to his family. I'll bet he worked a lot, spent time away from home.'

'He did, yes. But I was busy too. My sister was sick—'

'Her heart condition.'

Oh, she could talk to this man for hours. She'd met him only thirty minutes ago and yet he *knew* her. Knew her cold. Better than Tate had in all those years of marriage.

'That's right.'

'But why are you taking the blame? I can see you're attractive, intelligent, have a mind of your own. If you wanted an independent life, why should you feel bad about that? It seems to me that *he's* the one to blame for all this. He went into the marriage knowing who you were and tried to change you. And probably in some less-than-honest ways.'

'Less than honest?'

'He *appeared* supportive, I'll bet. He probably said, "Honey, do whatever you want to do. I'll be behind it."'

She was stunned. It was as if Dr Peters were looking directly into her memories. 'Yes, that's exactly what he'd say.'

'But in fact, what he was doing was the opposite. Little comments, even body language, that'd whittle away at your spirit. He wanted you barefoot and pregnant and wanted you to give up your life, have dinner on the table for him, give him a brood of kids, ignore your poor sister. And meanwhile he was going to make a name for himself as a prosecutor and to hell with everybody else.' His eyes flickering with pain – *her* pain. 'It was horrible what he did to you. Inexcusable. But I suppose it's understandable. His character, you know.'

'Character.'

'You know the old expression? "A man's character is his fate." That's your ex-husband. He's reaping now what he sowed. With Megan running away.'

I wish I could believe that, Bett thought. Please . . . Tears now. From the wine, from the astonishing comfort she felt, years and years of pain being stripped away. 'I . . .' She caught her breath. 'He'd sit down and talk to me and say that he loved me and what could he do for me—'

'Tricks,' Dr Peters said quickly. 'All tricks.'

'I couldn't argue with him. He had an answer for everything.'

'He's smooth, isn't he? A slick talker. Megan told me that.'

'Oh, you better believe it. I couldn't win against him. Not at words. Never.'

'Bett, most women would've put up with that. They would've stayed and stayed and destroyed themselves. And their children. But you had the courage to do something about it. Strike out on your own.'

'But Megan . . . she's suffered . . .'

'Suffered?' He laughed. 'Because of him, yes. Not because of you. You've done a *miraculous* job with her. Here's to you.'

He handed her the wineglass, filled again, and they drank. The room was swimming. He was very close to her, gazing into her eyes.

'A miraculous job?' Bett shook her head, felt her eyes swimming with tears. 'Oh, I don't think so.'

'Are you serious? Why, if every mother cared for their children the way you care for Megan I'd be out of business.'

'Do you really think that?' The tears were coming fast now. But she wasn't the least embarrassed. Not in front of this man. She could tell him anything, do anything in front of him. He'd understand, he'd forgive, he'd comfort. She said wistfully, 'Too bad Megan doesn't think so.'

'Oh, but she does.'

'No, no . . . there's a letter . . .' She glanced toward her purse, where the girl's note sat like a puddle of cold blood.

'The detective told me about it. That's the main reason why I wanted to see you. Alone, without your husband here.' He took the wineglass from her and sat forward, took her hands in his. Looked at her until she was gazing hypnotically into his dark eyes. 'Listen to me. Listen carefully. She didn't mean what she wrote you.'

'She—'

'She. Didn't. Mean. It. Do you hear what I'm saying?'

Bett was shaking with sobs. 'But what she wrote, it was so terrible . . .'

'No,' he said in a firm whisper. 'No.' He was completely focused on her. She thought of the other men in her life with whom she'd had serious talks. Tate was often elsewhere – thinking of cases or trying to dissect what she was saying.

Brad would smother her with an adoring gaze. But Dr Peters was looking at *her* as a person.

'Here's what you have to understand. Your letter doesn't mean anything.'

Oh, please, she thought, her eyes filling again. Yes, please explain how this happened. Please explain to me why I'm not a witch, please explain how my daughter still loves me. She thought of an expression she'd heard once and believed was true. You'd kill for your mate; but you'd die for your child. Well, I would, she thought. If only Megan knew that she felt that way.

He squeezed her hands. 'Your daughter hates your husband. I don't know what the genesis of that is but it's a very deeply ingrained feeling.'

'So many little things,' Bett began, feeling the impossibility of compressing seventeen years into a few minutes. Her eye went to a board game, Monopoly, sitting dusty on the shelf. 'Megan wanted us to play games together, Tate, her and me. But he never would. And then—'

'It doesn't matter,' he interrupted. 'The fact is that she was a child and he was the adult and failed her. Megan knows it and she hates him. The anger inside her is astonishing. But it's only directed at *him* – I guarantee you that. She loves you so much.'

Shaking with tears. 'But the letter . . .'

'You know the Oedipus and Electra principles? The attractions of sons and mothers and daughters and fathers?'

'A little, I guess.'

'In Megan's subconscious her anger at your husband makes her feel terribly guilty. And directing it *only* at him is intolerable. With the natural attraction between fathers and daughters she either had to write no letter at all or write you both. She was psychically unable to point her anger only at its true source.'

'Oh, if I could believe that . . .'

'During our sessions she did nothing but talk about you. How proud she was of you. How she wants to be like you. How hard you've had it. I promise you, without a doubt, she regrets writing that letter. She doesn't mean it. She'd give anything to take it back.'

Bett lowered her head and put her face in her hands. Why was the room swimming so badly? Well, no sleep. Exhaustion. The wine too. His arm went around her shoulders.

'You okay?'

She nodded.

'Will she be coming back?' Bett asked.

'I don't doubt it for a minute. It might be a while – your husband's caused some serious damage, But nothing that's irreparable. Megan knows that she couldn't ask for a better mother in the world. You've done everything right. She loves you and misses you.'

Bett leaned against his chest, felt the muscles in his arms tighten around her. Oh, when was the last time she'd felt this good, this easy, this comforted? Years. She felt his hot breath on the top of her head. She smelled a faint aftershave.

'I feel so light-headed.'

Did she say that or think it?

She wept and she laughed.

The doctor's hand went to her forehead. 'You're so hot . . .'

He hugged her harder and his hands slid downward, fingers encircling her neck. An electric chill went through her and then her arms were snaking around him, pulling him to her. Her head was up and she pressed her cheek against his.

No, no, she thought. I can't be doing this . . .

But she was thinking these words from a very different place, very remote. And it was impossible for her to release her grip on the man who'd repaired her torn soul.

He thinks I'm a good mother, he thinks I'm a good mother.

He leaned down and kissed her tears away.

The light touch of his lips felt so good . . .

She was so giddy, so happy . . .

Stretching out, getting comfortable . . . The room was hot, the room was wonderful . . .

And what was this?

He was kissing her on the mouth. Or am I kissing him? She didn't know. All she knew was that she wanted to be close to him. To the man who'd found her single worst fear and killed it dead.

'No,' he protested, 'really.' Whispering.

But she was not letting him go. She knew she should stop but she couldn't. She pulled him down next to her on the couch, refusing to let go, arms fixed forever around his neck. The room spinning, orange lights, yellow lights.

Kissing harder now.

Hands on her belly, then her chest. She glanced down and wasn't surprised to see her blouse was undone. Her bra up, his fingers cupping her breast. This seemed completely natural. A pop, the snap of her jeans opened. Had he done that or had she? It didn't matter. Getting close to him mattered, hearing him whisper what he would whisper in her ear as he lay on top of her. *That* was what she wanted, hearing him speak to her. The sex wasn't important but she'd gladly give him that if only he'd keep speaking . . .

She opened her mouth and kissed him . . .

And then the world ended.

The front door was swinging open.

A familiar voice was crying, 'Bett . . . why, Bett!'

Gasping, she sat up.

Dr Peters backing away, a shocked look on his face.

Brad Markham stood in the doorway, his face a horrified mask. His key to her house dropped to the floor with a loud ring. 'What . . .' He was breathless. 'What . . .'

'Brad, I thought . . .'

'I was in Baltimore?' he spat out. He shook his head. 'I was. A policeman called and told me about Megan. Your daughter's missing and you're fucking somebody. You're *cheating* on me?'

'No,' she said, feeling faint and nauseous from the wine and shock. Tears coming again. Tears of horror. 'You don't understand.'

Too much wine, the emotion. She felt drugged . . . 'I didn't mean it. I didn't know what I was doing.'

'I'm sorry.' Dr Peters looked horrified. 'I didn't know you had a boyfriend. You never said anything.'

'Boyfriend?' Brad spat out. 'We're engaged.'

'You're *what*?' The doctor stared at Brad. 'I'm so sorry. She never said anything.'

'How could you?' Brad spat out. 'After everything I've done for you? And Megan? How could you?'

'I don't know what happened . . .'

Leaving the door open, Brad stalked outside.

'No!' Bett cried, sobbing, pulling her bra down and buttoning her blouse as she stumbled toward the door. 'Wait.'

Through her tears she saw Brad's car squeal off down the street.

Leaning against the door jamb, sobbing, sinking to the floor. Close to fainting, wishing to die . . .

'No, no, no . . .'

Then the doctor was standing next to her, crouching down. His mouth close to her ear. When he spoke the voice was so different from the soothing drone of ten minutes ago. It was flint, it was ice water.

'What I told you Megan said about you? That wasn't true. I only said it to make you feel better . . . All she told me was that you were a selfish whore. I didn't believe her. But I guess she was right.' He took a final sip of wine. 'What a pitiful excuse for a mother you are.'

The doctor rose, set the glass on the table and stepped over her, out the door. It seemed he was smiling, though Bett was blinded by the tears and couldn't say for certain.

Tate Collier hung up the phone. Sighed.

No, man, Josh still isn't home. I don't know where he is. You called, like, three times already. Maybe we'll give it a rest now? Okay?

Well, where the hell was he – the boy?

Konnie too was still out of the office. And it irked Tate that the detective hadn't returned his page.

He fed the Dalmatian and paced up and down his front porch, looking at the clear early evening skies and the dusting of April growth over his fields.

No more Dead Rebs that he could see.

Again his eye settled on the dilapidated picnic bench in the back yard. Remembering Bett unhooking the Japanese lanterns, feeling the odd heat of that fall fifteen years ago, the residual exhaustion of the funeral. Sweating in November, the way he was sweating now in April, the hot wind pushing crisp, curled leaves over the shaggy grass.

He remembered:

Bett looking down at him. Asking, 'What is it?'

Alarmed, as she gazed at the expression on his face.

What is it, what is it, what is it? . . . A simple question.

Yet simple words can't convey the answer – that two people who were once in love no longer were.

He'd closed his eyes.

'I don't want to be married to you anymore,' he'd said.

Goodbye . . .

Tate now looked impatiently at the cordless phone, sitting on the porch swing. Why wasn't—

It rang. He blinked and snagged it from the cradle.

'Hello?'

Silence for a moment. Then: 'Tate?'

'I'm here, Bett. What's wrong?'

'I'm on my way to Baltimore.'

'You are? Why?'

More silence. 'Brad left me.'

'What? At a time like this?'

'It's not him. I did something stupid. I don't know . . . I don't want to go into it. It's . . . Oh, Jesus, it's a mess.'

'Bett, you sound terrible. Are you crying?'

'I can't talk about it. Not now.'

'When'll you be back? What about Megan?'

'I don't care.'

He heard utter defeat in her voice. 'What do you mean?'

'Oh, Tate. We've blown it. There's nothing we can do. We've ruined her life, she's ruined ours. Maybe she'll come back, maybe she won't. Let's just let her go and hope for the best. I don't care anymore.'

'This doesn't sound like you.'

'Well, it *is* me, all right? It was stupid looking for her, it was stupid getting together like this, you and me. We should have kept our lives on different sides of the universe, Tate. What've we got to show for it? Just pain.'

'We're going to find her.'

'She doesn't *want* to be found. Don't you get that? Let her go and don't worry about it. She's part of the past, Tate. Let her go. The phone's breaking up. I'm coming to a tunnel. Goodbye, Tate . . . Goodbye . . .'

Chapter TWENTY

Bait.

That's me, yessir. That's me.

He's on to you, Crazy Megan says. *Move, move, move.*

She went to the right and Peter Matthews went to the right.

Left and left, straight and straight.

Getting closer all the time.

Whispering, 'Megan, Megan, Megan.'

Other words too. She wasn't sure but she thought he was muttering, 'I want to fuck you, I want to fuck you.' Or maybe 'cut you'.

She was part of his fantasy now. From those disgusting comic books. The tentacles, the monsters, the purple dicks, the claws and pinchers . . .

And was a game to the boy – if you can call a six-foot, two-hundred-pound *thing* a boy.

As she moved up and down the corridors, gripping the handle of her glass knife in her right hand, stinging fiercely from the blisters, she had all sorts of terrible thoughts.

She suspected why the father had brought her here. As a bride for his son. Maybe Aaron Matthews had wanted grandchildren. Maybe Peter'd been at Jefferson High – they had a special ed department – and he'd gotten obsessed with her. That might be it. And his father had arranged her to be a present for his son.

Down the corridor toward the kitchen.

No sign of him.

Down the corridor that led past the door to the basement. The lock looked flimsy but not *that* flimsy. Breaking it open would make a hell of a noise. And what was down there anyway?

No, Crazy Megan tells her. *Stick to your plan. He's gotta go down.*

Well, one of us does, thought the less confident half of the duo.

Keep going, keep looking for him. Up and down the dim halls.

It didn't seem that late but the hospital was in a valley and the sun was behind a mountain to the west. The whole place was bathed in cold blue light and she was having trouble seeing.

She stopped. Footsteps getting closer.

This is it, Crazy Megan says. *Just stab the fucker in the back and get it over with.*

But Megan reminded her that she'd thought about it and couldn't do that. As much as she hated him, she couldn't kill.

He wants to fuck you. He wants to pretend he's one of those insect monsters and fuck you till you bleed.

Be quiet! I'm doing the best I can.

Closer. The steps got closer. The sound coming from around the corner. She didn't have time to get into the main corridor – he was too close.

She stepped into a little nook. Trapped.

He stepped closer, paused. Maybe hearing her.

Maybe *smelling* her.

He'd stopped whispering her name. Which scared her more. Because now he didn't want to be heard. He was sneaking up on her. He was playing the invisible monster; she'd seen that story too in one of the comic books. Some creature you couldn't see snuck into girls' locker rooms and raped stragglers after gym class. The comic had been limp. Looked like Peter'd read that one a thousand times.

He moved forward another few cautious steps.

Her hand started to shake.

Should she jump out into the corridor and just run like hell?

But he couldn't be more than ten feet away. And he'd looked so big in the photographs! He could lunge like a snake and grab her by the throat in two steps.

Suddenly a flash of pain went through her hand – from one of the blisters – and she dropped the knife. Gasped involuntarily.

Megan froze, watching the knife tumble to the floor. It can't break! No . . .

Just before the icy glass hit the floor she shoved her foot under it, waiting for the pain as the tip of the blade sliced into the top of her foot.

Thunk. The knife hit her right foot flat and rolled, unbroken, to the floor.

Thank you, thank you . . .

She bent down and picked it up.

Another two footsteps, closer, closer.

No choice. She had to run. He was only three or four feet away.

Megan took a deep breath, another. Jump out, slash with the knife and run like hell toward the trap.

Now!

She leapt out, turned to the right.

Froze. Gasping. Her ears had played tricks on her. No one

was there. Then she looked down. The rat – a large one, big as a cat – standing on his haunches, sniffing the air, blinked at her, cowering. Then indignantly it turned away as if angry at being startled.

Megan sagged against the wall, tears welling as the fear dissipated.

But she didn't have much time for recovery.

At the far end of the dim corridor a shadow materialized into the loping form of Peter Matthews, hunched over and moving slowly. He didn't see her and disappeared from view.

Megan paused for only a few seconds before she started after him.

The Shenandoahs and the Massanuten Mountains keep the air in northwest Virginia clean as glass in the spring, and when the sun sets, it's a fierce disk, bright as an orange spotlight.

This radiant light behind Tate, from the sun melting into the horizon, lit every detail in the trees and buildings and oncoming cars. He sped down Route 66 at eighty miles an hour.

He skidded north on the Parkway then east on Route 50, pulled into the County Police station house and climbed out of the car. He practically ran into Dimitri Konstantinatis as he too arrived, carrying two large Kentucky Fried Chicken bags.

'Oh-oh,' the detective muttered.

'What oh-oh?'

'That look on your face.'

'I don't have a look,' Tate protested.

'You had it comin' into my office when you were CA and needed that little bit of extra evidence – which'd mean I'd lose a weekend. And you've got it now. *That* oh-oh.'

They walked inside the building and into Konnie's small office.

'You didn't call me back,' Tate said.

'Did so. Ten minutes ago. You musta left. What's that?'

Tate set the letter Megan had written him and the knuckle bone he'd found in his house that morning, both in Baggies, on the cop's desk.

'Prints,' Tate said.

'A prince among men, yes I am. So, what's going on?'

'I want you to run the letter through Identification. Something's up. Bett's acting funny.'

'You complained about that when you were married. Crystals, mumbo-jumbo, long-distance calls to people'd been dead a hundred years.'

'That was cute funny. This's weird funny. Witnesses've been disappearing and not calling back and it's just too much of a coincidence. And I think I know who's behind it.'

He also told Konnie about his run-in with Jack Sharpe.

'Ooo, that was bright, Counselor, and you were packing your gun to boot?'

Tate shrugged. 'Was your idea for me to get one.'

'But it *wasn't* my idea to threaten an upstanding member of the Prince William mafia with it. Grant me that at least.'

'I've been on his bad side since I routed his lawyers at the injunction hearing last week.'

'What's wrong with a nice theme park round here, Tate? What'd you rather have, an amphitheater fulla big wheels slugging it out in a mud pit or them fun rides and cotton candy and knock the clown in the water shit?'

'Talk to my clients about it. I'm just telling you that Sharpe would love for me to be out of commission come that argument in Richmond next week. And I think he's had somebody in a van following me. Sorry, no tag, no model.'

Konnie nodded slowly. Then added, 'But he's got boys he'd hire for that. And they could hire other boys. No way could you trace it back to him. And you think anybody'd snitch on Jack Sharpe?'

'I'm not a prosecutor anymore, Konnie. I don't want to make a case. I want to find Megan. Period. End of story.'

'And kneecap the prick did it.'

'I wouldn't mind that. But it's optional.' He pushed the bags containing the letter and the bone toward Konnie again. 'Please.'

Another mournful glance at his cooling dinner. 'Be right back.'

'Wait.' Tate handed him another Baggie. 'Exemplars of Megan's prints on the keys and mine on that glass. And remember you handled the note too.'

Konnie nodded. 'The prosecutor in you ain't dead, I see.' Carrying the bags, he walked down the hall toward the forensic lab. He returned a moment later.

'Won't be long. I *was* looking forward to supper.'

Tate ignored the red-and-white KFC bag and continued. 'Now, there was a gray Mercedes following her. Can you check that out?'

'Check what out?'

'Registered owners of gray Mercedes.'

'I was asking before: year, model, tag?'

'Still none. Only that it's a Merc.'

Konnie laughed. He typed heavily on his computer keyboard. 'This'll be worth it just to see your expressions.'

As he waited for the results Konnie peeked into the tallest Kentucky Fried bag, kneaded his ample stomach absently. 'You know what the worst is? The worst is when the mashed potatoes get cold. You can eat the chicken when it's cold because everybody does that. On a picnic, say. Same with the beans. But when mashed potatoes get cold you have to throw them out. Which is bad enough but then you think about them all night. How good they would've been. *That's* what I mean by the worst.'

The screen fluttered. Konnie leaned forward.

'Here's what we got. I did Fairfax, Arlington, Alexandria, Prince William and Loudon. Mercedes, all types, all years, gray.'

Tate leaned forward and read: *Your request has resulted in 2,603 responses.*

'Two thousand,' Tate muttered. 'Man.'

'Two thousand *six* hundred.'

Tate knew from his prosecuting days that too much evidence was as useless as too little.

'Forensics're one way to go. But if you're just not buying the runaway stuff—' Konnie sighed. '—we're gonna have to do more thinking. All right, you think Sharpe's a possibility and I don't think he's above snatching a girl. But there anybody else? Think hard now, Tate. Anybody hassling her?'

'Recently?'

'Like last year's weirdos don't count?' Konnie snorted. 'Anytime!'

'Not that I know of. I have to say there was a rumor . . . it was just a rumor . . . she might've been seeing . . . well, having sex with some older men. And maybe there was some money involved. I mean, they were paying her.'

If Konnie felt anything about this he didn't show it. 'You have any idea who? Where?'

'Some kids at this place called the Coffee—'

'—Shop. They been trying to close that piss hole down for a year. Well, I can poke around there. Ask some questions. Now, was she in any cults or anything?'

'No, don't think so.'

'You or Bett in anything like that?'

'*Me?*'

'All right, your wife.'

'Ex,' Tate corrected.

'Whatever. She did that sort of stuff.'

'It was strictly softball with her. No Heaven's Gate or

Jonestown or anything like that. Bett wouldn't even put up these Indian posters because they had reverse swastikas on them. Nothing to do with Nazis; she just thought it was bad karma.'

'Karma,' Konnie scoffed. 'Any relationships of yours go south in a big way recent?'

'I—'

''Fore you answer, think back to everyone of them twenty-one-year-olds you promised diamonds to and then run for the hills from.'

'I never proposed to a single one,' Tate said.

'Never proposed to *marry* 'em, maybe.'

'You don't get *Fatal Attraction* after three dates. That's about the longest term I went.'

'Sad, Tate, sad. How 'bout Bett?'

'I don't know. But I don't think so.'

'Any relatives acting squirrely? Might've wanted to take the girl and run?'

'Only relative near by's Bett's sister, Susan. Outside of Baltimore. She'd never do anything to hurt her. Hell, she was always joking about adopting Megan.'

'You sure she's okay? Maybe she went over the edge, decided to get herself a daughter.'

'Imagine Bett but fifteen pounds lighter. She couldn't kidnap a bird.'

'But she could've *hired* somebody to. She could have a wacko boyfriend.'

'I just can't see it, Konnie.'

'Gimme her name anyway.'

Tate wrote it down.

'Okay, how 'bout any associates of either of y'all? Clients? Or the bad guys? Other than Sharpe.'

'Bett's got this interior design business. But I don't think her clients're the sort for this kind of thing. Me, I've been doing wills, trusts and house closings except for the Liberty Park case.'

Konnie grunted. The detective got a call. Grabbed the phone. Nodded. Slammed it down. 'Interesting . . . That was the lab. Only her prints and yours on the bone and mine, yours and hers on the letter. But . . . there were some smudges on the bone that might've been from latex gloves. Can't say for certain. But that starts me wondering. Think it's about time to do a Title Three.'

'A wiretap?'

'Yours and your wife's phones both.'

'Ex.'

'You keep saying that. Broken record. That's in case you get a ransom call.'

'I thought this wasn't a case.'

'It's becoming one. Tell me again what happened this morning at your place. I mean exact.'

Tate remembered this about Konnie: he was a working dog when it came to hammering on suspects and witnesses. Only exhaustion would slow him down – and even then it never stopped him.

Tate gave another recap of the events.

'So you never actually saw her at your house?'

'No,' Tate said. 'I got back home about ten then got suited up and went to check on a busted pipe.'

'The sharecroppers there?'

'No. Not on Saturday. I never saw anybody at all. Just the lights go out around ten-twenty.'

'All of 'em?'

'Yeah.'

'Didn't you think that was funny?'

'No. Megan doesn't like bright lights. She likes candlelight and dimmers.'

This gave him a burst of pleasure – proving to Konnie that he knew *something* about the girl after all.

'It was dark as pitch this morning,' the detective mused. 'With all that rain. Most people'd want *some* light, you'd think. 'Less they didn't want to be seen from the outside.'

'True.'

'And shit, Tate, wait a minute. Why'd she go to your place at all?'

'To leave the letters and get the backpack.'

'Well, doesn't she have any suitcases or bookbags at your wife's? Sorry, your *ex's*? Your dee-vorced spouse's?'

'Sure she does, you're right! Most of them are there, as a matter of fact. And she had her bookbag with her at Amy's. And a lot more clothes and makeup at Bett's place than mine.'

The cop continued, 'You and Megan hardly ever saw each other.'

'True again.'

'So you wouldn't go into her room much, would you?'

'Once a month maybe.'

'So why'd she leave the letters there? Why not at her mother's?'

That would've made more sense, true. The detective added, 'And, hell, why go to the house and leave some letters this morning around the time you were going to meet her? I tell you, if I was going to leave a note to diss my folks and run I'd leave it someplace they *weren't* going to be. Dontcha think?'

'So he made her write 'em and planted them himself. Whoever he is.'

'That's what I think, Counselor. Here's what I'm gonna do. Order some serious forensic work and then have a chat with the captain. Guess what? This's just become a case. And in a big way.'

Tate returned home.

No messages and no one had called; the caller ID box was blank.

Twelve hours ago he had wanted Megan and Bett out of his life again. He'd gotten his wish and he didn't like it one bit.

So Brad had left Bett. He didn't know what to make of that. Why? And why now? He had a feeling that whoever was behind Megan's disappearance was behind their problems too.

Then his thoughts segued to Belize, the trip they'd planned to take. A second honeymoon. Well, a first honeymoon – since they'd never taken one after their wedding.

He looked out over the dark sky, at the spattering of a million stars.

Tate laughed to himself. What a kick if they'd run into each other. He wondered how Bett would have reacted to Karen. No, Cathy. Or was it Kate?

Probably not well.

Not a jealousy thing so much as a matter of approval. She'd never liked his taste in women.

Well, Tate didn't either, now that he looked back over the last ten years.

Belize . . .

Was there actually a possibility that they might take that trip together still, after this thing with Megan got sorted out?

Whatever happened with Brad, the presence of a fiancé didn't seem as insurmountable as simply the concept of Tate and Bett taking a trip together. At one time their joined names had been a common phrase. But that was a long, long time ago.

Yet – this was *feelings* again, not Cartesian logic – yet somehow he believed that they'd get along just fine. The fight today had been as bad as any they'd had fifteen years ago. And what had happened? A reconciliation. This astonished him.

He sighed, sipped his wine, looked out at the Dalmatian nosing about in the tall grass. Thinking now of Megan.

But even if they did get together again, what would the girl come home to? And more important . . . *who* was the person coming home?

Was the drinking and the water tower more than just a one-time fluke? Was that the real Megan McCall? Had she really slept with men for money? Or was there another young woman within her? One Tate didn't know well – or maybe one he hadn't yet met?

Tate Collier felt a sudden desperation to know the girl. To know *who* she was. What excited her, what she hated, what she feared. What foods she liked. What clothes she'd pick and which she'd shun. What bad TV shows she'd want to watch.

What made her laugh. And what weep.

And he was suddenly stung by a terrible thought: that if Megan had *died* this morning, the victim of a deranged killer or an accident, he'd have been distraught, yes, terribly sad. But now, if that had happened or – the most horrifying – if she simply vanished for ever, never to be found at all, he'd be destroyed. It would be one of those tragedies that diminishes you forever. He remembered something he'd told Bett when they'd been married, a case he was working on – prosecuting an arson murder. The victim had run into a burning building to save her child, who'd lived, though the mother had perished. He'd read the facts, looked up to her and said, 'You'll kill for your spouse, but you'll die for your child . . .'

In rhetoric, lawyers use the trick of personification – picking words to make their own clients seem human and their opponents' less so. 'Mary Jones' instead of 'the witness' or 'the victim'. Juries find it far easier to be harsh to inanimate abstractions. The 'defendant'. The 'man sitting at that table there'.

It's a very effective trick, and a very dangerous one.

And it's just how I've treated Megan over the years, Tate

now thought. Referring to her usually as 'the girl'. Not by her name.

He walked into the den and spent a long time looking for another picture of her. Was terribly disappointed he couldn't find one. He'd given his only snapshot to Konnie and Beauridge that afternoon.

He sat down in his chair, closed his eyes and tried to create some images now. Images of the girl. Smiling, looking perplexed, flirtatious, exasperated. . . . A few came to mind. He tried harder.

And harder still.

Which was why he didn't hear the man come up behind him.

The cold finger of a pistol touched his temple. 'Don't move, Mr Collier. No, no. I really mean that. For your sake. Don't move.'

Chapter TWENTY-ONE

Jimmy, Tate recalled.

His name was Jimmy. The man who'd been far more willing than Tate to engage in some gunplay in Jack Sharpe's immaculate foyer.

Tate glanced at the phone.

Jimmy shook his head. 'No.'

'What do you want?'

'Mr Sharpe sent me.'

'Figured that.'

The gun was really very large. The man's finger was on the outside of the trigger guard. This didn't reassure Tate at all.

'I have something for you to look at.'

'Look at?'

'I'm going to give it to you to look at. Then I'm going to take it back. And neither me or Mr Sharpe'll ever admit we know what you're talking about if you ever mention it. You understand?'

Tate didn't have a clue. But he said, 'Sure. Say, is that loaded?'

Jimmy didn't respond. From the pocket of his leather jacket he took a videocassette. Set it on the table. Backed up.

Nodded toward it. Tate walked over, picked it up. 'I should play it?'

Jimmy's face scrunched up impatiently.

Tate put the cassette in the player and fiddled with the controls until the tape started to play. He was looking at a building, some bushes. The date and time stamp showed that it had been made that morning, at 9:42. He didn't recognize where. The tape jumped ahead four minutes and now whoever was making the tape was moving, driving in a car following another car down a suburban street. Tate still didn't recognize the locale but he did the car being followed. It was Megan's Tempo. Because of the rain he couldn't make out who was driving.

'Where did you get this?' Tate demanded.

'Watch, don't talk,' Jimmy muttered. The gun was pointed directly at Tate's back.

Another jump on the tape. To 9:50 that morning. Tate recognized the Vienna Metro station. The man taping – of course, one of the private eyes hired by Sharpe, despite his protests to the contrary – must have been afraid of getting too close to his subject. He was about fifty yards away and shooting through the mist and rain. Megan's car stopped at a row filled with other cars. There was a pause and then motion. After a moment he caught a glimpse of someone. A white man, it seemed, wearing a dark jacket, though he couldn't be sure. Tate could see no distinguishing features. Then there was more motion. Finally a gray Mercedes pulled out of a space and a moment later Megan's car eased into where the Merc had been. At 10:01 the Mercedes sped out of the lot.

The tape went fuzzy. Then black.

Tate stared, his heart pounding. Thinking of the vague motion he'd seen – pixels of light on the screen, distorted to start with, more distorted in the rain and fog. But he believed it might have been the man lifting a heavy object from the trunk of Megan's car and putting it into the Mercedes. An object about the size of a human body.

'That's all,' Jimmy said. 'Could you eject it?'

Tate did. 'Did he see anything else?' he asked.

'Who?' Jimmy asked.

'You know who. The private eye. Can I talk to him? Please?'

Jimmy nodded at the table. 'If you could just set the tape there and back up.'

Tate did. He knew he wouldn't get an answer. This was as far as the old bastard was willing to go. But he asked one more question. 'Why did Sharpe show this to me? He didn't have to.'

Jimmy pocketed the cassette, gun still held steadily at Tate. He backed to the door. 'Mr Sharpe asked me just to mention the old adage that one good deed deserves another. He hopes you'll remember that next Thursday at the argument down in Richmond.'

'Look—'

'He said he didn't think you'd agree. He just asked me to mention it.'

Jimmy walked to the sliding door, through which he'd apparently entered. He paused. 'The answer to your question? I myself would guess it's because he's got two daughters of his own. Goodnight.'

After he'd gone Tate drained his wineglass with a shaking hand and picked up the phone.

When Konnie answered Tate said, 'Gotta lead.'

'Asking or telling?'

'Telling.'

'Go on.'

'Long story. That case with Sharpe?'

'Right.'

'It wasn't just me he had a PI tailing. It was Megan too.'

'Why? Dig up dirt?'

'That's my guess. Lawyer's daughter scores drugs. Sleeps around. Something like that. Anyway a friend of his just showed me a tape.' Tate described it.

'Hot damn. Get it over here—'

'Forget it. It's been atomized. But I think it was Megan he was moving from one trunk to another. She was probably drugged. At least I hope she was just drugged.'

'Tags?'

'Nope. Sorry.'

'Damn, Tate. Why'd you think they put those cute little signs on cars?' After a pause Konnie continued. 'Okay. You don't think it's Sharpe?'

'He didn't have to show me diddly. He didn't even bargain – well, not too hard. Get off the case and I'll tell you what the PI saw. He could've done that.'

'Would you've agreed?'

Tate didn't hesitate for an instant. 'Yes, I would have.'

'Okay, so it's not him. Then let's think. She's got a stalker after her. He's checking out her routine. Following her. When she goes to school, when she goes to pom-pom practice.'

Tate thought of Megan as a cheerleader. 'As if.'

'He knows where she's going to be this morning. He gets her, drugs her, drives her to Vienna, where he's left his own car. He's got switch wheels. The Mercedes.'

'Right.'

'Leaves her car with the timetable. So it looks like she's headed off on Amtrak. . . . He took off to wherever he was going to stash her. Which means what, Counselor?'

Tate couldn't think.

When he said nothing Konnie gave a harsh laugh. 'Damn, I'd forgot how I had to hold your hand when we were putting all those bad guys away. What's sitting right *under* her car at the moment?'

'Tread marks! The Mercedes's tread marks.'

'There's hope for you after all, boy. If you apply yourself and work real hard to make up for all the brain cells you're lacking. Okay, Counselor, this's gonna take some time. Listen, you sit tight and have some nice hot mashed potatoes. And think of me when you eat 'em.'

Konnie Konstantinatis's first lesson in police work was to watch his father run the taxmen like 'coons tricking hounds.

The old Greek immigrant was petty, weak, dangerous, a cross between a squirrel and a ferret. He was a born liar and had an instinct for knowing human nature cold. He put stills next to smokehouses, stills next to factories, stills in ships, disguised them like hen-houses. Hid his income in a hundred small businesses. Once he smooth-talked a revenuer into arresting his innocent brother-in-law instead of him and swore an oath at the trial that cost the bewildered man two years of his life.

So from the age of five or six Konnie learned the art of evasion and deception. And therefore he learned the art of unraveling deceit.

Slowly and tediously. This was the only way to make cases. And this was how he was going to find the man who'd kidnapped Tate Collier's daughter.

Konnie arranged for a small crane to lift Megan's car out of its spot, rather than drive it out and risk obliterating the Merce's tread marks.

He then spent the next two hours taking electrostatic prints of the twelve tire treads that he could find – ones he determined weren't from Megan's car. He then identified the matching left and right tires and measured wheelbases and lengths of the cars they'd come from. Jotted all this in his lyrical handwriting.

He then went over the entire parking space with a Dustbuster and – in the front seat of his car – looked over all the trace evidence picked up in the paper filter. Most of it was meaningless without a gas chromatograph. But Konnie found one thing helpful. A single fiber he recognized as coming from cheap rope. He recognized it because in one of the three kidnapping cases he'd worked over the past ten years the victim's hands had been bound with rope that shed fibers just like this.

Speeding back to the office, he sat down at his computer and ran the wheel dimensions through the motor vehicle specification database. One set of numbers perfectly fit the dimensions for a Mercedes sedan.

He examined the electrostatic prints carefully. Flipping through Burne's Tire Identifier, he concluded that they were a rare model of Michelin and because they showed virtually no wear he guessed the tires were no more than four months old. Encouraging, on the one hand, because they were unusual tires and it would be easier to track down the purchaser. But troubling too. Because they were expensive, as was the model of the car the man was driving. It was likely that the perp was intelligent. An organized offender. The hardest to find.

And the sort that presented the most danger.

Then he started the canvassing. It was Saturday evening, and although most of the stores were still open – General Tire, Sears, Merchants, Mercedes dealerships – the managers had gone home. But nothing stopped Konnie. He blustered and bullied until he had home phone numbers and the names of night staff managers of data processing departments. He was good at this, though he gave credit to his mentioning that a seventeen-year-old girl had been kidnapped – which opened doors that might otherwise have remained closed until Monday.

He made thirty-eight phone calls and by the time he hung up from speaking with the last parts department manager on his list, faxes of bills of sale were starting to roll in to police headquarters.

But the information wasn't as helpful as he'd hoped. Most

of the sales receipts included the manufacturer of the customer's car and the tag number. Some had the model number but virtually none had the color. The list kept growing. After an hour he had copies of 142 records of the sales of that model of Michelin in the last twelve months to people who owned Mercedes.

He looked over the list of names. It was discouraging.

Standard procedure was to run the names through the outstanding warrants/priors database. But a net like that didn't seem to be the sort that would catch this perp – he wasn't a chronic 'jacker or a shooter with a long history of crime. Still, Konnie was a cop who dotted his i's and he handed the stack to Genie.

'You know what to do, darling.'

'It's seven forty-two on a Saturday night, boss.'

'*You* had dinner at least.'

'Lemme tell you something, Konnie,' the huge woman said, nodding at the KFC bags. 'Throw them out. They're starting to stink.'

Dutifully, he did. As he returned to his desk he grabbed his ringing phone.

''Lo?'

'Detective Konstantinatis, please?'

'Yeah.'

'This is Special Agent McComb with the FBI. Missing and Exploited Child Unit.'

'Sure, how you doin'?' Konnie'd worked with the unit occasionally. They were tireless and dedicated and top-notch.

'I'm doing a favor for my boss in Quantico. He asked me to take a look at the Megan McCall case. You're involved in that, right?'

'Yup.'

'It's not an active case for us but you know Tate Collier's the girl's father, right?'

'Know that.'

'Well, he did some pretty good work for us when he was a commonwealth's attorney so I said I'd look into her disappearance. As a favor.'

'Just what I'm doing, more or less. But I'm gonna present it as an active case to my captain tonight.'

'Are you really?'

'Found some interesting forensics.' Konnie was thinking: Man, if he could turn the tire data over to them . . . the FBI had a whole *staff* of people who specialized in tires. That was all they did. In-fucking-credible.

'That's good to know. We ought to coordinate our approaches. Do some proactive thinking.'

'Sure.' Konnie's thinking was: They might be the best cops in the world but feebies talk like assholes.

The agent said, 'I'm up at Ernie's, near the Parkway. You know it?'

'Sure. It's a half-mile from me.'

'I was about to order dinner and was reading the file when I saw your name. Maybe I could come by in an hour or so. Or maybe – this might appeal to you, Officer – you might want to join me? Let Uncle Sam pick up the dinner tab.'

He paused for a moment. 'Why not? Be there in ten minutes.'

'Good. Bring whatever you've got.'

'Will do.'

They hung up. Konnie stuck his head in Genie's office, where she was looking over the warrants request results. 'Everything's negative, Konnie.'

'Don't worry. We got the feds on the case now.'

'My.'

He took the stack of faxed receipts from her desk, shoved them into his briefcase and headed out the door.

Konnie was feeling pretty good. Ernie's served some great mashed potatoes.

Chapter TWENTY-TWO

Aaron Matthews sat at a booth in a dark corner of the restaurant, looking out the window at a tableau of heavy equipment, bright yellow in the dusk, squatting on a dirt hillside near by.

This was an area that five years ago had been fields and was now rampantly overgrown with townhouses and apartments and strip malls. Starbuck's, Bruegger's Bagels, Linens 'n' Things. Ernie's restaurant fit in perfectly. An upscale franchise. Looked nice on the surface but beneath the veneer it was all formula.

He stirred as the waddling form of Detective Konstantinatis entered the restaurant and maneuvered through the tables.

Good, he thought. Good.

Watching the man's eyes, seeing where they slid – furtively, guiltily.

Always the eyes.

Matthews waved and Konstantinatis nodded and steered toward him. Matthews had no idea what official FBI identification looked like and wouldn't have known how to fake some if he had but he'd dressed in a suit and white shirt – what he always wore when seeing patients – and had brought several dog-eared file folders, on which he'd printed 'FBI

PRIVILEGED AND CONFIDENTIAL' with stencils he'd made from office materials he'd bought at Staples. These sat prominently in front of him.

He hoped for the best.

But after glancing at the files the detective merely scooted into the seat across from Matthews and shook his hand.

They made small talk for a few moments – Matthews using his best government-speak. Stiff, awkward. If the fake files hadn't fooled the cop the stilted language surely would have.

The waitress came and they ordered. Matthews wasn't surprised when the detective ordered milk with dinner. Matthews himself ordered a beer.

He said, 'I'm afraid we don't have many leads. But from what you were telling me you think there's a chance she was kidnapped?'

'First I just thought she ran off. But there's apparently a tape that shows somebody switching her car with this gray Mercedes around the time she vanished.'

'I see,' said Aaron Matthews, who felt fire burn right through him. His battleship-gray 560 sat in the parking lot, fifty feet from them. Resplendent with its stolen license plates. Tape? Who'd taken it? He was furious for a moment but anger was a luxury he had no time for.

'What's this tape?'

'Vanished into thin air. Long story.'

'Oh.'

'Don't envy you that job,' the detective said, revealing a sentimental side Matthews wouldn't have guessed he had. 'Looking for missing kids all day long. Must be hard.'

Matthews said in a soft voice, 'It's where I feel I can make the most difference.'

Their drinks came. They clinked glasses. Matthews spilled some beer on the table. Wiped it up sloppily with a cocktail napkin.

'Detective—'

'Call me Konnie, everybody else does.'

'Okay, Konnie. I hate to ask but I don't know this Collier and the question's come up. Do you think there was anything between him and the girl?'

'Naw. Not Tate. If anything, just the opposite.'

'How's that?'

'Hell, I didn't even know he *had* a daughter until we'd been working together a while. Anyway, naw, naw, it's not that. I do think somebody 'napped her. No motive yet though might be a case Tate's working on. He's decided this local real estate guy didn't do it. But I'm not so sure. I also have some thoughts about the girl's aunt. I was hoping you could help.'

'Of course. What can we do?' Bett's sister, Susan . . . How did Konnie know about *her*?

'I 'statted some tire treads and got a list of a hundred and a half people bought that brand of tire in the past year. Could I give you the list—' He patted the briefcase. '—have your people check 'em out?'

'Be happy to. Have you done anything with them yet?'

'Just run 'em through the outstanding warrants computer. Nothing showed up.'

Planning for the kidnapping, Matthews had bought new tires for the car two months ago; he couldn't afford a flat. At least when he'd taken the car into General Tire he'd given a fake name and paid cash.

'But then I got to thinking,' Konnie continued, 'on the way over here, what I shoulda done – I shoulda looked at the receipts and found out who paid cash. Anybody who did, I figure it'd be a fake name. I mean, those tires cost big money. Nobody pays cash for something like that. So what your folk could do is check the tags and see if the name matches. If not then they're somebody I've gotta talk to.'

Jesus in heaven. Matthews hadn't swapped plates when

he'd taken the car in to have the new tires mounted. The tag would reveal his real name and the address of his rental house in Prince William County. Which didn't match the fake information he'd given the clerk at the tire store.

'That's a good idea,' Matthews said. 'A proactive idea.'

He wanted to scream. A dark mood hovered over him.

The food came and Konnie ate hungrily, hunched over his meal.

Matthews picked at his. He'd have to act soon. He flagged the waitress down and ordered another beer.

'You want to give me those receipts?' Matthews nodded at the briefcase.

'Sure, but let's go back to headquarters after. It's right up the street here. You can fax 'em to your office.'

'Okay.'

The second beer came. Konnie glanced at it for a second, returned to his food.

'This Tate Collier,' Matthews said slowly, savoring his microbrew. 'Sounds like a good man.'

'None better. Fucking best lawyer in the commonwealth. I get sick of these shits getting off on technicalities. When Collier was arguing the case they went away and stayed away.'

Matthews held up the beer. 'To your theory of tires.'

The detective hesitated then they tapped glasses.

Matthews drank half the beer, exhaled with satisfaction and set it down. 'Hot for April, don't you think?'

'Is,' the detective grunted.

Matthews asked, 'You on duty now?'

'Naw, I been off for three hours.'

'Then hell, chug down that milk and let me buy you a real drink.' He tapped the beer.

'No thanks.'

'Come on, nothing like a nice beer on a hot day.'

'Fact is, I give up drinking a few years back.'

Matthews looked mortified. 'Oh, I'm sorry.'

'Not at all.'

'I wasn't thinking. A man drinking milk. Shouldn't have ordered this. I *am* sorry.'

The cop held up a calm hand. ''S no problem at all. I don't hold with making other folk change their way of life 'cause of me.'

Matthews lifted the glass of beer. 'You want me to get rid of it or anything?'

As the cop glanced at the beer his eyes flashed – the same as they had when he'd walked through the bar, looking longingly at the row of bottles lined up like prostitutes on a street corner.

'Nope,' the detective said. 'You can't go hiding from it.' He ate some more mashed potatoes then said, 'Where you find most of the runaways go?'

Matthews enjoyed each small sip of the beer. The detective eyed him every third or fourth. The aroma from the liquid he'd spilled – on purpose – filled the booth with a sour malty scent. 'Always the big city. What a lure New York is. They think about getting jobs, becoming Madonna or whoever the girls want to become nowadays. The boys think they'll get laid every night.' Matthews sipped the beer again and looked outside. '*Damn* hot. Imagine that battle.'

'Bull Run?'

'Yep, well, I call it First Manassas but that's because I'm from Pennsylvania.' Matthews enjoyed another sip. 'You married?'

Or did the wife leave the drunk?

'Was. Divorced now.'

'Kids?'

Or did they cut Daddy off cold when they got tired of him passing out during *Jeopardy!* on weeknights and puking to die every Sunday morning?

'Two. Wife's got 'em. See 'em some holidays.'

Matthews poured down another mouthful. 'Must be tough.'

'Can be.' The fat cop took refuge in his potatoes.

After a minute Matthews asked, 'So you a graduate?'

'How's that?'

'Twelve steps.'

'AA? Sure.' The cop glanced down at his beefy hands. 'Been two years, four months.'

'Eight years for me.'

Another flicker in the eyes. The cop glanced at the beer.

Matthews laughed. 'You're where you are, Konnie. And I'm where I am. I was drinking a fifth of fucking bad whisky every day. Hell, at least that. Sometimes I'd crack the revenue of a second bottle just after dinner.' Konnie didn't notice how FBI-speak had turned into buddy talk, with syntax and vocabulary very similar to his.

'"Crack the revenue."' Konnie laughed. 'My daddy used to say that.'

So had some of Matthews's patients.

'Bottle and a half? That's a hell of a lot of drinking.'

'Oh, yes, it was. Yessir. Knew I was going to die. So I gave it up. How bad was it for you?'

The cop shrugged and shoveled peas and potatoes into his mouth.

'Hurt my marriage bad,' he offered. Flicker. Reluctantly the cop added, 'I guess it *killed* my marriage.'

'Sorry to hear that,' Matthews said, thrilling at the sorrow in the man's eyes.

'And it was probably gonna kill me some day.'

'What was your drink?' Matthews asked.

'Scotch. And beer.'

'Ha! Mine too. Dewars and Bud.'

Konnie's eyes softened at this unexpected camaraderie. 'So you . . . what?' The cop nodded at the tall-neck bottle. 'What happened? You fell off, huh?'

Matthews's face went reverential. 'I'll tell you the God's truth, Konnie.' He took a delicious sip of beer. 'I believe in meeting your weaknesses head-on. I won't run from them.'

The cop grunted affirmatively.

'See, it seemed too easy to give up drinking completely. You understand me?'

'Not exactly.'

'It was the coward's way. A lot of people just stop drinking altogether. But that's as much a failure to me . . . sorry, don't take this personal.'

'Not at all, keep going. I'm interested.'

'That's as much a failure to me as somebody who drinks all the time.'

'Guess that makes some sense,' the cop said slowly.

Matthews swirled the beer seductively in his glass.

'Take a man addicted to sex. You know that can be a problem?'

'I've heard. They got a Twelve Step for that too, you know?'

'Right. But he can hardly give up sex altogether, right? That'd be unnatural.'

Konnie nodded.

Oh, he's with me, Matthews thought. Hell, *this* is like sex. He felt so high. 'So,' he continued, 'I just got back to the point where I could control it.'

'And that worked?' Konnie asked. The toady little man seemed awestruck.

'What it was, I stopped cold for two years. Just like I told myself I'd do. This was all planned out. Sometimes it was tough as hell. I'm not gonna sugarcoat it. But God helped me. As soon as I had it under control, two years to the day I stopped, I took my first drink. One shot of Dewars. Drank it down like medicine.'

'What happened?'

'Nothing. Felt good. Enjoyed it. Didn't have another. Didn't have anything for a week. Then I had another shot and a Bud. I let a month go by.'

'A month?' Konnie whispered.

'Right. Then I poured a glass of Scotch. Let it sit in front of me. Looked at it, smelled it, poured it down the drain. Let another month go by.'

The cop shook his head in wonder. 'Sounds like you're one of them masochists or whatever you call 'em.' But there was a desperation in his laugh.

'Sometimes we have to find the one thing that's hardest for us and turn around and stare right at it. Go deep. As deep as we can go. That's what courage is. That's what makes men out of us.'

'I can respect what you're saying.'

'I've been drinking off and on for the past five years. Never been drunk once.' He leaned forward and rested his hand on the cop's hammy forearm. 'Remember that feeling when you were first drinking?'

'I think—'

'It made you relaxed, peaceful, happy? Brought out your good side? That's the way it is now.' Matthews leaned back. 'I'm proud of myself.'

'To you.' The cop swallowed and tipped his milk against the beer glass. His eyes slid over the golden surface of the brew.

Oh, you poor fool, thought Aaron Matthews. You don't have a soul in the world to talk to, do you? 'Sometimes,' he continued pensively, 'when I have a real problem, something eating at me, something making me feel so guilty it's like a fire inside . . . Well, I'll have a shot. That numbs it. It helps me get through.'

The fork probed the diminished pile of potatoes.

Let's go deep.

Touch the most painful part . . .

'If I found myself in a situation where there was somebody I loved and she was drifting away because of the way I'd become – well, I'd want to be able to face whatever had driven her away. I could show her I was in control again, and – who knows? – maybe I could just get her back.'

The cop's face was flushed and it seemed that his throat had swollen closed.

Matthews sipped more beer, looked out the window, at the dusk sky. 'Yessir, I hated living alone. Waking up on those Sunday mornings. Those March Sunday mornings, the sky all gray . . . The holidays by myself . . . God, I *hated* that. My wife gone . . . The one person in the world I needed. The one person I was willing to do anything for . . .'

The detective was paralyzed.

Now, Matthews thought. Now! 'Let me show you something.' He leaned forward, winking. 'Watch this.' He waved to the waitress. 'Shot of Dewars.'

'One?' she called.

'Just one, yeah.'

Numb, the cop watched the glass arrive.

Matthews made a show of reaching down and picking up the brimming glass. He leaned forward, smelled the glass, then took the tiniest sip. He set the glass down on the table and lifted his hands, palm up.

'That's it. The only hard liquor I'll have for two, three weeks.'

'You can do that?' The cop was dumbfounded.

'Easiest thing in the world. Without a single problem.' He returned to his beer and called the waitress over. 'I'm sorry, honey. I'll pay you for it but I changed my mind. I think I better keep a clear head tonight. You can take it.'

'Sure thing, sir.'

The cop's hand made it to the glass before hers. She blinked in surprise at the vehemence of the big man's gesture.

'Oh, you want me to leave that after all?'

The cop looked at Matthews but then turned his dog eyes to the waitress. 'Yeah. And bring my friend here another beer.'

A fraction of a pause. Their eyes met. Matthews said, 'Make it two.'

'Sure thing, gentlemen. Put it on your tab?'

'Oh, no,' Matthews insisted. 'This's on me.'

Matthews, wearing his surgical gloves, drove Konnie's car out of the parking lot of the strip mall and toward the interstate. The cop was in the passenger seat, clutching the bottle of Scotch between his legs like it was the joystick in a biplane. His head rocked against the Taurus's window. Spit and whiskey ran down his chin.

Matthews parked on a side road, not far from Ernie's, lifted the bottle away from Konnie and splashed some on the dashboard and seat of the car, handed it back. Konnie didn't notice. 'How you doing?' Matthews asked him.

The big man gazed morosely at the open mouth of the bottle. A declaration of intent, Aaron Matthews concluded, to his great pride and pleasure.

At the strip mall where they'd bought the Scotch Matthews had pitched a trash bag containing the tire receipts and all the rest of the notes on the Megan McCall investigation into a dumpster.

Matthews now climbed out of the car, pulled Konnie into the driver's seat.

Konnie gulped down two large slugs of liquor. He wiped his sweating, pasty face. 'Where'm I going?'

'You're going home, Konnie.'

'Okay.'

'You go on home now.'

'Okay. I'm going home. Is Carol there?'

'Your wife? Yeah, she's there, Konnie. She's waiting for you to come home. You better hurry.'

'I really miss her.'

'You know where to go, don't you?' Matthews asked.

'I think . . .' His bleary eyes looked around. 'I don't know.'

'That road right there. See it?'

'Sure. There?'

'Right there,' Matthews said. 'Just drive down there. That'll get you home. That'll get you home to Carol.'

'Okay.'

'Goodbye, Konnie.'

'Goodbye. That road there?'

'That's right. Hey, Konnie?'

Matthews looked at the rheumy eyes, wet lips.

'You say hi to Carol for me, won't you?'

The cop nodded.

Matthews flicked the gearshift into drive and stepped back as Konnie accelerated. He was driving more or less down the middle of the road.

Matthews was walking back to Ernie's to pick up the Mercedes when he heard the sudden squealing of brakes and the blares of a dozen horns, signaling to Konnie in his dark blue Taurus that he'd turned on to the exit, not entrance, ramp of I-66 and was driving the wrong way down the interstate. It was no more than thirty seconds later that he heard the pounding crash of what was probably a head-on collision and – though perhaps only in his imagination – a faint scream.

Chapter TWENTY-THREE

Night now.

The corridors of the asylum were murky, illuminated only by the light from two outdoor security lamps, bleeding in through the greasy windows.

Megan McCall, gripping her glass sword, moved silently through the main wing. She couldn't get the comic books out of her mind, the tentacles gripping screaming women, the monsters raping them. In some of the mags, Peter'd circled pictures a dozen times with different colored pens.

Moving toward the boy's room. Closer, closer.

She stepped into the large lobby. In the dim light shadows filled the space. She *believed* he was in his room but he could have been anywhere. She spun around, practically feeling the metal rod he carried swinging toward her head. Gasping.

Nothing.

Was he asleep in there? Reading? Jerking off?

Fantasizing about her.

About what he was going to *do* to her.

The corridors were like a maze. She wasn't sure anymore where his rooms were. She made several false turns and found herself back where she'd started. Feeling desperate now. Afraid that he'd find the trap.

She walked more quickly, listening carefully. But she heard no obscene breathing, no lewd whispering of her name. In a way the silence was *more* frightening; she didn't know where he was.

Then she turned a corner and there it was! She saw light spilling into the corridor from the open door of Peter's room. She was sure the lights had been off when she'd been in there.

The light flickered. A shadow.

He was inside.

Megan, sweating. Megan, scared.

Scared of dying, scared of the monster who lives up the hall, scared of the whispering bears.

Well, you wanted him, Crazy Megan whispers. *What're you waiting for? Go get him.*

She started to tell C.M. to be quiet. But suddenly she stopped. Because a thought hit her with the strength of the cinder blocks piled up in her trap. It was this: that Crazy Megan not only isn't crazy, she's the only one of them that's real.

Crazy Megan is the genuine Megan. The Megan who danced on the scaffolding of the water tower on a dare to make herself known. The Megan who was secretly dreaming of going to San Francisco for a year after high school and then to college in Paris. The Megan who made fierce love with a sexy black boyfriend who – fuck you, Dr Hanson – I *do* love after all! The Megan who wanted to poke her finger into her father's face and scream at him, 'The inconvenient child's back and you've got her whether you like it or not!'

Oh, yeah, Crazy Megan's the sane one. And the other one's just a loser.

'Okay,' she said out loud. 'Okay, prick, come and get me.'

The shadow of Peter Matthews froze on the wall.

The light clicked out.

'Come on, you fucker!' she shouted.

There was a ring of metal – he must have picked up the rod.

She couldn't see clearly but she was suddenly aware of his form lumbering slowly from the doorway. He looked up and down the hall and then turned toward her. 'Megan . . .'

God, he's big.

'*Megan!*' he rasped.

He started toward her. Moving much faster than she'd expected from the shuffling lope she'd heard earlier.

Her courage dissolved. What a fucking stupid idea this is! Hell, it's not going to work. Of course it isn't. He'll get her.

'No!' she screamed in panic.

Get going! Crazy Megan shouts. *Run.*

Stupid, stupid . . . Just like everything else I do. Everything else I get wrong. I'll lead him back to the trap and he'll dodge the cinder blocks, laughing the whole time, and move in slowly, pinning me against the wall and jabbing the rod up into me the way one of his damn monsters would do.

She backed up fast, knowing that she should be watching where she was going but afraid to take her eyes off him for an instant.

Feeling the wall behind her. Nearly tripped on a table. She spun around, pushed it aside.

And when she looked back he was gone.

We're fucked, Crazy Megan says.

He could be anywhere now! Coming up around her from the left or the right.

And, of course, she remembered, he had keys to the place. He could move from room to room and come up behind her.

There was nothing she could do now except get into the dead end corridor where she'd set up the trap. Get there as fast as she could and wait.

But in her panic she was turned around. Was it back that way? Or to the side? She gazed down two corridors. Which? He could be down either of them. She could hardly see a thing in the darkness.

There, she thought. It's got to be that one. I'm sure.

Almost sure.

She sprinted. She slammed into a fiberglass chair, sending it flying. She stayed upright but the noise of the furniture hitting the wall was very loud.

Megan froze. Had he heard? Had—

Suddenly a huge form stepped from the corridor about two feet away, lunging toward her. 'Megan . . .'

Megan screamed, couldn't get the knife up in time. She closed her eyes, swinging her left fist toward where his face was. She connected hard and must have broken his nose because he wailed in pain and dropped back, around the corner.

She ran.

Turned one corner and paused at the entrance to the hallway that led to the trap.

He followed, moving toward her.

She made sure he got a good look at her, to see which way she was going, then started toward the trap.

But she stopped. Wait! Was it *this* corridor? No, the next. Wait. Was it?

She glanced into the murky shadows and couldn't see the denim rope. Was it there? Yes or no?

Peter was getting closer.

Which fucking corridor? Crazy Megan shouts.

I don't know, I don't know, they all look alike . . .

He was twenty feet away.

Come on, snaps C.M. *Get it together.*

No choice. It better be this one.

Megan ran to the end of the corridor.

Yes! She'd been right. There was the trap. She crouched

down and picked up the end of the rope. At the far end of the corridor Peter paused and glanced toward her.

More muttering. Like an animal. She remembered the newspaper picture: his odd mouth, probing tongue, the crazy eyes. The grin of his mother's funeral.

I'm so fucking scared . . .

You're gonna nail him, Crazy Megan says.

In the darkness he didn't even seem to be walking. He just floated closer to her, growing larger and larger, filling the corridor. He stopped right before the trap. She couldn't see his eyes or face in the shadow but she knew he was leering at her.

More muttering.

He stepped closer.

Now!

She pulled the rope.

The denim snapped neatly in half. The cinder blocks shifted slightly but stayed where they were.

Oh, no. Oh, Christ, no! *That's it*, Crazy Megan cries. *It's over with.*

He moved forward another two steps.

She swept the knife from her pocket, looked at his shadowy form.

I'm going to die. This is it. I'm dead. He'll break my arm, take the knife away from me and fuck me till I die . . .

Crazy Megan has gone away. Crazy Megan is dead already.

He stepped forward one more foot. The dim light from outside fell on his face.

No . . .

She was hallucinating.

Megan gasped. 'Josh!'

'Megan,' he mumbled again. Joshua LeFevre's face and neck were bloody messes, his hands, arms and legs too. Large gouges were missing from his skin all over his arms and legs. He dropped to his knees.

Just as the cinder blocks started to tumble toward him.

'No!'

Megan leapt forward and pushed him aside. The blocks crashed into the floor, firing splinters of stone through the air. He fell backwards, hard. She cradled his bloody head.

'Megan,' he said, the name stuttering from his torn throat. Blood sprayed her face. Then he passed out.

Tate Collier's Lexus skidded up to the pay-phone on Route 29.

He leapt out, looking around desperately.

He saw no one.

'Hello?' he called in a harsh whisper. 'Hello!'

He glanced at the old diner – or what was left of it after an arson fire some years ago – and piles of trash. Deserted.

He heard a moan. Then some violent retching.

Tate ran into the bushes. There Konnie sat, bloody and drenched in sweat, vomit on his chin, eyes unfocused. He'd been crying.

'Jesus. What happened?' Tate bent down, put his arm around the man. When Konnie'd called him twenty minutes ago he'd said only to meet him here as soon as possible. Tate knew he was drunk, only half conscious, but had no other clue as to what was going on.

'I'm going down, Tate. I fucked up bad. Oh, Christ . . .'

Bett . . . now Konnie . . . What a day, Tate thought. What a day.

'You're hurt.'

'I'm okay. But I may've killed people, Tate. There was an accident. I left the scene.' He gasped and retched for a minute. 'They're looking for me, my own people're looking for me.' He coughed violently.

'I'll call an ambulance.'

'No, I'm turning myself in. But—'

He rolled over on his side and retched for a few minutes. Then caught his breath and sat up.

A squad car with flashing lights cruised past slowly. The searchlight came on but it missed the bushes where Tate crouched beside the detective.

'They're all over the place, looking for me. But listen to me, you have to get to the office. I couldn't find my briefcase, I don't know where I left it. You need to look at the receipts.'

'Receipts.'

'For the tires. Go to the office, Tate. Genie should've made a copy of them. I'm praying she did. Ask her for them. But move fast 'cause they're going to impound my desk.'

'Genie? That's your assistant?'

'You remember her. The list of receipts, okay?'

'All right.'

'Then look for whoever paid cash for the tires.'

'Cash for the tires. All right.'

'She ran warrants but that's not . . . that's not what I shoulda been looking for. Tate, you listening?'

'I'm listening.'

'Good. Look for the receipts where the customers paid cash. Then run the tag numbers of their cars. If the registered owner doesn't match the name on the receipt that's our boy. The one took your daughter. I got a look at . . .' He caught his breath. 'I got a look at him.'

'You saw him?'

'Oh, yeah. The prick suckered me good. He's white, forties, dark hair. About one seventy. Said he . . . Claimed he was Bureau. He suckered me just like my daddy suckered people. Shit. God, I'm sick.'

'Okay, Konnie. I'll do it. But now I'm getting you to the hospital.'

'No, you're not. You're not wasting another fucking minute.

You're going do what the hell I told you. And fuck, be there for my arraignment. I can't believe what I did. I can't believe it.' His voice disappeared in a cascade of retching.

Tate found his old commonwealth's attorney ID badge at home and ran back to his car, hanging the beaded chain around his neck.

The date was four years old but was in small type; he doubted anyone would notice.

In twenty minutes he was walking into the police station. No one paid him any attention. He signed the log-in book and walked into Konnie's office.

A heavy-set woman, red-eyed and crying, looked up.

'Oh, Mr Collier. Did you hear?'

'He's going to be all right, Genie.'

'This's so terrible,' she said, wiping her face. 'So terrible. I can't imagine he'd take to drinking again. I don't know why. I don't know what's going on.'

'I'm going to help him. But I've got to do something first. It's very important.'

'He said I should help you when he called. Oh, he sounded so drunk on the phone. I remember he used to call me up and say he wouldn't be coming in today because he had the flu. But it wasn't the flu. He sounded the way he was tonight. Just plain drunk.'

Tate rested his hand on her broad shoulder. 'He's going to be all right. We'll all help him. Did you make a copy of the receipts?'

'I did, yes. He always tells me, "Make a copy of everything I give you. Always, always, always make a copy."'

'That's Konnie.'

'Here they are.'

He took the stack of receipts, owners of Mercedes who'd bought new Michelins. On four receipts the cash/check box was marked. He didn't recognize any of the names.

'Could you run these tag numbers through DMV and get me the names and addresses of the registered owners?'

'Sure.' She sniffed and waddled to her chair, sat heavily. Then she typed furiously.

A moment later she motioned him over.

The first three names matched those on the receipts.

The fourth didn't.

'Oh my God,' Tate muttered.

'What is it, Mr Collier?'

He didn't answer. He stood, numb, staring at the name Aaron Matthews, Sully Fields Drive, Manassas, the letters glowing in jaundice-yellow type on the black screen.

Chapter TWENTY-FOUR

The Court: *The prosecution may now present its summation. Mr Collier?*

Mr Collier: *My friends . . . The task of the jury is a difficult and thankless one. You're called on to sift through a haystack of evidence, looking for that single needle of truth. In many cases, that needle is elusive. Practically impossible to find. But in the case before you, the Commonwealth versus Peter Matthews, the needle is lying out in the open, evident for everyone to see.*

There is no question that the defendant killed Joan Keller. He was seen walking with the victim, a sixteen-year-old girl, by Bull Run Marina. He was seen leading her into the woods. He was later seen running from the park five minutes before Joan's body was found, strangled to death. The mud in which her cold corpse lay matched the mud found on the knees of the defendant's jeans. When he was arrested, as you heard from the testimony, he blurted out to the officers, 'She had to die.'

And in the trailer where he lived, the police found hundreds of comic books and horror novels, depicting big, hulking men doing unspeakable things to helpless women victims – victims just like Joan Keller.

The defense can see that shiny needle of truth as clearly as you and I can. There's no doubt in their minds either that the defendant killed that poor girl. And so what do they do? They try to distract us. They raise doubts about Joan's character. They suggest that she had loose morals. That she'd had sex with local boys . . . sometimes for money. Or for liquor or cigarettes. A sixteen-year-old girl! These are vile attempts to distract you from finding the needle.

Oh, they talk about accidental death. 'Just playing around,' they say. The killer was a troubled young man, they say, but harmless.

Well, the facts of the case prove that he wasn't harmless at all.

Harmless men don't strangle innocent young women, seventy pounds lighter than they are.

Harmless men don't act out their sick and twisted fantasies on helpless youngsters like Joanie Sue Keller.

Ladies and gentlemen, don't let the defense hide that needle from you. Don't let them cover it up. This case is simple, extremely simple. The defendant, through his premeditation, his calculation, his knowing, purposeful intent, has taken a life. The life of a young girl. Someone's friend . . . someone's sister . . . someone's daughter. There is no worse crime than that. And he must be held fully responsible for it.

The great poet Dante said that the most righteous requests are answered in the silence of the deed. I'm not asking for hollow words, ladies and gentlemen. No, I'm asking for your courageous deed – finding this dangerous killer sane, finding him guilty and recommending to the court that he pays for young Joan Keller's life with his own. Thank you.

Tate Collier had done everything right in the closing statement. It was short, colloquial, filled with concrete imagery. He'd referred to Peter Matthews as the 'defendant' and to the girl as 'Joan' – depersonalizing the criminal, humanizing the victim. He'd played with shadows and light. The reference to the 'needle' – getting the jury used to the thought of the needle used in lethal injections – was a particularly good touch, he'd thought.

He'd even added the request for the death penalty because that was something they could bargain with in their minds – trading the boy's life for a finding of sanity and a long prison sentence.

And that was exactly what happened.

He won, the boy was found sane and guilty. And was sentenced to life without parole. Which had been Tate's goal all along.

And a week later the young man who'd beaten capital punishment was executed by a far more informal means than lethal injection – a dozen prison inmates, identities unknown, had used broomsticks and sharpened spoons to carry out the sentence. And it took them three hours to do so.

Justice?

After he'd heard of Peter's death, Tate had sat at his desk for a long moment then walked into the commonwealth's attorney's file room and read through evidence in the case once again.

They were the same files and documents he'd read before the trial, of course. But he examined them now untainted by the passionate drive to convict the young man. He looked more carefully at the picture they painted of the boy. Not of 'the defendant'. But of Peter Thomas Matthews. A seventeen-year-old boy, a resident of Fairfax, Virginia.

Yes, Peter had a collection of eerie comics and Japanamation tapes. But many of them, Tate learned, were bestsellers in Japan – where they'd taken on an artsy, cult status and were reviewed seriously and collected by young people and adults alike. What was more, the boy also had a collection of serious science fiction and fantasy writers like Ray Bradbury, Isaac Asimov, William Gibson, C. S. Lewis, J. R. R. Tolkien, Jules

Verne, Edgar Rice Burroughs. Peter had spent hours copying long, poetic passages from these books and had tried his hand at illustrating scenes from them. He also wrote pretty good fantasy short stories of his own.

Yes, some psychiatric evaluations called the boy dangerous. But others said he merely had a paranoid personality and was given to panic in stressful situations. He had no history of violence.

Tate had also read about Joan Keller – the victim – who'd been sexually active since age twelve. She'd experimented with 'weird things', possibly erotic asphyxia. She'd seduced older men on several other occasions and would have been the complaining witness in at least one statutory rape case, except that she'd refused to cooperate. She'd been treated for being a borderline personality and had been suspended twice for assaults – against both girls and boys at her school, including one involving a knife.

Peter had abrasions on his face and neck when he was brought to the lockup. He claimed that Joan had struck him with a rock when she got tired of his awkward groping – after she'd taken his hand and slipped it into her panties.

And the statement the boy had made – about how Joan 'had to die' – was disputed by a local fisherman near the scene of the arrest. He claimed the boy might have said, 'She never had to die . . . She shouldn't have hit me.'

But silver-tongued Tate Collier had managed to keep all of this damning evidence out of the jury's earshot or had shattered the credibility of the witnesses presenting it.

Your honor we will not try the victim in this case your honor a well-written short story has no probative value in this case whatsoever your honor that fact is immaterial and has to be stricken please instruct the witness . . .

The defense lawyers had come to him with a plea bargain. Criminally negligent homicide, suspended sentence, three years' probation and two years' mandatory counseling.

But, no. Peter Matthews had laid his hands upon the neck

of a sixteen-year-old girl and had pressed, pressed, pressed until she was lifeless. And so a plea bargain wouldn't do.

The Court: *The defendant will rise. You have heard the verdict of the jury and have been adjudged guilty of murder in the first degree. The jury has not recommended the death penalty and accordingly I hereby sentence you to life in prison . . .*

He went to prison and the last thing anyone remembered about Peter was a giggling fit and his telling a guard he was going to play with his new friends. 'Won't that be way cool?' Peter asked. 'We're going to play ball, a bunch of us. They want me to play ball. Awesome.' Then he disappeared into the laundry room and was found, in several pieces, five hours later.

Why, Tate had wondered then, sitting alone in the musty file room, had he been so vehement about prosecuting the boy? *Why?*

The question he'd asked himself often in the past few years.

The question he asked himself now.

What would have been so bad if the defendant . . . if *Peter* had gone into a hospital? Gone to see a counselor.

Wasn't that reasonable? Of course it was. But it hadn't been then, not to the Tate Collier of five years ago. Not to Tate Collier the whiz-kid commonwealth's attorney, the man who spoke in tongues, the Judge's grandson.

Why?

Because the thought of a killer depriving parents of their child was unbearable to him. *That* was the answer. *That was* all he thought. Someone stole away a girl just like Megan. And he had to die. To hell with justice.

Tate had never seen Peter's father at the trial or hadn't paid any attention to him if he'd been there. He was a therapist, Tate remembered from reading the boy's history and evaluations. Lived alone. His wife – a therapist as well, and reportedly more successful than her husband – had committed suicide some years before.

Aaron Matthews . . .

Well, he could give the police a name and address now. They'd find him. He only prayed Megan was still alive.

Now, in Konnie's office, he dialed Bett's home phone. Her voice mail gave her cellphone number and he dialed that. She didn't answer. He left a message about what he'd learned and told her that he was at the county police station.

He started down the hall, striding the way he'd walked when he'd been a commonwealth's attorney and cut up these offices as if he owned them, playing inquisitor to the young officers as he grilled them about their cases and the evidence they'd collected.

He pushed through the door to the Homicide Division and was surprised to see three startled detectives stop in the tracks of their conversations.

He smiled ruefully, remembering only then that he was a trespasser.

One detective looked at another, an astonished gaze on his face.

'I'm sorry to barge in,' Tate began. 'I'm Tate Collier. It's about my daughter. I don't know if you heard but she's disappeared and—'

In less than twenty seconds he was face down on a convenient desk, the handcuffs ratcheting on to his wrists with metallic efficiency, his Miranda rights floating down upon him from a gruff voice several feet above his head.

'What the hell's going on?' he barked.

'You're under arrest, Mr Collier. Do you understand these rights as I've read them to you?'

'For what? What're you arresting me for?'

'Do you understand your rights?'

'Yes, I understand my fucking rights. What for?'

'For murder, Mr Collier. The murder of Amy Walker. If you'll come this way, please.'

Chapter TWENTY-FIVE

She cradled him, sobbing.

Megan had eased Joshua LeFevre into the pale light from the outside lamp. He was even more badly injured than she'd thought at first – terribly battered – cut with slashes and bite marks, the wounds covered with dirt and dried blood. A stained scarf was tied around his neck as a bandage. One eye was swollen completely closed. Most of his dreads had been torn off his scalp, which was covered with mud and scabs.

He could speak only in a ghostly, snapping wail. No, it hadn't been Peter Matthews's leering voice, she'd heard; it was Josh's. His throat was split open with a terrible wound. His vocal cords had been cut and she thought, sobbing, of his beautiful baritone. When he breathed, air hissed in through both his mouth and the slash. The bleeding seemed to have stopped but she bound the denim rope around his throat anyway. She could think of nothing else to do.

'I thought it was you,' he gasped. 'I couldn't see. My eyes, my eyes. I thought it was you. But you didn't answer.'

Megan lowered her head to his chest. 'And I thought you were his son. I thought you were going to kill me. Oh, Josh, what happened? Was it the dogs? Outside?'

He nodded, shivered – from the pain, she guessed, as much as the cold.

'That . . . man?' he struggled to ask. 'He kidn—'

She nodded. 'Did you call the police?'

'No,' he gasped. 'I didn't know what was going on. I stopped him but he tricked me . . .' He coughed for a moment. 'Thought you . . . thought you were going with him.'

'What happened?' she asked tearfully.

The stuttering explanation: he'd followed her and Matthews here then the doctor had attacked him and left him for the dogs. But before they could finish him off a young deer had trotted past and they left Josh to pull her down.

His beautiful voice, Megan thought, crying. It's gone. She had to look away from his face.

He'd found a tire iron to use as a cane, he continued, and made his way into the hospital to find a phone. But there weren't any and he found that the doors didn't open outward, that the place was a prison.

She gently touched a terrible wound on his face. Even if they found a doctor soon would he survive?

'Were you . . . you weren't his lover, were you?'

'What?' she blurted.

'He said you were. He said . . . He said you wanted to get rid of me.'

'Oh, Josh, no. It was . . . whatever he said, it was a lie.'

'Who is he?' LeFevre rasped.

'We don't have time now. Can you walk?'

'No.' He breathed heavily and winced. 'Can't do anything. I've about had it.'

She pulled him further into the alcove, hid him from view. 'Wait here.'

'Where . . . you going?'

'Lie still, Josh. Be quiet.'

'I'll get something to use for bandages,' she said, rising.

'But he might be there.'

She showed him the glass knife. 'I really hope he is.'

'I'll tell you whatever you want to know. But for God's sake send somebody after my daughter.'

'Once more from the top, please, sir.' Tate was still stunned from the news that Amy had been found naked and stabbed to death in Tate's north thirty field.

'There's a man named Aaron Matthews. He drives a gray Mercedes. He lives on Sully Field, off Route 29 near Manassas. He's been following my daughter for the past couple weeks. Or months. I don't know. And—'

'We've got our own agenda here, Collier,' the young homicide detective – a dead ringer for the security guard at Megan's high school – said gruffly, his patience gone. 'You don't mind, we got a lotta ground to cover.'

'Is Ted Beauridge around?'

'No. One more time, sir. From the top.'

He was in an interrogation cubicle. At least the cuffs were off.

'Matthews killed Amy. Megan had told her about being followed. He thought she might have some information – Maybe he just killed her to get me out of the picture.'

And *I* gave him her name, Tate thought. He was sure the man who called from the FBI – special agent McComb – was Aaron Matthews, probing to get information. Trying to stop them from looking for her. He forced or tricked Megan into writing those notes and when they kept looking for her anyway, he turned on them.

'How'd you find out about the body?' Tate asked. 'An anonymous call, right?'

The detectives looked at each other. They were slim and in perfect shape. Trimmed hair. Shoes polished, guns tucked neatly away. Law enforcement machines.

'It was *Matthews* who called. Don't you get it?'

'Her mother said you'd been stalking Amy. That Child Protective Services has been investigating you.'

'What? That's bullshit. Call them.'

'On Saturday night, sir? We'll call on Monday.'

'We don't have until Monday.'

The cop continued lethargically, 'Mrs Walker also said you tried to break into her house today.'

'Amy was going to give us Megan's bookbag. I knocked on the door and tried to open it when no one answered.'

'Uh-huh.'

'There *is* no Child Protective investigation. It's him! It's Matthews. He's trying to stop me from finding Megan. Can't you see?'

'Not exactly, sir. No.'

'Okay. When did this anonymous call come in? Within the last half-hour? Believe me, Matthews killed Amy and dumped the body on my land. I saw somebody watching the house this morning.'

'Did you report it?'

'Well, no, I didn't.'

'Why not?'

Tate remembered thinking, as he stood in the rain-swept field that morning, Hey, looks like the Dead Reb. But it wasn't. It was Aaron Matthews, waiting until I left the house then tossing the dog a bone, planting Megan's letters, shutting the light out, leaving fast.

'I just didn't. Look, he knows I'm after him – Konnie was running a check on the Mercedes. It turned out to be his. That's not a coincidence.'

'How do you account for the fact that this girl was murdered with a kitchen knife that had your fingerprints on it?'

'Because it was probably from *my* kitchen. Talk to Konnie about this morning. He—'

'Detective Konstantinatis is in custody and he's also in no shape to talk to anybody. As I'm sure you know.'

'Beauridge, then. They were out to my house. Matthews broke in, planted some fake letters that Megan supposedly wrote and he must've stolen the knife at the same time. Or stole it tonight. It's an easy house to break into.'

'The cause of death was shock due to blood loss after her throat was slashed and her chest and abdomen punctured thirty-two times. There was some mutilation too.'

'Fuck of a way to kill someone,' the other detective added.

Tate's face grew hot. Megan's terrified eyes were the most prominent image in his thoughts.

'We've checked out your house and found you'd packed most of your girl's stuff away. Her bedroom looked about as personal as a storeroom.'

'She lives with her mother.'

'No pictures of her, no clothes, nothing personal. The impression we got was you'd been planning to say adios to Megan for some time. That's making us wonder about this whole kidnapping story.'

'There were some witnesses. There's a teacher . . . Robert Eckhard. He saw—'

But he stopped talking when he saw the expression on their faces.

'You a friend of Eckhard?'

'I don't know him,' Tate said cautiously. 'I just heard that he'd seen the car that was following Megan.'

'Have you ever talked to him?'

'No. I just told you – Why?'

'Robert Eckhard was arrested today on numerous counts of child pornography and endangering the welfare of minors.'

'What?'

'Could you describe your relationship with him?'

'With Eckhard? There *is* no relationship . . . Jesus Christ.

I don't know him! Please! Just send somebody out to check out this Matthews!'

A rhetorician never pleads. Tate's talents were deserting him in droves. Think smarter, he raged at himself. He could talk his way out of this. He *knew* he could. There must be some way. What would his grandfather, the Judge have done?

All cats see in the dark . . .

Midnight is a cat . . .

'Officer,' Tate said calmly, offering a casual smile, 'you've got nothing to lose. Absolutely nothing. I'm not going anywhere. If you check him out, if you send a couple officers out to his place then I'll tell you whatever you want to know. Anything. No hassle. We have a deal?'

One of the detectives sighed. He shrugged and stepped out the door.

Therefore Midnight sees in the dark.

Tate pictured Megan, bound and gagged, lying somewhere in a basement. Matthews standing over her. Undressing.

It was a terrible image and, once thought, wouldn't go away.

'Have you ever had sexual relations with Amy Walker?'

He tamped down his anger. 'I've never met her,' he answered.

'Did you send your daughter off somewhere because she knew you were stalking Amy Walker? And fabricate a kidnapping charge?'

'No, I didn't do that.' Struggling now to stay calm, to stay *helpful*. Really struggling. He looked at the doorway through which the other cop had disappeared. Were they sending a hostage rescue team to Matthews's house? Or just patrol officers? Matthews could trick them. He could lull them into complacency – oh, yes, *he* had the gift too, Tate now understood the dicey talent of persuasion.

They can't negotiate with someone like Matthews.

The silence of the deed.

'Did you kill Amy Walker?'

'No, I did not.'

'When was the last time you drove your daughter's car?'

'A month or so ago, I think.'

'Is that how your fingerprints got on the door handle of her car?'

'It would have to be.'

'Could we run through the events just prior to her disappearance once more?'

'Prior?'

'Say, for the week before.'

Tate glanced out the door, squinted. Looked again. The second detective came back into the cubicle. Tate asked, 'Did you send a team to his house? I should have told you to send hostage rescue. Tactical. Don't listen to him. Whatever he says, Megan's there, in the house. Tell whoever's on their way not to listen to him.'

'He wasn't home.'

'What?' Tate asked. He didn't understand. The officers couldn't have gotten there so quickly.

'I called him. He wasn't home.'

'You *called* him?' Tate's heart stuttered.

'Relax, sir, I didn't tell him anything. Just asked him to give us a call about some parking tickets.' The slick young cop seemed proud of his cleverness.

'Jesus Christ, you don't *have* to tell him anything. He's going to know. Are you crazy?'

'Sir, we don't have to pay any attention to your story at all, you know. We're doing you a favor.'

Tate sat back, glanced into the hall again.

After a moment he looked back at the officers again. Closed his eyes and sighed 'You win. Okay, you win.'

'How's that, sir?'

'I'll waive my rights and tell you everything I can think of. No confession but a full statement about my daughter and Amy

Walker. But I want some coffee and I've got to use the john.'

They looked at each other and nodded.

'I'm coming with you,' the detective muttered.

Tate laughed. 'I was a commonwealth's attorney for ten years. I'm not going to escape.'

'I'm coming with you.'

Tate gave a disgusted sigh and walked out of the Detective Division into the scuffed halls, which resembled a suburban grade school. He ambled to the men's room and pushed inside. The detective was directly behind him.

He stood at the urinal for an inordinately long time.

When he'd finished and washed his hands he stepped to the door and pushed it open, bumping into the woman who was juggling three large law books and several pads of foolscap, which tumbled to the floor.

'Sorry,' Tate said, bending down to pick up the books.

Bett McCall glanced at him, said, 'No problem.' And slipped the pistol out of her purse and into his hand.

Tate didn't even pause to think – that would've been disastrous. He simply spun around, shoved the Smith & Wesson into the belly of the shocked detective and pushed him back into the men's room as Bett calmly retrieved the books.

In one minute Tate had gagged and cuffed the furious cop and relieved him of his gun. He tossed it in the wastebasket.

'The cuffs too tight?' he asked.

The detective stared angrily.

'Are they too tight?'

A nod.

Tate snapped, 'Good.'

And stepped out into the corridor as a faint rumble arose in the john, like a low-Richter earthquake. The detective was trying to pull down the stall.

When he'd looked into the hallway from the interrogation room he couldn't believe that he'd seen her standing there, motioning with her head down the hall. 'How did you get in here?' he asked as they walked briskly toward the exit.

'Told them I was a lawyer.'

'You cite a case or two?'

'I could have.' She smiled. 'I memorized the names of a couple on your desk. I was going to tell the desk sergeant I had to see my client because these new cases had just been put down.'

'It's "handed down",' Tate corrected.

'Oh. Glad he didn't ask.'

'I don't know if we can get out that way. I came in under my own steam but the desk officer might know I've been arrested.' He looked back down the corridor. 'Five minutes, tops, till they come looking.'

She rearranged the books she was carrying so the cover showed. A school hornbook, *Williston on Contracts.*

He laughed. 'That'll fool 'em.' Then asked, 'You got my message?'

She nodded. 'I called Konnie and his assistant told me you'd been arrested. I couldn't decide whether to get a lawyer or the gun. I figured we didn't have time to wait for public defenders. My car's outside.'

The old Bett McCall might have meditated for days, hoping for guidance. The new one went right for the Smith & Wesson.

They paused just before they turned the corner beside the guard station. He took a breath. 'Ready?'

'I guess.'

'Let's go.'

Mentally crossing his fingers, Tate started forward, Bett at his side. The guard glanced at them but out they strolled without a hitch, signing the 'time departed' line in the log book scrupulously – one a phony prosecutor and one a phony defense lawyer and both of them now fugitives.

* * *

Aaron Matthews was driving, seventy, then eighty miles an hour.

Anger had given way to sorrow. To the same piercing hollowness he'd felt in the months after Peter had died in prison.

Sorrow at plans gone wrong, terribly wrong.

Matthews had been at his rental house off Route 29, waiting to see if he'd finally stopped Tate Collier. He believed he had. He'd given up on the subtlety, given up on the words, given up on the delicious art of persuasion. Stiff with anger, he'd dragged the Walker girl, screaming, from the trunk of his car. Said nothing, convinced her of nothing – he'd just slashed and slashed and slashed . . . All of his anger flowing from him as hot and sudden as the blood from her body. And then he'd sped home.

There the phone had rung. He hadn't answered but listened to the message as the officer left it. Some bullshit about the traffic tickets. 'Give us a call when you get home. Thank you.'

It meant of course that they knew. Or suspected, at least.

How had it happened? Why hadn't they just tossed Collier into the lockup and ignored him? Maybe he had actually convinced them that he was innocent and that Matthews had kidnapped the girl. The fucking silver-tongued devil! The mood exploded within Matthews like napalm.

It was only a matter of time now before they found Blue Ridge Hospital. They knew his name, they'd find out his connection there, and they'd find Megan.

In a perfect world, moods don't burn you like torches, juries work pure justice, and revenge befalls sinners in exact proportion to their crimes. In a perfect world Matthews would have kept Megan McCall as his child forever, a replacement for Peter. And Tate Collier would have lived in despair all his life, never knowing where she was – knowing only that she'd fled from him, propelled by undiluted hate.

But there was no chance for such symmetry now. All his hopes had unraveled. And there was only one answer left. To kill the girl and leave. Flee to the West Coast, New England, maybe overseas.

He'd lost his son, Tate Collier would lose his daughter.

A kind of cure, a kind of justice, a kind of revenge . . .

He sped out on to the highway, toward the distant humps of mountains, a sensuous dark line above which no stars became stars and the moon showed as a faint, white crescent of frown.

Cleaning the deep wounds was the hardest part.

She'd found a cheap sewing kit in the bedroom and a bottle of rubbing alcohol in the medicine cabinet.

He took the stitches fine (even though *she* cringed every time the needle pierced his skin). But when Megan poured a capful of alcohol on the wound he shivered frantically at the pain.

'Oh, I'm sorry.'

'No, no,' came his liquid voice. 'Keep at it, Ms Beautiful . . .'

Her eyes teared when she heard the nickname he'd used the night he picked her up.

'Even if you get out, you'll never get past 'em. The dogs. He's got four or five of the big fuckers.'

'You're sure you can't walk?'

'I don't think so,' his voice gurgled. 'No.'

'Okay, you stay here. I saw a door going to the basement. I think I can break it open. I'm going to see if there's a door or window down there. Maybe it'll lead outside.'

He nodded, breathed 'I love . . .' and passed out.

She stacked the cinder blocks around him so that Matthews, glancing down here from the corridor, wouldn't see him.

She listened for a moment to his low, uneven breathing. Then, knife in one hand, she started down the corridor.

Megan was almost to the intersection of the corridors when she heard the creak of a door opening. Then it slammed. Aaron Matthews had returned.

Chapter TWENTY-SIX

They drove in silence through destitute parts of Prince William County. They passed tilled fields, where the taproots of corn were reaching out silently into the dark, red-tinted earth. Barns long ago abandoned. Decaying tract bungalows, where postwar dreams had withered fast – tiny cubes of vinyl – and aluminum-sided homes. Shacks and cars on blocks.

Through Manassas, where the fearsome Rebel Yell was first heard, then through the outlying farms and past the Confederate Cemetery.

'It was him, Tate,' Bett said finally.

'Who?'

'A man came to see me. He said he was her therapist but he wasn't.'

'It was Matthews?'

'He called himself Peters.'

'His son's name was Peter,' Tate mused. Glanced at her. 'What happened?'

She shook her head. 'He seduced me. Nothing really happened but it was enough . . . Oh, Tate, he looked right into my soul. He knew what I wanted to hear. He said exactly the right things.'

You can talk your way into somebody's heart and get them to do whatever you want. Judge or jury, you've got that skill. Words, Tate. Words. You can't see them but they're the most dangerous weapons on earth. Remember that. Be careful, son.

She continued, 'He'd called Brad. I think he pretended he was a cop and told him to get to my house. We were together on the couch . . . I was drunk . . . Oh, Tate.'

Tate put his hand on her knee, squeezed lightly. 'There was nothing you could've done, Bett. He's too good. Somehow, he's done all of this. Dr Hanson, Konnie . . . probably Eckhard too, the teacher. Just to get even with me.' They drove on in silence. Then Tate realized something. 'You got here too quickly.'

'What?'

'You couldn't have been in Baltimore when you got my message.'

'No, I got as far as Takoma Park and turned back.'

'Why?'

A long pause.

'Because I decided it had to stop.' Instinctively she flipped the mirror down and examined her face. Poked at a wrinkle or two. 'I was running after Brad and I should have been going after Megan.' She continued, 'I realized something, Tate. How mad I've been at her.'

'At Megan? Because of what we heard at the Coffee Shop?'

'Oh, Lord, no. That's *my* fault, not hers.' She took a deep breath, flipped the mirror back up. 'No, Tate. I've been mad at her for years. She ended up right in the middle of all our problems. It wasn't her fault. She was born at the wrong time and the wrong place.'

'Yes, she sure was.'

'I neglected her and didn't do the things I should have. . . . I dated, I left her alone. I did the basics, sure. But kids know. They know where your heart is. Here I was running after Joe or Dave or Brad and leaving my daughter. Time for that to stop. I'm just praying it's not too late.'

'We'll get her.'

The roads were deserted here and the air aromatic with smoke from wood cooking fires. The Volvo streaked through a stop sign. Tate skidded into a turn and then headed down a bad road, surrounded by scrub oak, brush and a rusted wire fence.

'We're in trouble, aren't we?' she asked.

'We sure are. They don't put out all-points bulletins anymore. But if they did we'd be the main attraction in one.'

'They don't know my car,' Bett pointed out.

He laughed. 'Oh, that took all of thirty seconds for 'em to track down. Look, there. That's his place.'

Matthews's small bungalow was visible through a stand of trees some distance away. A rusting heating-oil tank sat in the side yard and the stands of uncut grass were outnumbered by patches of red mud. The house was only two miles away from Tate's farm. Convenient staging point for a break-in and kidnapping, he noted.

'What are we going to do?' Bett asked.

Tate didn't answer her. Instead he took the gun out of his pocket. 'We're going to get our daughter,' he said.

Thirty yards, twenty, fifteen.

Tate paused and listened. Silence from inside Matthews's house.

He smelled the scent of woodsmoke and pictured the kidnapper sitting beside the fireplace with Megan bound and gagged at his feet.

The shabby house chilled his heart. He'd seen places like it often. Too often. When he was a commonwealth's attorney he'd always – unlike most big-city prosecutors – visit the crime scenes himself. This was what detectives dubbed a Section

Sixty cottage, referring to the Virginia Penal Code provision for murder. Shotgun killings, domestics, love gone cruel then violent . . . There was a common theme to these houses: small, filthy, silent, brimming with unspoken hate.

The Mercedes wasn't here so it was possible that Matthews hadn't heard the message from the police. Maybe Megan was here now, lying in the bedroom or the basement. Maybe this would be the end of it. But he moved as silently as he could, taking no chances.

He glanced through the window.

The living room was empty, lit only by the glow of embers in the fireplace. He listened for a long moment. Nothing.

The windows were locked but he tested the handle on the door and found it was open. He pushed inside, thinking only as he did so: Why a fire on a warm night?

Oh, no! He lunged for the doorknob but it was too late. The door knocked over the large pail of gasoline.

'God!'

Instinctively Tate grabbed for the bucket as the pink wave of gas flowed on to the floor and into the fireplace.

'What?' Bett cried.

The gas ignited and with a whoosh a huge ball of flame exploded through the living room.

'Megan!' Tate cried, turning away from the flames and falling on to the porch. His sleeve was on fire. He slapped out the flames.

'She's in there? *She's in there?*' Bett shouted in panic and ran to the window.

Scrabbling away from the flowing gasoline, Tate grabbed Bett and pulled her back. He covered his face with his hand, felt the searing heat take the hairs off the back of his fingers.

'Megan!' Bett cried. She broke the window in with her elbow. She peered inside for a moment but then leapt back as a hand of flame burst through the window at her. If she hadn't leapt aside the fire would have consumed her face and hair.

Tate ran around the back of the cottage, broke in the window in one of the bedrooms, which was already filling with dense smoke.

No sign of the girl.

He ran to the other bedroom – the cottage had only two – and saw that she wasn't there. The flames were already burning through the door, which, with a sudden burst, exploded inward. In the light from the fire Tate could see that Megan wasn't in this room either. He could also see that it wasn't a bedroom but an office. There were stacks of newspaper clippings, magazines, books and folders. Maps, charts and diagrams.

Sirens sounded in the distance.

Bett came up behind him. There was a burn on her arm but she was otherwise okay. 'Tate, I can't find her!' she screamed.

'I don't think she's here. She's not in either of these rooms and there's no basement.'

'Where *is* she?'

'The answer's in there,' he shouted. 'He only set the trap so nobody could find any clues to where he's got her.'

He picked up several bricks and shattered the glass and wooden grid in the window. 'Oh, brother,' he muttered. And climbed inside, feeling the unnerving pain as a shard of glass sliced through his palm.

The heat inside was astonishing, smoke and embers and flecks of burning paper swirling around him, and he realized that the flames weren't the worst problem – it was the heated air and lack of oxygen. He didn't think he could stay here for more than a minute.

He raced to the desk and grabbed all the papers and notebooks he could, ran to the window and flung them outside, crying to Bett, 'Get it all away from the house.' He went back for more. He got two more armfuls before the heat grew too much. He dove out the window and rolled to the ground heavily as the ceiling collapsed and a swell of flame puffed out the window.

He lay, exhausted, gasping, on the ground. Dizzy and hurt. Wondering why on earth Bett was doing a funny little dance around his arm. Then he understood. The file folder he held had been burning and she was stamping out the flames.

The sirens were getting closer.

'Great,' he muttered. 'Now they're gonna add arson to my rap sheet.'

Bett helped him up and they gathered all the notebooks and files he'd flung into the back yard. They ran to the car, started up and skidded out of the drive, passing the first of the fluorescent green fire trucks that were speeding toward the house.

They turned north and drove for ten minutes until Tate figured there was no chance of being spotted. He parked near the quarry in Manassas. A grim, eerie place that looked like it should have been a serial killer's stalking ground though to Tate's knowledge there'd never been any crime committed here worse than pot-smoking and drinking beer and sloe gin from open containers.

Tate in fact had snuck past the gate himself last year, with a date, to park and make out. He shamefully remembered that night briefly now, recalling that he'd been excited that the young woman had wanted to come here for the adventure of it – then realizing soberly that the only reason she'd suggested it was that she couldn't invite him home: she was twenty-one and still lived with her parents.

Tate and Bett pored over the singed files and papers, looking for some clue as to where Matthews might have taken Megan.

The files were mostly articles, psychiatric diagnostic reports, medical evaluations. He also found surveillance photos of Megan. Dozens of them. And of Tate's house and Bett's. Matthews had been planning this for months; some of the pictures had been taken during the winter. In one notebook Megan's daily routine was described in obsessive detail.

More patient reports.

More articles.

More diaries. With shaking hands Tate and Bett read through them all but there was no clue as to any other residences, apartments, houses where he might have taken the girl.

'There's nothing,' Bett barked in frustration. 'We've looked at everything.' Tears on her face.

Tate gazed at the mess of scorched papers and files on their laps. His eye fell on the patient diagnostic report. Then another. He flipped through them quickly. Then read the name and address of the hospital where the patients had been evaluated.

He snatched up his cellphone and, eyes on one of the reports, made a call to directory assistance for Calvert, Virginia. He asked for the number for the Blue Ridge Mental Health Facility.

'Please be out of order,' he whispered.

'Why on earth?' Bett asked.

'Please . . .'

'We're sorry,' the electronic voice reported, 'there is no listing for that name. Do you have another request?'

He clicked the phone off. 'That's where she is. An old mental hospital in the Shenandoahs.' He tapped the reports. 'Matthews was a shrink. I'd guess he was on the staff there a few years ago. It's probably closed and that's where he's taken her.'

'You sure?'

'No. But do we have any other leads?'

'Go, Tate.'

He pulled out on to the highway and steered toward the interstate. Thinking with frustration that they'd have to drive the entire way right on the speed limit. They could hardly afford to be stopped now.

Glass knife in front of her, Megan walked through the hallways.

There was silence, then the shuffling of footsteps. More silence.

I hate the quiet worse than his footsteps.

I'm with you there, Crazy Megan shares.

Then the steps again but from a different place as if the intruder were a ghost materializing at will.

Five minutes passed. Then another noise near by, behind her. A sharp inhalation of breath. Megan gasped and turned quickly. Aaron Matthews was twenty feet away. His eyes widened in surprise. She stumbled backwards and fell over a table, went down hard. Grunted in pain as the edge of the table dug into her kidney.

Despite the pain, though, she leapt to her feet, lifting the knife. She assumed he'd charge at her.

But he didn't. He merely frowned and said, 'Oh, my God, Megan, are you all right?'

In a crouch, eyes fiery, breath hard, gripping the cloth handle of her wicked knife. Staring at his dark eyes, his large shoulders and long arms. Why wasn't he coming at her?

'Wait,' he said with a heart-tugging plea in his voice. 'Please, don't run. *Please.*'

She hesitated.

He sighed. 'Oh, I know you're upset, Megan, honey. I know you're scared, . . . You hate me and you have every right to. But please. Just listen to me.' He held his hands up. 'I don't have a knife or gun or anything. Please, will you listen?'

His eyes were so sincere and his voice so imploring . . .

'Please.'

Megan kept her tight grip on the knife. But she straightened up. 'Go ahead,' she whispered uneasily. 'I'm listening.'

'Good,' he said. And offered her a smile.

Chapter TWENTY-SEVEN

'I didn't know you'd gotten out of your room,' Aaron Matthews said.

'Cell,' she corrected bluntly.

'Cell,' he conceded, watching her eyes carefully. 'But I should've guessed.' He laughed. 'You're the independent sort. Nobody was going to lock you away. It's one of the things I love about you.'

Matthews noted how she fixed her gaze on his eyes. How her pale lashes stuttered when he'd said the word 'love'.

How had she done it? he wondered. He'd been over the cell so carefully – and the lock was still on the door. Had she gotten through the ceiling? The wall? And she was wearing some of his clothes. So she'd found his living area. What else did she know?

However it had happened, Matthews was surprised. It showed more mettle than he'd expected from the spoiled little whiner.

'Are you all right? Just tell me that.' He looked her up and down.

No answer.

He continued, 'I'm sorry about your clothes. When you

passed out from the medicine I gave you . . . well, you had an accident. I'm sorry. I didn't think it would happen. I'm washing your clothes in the laundry room here. They're drying now. They should be ready soon.'

He glanced at the knife in her hand. A long shard. He thought at first that there was something about the glass itself that was particularly unnerving, the sharp, green edge of the triangle. But then he decided that, no, it was her *face* that scared him. She was prepared – no, eager – to use the weapon. And so much in control . . . she'd be a hard one to crack. Harder than in Hanson's office, where her defenses were down and her self-esteem bubbling near empty.

He eased forward. 'Oh, Megan, I'm so sorry.'

The point of the knife tilted toward him and Matthews froze. He said in his best therapist's tone, 'I didn't want it to happen this way.'

He fell silent. And to fill the intolerable gap of silence she asked, 'What way?'

'This . . .' He lifted his arms to the hallways. 'If there'd been anything else I could have done, I would have. I promise you.'

'What do you mean?'

He leaned against the wall, closed his eyes. 'You don't really know me. But I know you. I've known you for a long time.'

She shook her heard, frowning, confused. The tip of the knife was pointed lower.

'My name's Aaron Matthews . . .'

She'd've learned his real name, of course – from looking through the desk in his rooms. But tell someone the truth – no matter how much you've lied to them in the past – and you nudge them closer toward you, if ever so slightly. He continued right away – Matthews had a spell to cast and spells work best when cast quickly. 'I worked with your father on a case last year. He hired me as an expert witness. To evaluate a suspect. We were talking before the trial. Just making conversation. And I asked about children, if he had any, and he said . . .' Matthews paused and his face grew somber. He continued, 'I'm sorry, honey, but he said no, he didn't.'

Megan's beautiful light eyes widened. Shocked for a moment. Then they grew deeply sad, as they had in Hanson's office. A child betrayed, a child alone.

What are the bears whispering to you?

'But I'd heard somebody mention his daughter and I asked him about you. He looked embarrassed and said that, well, yes, he *did* have a daughter. But she lived with her mother. He said you were technically his child but that was all. I told him about my son. Peter. See, he had some problems at birth. Serious mental problems.'

Another flicker of lash. So she knew about him too. He said, looking down, 'But I've always felt that, despite all that, I loved my boy and wanted him to be with me. I mentioned that to your father. But he didn't say anything. I asked him how often he saw you . . . He said virtually never. I asked him about you and he didn't seem to know much at all. And then—' Matthews stopped abruptly, like a man finding himself in a minefield.

'What?'

'Nothing.'

'No, tell me,' she said with faint desperation in her voice.

'He said some things about you.'

'Please.' The knife was pointed straight down. 'I want to know.'

'He said being more involved with a child would be . . . awkward.'

'No he didn't,' she whispered. 'He didn't say that at all, did he?'

'I'm not sure . . .' Matthews stammered, putting a vulnerable look on his face.

She muttered, 'He said being involved with a child would be inconvenient. Right?'

'Yes,' Matthews conceded, sighing. 'I'm so sorry, Megan. But that's what he said. And when I heard it, all I could think of was how I hoped you had a good relationship with your mother. I hoped *someone* cared. I felt so bad for you.'

A faint laugh then her face went still. 'My mother. Yeah, right.'

He cocked his head, offering her another sympathetic glance. And continued, 'Well, I went to see her. When you were in school one day.'

'You did?'

Matthews eased a few inches closer. He decided that anger wouldn't work with Megan, unlike with her boyfriend, Josh. The madder she got the more dangerous she'd be. No, the way to get inside her defenses was to tap into her sorrow and loneliness.

'I lied, Megan. I'll admit it. I told Bett I was a counselor with your school and I wanted to know how you were doing. I was shocked to find that she didn't have much time for you either. She told me she was engaged, trying to make that relationship work, was totally absorbed with Brad, didn't have much time for . . . well, she said, for babysitting.'

'She said *that*?' Megan gasped.

'In fairness she said you were very mature and didn't need a lot of hand-holding.'

'How would she know?' Megan muttered.

Matthews swayed toward her but the coldness returned to her eyes and she asked, 'But why the fuck did you kidnap me?'

He stopped.

'Because I wanted to give you a second chance, Megan.'

'Kidnapping me? What kind of chance is that?'

He looked down and rocked back and forth on his feet, moving a good six inches closer to her. 'Oh, Megan, yes, I kidnapped you. But I'd never hurt you. That was the last thing on my mind.' If she'd seen the room, she'd probably also seen the kitchen. He said, 'I can prove it. I'll show you the kitchen. It's filled with food that you like. I found out what you liked and I bought a lot of it.'

She nodded. Her defenses slipped a bit more. 'You were the one following me for the past couple weeks.'

'That's right. I followed you. And I talked to people about you too. Teachers, students. And the more I learned about you, the more I couldn't understand your parents. You're creative, you're funny, you're pretty, you have a sense of humor, you were artistic . . . You were everything a teenage girl ought to be. Why didn't they want you? Your parents, I mean?'

Her lip began to tremble. She wiped tears.

'It was so unfair,' he whispered. 'I wanted to give you the love that they never did. Parental love, I'm speaking of. I hope you know that . . . I think you're beautiful but I don't desire you physically.' He nodded toward her padded cell. 'I could have done that when you were unconscious if I'd wanted to.'

Her eyes told him that she understood it. That she'd checked her body for tenderness, for moisture.

But, once again, the eyes hardened. She asked, 'But there's more, isn't there? There's another side to it.'

He smiled. 'Oh, you're smart, Megan. You're very smart. Yes, there's another side. *I* wanted another chance too. I told you about my son. The problems I mentioned? They were pretty serious. My wife . . . she drank and had a Valium habit when she was pregnant. I tried to get her to stop but she wouldn't. Permanent prenatal damage . . . Oh, I wanted a normal child. Someone I could spend time with. Have fun with. Someone I could spoil.' He remembered something Bett had told him a few hours before. 'I wanted someone to play games with, to spend Christmas and Easter with, Thanksgiving. To make oatmeal and pancakes for. To hang out with on Sunday in sweats and sneakers and read the paper and rake leaves.'

From somewhere, he summoned a tear.

'You wanted me to be your daughter,' Megan said.

'Yes! But there was no way you would've agreed on your own. Or even listened to me. You would've thought I was some kind of crank and called the police. So I did what I had to. I waited until I had a chance – Dr Hanson's mother getting sick – and I arranged with him to see you.'

'That part was true?'

'Oh, yes. Of course it's true. We're friends, Hanson and me.' He smiled indulgently. 'Though I think I'm a better therapist than he is. I get right to the core of the problem.'

'Yeah, you sure do.' She offered a faint smile in return.

'You didn't like those letters, I know. But I had to make you see how angry you were with your parents. I had to make you see the truth.'

'That's why you made me write them?'

'Yes.'

'What did you do with them? Did you send them?'

He frowned. 'The letters? No, I threw them out. Writing them was just for you, Megan. I thought maybe, here, we could get to know each other for a while. I'd hoped you'd stay maybe for a few weeks, a month. If it worked out, fine. We could move to San Francisco, you could start college there in the fall.'

He'd moved another few feet closer to her. He was slumped, diminished, looking mournfully at the floor. Matthews had decided how she'd die. He'd strangle her. Her eyes would grow wide and he'd stare at them, drink them in as she died. Pull the glass knife from her hand and get a grip on her neck. Squeeze and squeeze and squeeze until the tip of her protruding tongue stopped quivering. And squeeze some more after that.

It was the way Peter had killed the slut who'd tried to seduce him. Maybe it was the way Peter himself had died.

The body was so mutilated the prison doctor hadn't been able to be certain of the cause of death.

Tears flooded the eyes of the inconvenient child.

'Oh, Megan, I'm sorry. I'm so sorry. I just thought that you deserved so much more than you had.'

She was shivering with the sobs.

'A father who wanted to be rid of you. What a terrible thing . . . He wanted to get you out of his life and get back to those ridiculous young women he chased after. And your mother . . . a dear woman but a child herself really. I thought about all sorts of things – how I could adopt you, get you into a foster home . . .'

'You really thought that?' she asked, wiping her face. Her attention was wavering from the glass blade. Her hand was in the shadows at her side. He couldn't tell whether it was pointed downward or at him.

'Yes, I sure did. I talked to a lawyer about adoption. He said I wouldn't have a chance, not with your natural parents around, however neglectful they were.' His voice was very soft, lulling.

Megan wiped her face again. 'I just wanted to be loved.' Her voice was choked.

'And they didn't love you, did they? They didn't give you any love at all.'

'No.'

'Oh, I would've done things so differently . . . and that's why I took this chance. I'm risking life in prison just to see if something might work out between us. I just wanted you to have a home.' He too was crying now. 'I just wanted a family! That's all *I've* ever wanted too.'

She was sobbing uncontrollably now, hand over her face. 'Yes! That's it. A home. I never had a home. I wanted a father so badly.'

Matthews stepped closer, reached out a tentative hand and

touched her cheek, wiped away a tear. He could almost feel her under his hands, peeing and thrashing as she died. He'd leave her out for the dogs. So that Collier would think she'd died as painfully as Peter had.

'I wish I could have done it differently,' he said. 'I mean, this place is so disgusting, Megan. But I didn't have any choice. For both our sakes.'

'I just—'

He reached out his other hand and put his arm around her shoulder. Rubbed her back.

'I just wanted a home . . . only a home.' She struggled to breathe.

'I know you did.' His right hand moved down her face to her neck. His left slipped down her arm until he gripped the glass knife she held.

He gently pulled it out of her hand.

Got you!

But then he glanced down, frowning. It wasn't a knife at all. In his hand was a plastic Bic pen. But he'd seen the blade . . . He looked into her face.

Saw the leering smile.

'Nice try,' Megan whispered.

And with her left hand she jammed the glass blade deep into his side. Once, then again. And again.

A flash of terrible pain shot through him and Matthews howled. He twisted hard away from her and the blade snapped on a rib, leaving a long glass splinter inside of him.

Now Megan screamed – an insane wail – and as her captor groped for the wound she slammed her open palm into his face. A huge pop as his nose broke and blood spurted. He went down on his knees. She kicked him near the knife wound and he coughed as his vision went black.

She came forward but he swam back to consciousness quickly and now it was his fist that connected with her jaw, sending her backwards into the wall. By the time he was on his feet she was disappearing down the dark corridor.

He touched the wound. The pain was astonishing, terrible.

But it was nothing compared with the feeling of shock that raged through him. *She's* the one who fooled me! Suckered me in nice and close, got *my* defenses down. My God, the whole time I thought I was playing her but she led me right into the trap . . .

Her father's daughter, Matthews thought in fury and disgust.

He dropped to his knees and began working the fragments of glass out of his wound, gasping and savoring the astonishing pain. He wanted to remember it. He wanted to feel what Megan was about to experience.

Chapter TWENTY-EIGHT

The basement . . .

Megan plunged into the dim corridors of the hospital looking for the basement.

Her jaw ached and the back of her head too – from where she'd slammed it into the wall after he hit her. For just a moment she'd thought about leaping on him again – seeing him lying there, blood filling his shirt, blood dripping from his nose. He'd looked half dead. But no, she wasn't sure that he was hurt as badly as he seemed.

He lied with words, he'd lie with actions.

So she ran – to find the basement door.

She heard Matthews's unearthly scream – it seemed to shake the walls – and then footsteps. Part of it was pain – the breathless sound. But part of it was rage too.

She made slow circles through the corridors until she found the door she'd seen earlier, the one leading to the basement. She grabbed a cinder block and smashed it down on the hasp and lock, which snapped off easily.

Megan flung the door open, looked down into the musty place. For a moment she was paralyzed.

No choice, girl, Crazy Megan the tour guide shouts. *Move, move, move.*

But Josh, she protested silently, I can't leave him.

Hey, you die, he dies. Go!

She clomped down the stairs and found herself in a dimly lit warren of corridors. Trotting slowly from room to room, she took care to avoid the standing water so she wouldn't leave footprints he could follow.

Please, a door, a window . . . Oh, please.

She heard the creak of footsteps from the ceiling above her as Matthews made his way to the door she'd just broken open. She found a door leading outside. It was locked. And the windows too were sealed. Another door. Nailed shut.

Goddamn him! C.M. blurts. *Why'd he padlock the fucking door upstairs if we can't get out this way?*

Megan didn't bother to answer. She couldn't figure it out either. She returned to a room near the base of the stairs and glanced again at one of the windows. The bars on these were wider than the ones on the main floor but she doubted that she could get through.

Fucking hips.

Don't start! Megan started to turn away. Then paused, looked back. Thinking: Okay, maybe I can't get through the bars. But I can make him *think* I did.

She smashed the glass and pushed an overturned plastic bucket beneath it so that it looked like she'd climbed out.

Then she ran back into the warren of dark storerooms to find someplace to hide.

Most of the cardboard boxes piled in the rooms were too small to conceal her. And she didn't have the strength to pull herself up into the pipes that ran along the ceiling.

His steps were approaching the door upstairs. Then he started down.

Megan ran into a cluttered storeroom, the farthest one from

the stairs. It was filled with cartons, small ones again. But over to the side, in the shadows, was a long metal box. It was almost too obvious a choice to hide in but this room was nowhere near the window where she'd faked her escape. And it was pitch dark. Matthews might not even see it.

Could she get it open? And was it empty?

But Megan stopped asking questions. Matthews was now in the basement. A shuffle of footsteps, a moaning wheeze from the pain of the wounds, words muttered to himself.

Now! Crazy Megan prods her. *Go, girl!*

Megan unlatched the trunk.

It took all her strength to lift the thick lid.

And it took all her willpower not to scream as she looked inside.

The blue-white flesh, the limp hair, the closed eyes, a dark, shriveled penis, the long yellow fingernails . . . The terrible Y incision that covered the young man's entire torso. And the cuts and black gouges over his body.

It was Matthews's son, Peter. She recognized the eerie face from the newspaper clipping.

Oh, God . . . My God . . . Tate, Bett . . . Somebody!

The footsteps were closer now. They sounded only thirty or forty feet away.

I can't do it, she thought. No way in hell.

Get inside, Crazy Megan chokes. *You have to.*

Fight him with your fists, she told herself, or you hide in here. Those're your choices.

A moment's pause. The moaning was now right outside the doorway, it seemed. Then Megan closed her eyes – as if that would lessen the horror – and climbed into the box, lying down on the corpse, on her back, shivering fiercely. She let the lid down. The air stank sweetly. Formaldehyde, rotting scents, old skin.

She felt the cold.

Nothing's colder than cold flesh.

Then she heard, faintly, a moan very near. Aaron Matthews was in the room.

Crossing a gap in the Shenandoahs, Tate glanced out the window of Bett's car at the darkened bungalows and ramshackle farmhouses, abandoned barns, the black pits that opened into the network of caverns that laced the earth beneath the Shenandoahs and the Blue Ridge.

They sped past walls of ominous forest – the stark pines, the scrub oak, the sedge, the young kudzu and Virginia creeper. Tate swore he saw eyes peering at them and he thought of the Dead Reb once again.

Ten minutes later, well into the Blue Ridge, Tate pulled Bett's Volvo into an all-night gas station. The elderly attendant glanced at them cautiously when he asked about the Blue Ridge Hospital.

'That old place. Phew.' The man cast a dark look westward.

'Where is it?'

'You get back on the interstate and go one more exit . . .'

'We'd rather stick to back roads, if we can.' The state troopers would be looking for him on the highway, a fact Tate didn't share.

The man cocked his head, shrugged. 'Well, that road there. Route one-seventeen? Take it west ten, twelve miles till you see a Buy-Rite gas station. Then go left on Palmer and just keep going.'

'We'll see the place? The hospital?'

'Oh, you'll see it. Can't miss it. But I'd wait till sunup. You don't wanna go there this time of night, no sir. But you asked for directions, not opinions.'

Tate handed over a twenty and they sped off down the road.

It was a half-hour later that a no-nonsense siren burst to

life a quarter-mile behind them. It was a county trooper. The light bar flashed explosively in Tate's rear-view mirror. He accelerated hard.

'You think he knows it's us?' Bett asked.

'Oh, yeah, he knows.' Tate's foot wavered. 'What do I do?'

'Drive like hell,' Bett suggested.

He did.

For about two miles.

The Swedes make a good car but it was no match for the souped-up engine of the pursuing Plymouth. 'Can't make it,' he told her.

He eased up on the gas. 'I'll talk to him. Maybe he'll at least send a car to the hospital.'

'No,' Bett said. 'Pull over.'

'What?' Tate asked, jockeying the skidding car on to the gravel shoulder.

Bett ripped her purse open and dug inside. She paused, took a deep breath, then sat upright, staring in the rear-view mirror at herself, stroking her cheek as Tate had seen her do so often.

What's she up to? he wondered.

'Bett!' he cried as she lifted the nail-file to her face and dragged it hard across her skin.

Blood poured from a gash deep in her cheek.

'Oh,' Bett wheezed. 'It hurts.'

Tate stared at the blood, running more black than red down her neck and falling on to her chest in delicate paisleys.

'Get out of the car!' reverberated the metallic voice through the rectangular mouth of the PA speaker atop the car.

The young trooper stood beside the open door of his squad car, aiming at Tate's head a blue-black pistol dwarfed by the lawman's huge hand. In his other he held the microphone.

'Get out of that vehicle! Keep your hands up.'

For a moment no one moved.

And then in a blur Bett's door was open – so fast Tate thought that another deputy had snuck up behind them unseen and pulled her out.

She screamed shrilly as she rolled on to the grassy shoulder. The leather strap of her purse was wound around her wrists as if she'd been tied up. Without the use of her hands she fell hard. Dust mixed with the blood covering her face.

'Help me!' she cried. 'He kidnapped me!'

'Don't move. Nobody move!' the trooper called, swinging the muzzle toward Bett. Tate sat perfectly still, hands on the wheel.

Bett scrabbled toward the cop.

'He's got a knife!' she cried. 'Help me, please. He cut me. I'm bleeding. Help me!' She put the harrowing wail of a frightened child into her voice as she stumbled forward. 'He was going to rape me! Get me away from him! Oh, please . . . Oh . . .'

The trooper gave in to his instincts. 'Over here, miss. You'll be all right. He's that fella from Prince William, isn't he? The one killed that girl? Where's the knife?'

'In his belt. He picked me up at a rest stop,' she cried. 'He kidnapped me!'

'Put your hands up!' the trooper called over the microphone. 'And I mean now!'

Tate did.

'What happened?' the cop asked Bett, who was stumbling closer.

'Cut me . . . I need a doctor . . .' The words were lost in the sobbing.

'You in the car. Leave your right hand up and with your left reach out the window and open the door. Don't lower that right hand.'

Tate didn't move.

'I'm not telling you again! I have a—'

'Put it down!' came Bett's raw scream from inches behind his head. Tate's pistol was resting at the cop's throat.

'Oh, shit.'

'Do it!'

'I've got him covered, lady. You do anything to me and he's gone. I'll shoot him. I swear . . .' But he said this out of shame, not resolve, and when Bett screamed, 'We're after my daughter and I'll kill you right now if I have to,' the cop's disgusted grunt was followed by the sound of his large pistol hitting the dirt.

Bett stepped away from the man, who towered over her. He went limp as he saw the ferocity in her face, realizing just how close to death he'd come. He sagged against the car.

'All right,' Bett muttered. 'Lie down on the ground. There. On your stomach.'

Tate was out of the car and jogging toward them.

'There're other troopers coming, lady. They'll be here in minutes.'

'All the more reason to *move*!'

He eased down. Bett handed the cop's pistol to Tate.

'Cuff him and let's go,' she said.

But Tate put his hand on her shoulder. 'No. You're staying.'

'No, Tate,' Bett said, holding a wad of Kleenexes up to her bloody chin. 'I want to come.'

What could he say to her? That there wasn't anything she could do and Tate needed to focus on saving Megan – if she could be saved? That it was important for her to stay here and tell the police exactly what had happened, send them out to the hospital? They were both sure-fire arguments. But Tate answered instead from his heart and told her the truth. Simply: 'I don't want to risk losing you.'

'But—'

'No, stay here.'

She looked at the dark blood on the Kleenex and up at

Tate once more. She nodded.

'Now, listen to me,' he said gravely, 'when they get here, just set the gun down and put your hands up. They'll be nervous and looking to shoot. Do exactly what they say. You hear me?'

She nodded. He touched her cheek, wiping away some blood.

'A sexy woman with a scar – won't be a man in the county'll keep his hands off you.'

'You'll get her, won't you, Tate?'

'I'll get her.'

He kissed her forehead and ran to the car.

He floored the accelerator, splattering the squad car with gravel and dirt. As he drove over a crest in the road, the tach nosing into the red crescent of the warning zone, he caught a glimpse of Bett in the rear-view mirror, crouching beside the prone trooper, undoubtedly apologizing earnestly. Still, the pistol that was clapped in both her hands was pointed steadily at his face.

She couldn't take it any more.

Crazy Megan was gone, dead and buried or sleeping with the fishes.

The depleted air suffocated her. The smells – the rot and the sweet scent from embalmed skin – wrapped themselves around her throat and squeezed.

Which was bad enough. But then the panic started to sizzle through her body like electricity. The claustrophobia.

'No, no, no,' she said or maybe she just thought it. 'No, no, nonono. Let me out, let me out, let me out . . .'

Not even worried that Matthews was outside, waiting for her. Maybe he was right there, waiting to kill her, maybe not. It didn't matter; she couldn't stay inside a moment longer.

Megan pushed against the lid of the coffin.

It didn't move.

She tried again. Nothing.

'Ah,' she gasped. 'Oh please, God, no . . .'

He'd locked her in! She heard a wild laugh outside. Words she couldn't distinguish. More laughter.

More words, louder: '. . . two having fun together . . . likes you . . . Peter likes you . . .'

'Let me out let me out letmeoutoutoutout!'

Her voice rose to a wild keening, her whole body shivered in violent spasms.

'You fucker you fuck let me outoutoutout!'

She didn't have any idea what words she was saying. It was too much for her.

With both her fists Megan pounded on the lid, banged it with her head, feeling with horror Peter's cold face against her neck, his cold penis against her thigh.

From outside Aaron Matthews beat on the lid too, responding to her pounding. Then more laughter. And finally more tapping, like a drummer, keeping perfect time with the rhythm of her raw screams. Five unbearable minutes later two latches clicked and the lid began to rise.

No subtlety, no nuance . . .

Tate Collier came to the end of Palmer Road and saw the hospital in front of him. He aimed Bett's car directly toward the gate, got his speed up to about forty and bounded over logs and potholes in the neglected surface. He saw the infamous gray Mercedes parked in the staff-only carport. He saw a faint light in one of the windows.

He had no plan other than the obvious and as he skidded around a fallen pine and straightened for the final assault on the gate he pressed the accelerator down harder, sealing his resolve.

Tires spat gravel. He pressed his hands into the steering

wheel, pinning himself into the seat. The car plowed through the wrought iron. The air bag popped with an astonishingly loud bang. He'd forgotten about it and hadn't closed his eyes. He was momentarily blinded and lost control of the car. When he could see again he found the vehicle skidding sideways, narrowly missing the Mercedes. The Volvo crashed obliquely into the cinder blocks, stunning him.

Tate leapt out of the car and ran to the first door he could find. Gripping his pistol hard, he flung all his weight against the double panels.

Expecting them to be locked.

But the doors swung open with virtually no resistance and he stumbled head first into a large, dim lobby.

He saw shadows, shapes of furniture, angles of walls, unlit lamps, dust motes circling in the air.

He saw faint shafts of predawn blue light bleeding in through the windows.

But he never saw the bat or tire iron or whatever it was that hummed through the air behind him and caught him with a glancing blow just above the ear.

IV

THE SILENCE OF THE DEED

Chapter TWENTY-NINE

A hand stroked his hair.

Tate slowly opened his eyes, which stung fiercely from his own sweat. He tried to focus on the face before him. He believed momentarily that the soft fingers were Bett's; she'd been the first person in his thoughts as he came to consciousness.

But he found that the blue eyes he gazed into were Megan's.

'Hey, honey,' he wheezed. 'Fancy meeting you here.'

'Dad.' Her face was pale, hair pasted to her head with sweat, her hands bloody. But she didn't seem too badly hurt.

They were in the lobby of the decrepit hospital. His hands were bound behind him with scratchy rope. His vision was blurry. He tried to sit up and nearly fainted from the pain that roared in his temple. He gasped and collapsed back against a moldy couch.

Aaron Matthews was sitting on a chair near by.

What astonishing black eyes he has, Tate thought. Like dark lasers. They turned to you as if you were the only person in the universe. Why, patients would tell him anything. He understood why Bett had been powerless earlier that night. Konnie too. And Megan.

Then he saw that Matthews was hurt. A large patch of

blood covered the side of his shirt and he was sweating. He glanced at Megan. She gave a weak smile and nodded. He lowered his head to the girl's shoulder. When the pain subsided Tate looked up. 'Hey, you've lost those five pounds you wanted to,' he said to her. 'You're lean and mean.'

'It was ten,' she joked.

Matthews said, 'Well, Tate Collier. Well . . .'

And such a smooth, baritone voice. But not phoney or slick. So natural, so comforting. Patients would cling to every word he uttered.

'I was just doing my job,' Tate finally said to him. 'Peter's trial, I mean. The evidence was there. The jury believed . . .'

Megan frowned and Tate explained about the trial and the boy's murder in prison.

The girl scowled, said to Matthews, 'I knew you'd never worked with him. What a liar.'

Matthews didn't even notice her. He crossed his arms. 'You probably don't know it, Collier, but I used to watch you. After Pete died I'd go to your trials. I'd sit in the back of the gallery for hours and hours. Just watching you. You know what struck me? You reminded me of myself in therapy sessions. Talking to the patients. Leading them where they didn't want to go. You did exactly the same with the witnesses and the juries.'

Tate said nothing.

Matthews smiled briefly. 'And I learned some things about the law. *Mens rea*. The state of a killer's mind – he has to *intend* the death in order to be guilty of murder. Well, that was you, all right, in Pete's trial. You *murdered* Pete. You intended him to die.'

'My job was to prosecute cases as best I could.'

'*If*,' Matthews pounced, 'that was true then why did you quit prosecuting? Why did you turn tail and run?'

'Because I regretted what happened to your son,' Tate answered.

Matthews lowered his sweaty, stubbly face. 'You looked at my boy and said, "You're dead." You stood up in court and felt the power flowing through you. And you *liked* it. You knew how dangerous it could be.'

Tate looked around the room. 'You did all this? And you went after all the others – Konnie and Hanson and Eckhard? Bett, too.'

'Mom?' Megan whispered.

'No, she's okay,' Tate reassured her.

'I had to stop you,' Matthews said. 'You kept coming. You wouldn't listen to reason. You wouldn't do what you were supposed to.'

'This is where you were committed, right?'

'Him?' Megan asked. 'I thought he'd worked here.'

'I thought so too,' Tate said, 'but then I remembered testimony at Peter's trial. No. He *was* a therapist but *he* was the one committed here.' Nodding at Matthews.

Mr Bogan: *Now, Doctor Rothstein, could you give an opinion of the source and nature of Peter's difficulties?*

Dr Rothstein: *Yessir. Peter displays socialization problems. He is more comfortable with inanimate creations – stories and books and cartoons and the like – than with people. He also suffers from what I call affect deficit. The reason, from reviewing his medical records, appears to be that his father would lock him in his room for long periods of time – weeks, even months – and the only contact the boy would have with anyone was with his father, Aaron. He wouldn't even let the boy's mother see him. Peter withdrew into his books and television. Apparently the only time the boy spent with his mother and others was when his father was committed in mental hospitals for bipolar depression and delusional behavior.*

Matthews said, 'I was here, let's see, on six intakes. Must have been four years altogether. I was like a jailhouse lawyer, Collier.

As soon as the patients heard I was a therapist they started coming to me.'

'So *you* were Patient Matthews,' Megan said, eyes widening.

'That's my Megan,' Matthews said with something that might have been real pride.

She said to Tate, 'They closed this place because of a bunch of suicides. I thought it was Peter who'd killed them. Or talked them into killing themselves.'

'But it was you?' Tate asked Matthews.

'The DSM-III claimed I was sociopathic – well, they call it an antisocial/criminal personality now. How delicate of them. I knew Richmond was looking for an excuse to close down places like this. So I simply helped them. Too understaffed and too incompetent to keep patients from killing themselves. The place was a poster boy for budget cuts. I got transferred to a halfway house and one bright, sunny May morning, I walked out the front door. Moved to Prince William. And started planning how to destroy you.' Matthews winced and pressed his side. The bleeding seemed to have stopped and the wound, unfortunately, didn't look that severe.

Tate recalled something else from the trial and asked, 'What about your wife?'

Matthews said nothing but his eyes responded. And Tate understood. 'She was your first victim, wasn't she? Did you talk her into killing herself? Or maybe just slip some drugs into her wine during dinner?'

'She was vulnerable,' Matthews responded. 'Most therapists are.'

Tate asked, 'What was she trying to do? Take Peter away from you?'

'Yes, she was. She wanted to place him in a hospital full-time. She shouldn't have meddled. *I* understood Peter. No one else did.'

'But you made Peter the way he was,' Megan blurted. 'You cut him off from the world.'

The girl was right. Tate recalled the defense's expert witness, Dr Rothstein, testifying that if you arrest development by isolation before the age of eight, social – and communications – skills will never develop. You've basically destroyed the child for ever.

Tate remembered too how he'd handled the expert witness's testimony.

The Court: *The Commonwealth may cross-examine.*

Mr Collier: *Dr Rothstein, thank you for that trip down memory lane about the defendant's sad history. But let me ask you: Psychologically, is the defendant capable of premeditated murder?*

Dr Rothstein: *Peter Matthews is a troubled—*

Mr Collier: *Your honor?*

The Court: *Please answer the question, sir.*

Dr Rothstein: *I—*

Mr Collier: *Is the defendant capable of premeditated murder?*

Dr Rothstein: *Yes, but—*

Mr Collier: *No further questions.*

'All he needed was *me*!' Matthews now raged. 'He didn't need anyone else in his life. We'd spend *hours* together – when my wife wasn't trying to sneak him out the door.'

'Did you love him that much?' Tate asked.

'You don't have a clue, do you? Why, you know what we did? Peter and I? We *talked*. About everything. About snakes, about stars, about floods, about explorers, about airplanes, about the mind . . .'

Delusional ramblings, Tate imagined. Poor Peter, baffled and lonely, undoubtedly could do nothing but listen.

Yet . . . with a sorrowful twist deep within him, Tate

realized that this was something Megan and he *didn't* do. They didn't talk at all. They never had.

And won't ever, he realized. We've lost that chance forever.

Their captor fell silent, looking into a corner of the hospital lobby, lost in a memory or thought or some confused delusion.

Finally Tate said, 'So, Aaron. Tell me what you want. Tell me exactly.' He closed his eyes, fighting the incredible pain in his head.

After a moment Matthews said, 'I want justice. Pure and simple. I'm going to kill your daughter and you're going to watch. You'll live with that sight for the rest of your life.'

So it's come to this . . .

Tate sighed and thought, as he had so often on the way to the jury box or the podium in a debate, *all right, time to get to work.*

'I don't know how you can have justice, Aaron,' Tate said to him. 'I just don't know. In all my years practicing law—'

Matthews's face writhed in disgust. 'Oh, stop right there.'

'What?' Tate asked innocently.

'I hear it,' the psychiatrist said. 'The glib tongue, the smooth words. You have the gift . . . sure. We know that. But so do I. I'm immune to you.'

'I won't try to talk you into a single thing, Aaron. You don't seem to be the sort I could do that to anyway.'

'It won't work! Not with me. The advocate's tricks. The therapist's tricks. "Personalize the discourse." "Aaron" this and "Aaron" that. Try to get me to think of you as a specific human being, *Tate*. But that won't work, *Tate*. See, it's Tate Collier the human being I despise.'

Undeterred, Tate continued, 'Was he your only child? Peter?'

'Why even try?' Matthews rolled his eyes.

'All I want is to get out of this and save our lives. Is that a surprise?'

'A perfect example of a rhetorical question. Well, no, it's not a surprise. But there's nothing you can say that's going to make any difference.'

'I'm trying to save your life too, Aaron. They know about you. The police. You heard the message from the detective, I assume? On your answering machine?'

'They may figure it out eventually but since you're here by yourself, an escapee, I think I have a bit of time.'

'What does he mean?' Megan asked. 'Escapee?'

He saw no reason to tell her now that her friend Amy was dead. He shook his head and continued, 'Let's talk, Aaron. I'm a wealthy man. You're going to have to leave the country. I'll give you some money if you let us go.'

'Leading with your weakest argument. Doesn't that mean you've just lost the debate? That's what you say on your American Forensics Society tape.'

The faint smile never wavered from Tate's face. 'You saw my house, the land,' he continued. 'You know I've got resources.'

A splinter of disdain in Matthews's eyes.

'How much do you want?'

'You're using a rhetorical fallacy. Appealing to a false need – for diversion.' Matthews smiled. 'I do it all the time. Soften up the patient, get the defenses down. Then, bang, a kick in the head. Come on, I didn't do this for ransom. That's obvious.'

'Well, whatever your motive *was*, Aaron, the circumstances've changed. They know about you now. But you've got a chance to get out of the country. I can get you a half-million in cash. Just like that. More by hocking the house.'

Matthews said nothing but paced slowly, staring at Megan, who gazed back defiantly.

Tate knew of course that money wasn't the issue at all; neither was helping Matthews escape. But his immediate purpose was simply to make the man indecisive, wear down his resistance. Matthews was right, this was a diversion. And even though the man knew it Tate believed the technique was working.

'I can't make you a rich man but I can make you comfortable. I can—'

'Pointless,' Matthews said, as if he were disappointed.

'But you can't change things. You can't make it the way it was. You can't bring Peter back. So will you just let us go?'

'Specific request within the opponent's power to grant, requiring only an affirmative or negative response. Your skills are still in top form, Collier. My answer, however, is negative.'

'You tell me you're after justice.' Tate shrugged. 'But I wonder if it's not really something else.'

Another flicker in the eyes.

'Have you really thought about why you're doing this?' Tate asked.

'Of course.'

'Why?'

'I—'

'It's to take the pain away, isn't it?'

Matthews's lips moved as he carried on a conversation with himself or his dead wife or dead son. Or no one.

What a man hears, he may doubt.

What a man sees . . .

Tate leaned toward him, ignoring the agony in his head. He whispered urgently. 'Think about it, Aaron. *Think.* This is very important. What if you get it wrong? What if killing Megan makes the pain *worse*?'

'Nice try,' Matthews cried. 'Setting up straw men. What you're saying—'

'Or what if it had no effect at all? What if this is your one chance to make the pain go away and it doesn't work? Did you ever *consider* that?'

'You're trying to distract me!'

'You lost someone you loved. You lie on your back for hours, paralyzed with the pain. You wake up at two a.m. and think you're going mad. Right?'

Matthews fell silent. Tate saw he'd touched a nerve.

'I know all about that. It happened to me.' Tate leaned forward and, without feigning, matched the agony he saw in Matthews's face with pain of his own. 'I've been there. *I* lost someone I loved more than life itself. I lost my wife. I can see it in your face. Yes, see! These aren't tricks, Aaron. I *do* know what I'm talking about. That's all you want – the pain to go away. You're not a lust killer, Aaron. You're not an expediency killer. You're not a hired killer. You only kill when there's a reason. To make the pain go away!'

And to Tate's astonishment he heard a woman's voice beside him. A smooth contralto. Megan, gazing into Matthews's eyes, was saying, 'Even those patients you killed here, Aaron. . . . You didn't *want* to kill them, not really. You just wanted to help them stop hurting.'

Excellent, Tate thought, proud of her.

'The pain,' he took over. 'That's what this is all about. You just want it to go away.'

Matthews's eyes were uncertain, even wild. How we hate the complex, the confusing, the unknown, and how we flock to those who offer us answers simple as a child's drawing.

'I'll tell you, Aaron, that I've lived with your son's death every day since the D of C called and told me what happened. I feel that pain too. I know what you're going through. I—'

In three steps Matthews was on top of Tate, slugging him madly, knocking him to the floor. Megan cried out and stepped toward the madman but he shoved her to the floor again. He screamed at Tate, 'You *know*? You know, do you? You have no fucking idea! The times, weeks and weeks, I haven't been able to do anything but lie on my back and stare at the ceiling, thinking about the trial. You know what I see? I don't see Peter's face. I see your *back*. You, standing in the courtroom with your back to my son. You sent him to die but you didn't even *look* at him! The jury were the only people in that room, weren't they?'

No, Tate thought. They were the only people in the universe. He said, 'I'm so sorry for you.'

'I don't want your fucking pity.' Another wave of fury crossed his face and he lifted Tate in powerful hands and shoved him to the floor again, rolled him on his back. He took a knife from his pocket, opened it with a click and bent down over Tate.

'No!' Megan cried.

Matthews slipped the blade past Tate's lips. Tate tasted metal and felt the chill of the sharp point against his tongue. He didn't move a muscle. Then Matthews's eyes crinkled with what seemed to be humor. His lips moved and he seemed to be speaking to himself. He withdrew the blade.

'No, Collier, no. Not you. I don't want you.'

'But why not?' Tate whispered quickly. 'Why not? Tell me!'

'Because you're going to live a long life without your daughter. Just like I'm going to do without my son.'

'And that'll take the pain away?'

'Yes!'

The lawyer smiled once more. 'Then you have to let her go.' He struggled to keep the triumph from his voice – as he always did in court or at the debate podium. 'Let her go and kill me. It's the only answer for you.'

'Daddy,' Megan whimpered. Tate believed it was the first time he'd heard her say the word in ten years.

'Only answer?' Matthews asked uncertainly.

Tate had known for years it would come to this, he supposed. But what a time, what a place for it to happen.

All cats see in the dark . . .

Therefore Midnight can see in the dark.

He leaned his head against the girl's cheek. 'Oh honey . . .'

Megan asked. 'What is it? *What?*'

Unless Midnight is blind.

Tate began to speak. His voice cracked. He started again. 'Aaron, what you want makes perfect sense. Except that . . .' It was Megan's eyes he gazed into, not their captor's. 'Except that I'm not her father.'

Chapter THIRTY

Matthews had stopped pacing. He seemed to gaze down at them but he was silhouetted by the backlit picture window and Tate couldn't see where his eyes were turned.

Megan, pale in the same oblique light, clasped her injured face. A pink sheen of blood was on her cheeks and breasts. She was frowning.

Matthews laughed but Tate could see that his quick mind was considering facts and drawing tentative conclusions.

'I'm disappointed, Collier. That's obvious and simple-minded. You're lying.'

'How often did you see us together?' Tate asked.

'That doesn't mean anything.'

'You followed us for how long?'

A splinter of doubt. Tate had seen this in the eyes of a thousand witnesses.

Matthews answered, 'Six months.'

'How many weekends was she with me?'

'That doesn't—'

'How many?'

'Two, I think.'

'You broke into my house to plant those letters. How

many pictures of her did you see?'

'Dad . . .'

'How many?'

Matthews finally said, 'None.'

'What did her bedroom look like?'

Another hesitation. 'A storeroom.'

'How much affection did you ever see between us? Did I *seem* like a father? I've got dark, curly hair and eyes. Bett's auburn. And Megan's *blonde*, for God's sake. Does she even look like me? Look at the eyes. Look!'

He did. He said uncertainly, 'I still don't believe you.'

'No, Daddy! No!'

'You went to see my wife,' Tate continued to Matthews.

The doctor nodded.

'Well, you're a therapist. What did you see in Bett's face when you were talking to her? What was there when she was telling you about us and about Megan?'

Matthews reflected. 'I saw . . . guilt.'

'That's right,' Tate said. 'Guilt.'

Matthews looked from one of his captives to the other.

'Seventeen years ago,' Tate began slowly, speaking to Megan, 'I was prosecuting cases here. Making a name for myself. The *Washington Post* called me the hottest young prosecutor in the commonwealth. I'd take on every assignment that came into the office. I was working eighty hours a week. I got home to your mother on weekends at best. I'd go for three or four days in a row and hardly even call. I was trying to be my grandfather. The lawyer-farmer-patriarch. I'd be a local celebrity. We'd have a huge family. An old manse. Sunday dinners, reunions, holidays . . . the whole nine yards.'

He took a deep breath. 'That was when your Aunt Susan had her first bad heart attack. She was in the hospital for a month and mostly bedridden after that.'

'What are you saying?' Megan whispered coldly.

'Susan was married. Her husband, you remember him.'

'Uncle Harris.'

'You were right in your letter, Megan. Your mother *did* spend a lot of time caring for her sister. Harris and your mother both did.'

'No,' Megan said abruptly, 'I don't believe it.'

'They'd go to the hospital together, Harris and Bett. They'd have lunch, dinner. Go shopping. Sometimes Bett cooked him meals in his studio. Helped him clean. Your aunt felt better knowing he was being looked after. And it was okay with me. I was free to handle my cases.'

'She told you all this?' Megan asked. 'Mom?'

His face was a blank mask as he said slowly, 'No. Harris did. The day of his funeral.'

Tate had been upstairs on that eerily warm November night fifteen years ago. The funeral reception, at the Collier farm, was over.

Standing at a bedroom window, Tate had looked out over the yard. Felt the hot air, filled with leaf dust. Smelled cedar from the closet.

He'd just checked on young Megan, asleep in her room, and he'd come here to open windows to air out the upstairs; several relatives would be spending the night.

He'd looked down at the back yard, gazing at Bett in her long black dress. She hiked up the hem and climbed on to the new picnic table to unhook the Japanese lanterns.

Tate had tried to open the window but it was stuck. He took off his jacket to get a better grip and heard the crinkle of paper in the pocket. At the funeral one of Harris's attorneys had given him an envelope, hand-addressed to him from Harris, marked personal. He'd forgotten about it. He opened the envelope. He read the brief letter inside.

Tate had nodded to himself, folded the note slowly and walked downstairs, then outside.

He remembered hearing a Loretta Lynn song playing on the stereo.

He remembered hearing the rustling of the hot wind over the brown grass and sedge, stirring pumpkin vines and the refuse of the corn harvest.

He remembered watching the serpentine arc of Bett's narrow arm as she reached for an orange lantern. She glanced down at him.

'I have something to tell you,' he'd said.

'What?' she'd whispered. Then, seeing the look in his eyes Bett had asked desperately: 'What, what?'

She'd climbed down from the bench. Tate came up close and, instead of putting his arm around his wife's shoulders, as a husband might do late at night in a house of death, he handed her the letter.

She read it. And nodded.

'Oh.'

Bett didn't deny anything that was contained in the note: Harris's declaration of intense love for her, the affair, his fathering Megan, Bett's refusal to marry him and her threat to take the girl away from him forever if Harris told her sister of the infidelity. At the end the words had degenerated into mad rambling and his chillingly lucid acknowledgment that the pain was simply too much.

Neither of them cried that night as Tate had packed a suitcase and left. They never spent another night under the same roof.

Despite the presence of a madman, holding a knife a few feet from them, Tate's concentration was wholly on the girl. To his surprise her face blossomed not with horror or shock or anger but with sympathy. She squeezed his leg. 'And you're the one that got hurt so bad. I'm sorry, Daddy. I'm sorry.'

Tate looked at Matthews. He said, 'So that's why your

argument doesn't work, Aaron. Taking her away from me won't do what you want.'

Matthews didn't speak. His eyes were turned out the window.

Tate said, 'You know the classic reasons for punishing crimes, Aaron? To condition away bad behavior – doesn't work. A deterrent – useless. To rehabilitate – that's a joke. To protect society – well, only if we execute the bad guys or keep them locked up for ever. No, you know the real reason why we punish? We're ashamed to admit it. It's barbaric. But, oh, how we love it. Good old biblical retribution. Bloody revenge is the only honest motive for punishment. Why? Because its purpose is to take away the pain.

'That's what you want, Aaron, but there's only one way you'll have that. By killing me. It's not perfect but it'll have to do.'

Megan was sobbing.

Matthews leaned his head against the window. He moaned as he gazed outside. The sun was up now and flashed on and off as strips of liver-colored clouds moved quickly east. He seemed diminished and changed. As if he were beyond disappointment or sorrow.

'Let her go. Hell, it doesn't even make sense to kill her because she's a witness. They know about you anyway.'

Matthews crouched beside Megan. Put the back of his hand against her cheek, lifted it away and looked at the glistening streak left by her tears on his skin. He kissed her hair.

'All right. I agree.'

Megan started to protest.

But Tate knew that he'd won. Nothing she could say or do at this point would change his decision.

'I'll call the dogs to the run. I'll be back in five minutes.'

Chapter THIRTY-ONE

'Is it true?' she asked, tears glistening on her cheeks.

'Oh, yes, honey, it's true.'

'You never said anything.'

'Your mother and I decided not to. Until after Susan died. You know how close Bett was to your aunt. She wanted her never to find out – it would have been too hard for her. The doctors only gave her a year or two to live. We were going to wait until she'd passed away.'

'But . . .' Megan whispered.

He smiled wanly. 'Oh, yes. She's still alive. Miracle of modern medicine. That's why we kept up the pretense that you were ours.'

'Why didn't you ever tell *me*? Aunt Susan wouldn't have to know.'

Tate examined wounds on her palms. Pressed his hands against them. He couldn't speak at first. Finally he said, 'The moment passed.'

'All these years,' she cried, 'I thought *I* must've done something.' She laughed, then lowered her head against his shoulder. 'What a terrible thing I must have been for you. What a reminder.'

'Honey, I wish I could tell you different. But I can't. You were half the person I loved most in the world and half the person I most hated.'

'One time I said something,' she said, weeping softly. 'I'd been with you for the weekend and Mom asked how it went. I said I'd had an okay time but what could you expect? You were just an adequate father. I thought she was going to whip me. She freaked out totally. She said you were the best man she'd ever met and I was never, ever supposed to say that again.'

Tate smiled. 'An adequate father for an inconvenient daughter.'

'Why didn't you ever try it again, the two of you?'

He echoed, 'The moment passed.'

'How much you must love her.'

Tate laughed sourly to himself at the irony. The child that drove them apart had now brought them back together – if only for one day.

How scarce love is, he thought. How rarely does it all come together: the pledge, the assurance, the need, the circumstance, the hungry desire to share minutes with someone else. And the dear desperation too. It seems impossible, miraculous, when it works.

He looked her over and decided that the two of them, his ex-wife and her daughter, would be fine – now that the truth had been dumped between them. A long time coming but better than never. Oh, yes, they'd do fine.

Gritty footsteps approached.

'Now, listen to me,' he said urgently. 'Find a phone and call Ted Beauridge at Fairfax County Police. He's a friend of mine. Tell him your mother's probably in jail in Luray or Front Royal—'

'What?'

'No time to explain. But she's there and tell him to get cops out here.'

The girl looked at him with eyes that reminded him of her mother's. Not the violet shade, of course – those were Bett's and Bett's alone – but the unique mix of the ethereal and the earthy.

Matthews appeared in the doorway.

They turned to look at the gaunt man standing before them, his muscular hand pressed to his bloody belly

'Okay, get going,' Tate said to her. 'Run like hell.'

'Go on,' Matthews said, and reached forward to take her arm.

She spun away from him and hugged Tate hard. He felt her arms around his back. Felt her face against his ear, heard her speaking to him, a torrent of fervid words flowing out, coming from a source other than the heart and mind of a seventeen-year-old high school junior.

'Megan . . .' he began.

But she took his face in both her hands and said, 'Shhh, Daddy. Remember, bears can't talk.'

Matthews grabbed her again and pulled her away. Took her to the door.

He unlocked it and shoved her outside. The door closed with a snap behind her. Through a dirty, barred window Tate saw her sprint down the driveway and disappear through the gate.

'So,' Collier said, glancing up at Matthews.

'So,' he echoed.

'Outside?' the lawyer asked, looking around at the gloomy place. 'Would that be all right? I'd rather.'

Matthews hesitated for a moment. But then decided, why not? 'Yes. That's all right.'

He unlocked the door again and they stepped into the parking area and walked around into the back grounds, past the wild Rottweilers in their cage.

Matthews was thinking back to the times he'd been committed here. The lawns and gardens. They were beautiful. Well, why wouldn't they be? Give five hundred crazy people grounds to tend and, brother, you've got a showplace. He'd sat for hours and hours and hours talking to other patients and – in his imagination – to his dead Peter. Sometimes the boy responded, sometimes not.

The dawn sun was still below the horizon but the sky was bright as they walked side by side lithely through the tall grass and goldenrod and milkweed while dragonflies zipped from their path. Grasshoppers bounced against their legs, leaving dots of brown spit on their clothing.

The dogs were in a frenzy behind them, sniffing the ground and bounding at the wire fence of their run, trying to escape and go after the intruder who walked beside their master.

'Look at this place,' Matthews said conversationally. He waved his arm. 'I remember it like it was yesterday. I remember the strange things people would say. The delusional ones, the paranoid ones, the depressed ones. The ones who were simply nuts – you know, Collier, the mind isn't an exact science, whatever the Diagnostic and Statistical Manual says. Some of the men and women were just plain crazy and that's all you could ever say about them. But I always listened to them. Why, people give themselves away like free samples at a grocery store. Hand themselves to you on platters. And what do they use? Words. Aren't words the most astonishing thing?'

Collier said, 'You bet they are.'

There wasn't much time, Matthews reflected. He supposed he had an hour or two until the police arrived. At best it would take Megan two hours to get to the nearest phone. Enough time to finish here, bury Peter, and get to Dulles for a flight to Los Angeles. Or maybe he should just drive west. Hide in the hills of West Virginia. He took a deep breath. 'Stop here.'

They were beside a shallow ditch. It would make a fine grave for Collier. And he'd decided that he'd kill the lawyer with a single shot to his head. No pain, no torment. And he wouldn't let the dogs have the body. Out of respect for a worthy adversary.

Then the lawyer stunned him by closing his eyes and whispering, 'Our Father, Who art in Heaven . . .' He slowly completed the Lord's Prayer.

Matthews laughed then asked, 'You believe in God?'

Collier nodded. 'Why does that surprise you?'

'When I'd see you in court it seemed that only the judge and jury were your gods.'

'No, no, I believe He exists. That He's merciful and He's just.'

'Just?' Matthews asked skeptically.

'Well, he's the reason I don't send people to death row anymore . . . Do *you*? Believe in God?'

'I'm not sure,' Matthews said.

'You know, I always wanted the chance to prove the existence of God in a debate.'

'How would you do it?' Matthews asked truly curious. 'Prove God existed? Rhetorically, Resolved: God exists. Isn't that how debates start?'

Collier looked up at the purple sky. 'You know Voltaire?'

'Not really. No.'

'I'd make his argument. He said there had to be a God because he couldn't imagine a watch without a watchmaker.'

Matthews nodded. 'Yes, I can see that. That's good. That's compelling.'

'But of course then you run into all of the counter-arguments. The con side.'

'Such as?'

'Incompatible religious sects, interpretations of holy scriptures proven wrong later, no empirical proof of miracles, the

Crusades, ethical and secular self-interest, terrorism . . . That's an uphill battle, all right.'

'No answer for that?'

'Oh, sure. I've got an answer.'

Matthews was suddenly fascinated. After Peter's death he'd prayed every night for six months. He believed that the boy had answered some of those communiqués. It gave him clues, but not proof, that Peter's soul floated near by. 'What is it, what's the answer?' he asked hungrily.

'That a watch,' Collier answered slowly, 'no matter how well made, can never *comprehend* its watchmaker. When we claim to, everything breaks down. If God exists then by definition he's unknowable, and souls – yours, mine, Megan's, Peter's – are beyond our understanding. When we create human institutions to represent God they have to be flawed.'

'Yes, it makes sense. How simple, how perfect.'

'You've thought about questions like this, haven't you? Because of Peter?'

'Yes.'

Eyes on Matthews's, Collier said, 'You miss him so much, don't you?'

'Yes, I do.' Matthews stared down at the ground. For all he knew he'd stood on this very spot two or three years ago, studying slugs or dung beetles or ants for hour upon hour, wondering how, in their worldless world, they communicated their passions and fears.

'You can get help, Aaron. It's not too late. You'll be in jail but you can still be content. You can find somebody to help you. Somebody who's as good as you were.'

'Oh, I don't think so. It's too late for that, I'm afraid. One thing I learned – you can't talk somebody out of his nature.'

'"Your character is your fate,"' Collier said.

Matthews laughed. 'Heraclitus.'

He'd learned the aphorism from one of Collier's closing

statements. He lifted the gun toward the lawyer.

Then Collier's eyes flickered slightly. He sighed. 'I'm sorry,' he said.

Matthews frowned. 'What do you mean?'

'I'm so sorry.'

He heard the snap behind him.

Matthews spun around. There stood Megan, holding the gun Collier had brought with him. Matthews had left it in the lobby of the hospital and had forgotten about it. The girl was ten feet away and was pointing the black muzzle at Matthews's chest.

Oh yes, Matthews laughed to himself. Oh yes . . . He understood. Remembered her whispering to Tate before he'd escorted her out the door. They'd planned this together. Collier would stall him, Megan would pretend to run but would return for the gun, propping open the door. He remembered Collier protesting as they'd hugged. But she'd had her way.

Maybe she wasn't his blood daughter but they were a family now.

He glanced at her eyes. 'Drop the gun,' she ordered.

But he didn't. He wondered, would she go through with it? She was only seventeen and, yes, she had anger in her heart – enough to attack him with a knife – but not enough to kill, he believed.

Character is fate . . .

He saw compassion, fear, weakness in her eyes. He could stop her. He could get her to put the gun down.

'Megan, listen to me—' he began in a soft voice, gazing into her blue eyes, which *were* so unlike Collier's. 'I know what you're—'

The first bullet tugged at his side, near the knife wound, and he felt a rib snap. He was swinging the gun toward her when another shot struck his shoulder and arm.

Collier dropped to his knees, clear of the line of fire.

Megan stepped closer.

'Peter . . .' Matthews whispered, struggling to lift his pistol.

Yet another shot burned into him striking his chest.

A step closer.

'Please . . .'

She shook her head.

The girl paused a foot away.

He looked into her eyes.

Always the eyes . . .

The gun fired one last time. And for an instant his vision was filled with a thousand suns. And in his ears was a chorus of noise – voices, perhaps.

Peter's among them, perhaps.

And then there was blackness and silence.

Epilogue

The beach at San Cristo del Sol in Belize is one of the finest in Latin America.

Even now, in May, the air is torrid but the steady breezes soothe the hordes of tourists during their endless trips from the air-conditioned bars and seafood joints to the pools to the beach and back again. Windsurfing, paragliding, jet-skis and waterskiing keep the surface of the turquoise water perpetually turbulent, and within the bay itself hundreds of snorklers and resort-course scuba divers engage in their elegantly awkward amphibious activities.

The town is also a well-known staging area for those who wish to see Mayan ruins; there are two beautifully preserved cities within five kilometers of the main drag in San Cristo.

The Caribe Inn is the most luxurious of all the hotels in town, a Spanish colonial hacienda that has four stars from Mobil and accolades from a number of other sources, proudly displayed behind the registration desk, at which Tate Collier now stood, hoping fervently that the clerk spoke English.

The man did, it turned out, and Tate explained that he had reservations, proffering passports and his American Express card.

'That's a party of . . . . ?' the clerk queried.

'Party of two.'

'Ah,' the desk clerk responded. Tate filled out the registration card with ungainly strokes.

'So, you are from Virginia,' the clerk said. 'Near Washington?'

'*Sí*,' Tate responded self-consciously, ready for his pronunciation to throw the conversation off kilter if not insult the clerk personally.

'I have been there several times. I like the Smithsonian especially.'

'*Sí*,' Tate tried again, forgetting even the words that conveyed some meaningless pleasantry – words he'd practiced on the flight. For a man who'd made his way in the world by speaking, Tate's command of foreign languages was abysmal.

He watched the clerk glance down at the reservation form with a momentarily perplexed frown on his dark, handsome face. Tate thought he knew why. The clerk had taken a good look at the attractive woman who'd entered the hotel on Tate's arm a moment before and though surely, in this line of work, the clerk had seen just about everything, he couldn't for the life of him figure out why these two would want separate rooms.

A man is, after all, a man . . . And an age difference of twenty years . . . well, that's nothing.

Megan came out of the lobby phone booth and walked to the desk just as the clerk was showing Tate a diagram of the available rooms. Tate pointed to two, first a smaller inside room, then a corner unit with a view of the beach. 'I'll take this one. My daughter'll have the corner room.'

'No, Dad, you take the nice one.'

'This is your daughter?' the clerk said, his curiosity satisfied. 'Of course, I should have known.'

'I'm sorry?' Tate asked him.

'I mean, the resemblance. The young lady takes after you.'

The man's suspicions crept back when he saw the two guests exchange fast glances and struggle to suppress laughter. Tate thought about pulling out driver's licenses and proving the relationship but then decided: It's none of this guy's business.

Besides, mystery has an appeal that documented fact will always lack.

They settled on the rooms and after Tate's card was imprinted they followed the bellhop through a veranda.

'Josh said his new physical therapist is great,' Megan told him.

'Glad to hear it.'

'But the way he put it was he said "she's" great. Think she's old and fat?'

'We'll be back in six days. You can find out for yourself. When do you say *de nada* again?'

'After somebody thanks you. It means, "It's nothing."'

'They say "*Gracias*" and then I say "*De nada*".' Tate repeated the words several times as if he were a walking Berlitz tape.

'Then I called Bett,' Megan continued. 'She's glad we got in okay. She said to take lots of pictures.'

'I'll call her later.'

'She, um, was going over to Brad's tonight. But she said it in a funny way. Like there was something going on. Is anything going on?'

'I don't have a clue.'

Megan shrugged. 'She said she talked to Konnie and he's coming to your office on Tuesday at nine to talk about the case.'

The previous week Tate had made his first appearance in a criminal court in nearly five years – Konnie's arraignment. He'd answered the judge's simple query with simpler words. 'Not guilty, your honor.'

He had a novel defense planned. It was called 'induced

intoxication', and although he'd promised Megan that they would be spending the week doing nothing but seeing the sights and partying he'd hidden three law books in his suitcase and suspected the last day of the trip would find him with at least a rough draft of his opening statement to the jury – if not a set of deposition questions or two. He knew that as soon as she met a handsome young windsurfer – probably at the cocktail party that night – he would have a few hours free on most of the evenings.

He and Megan arrived at their rooms.

'*Gracias de nada,*' Tate said, and slipped the confused bellhop an outrageously generous tip.

A half-hour later they'd showered and were in khaki shorts, T-shirts and wicker hats. Every inch *los turistas.* They walked down to the lobby and asked about how they might bicycle to the nearest Mayan ruin. The clerk arranged for the bike rental and gave them directions. It was just past the afternoon siesta and most of the guests were headed for the white-sand beach. But Tate and Megan snagged two battered bicycles from the rack in front of the inn and headed away from town.

'Which way?' she called.

He pointed and they mounted up.

Despite the opposing foot traffic and the astonishing heat, they sped along the cracked asphalt path straight into the dense, fragrant jungle, standing on the pedals, hollering and laughing, racing each other, as if every moment counted, as if they had many, many hours of missed exploration to make up for.

JEFFERY DEAVER

Manhattan Is My Beat

The land of faery:
where nobody gets old and godly and grave,
where nobody gets old and crafty and wise,
where nobody gets old and bitter of tongue.

—*William Butler Yeats*

CHAPTER ONE

He believed he was safe.

For the first time in six months.

Two identities and three residences behind him, he finally believed he was safe.

An odd feeling came over him—comfort, he finally decided. Yeah, that was it. A feeling he hadn't experienced for a long time, and he sat on the bed in this fair-to-middling hotel, overlooking that weird silver arch that crowned the riverfront in St. Louis. Smelling the midwestern spring air.

An old movie was on television. He loved old movies. This was *Touch of Evil*. Orson Welles directing. Charlton Heston playing a Mexican. The actor didn't look like a Mexican. But then, he probably didn't look like Moses either.

Arnold Gittleman laughed to himself at his little joke and told it to a sullen man sitting nearby, reading a *Guns & Ammo* magazine. The man glanced at the screen.

"Mexican?" he asked. Stared at the screen for a minute. "Oh." He went back to his magazine.

Gittleman lay back in the bed, thinking that it was damn well about time he had some funny thoughts like the one about Heston. Frivolous thoughts. Amount-to-nothing thoughts. He wanted to think about gardening or painting lawn furniture or taking his grandson to a ball game. About taking his daughter and her husband to his wife's grave—a place he'd been too afraid to visit for over six months.

"So," the sullen man said, looking up from the magazine, "what's it gonna be? We gonna do deli tonight?"

Gittleman, who'd lost 30 pounds since Christmas—he was down to 204—said, "Sure. Sounds good. Deli."

And he realized it *did* sound good. He hadn't looked forward to food for a long time. A nice fat deli sandwich. Pastrami. His mouth started to water. Mustard. Rye bread. A pickle.

"Naw," said a third man, stepping out of the bathroom. "Pizza. Let's get pizza."

The sullen man who read about guns all the time and the pizza man were U.S. marshals. Both were young and stony-faced and gruff and wore cheap suits that fit very badly. But Gittleman knew that these were exactly the kind of men you wanted to be watching over you. Besides, Gittleman had led a pretty tough life himself, and he realized that when you looked past their facade these two were pretty decent and smart guys—street-smart, at least. Which was all that really counted in life.

Gittleman had taken a liking to them over the past five months. And since he couldn't have his family around him he'd informally adopted them. He called them Son One and Son Two. He told them that. They weren't sure what to make of it but he sensed they got a kick out of him saying the words. For one thing, they said, most of the people they protected were complete shits and Gittleman knew that, whatever else, he wasn't that.

Son One was the man reading the guns magazine, the man who'd suggested deli. He was the fatter of them. Son Two grumbled again that he wanted pizza.

"Forgetaboutit. We did pizza yesterday."

An irrefutable argument. So it was pastrami and cole slaw.

Good.

"On rye," Gittleman said. "And a pickle. Don't forget the pickle."

"They come with pickles."

"Then *extra* pickles."

"Hey, go for it, Arnie," Son One said.

Son Two spoke into the microphone pinned to his chest. A wire ran to a black Motorola Handi-Talkie, clipped onto his belt, right next to a big gun that might very well have been reviewed in the magazine his partner was reading. He spoke to the third marshal on the team, sitting by the elevator up the hall. "It's Sal. I'm coming out."

"Okay," the staticky voice responded. "Elevator's on its way."

"You wanta beer, Arnie?"

"No," Gittleman said firmly.

Son Two looked at him curiously.

"I want *two* goddamn beers."

The marshal cracked a faint smile. The most response to humor Gittleman had ever seen in his tough face.

"Good for you," Son One said. The marshals had been after him to lighten up, enjoy life more. Relax.

"You don't like dark beer, right?" asked his partner.

"Not so much," Gittleman responded.

"How do they make dark beer anyway?" Son One asked, studying something in the well-thumbed magazine. Gittleman looked. It was a pistol, dark as dark beer, and it looked a lot nastier than the guns his surrogate sons wore.

"Make it?" Gittleman asked absently. He didn't know. He knew money and how and where to hide it. He knew movies and horse racing and grandchildren. He *drank* beer but he didn't know anything about making it. Maybe he'd take that up as a hobby too—in addition to gardening. Home brewing. He was fifty-six. Too young for retirement from the financial services and accounting profession—but, after the RICO trial, he was definitely going to be retired from now on.

"Clear," came the radio voice from the hallway.

Son Two disappeared out the door.

Gittleman lay back and watched the movie. Janet Leigh was on screen now. He'd always had a crush on her. Was still pissed at Hitchcock for killing her in the shower. Gittleman liked women with short hair.

Smelling the spring air.

Thinking about a sandwich.

Pastrami on rye.

And a pickle.

Feeling safe.

Thinking: the Marshals Service was doing a good job at making sure he stayed that way. The rooms on either side of this one had adjoining doors but they'd been bolted shut and the rooms were unoccupied; the U.S. government actually paid for all three rooms. The hallway was covered by the marshal near the elevator. The nearest shooting position a sniper could find was two miles away, across the Mississippi River, and Son One—the *Guns & Ammo* subscriber—had told him there was nobody in the universe who could make a shot like that.

Feeling comfortable.

Thinking that tomorrow he'd be on his way to California, with a new identity. There'd be some plastic surgery. He'd be safe. The people who wanted to kill him would eventually forget about him.

Relaxing.

Letting himself get lost in the movie with Moses and Janet Leigh.

It was really a great film. The very opening scene was somebody setting the hands of the timer on a bomb to three minutes and twenty seconds. Then planting it. Welles had made one continuous shot for that exact amount of time, until the bomb went off, setting the story in motion.

Talk about building the suspense.

Talk about—

Wait. . . .

What was that?

Gittleman glanced out the window. He sat up slightly.

Outside the window was . . . What *was* that?

It seemed like a small box of some sort. Sitting on the window ledge. Connected to it was a thin wire, which ran upward and disappeared out of view. As if somebody'd lowered the little box from the room above.

Because of the movie—the opening scene—his first thought was that the box was a bomb. But now, as he lunged forward, he saw that, no, it looked like a camera, a small video camera.

He rolled off the bed, walked to the window. Looked at the box closely.

Yep. That's what it was. A camera.

"Arnie, you know the drill," Son One said. Because he was heavy he sweated a lot and he sweated now. He wiped his face. "Stay away from the windows."

"But . . . what's that?" Gittleman pointed.

The marshal dropped the magazine to the floor, rose, and stepped to the window.

"A video camera?" Gittleman asked.

"Well, it looks like it. It does. Yeah."

"Is it . . . But it's not yours, is it?"

"No," the marshal muttered, frowning. "We don't have surveillance outside."

The marshal glanced at the thin cable that disappeared up, presumably to the room above them. His eyes continued upward until they came to rest on the ceiling.

"Shit!" he said, reaching for his radio.

The first cluster of bullets from the silenced machine gun tore through the plaster above them and ripped into Son One, who danced like a puppet. He dropped to the floor, bloody and torn. Shivering as he died.

"No!" Gittleman cried. "Jesus, *no!*"

He leapt toward the phone. A stream of bullets followed him; upstairs the killer would be watching on the video camera, knowing exactly where Gittleman was.

Gittleman pressed himself flat against the wall. The gunman fired another shot. A single. It was close. Then two more. Inches away. Teasing him, it seemed like. Nobody would hear. The only sound was the cracking of plaster and wood.

More shots followed him as he dodged toward the bathroom. Debris flew around him. There was a pause. He hoped the killer had given up and fled. But it turned out that he was after the phone—so Gittleman couldn't call for help. Two bullets cracked through the ceiling, hit the beige telephone unit, and shattered it into a hundred pieces.

"Help!" he cried, nauseated with fear. But, of course, the rooms on either side of this one were empty—a fact so reassuring a few moments ago, so horrifying now.

Tears of fright in his eyes . . .

He rolled into a corner, knocked a lamp over to darken the room.

More bullets crashed down. Closer, testing. Trying to find him. The gunman upstairs, watching a TV screen of his own, just like Gittleman had been watching Charlton Heston a few minutes ago.

Do something, Gittleman raged to himself. *Come on!*

He eased forward again and shoved the TV set, on a roller stand, toward the window. It slammed into the pane, cracked it, and blocked the view the video camera had of the room.

There were several more shots but the gunman was blind now.

"Please," Gittleman prayed quietly. "Please. Someone help me."

Hugging the walls, he moved to the doorway. He fumbled the chain and dead bolt, shivering in panic, certain the man was right above him, aiming down. About to pull the trigger.

But there were no more shots and he swung the door open fast and leapt into the hallway. Calling to the marshal at the elevator—not one of the Sons, an officer named Gibson. "He's shooting—there's a man upstairs with a gun! You—"

But Gittleman stopped speaking. At the end of the hallway Gibson lay facedown. Blood pooled around his head. Another puppet—this one with cut strings.

"Oh, no," he gasped. Turned around to run.

He stopped. Looking at what he now realized was the inevitable.

A handsome man, dark-complected, wearing a well-cut suit, standing in the hallway. He carried a Polaroid camera in one hand and, in the other, a black pistol mounted with a silencer.

"You're Gittleman, aren't you?" the man asked. He sounded polite, as if he were merely curious.

Gittleman couldn't respond. But the man squinted and then nodded. "Yeah, sure you are."

"But . . ." Gittleman looked back into his hotel room.

"Oh, my partner wasn't trying to hit you in there. Just to flush you. We need to get you outside and confirm the kill." The man gave a little shrug, nodding at the camera. " 'Causa what we're getting paid they want proof. You know."

And he shot Gittleman three times in the chest.

In the hotel corridor, which used to smell of Lysol and now smelled of Lysol and cordite from the gunshots, Haarte unscrewed the suppressor and dropped it and the Walther into his pocket. He glanced at the Polaroid picture of the dead man as it developed. Then put it in the same pocket as the gun.

From his belt he took his own walkie-talkie—more expensive than the Marshals' and, unlike theirs, sensibly equipped with a three-level-encryption scrambler—and spoke to Zane, his partner, upstairs, the one so proficient with automatic weapons. "He's dead. I've got the snap. Get out."

"On my way," Zane replied.

Haarte glanced at his watch. If the other marshal had gone to get food—which he probably had, since it was dinnertime—he could be back in six or seven minutes. That's how much time it took to walk to the restaurant closest to the hotel, order take-out, and return. He obviously hadn't gone to the restaurant *in* the hotel because they would just have ordered room service.

Haarte walked slowly down the four flights of stairs and outside into the warm spring evening. He checked the streets. Nearly deserted. No sirens. No flashing lights of silent roll-ups.

His earphone crackled. Haarte's partner said, "I'm in the car. Back at the Hilton in thirty."

"See you then."

Haarte got into their second rental car and drove out

of downtown to a park in University City, a pleasant suburb west of the city.

He pulled up beside a maroon Lincoln Continental.

Overhead a jet, making its approach to Lambert Field, roared past.

Haarte got out of the car and walked to the Lincoln. He got in the backseat, checking out the driver, kept his hand in his pocket around the grip of the now-unsilenced pistol. The man sitting in the rear of the car, a heavy, jowly man of about 60, gave a faint nod, his eyes aimed toward the front seat, meaning: The driver's okay; you don't have to worry.

Haarte didn't care what the man's eyes said. Haarte worried all the time. He'd worried when he'd been a cop in the toughest precinct of Newark, New Jersey. He'd worried as a soldier in the Dominican Republic. He'd worried as a mercenary in Zaire and Burma. He'd come to believe that worry was a kind of drug. One that kept you alive.

Once he finished his own appraisal of the driver he released his grip on the pistol and took his hand out of his pocket.

The man said in a flat midwestern accent, "There's nothing on the news yet."

"There will be," Haarte reassured him. He flashed the Polaroid.

The man shook his head. "All for money. Death of an innocent. And it's all for money." He sounded genuinely troubled as he said this. He looked up from the picture. Haarte had learned that Polaroids never show blood the right color; it always looks darker.

"That bother you?" the man asked Haarte. "Death of an innocent?"

Haarte said nothing. Innocence or guilt, just like fault and mercy, were concepts that had no meaning to him.

But the man didn't seem to want an answer.

"Here." The man handed him an envelope. Haarte had received a lot of envelopes like this. He always thought they felt like blocks of wood. Which in a way they were. Money was paper, paper was wood. He didn't look inside. He put the envelope in his pocket. No one had ever tried to cheat him.

"What about the other guy you wanted done?" Haarte asked.

The man shook his head. "Gone to ground. Somewhere in Manhattan. We aren't sure where yet. We should find out soon. You interested in the job?"

"New York?" Haarte considered. "It'll cost more. There's more heat, it's more complicated. We'd need backup and we probably should make it look accidental. Or at least set up a fall guy."

"Whatever," the man said lackadaisically, not much interest in the details of Haarte's craft. "What'll it cost?"

"Double." Haarte touched his breast pocket, where the money now rested.

A lifted gray eyebrow. "You pick up all expenses? The cost of backup? Equipment?"

Haarte waited a moment and said, "Add ten points for the backup?"

"I can go there," the man said.

They shook hands and Haarte returned to his own car.

He called Zane on the radio once more. "We're on again. This time in our own backyard."

CHAPTER TWO

Rune got elected to pick up the videotape and her life was never the same after that.

She argued with her boss about picking up the tape—Tony, the manager of Washington Square Video on Eighth Street in Greenwich Village, where she was a clerk. Oh, she argued with him.

Rewinding a tape, playing with the VCR, snapping the controls, she stared at the fat, bearded man. "Forget it. No way." She reminded him how he'd agreed she didn't have to do pickups or deliveries and that was the deal when he'd hired her.

"So," she said. "There."

Tony peered at her from under flecked, bushy eyebrows and, for some reason, decided to be reasonable. He explained how Frankie Greek and Eddie were busy fixing monitors or something—though she guessed they were probably just figuring out how to get comped into the Palladium for a concert that night—and so she *had* to do the pickups.

"I don't see why I *have* to at all, Tony. I mean, I just don't see where the have-to part comes in."

And right about then he changed his mind about being reasonable. "Okay, here's where it comes in, Rune. It's the part where I'm fucking *telling* you to. You know, as your boss. Anyway, whatsa big deal? There's only one pickup."

"That's like a total waste of time."

"Your life is a waste of time, Rune."

"Look," she began, not too patiently, and went on with her argument until he said, "Thin ice, honey. Get your ass outa here. Now."

She tried, "Not in the job description." Only because it wasn't in her nature to give in too quickly and then she saw him go all still and before he exploded she stood up and said, "Oh, will you just *chill,* Tony?" In that exasperated, sly way of hers that would probably get her fired someday but so far hadn't.

Then he'd looked at an invoice and said, "Christ, it's only a few blocks from here. Avenue B. Guy's name is Robert Kelly."

Oh, Rune thought, Mr. Kelly? Well, that was different.

She took the receipt, snagging the retro, fake-leopard-skin bag she'd found in a used-clothing store on Broadway. She pushed out the door, into the cool spring air, saying, "All right, all right. I'll do it." Putting just the right tone in her voice to let Tony know he owed her one for this. In her two decades on earth Rune had learned that if she wanted to live life the way she did, it was probably a good idea to collect as many obligations from people as she could.

Rune was five two, one hundred pounds. Today she wore black stretch pants, a black T-shirt under an businessman's Arrow shirt she'd cut the sleeves out of, so it looked like a white pinstripe vest. Black ankle boots. There were twenty-seven silver bracelets, all different, on her left forearm.

Her lips varied in size, compressing, expanding. A barometer of her mood. She had a round face; her nose pleased her. Her friends sometimes said she looked like certain actresses who appeared in independent films. But there were few present-day actresses she cared about or tried to look like; if you took Audrey Hepburn and put her in a Downtown, New Wave version of *Breakfast at Tiffany's*—that's who Rune wanted to resemble and in many ways she did.

She paused, looked at herself in a mirror sitting in an antiques shop window, the words WHOLESALE ONLY larger than the name of the place. Several months ago she'd gotten tired of her spiky black-purple haircut, had rinsed out the frightening colors, and had stopped trimming the do herself. The strands were longer now and the natural chestnut was emerging. Staring at the mirror, she now teased the hair out with her fingers. Then patted it back down. It wasn't long, it wasn't short. The ambivalence of it made her feel more homeless than she normally did.

She started once more on her journey to the East Village.

Rune glanced down at the receipt again.

Robert Kelly.

If Tony'd told her right away who the customer was, she wouldn't have given him so much crap.

Kelly, Robert. Member since: May 2. Deposit: Cash.

Robert Kelly.

"My boyfriend."

That's what she'd told Frankie Greek and Eddie at the store. They'd blinked, trying to figure out what *that* meant. But then she'd laughed and made it sound like a joke—before they grinned and sneered and asked what was it like to be in bed with a seventy-year-old man?

Though she'd added, "Well, we *have* been out on a date." Which left enough doubt to make it fun.

Robert Kelly *was* her friend. More of a friend than most of the men she'd met in the store. And he *was* also the only one she'd ever gone out with—in her three months' working there. Tony had a rule against going out with customers—not that any rule of Tony's would slow her up for more than a half-second. But the only men she ever seemed to meet at the store were either long domesticated or about what you'd expect from somebody who picks up clerks in a Greenwich Village video store.

Hi, I'm John, Fred, Stan, Sam, call me Sammie, I live up the street, this's an Armani, you like it, I'm a fashion photographer, I work for Morgan-Stanley, I got some blow, hey, you wanna go to my place and fuck?

Kelly, Robert, deposit: cash, wore a suit and tie every time she'd seen him. He was fifty years older than she was. And when she'd offered to do him a favor, a little thing, copy a tape for him, for free, he'd looked down, blushing, and he'd asked her out to lunch to thank her.

They'd gone to a highly turquoise 1950s revival soda shop, called the Soda Shop, on St. Marks, and, surrounded by NYU students who managed to be both morbidly serious and giddy at the same time, had eaten grilled cheese sandwiches with pickles. She'd ordered a martini. He'd laughed in surprise and said in a whisper he'd thought she was sixteen. The waitress had somehow accepted the fake ID, which showed her age to be 23. According to the authentic documentation—her Ohio driver's license—Rune was twenty.

At lunch he'd been a little awkward at first. But that didn't matter. Rune was an old hand at keeping the conversation going. Then he warmed up and they'd had a great time. Talking about New York City—he knew it real well even though he'd been born in the Midwest. How he used to go to clubs in Hell's Kitchen, west of Midtown. How he'd have picnics in Battery Park. How he used to go for hikes in Central Park with a "lady friend" of his—Rune loved that expression. When she was old she hoped she'd be somebody's lady friend. She'd—

Oh, damn . . .

Rune stopped in the middle of the sidewalk. *God-damn.* She reached into her bag and found that she'd forgotten the tape she'd made for him. Which was too bad for Mr. Kelly because he'd be looking forward to it. But mostly it was too bad for her—because she'd left it at the store and if Tony found she'd made a bootleg of a store tape, Jesus, he'd kick her right out on her ass. No pleas for mercy accepted at Washington Square Video.

But she couldn't very well go back now and pull it out from underneath the counter where she'd hidden it. She'd bring it to Mr. Kelly in a day or two. Or slip it to him the next time he stopped in.

Would Tony find it? Would he fire her?

And if he did? *Well, them's the breaks.* Which is what she usually said, or at least *thought,* when she found herself back in line at the New York State Department of Labor, a place where she was a regular and where she'd made some of her best friends in the city.

Them's the Breaks. Her mantra of unemployment. Of fate in general too, she supposed.

Except that today, trying to be cavalier about it, she decided she didn't want to get fired. For her, this was a curious sensation—one that went beyond the usual pain-in-the-butt inconvenience of job searching that began to loom when a boss would motion her over and say, "Rune, let's you and me talk." Or "This isn't going to be easy . . ."

Though it usually was *very* easy.

Rune took the firings better than most employees. She had the routine down. So why was she worried about getting canned now?

She couldn't figure. Something in the air maybe . . . As good an explanation as any.

Rune continued east, through the area that NYU and the real estate developers were decimating for dorms and boring cinder-block apartments. A large woman thrust a petition toward her. "Save our Neighborhood" it said. Rune passed the woman by. That was one thing about New York. It always changed, like a snake shedding skins. If your favorite area vanished or turned into something you didn't like, there was always another one that'd suit you. All it took was a subway token to find it.

She glanced again at Mr. Kelly's address. 380 East Tenth. Apartment 2B.

She crossed the street and continued past Avenue A, Avenue B. Alphabet soup, alphabet city. The neighborhood growing darker, shabbier, more sullen.

Scarier.

Save our neighborhood . . .

CHAPTER THREE

Haarte didn't like the East Village.

When it came to the coin-toss to see who was going to stake out the target's apartment three weeks ago, after they'd gotten back from the Gittleman hit in St. Louis, he was glad Zane'd won.

He paused on East Tenth and looked for surveillance in front of the tenement. Zane'd been there for a half hour and had said the block looked clean. They'd learned that a while ago the target had vanished from his apartment on the Upper West Side—the apartment the U.S. Marshals Service had provided for him—and he'd given the slip to his minders. But that info was old. The feds might've tracked him down again—those pricks could find anybody if they wanted to—and be checking this building out. So this morning Haarte paused, scanned the street carefully, looking for any signs of baby-sitters. He saw none.

Haarte continued along the sidewalk. The streets

were piled with garbage, moldy books and magazines, old furniture. Cars doubled-parked on the narrow streets. Several moving vans too. People in the Village always seemed to be moving out. Haarte was surprised anybody moved *in*. He'd get the fuck out of this neighborhood as fast as he could.

Today Haarte was wearing an exterminator's uniform, pale blue. He carried a plastic toolbox which contained not the tools of the bug-killers' trade but his Walther automatic on which was mounted his Lansing Arms suppressor. Also inside the box was the Polaroid camera. This uniform wouldn't work everywhere but whenever he had a job in New York—which wasn't often because he lived there—he knew the one thing that people would never be suspicious about was an exterminator.

"I'm almost there," he said into his lapel mike. The other thing about New York was that you could seem to be talking to yourself and nobody thought it was weird.

As Haarte approached the building, 380 East Tenth Street, Zane—parked a block away in a green Pontiac—said, "Street's clear. Saw a shadow in his apartment. Asshole's in there. Or somebody is."

For this hit, the way they'd worked it out, Haarte was going to be the shooter, Zane was getaway.

He said, "Three minutes till I'm inside. Drive around back. Into the alley. Anything goes wrong we split up. Meet me back at my place."

"Okay."

He walked into the foyer of the building. Stinks in here, he thought. Dog pee. Maybe human pee. He shivered slightly. Haarte made over a hundred thousand dollars a year and lived in a very nice town house several miles from here, overlooking the Hudson River and New Jersey. So nice he didn't even *need* an exterminator.

Haarte checked out the lobby and hallway carefully. The target might not be thinking about a hit and Haarte could possibly just call up on the intercom and say that he was there to spray for roaches. The target might just let him in.

But he might also come to the top of the stairway, aim into the foyer with his own piece, and start shooting.

So Haarte decided on the silent approach. He jimmied the front-door lock with a thin piece of steel. The cheap lock clicked open easily.

He stepped inside and took the pistol from his toolbox. Started down the hall to Apartment 2B.

Rune was surprised, seeing Robert Kelly's building.

Surprised the way people sometimes are when they come to visit a friend for the first time. She'd seen his modest clothes and had expected modest quarters. But she was looking at piss-poor. The brick was scaly, diseased, shedding its schoolhouse-red paint in dusty flakes. The wooden window frames were rotting. Rust water had trickled down from the roof and left huge streaks on the front step and sidewalk. Some tenants had patched broken panes with cardboard and cloth and yellowing newspaper.

Of course she'd known that the East Village wasn't the greatest neighborhood—she came to clubs here a lot and hung out with friends in Tompkins Square Park on Avenue A, dodging the druggies and the wanna-be gangsters. But, picturing the gentlemanly Mr. Kelly, the image that had come to mind of his home was a proper English town house with frilly plaster moldings and flowered wallpaper. Outside would be a black wrought-iron fence and a neat garden.

Like the set in a movie she'd seen as a little girl, sitting next to her father—*My Fair Lady*. Kelly would sit in the parlor like Rex Harrison, in front of the fire, and drink tea. He would take small sips (a cup of tea lasted forever in English movies) and read a newspaper that didn't have any comics.

She felt uncomfortable, embarrassed for him. Almost wished that she hadn't come.

Rune walked closer to the building. A three-legged chair lay on its side in the bare-dirt garden outside the front stairs. A bicycle frame was fastened with a Kryptonite lock to a no-parking sign. The wheels, chain, and handlebars had been stolen.

Who else lived in the building? she wondered. Elderly people, she supposed. There were a lot of retirees around there. She herself would rather spend her final years there than in Tampa or San Diego.

But how had they happened to end up there? she wondered.

There'd be a million answers.

Them's the breaks. . . .

The building just across the alley from Mr. Kelly's was much nicer, painted, clean, a fancy security gate on the front door. A blond woman in an expensive pink jogger's outfit and fancy running shoes pushed out the doorway and stepped into the alley. She started her stretching exercises. She was pretty and looked disgustingly pert and professional.

Save our neighborhood . . .

Rune continued to the front stairs of Mr. Kelly's building. An idea occurred to her. She'd pick up the tape but instead of going back to the store she'd take a few hours off. She and Mr. Kelly could go have an adventure.

She'd take him for a long walk beside the Hudson.

"Let's look for sea monsters!" she'd suggest.

And she had this weird idea that he'd play along. There was something about him that made her think they were similar. He was . . . well, mysterious. There was nothing literal about him—being *un*literal was Rune's highest compliment.

She walked into the entryway of his building. Beneath the filth and cobwebs she noticed elaborate mosaic tiles, brass fixtures, carved mahogany trim. If it were scrubbed up and painted, she thought, this'd be a totally excellent place. . . .

She pushed the buzzer to 2B.

That'd be a fun job, she thought. Finding junky old buildings and fixing them up. But people did that for a living, of course. Rich people. Even places like this could cost hundreds of thousands. Anyway, she'd want to paint murals of fairy tales on the walls and decorate the place with stuffed animals and put magical gardens in all the apartments. She supposed there wasn't much of a market for that kind of look.

The intercom crackled. There was a pause. Then a voice said, "Yes?"

"Mr. Kelly?"

"Who is it?" the staticky voice asked.

"Here's Johnnyyyyyyy," she said, trying to impersonate Jack Nicholson in *The Shining*. She and Mr. Kelly had talked about horror films. He seemed to know a lot about movies and they'd joked about how scary the Kubrick film was even though it was so brightly lit.

But apparently he didn't remember. "Who?"

She was disappointed that he didn't get it.

"It's Rune. You know—from Washington Square Video. I'm here to pick up the tape."

Silence.

"Hello?" she called.

Static again. "I'll be there in a minute."

"Is this Mr. Kelly?" The voice didn't sound quite right. Maybe it wasn't him. Maybe he had a visitor.

"A minute."

"I can come up."

A pause. "Wait there," the voice commanded.

This was weird. He'd always seemed so polite. He didn't sound that way now. Must be the intercom.

Several minutes passed. She paced around the entryway.

She was looking outside when, finally, she heard footsteps from inside, coming down the stairs.

Rune walked to the inner door, peered through the greasy glass. She couldn't see through it. A figure walked forward slowly. Was it Mr. Kelly? She couldn't tell.

The door opened.

"Oh," she said in surprise, looking up.

The woman in her fifties, with olive-tinted skin, stepped out, glanced at her. She made sure the door closed before she left the entryway so Rune couldn't get inside—standard New York City security procedures when unknown visitors were in the lobby. The woman carried a bag of empty soda and beer cans. She took them out to the curb and dropped them in a recycling bin.

"Mr. Kelly?" Rune called again into the intercom. "You all right?"

There was no answer.

The woman returned and looked over Rune carefully. "Help you?" She had a thick Caribbean accent.

"I'm a friend of Mr. Kelly's."

"Oh." Her face relaxed.

"I just called him. He was going to come down."

"He's on the second floor."

"I know. I'm supposed to pick up a videotape. I called five minutes ago and he said he'd be right out."

"I just walked past his door an' it was open," she said. "I live up the hall."

Rune pushed the buzzer and said, "Mr. Kelly? Hello? Hello?"

There was no answer.

"I'ma go see," the woman said. "You wait here."

She disappeared inside. After a moment Rune grew impatient and buzzed again. No answer. She tried the door. Then she wondered if there was another door—maybe in the side or in the back of the building.

She stepped outside. Walked to the sidewalk and then continued on to the alley. The pert yuppie woman was still there, stretching. The only exercise Rune got was dancing at her favorite clubs: World or Area or Limelight (dancing was aerobic and she also built upper-body strength by pushing away drunk lawyers and account execs in the clubs' co-ed rest rooms).

No, there was nobody else. Maybe she—

Then she heard the scream.

She turned fast and looked at Mr. Kelly's building. Heard a woman's voice, in panic, calling for help. Rune believed the voice had an accent—maybe the woman she'd just met, the woman who knew Mr. Kelly. "Somebody," the voice cried, "call the police. Oh, please, help!"

Rune glanced at the woman jogger, who stared at Rune with an equally shocked expression on her face.

Then a huge squeal of tires from behind them.

At the end of the alley a green car skidded around the corner and made straight for Rune and the jogger. They both froze in panic as the car bore down on them.

What's he doing, what's he doing, what's he doing? Rune thought madly.

No, no, no . . .

When the car was only feet away she flung herself backward out of the alley. The jogger leapt the opposite way. But the woman in pink hadn't moved as fast as Rune and she was struck by the side-view mirror of the car. She was thrown into the brick wall of her building. She hit the wall and tumbled to the ground.

The car skidded onto Tenth Street and vanished.

Rune ran to the woman, who was alive but unconscious, blood pouring from a gash on her forehead. Rune sprinted up the street to find a pay phone. It took her four phones, and three blocks, before she found one that worked.

CHAPTER FOUR

Mr. Kelly's door was open.

Rune stopped in the doorway, stared in shock at the eight people who stood in the room. No one seemed to be moving. They stood or crouched, singly or in groups, like the mannequins she'd seen in the import store on University Place.

Gasping, she rested against the doorjamb. She'd raced back from the pay phone and charged up the stairs. No trouble getting in this time; the cops or the Emergency Medical Service medics had wedged the building door open.

She watched them: six men and two women, some in police uniforms, some in suits.

Her eyes fell on the ninth person in the room and her hands began to tremble.

Oh, no . . . oh, no . . .

The ninth person—the man whose apartment it was. Robert Kelly. He sat in an old armchair, arms outstretched, limp, palms up, eyes open and staring skyward, like Jesus or some saint in those weird religious paintings at the Met. His flesh was very pale—everywhere except his chest. Which was brown-red from all the blood. There was a lot of it.

Oh, no . . .

Her breath shrank to nothing, short gasps, she was dizzy. Oh, goddamn him! Tony! For making her pick up the tape and see this. God*damn* Frankie Greek, god*damn* Eddie for pretending to fix the fucking monitors when all they were really doing was figuring out how to get into a concert for free . . .

Her eyes pricked with tears. *Goddamn.*

But then Rune had a curious thought. That, no, no, if this *had* to happen, it was better that *she* was there, rather than them. At least she was Mr. Kelly's friend. Eddie or Frankie would've walked in and said, "Wow, cool, a shooting," and it was better for her to be the one to see this, out of respect for him.

No one noticed her. Two men in business suits gave instructions to a third, who nodded. The uniformed cops were crouched down, writing notes, some were putting a white powder on dark things, a black powder on light.

Rune studied the faces of the cops. She couldn't look away. There was something odd about them and she couldn't figure it out at first. They just seemed like everybody else—amused or bored or curious about something. Then she realized: *that's* what was odd. That there was nothing out of the ordinary about them. They all had a workaday glaze in their eyes. They weren't horrified or sickened by what they were looking at.

God, they seemed just like the clerks in Washington Square Video.

They looked just like me, doing what I do, renting movies eight hours a day, four days a week: just doing the job. The Big Boring J.

They didn't even seem to notice, or to care, that somebody had just been killed.

Her eyes moved around the apartment slowly. Mr. Kelly lived *here*? Grease-spotted wallpaper sagged. The carpet was orange and made out of thick, stubby strands. The whole place smelled like sour meat. There was no art on the walls: some old-time movie posters in frames leaned against a shabby couch. A dozen boxes were scattered on the floor. It seemed he'd been living out of them. Even his clothes and dishes were stacked in cartons. He must have moved in recently, maybe around the time he'd joined the video club, a month before.

She remembered the first time he'd come into Washington Square Video.

"Can you spell your name?" Rune'd asked, filling out his application.

"Yes, I can," he'd answered, offhand. "I'm of above-average intelligence. Now, do you *want* me to?"

She'd loved that and they'd laughed. Then she'd taken down the rest of the facts about Kelly, Robert, deposit: cash. Address: 380 East Tenth Street, Apt. 2B. He'd wanted a detective film, and, thinking about the old *Dragnet* series, she'd said, "All we want is the facts, sir, just the facts."

He'd laughed again.

No credit cards. She remembered thinking that was definitely one thing they had in common.

What were the words? You knew them real well at one time. How did they go?

Rune's eyes were on *him* now. A dead man who was a little heavy, tall, dignified, seventh-decade balding.

All that the father giveth me, he that raised up Jesus from the dead will also quicken up our mortal bodies . . .

What bothered her most, she decided, was the completely still way Mr. Kelly lay. A human being not moving at all. She shuddered. That stillness made the mystery of life all the more astonishing and precious.

I heard a voice from Heaven saying ashes to ashes, dust to dust, sure and certain I hope for Resurrection, and the sea shall give up . . .

The words coming fast now. She pictured her father, laid out by the talented siblings of Charles & Sons in Shaker Heights. Five years before. Rune had a vivid recollection of the man, lying in the satiny upholstery. But that day her father had been a stranger—a caricature of the human being he'd been when alive. With the makeup, the new suit, the smoothed hair, there was something slick and phony about him. He didn't even seem dead: he just seemed odd.

There was something far more real about Mr. Kelly. He wasn't a sculpture, he wasn't unreal at all. And death was staring right back at her. She felt the room tilting and had to concentrate on breathing. The tears tickled her cheeks with a painful irritation.

The Lord be with you and with thy spirit blessed be the name of the Lord. . . .

One of the men near the body noticed her. A short man in a suit, mustachioed. Trimmed black hair flowing away from his center part, held close to his head with spray. His eyes were close together and that made Rune think he was stupid.

"You're one of the witnesses? You're the one called nine one one?"

She nodded.

The man noticed where her eyes were aimed. He stepped between her and Mr. Kelly's body.

"I'm Detective Manelli. You know the deceased?"

"What happened?" Her mouth was dry and the words vanished in her throat. She repeated the question.

The detective, watching her face, probably trying to figure out where she fit on the spectrum of relationships, said, "That's what we're trying to find out. Did you know him?"

She nodded. She couldn't see the body; her eyes fell to a small metal suitcase stenciled with the words CRIME SCENE UNIT. They fixed on the case, wouldn't let go.

"The tape. I was supposed to pick up the tape. For my job."

"Tape? What tape?"

She pointed to a plastic bag with blue letters, WSV, printed on it. "That's my store. He rented a movie yesterday. I was supposed to pick it up."

"You have some ID?"

She handed Manelli her real driver's license and her employee discount card. He jotted down some information. "You have a New York address?"

She gave it to him. This he wrote down too. Handed back the cards. He didn't seem to think she was involved. Maybe in his line of work you got a feel for who was a real killer.

In a soft voice Rune said, "I was the one who rented the tape to him. It was me. Yesterday." She whispered manically, "I just saw him yesterday. I . . . He was fine then. I talked to him just a few minutes ago."

"You talked to him?"

"I just called on the intercom."

"You're sure it was him?" the detective asked.

She felt a thud in her chest. Recalling that the voice sounded different. Maybe it was the killer she'd talked to. Her legs went weak. "No, I'm not."

"Did you recognize the voice?"

"No. But . . . it didn't sound like Mr. Kelly. I didn't think anything about it. I don't know—I thought maybe I woke him up or something."

"The voice? Young, old, black, Hispanic?"

She shook her head. "I don't know. I couldn't tell."

"You were outside? Did you see anything?"

"I was in the alley. This green car tried to run us down."

"Us?" Manelli repeated. "You and the woman from next door?"

"Right."

"What kind of car was it?"

"I don't know."

"Dark green or light?"

"Dark."

"Tags?"

"What?" Rune asked.

"The license plate number. You notice it?"

"He was trying to run me down, the driver."

"You didn't see the number, you mean?"

"That's what I mean. I didn't see it."

"How 'bout the state?" the detective asked.

"No."

He sighed. "You see the driver?"

"No. There was too much glare."

Another man in a suit came up to them. He smelled of bitter cigarettes. "Whatta we got?"

Manelli said to him, "Here's what it looks like, Captain. This lady comes to pick up a videotape. She calls on the intercom and we think the perp answers. Probably after he does the vic."

Does the vic. Rune stared at the detective, furious at the callousness.

"Pops him three in the chest. No defensive wounds, so it happened fast. He never even tried to dodge. And one in the TV."

"The TV?"

Rune followed their eyes. The killer had shot out the TV set. A spidery fracture surrounded a small black hole in the upper right. It was, she noticed, a very old, cheap set.

Manelli continued. "Then this neighbor up the

hall—" He looked at his notebook. "Amanda LeClerc. She comes upstairs and finds him dead."

"Nobody hears anything?" the captain asked.

"No. Not even the shots . . . Okay, then the killer or his backup's in a car in the alley. He bolts and takes out one witness."

And nearly me too, Rune thought. As if they care.

Manelli consulted his notebook again. "Name's Susan Edelman. Lives next door." He nodded toward the building where Rune had seen the jogger stretching.

"Ice her?" the captain asked.

Ice . . . do . . . These people had no respect for human beings.

"No," Manelli said. "But Edelman's in no shape to say anything. Not for a while."

Rune remembered the woman lying on the greasy cobblestones of the alley. Blood on her pink jogging suit. Remembered feeling guilty that she'd put down the poor woman for being a yuppie, for being pert.

"This young lady"—Nodding at Rune—"saw the car too. Says she didn't see much."

"Yeah?" the captain asked. "You get a look at the perp?"

"The what?"

"Perp."

Rune shook her head. "I speak English. It's my native language."

"The driver."

"No."

"How many people were in the car?" the captain continued.

"I don't know. There was glare. I told *him* that."

"Yeah," the captain said doubtfully. "Some people think there's glare when they just don't *want* to see anything. But you don't hafta worry. We take care of witnesses. You'll be safe."

"I wasn't a witness. I didn't see anything. I was getting out of the way of a car that was trying to run me over. It's a little distracting. . . ."

Her eyes strayed again to the corpse; she found she'd eased to the side of the slow detective. Finally she forced herself to look away. She glanced up at Manelli.

"The tape," she said.

"What?"

"Can I get the tape? I'm supposed to take it back to where I work."

She saw the cover for the cassette. *Manhattan Is My Beat.*

Manelli walked over to the VCR and pushed eject. A clatter of the mechanism. The tape eased out. Manelli motioned to a crime-scene cop, who walked over. The detective asked, "Whatta you think? Can she have it?"

"One of my biggest fears." The crime-scene officer's latex-gloved hand lifted the cassette out of the VCR; he looked it over.

"What's that?" Manelli asked the officer.

"I rent *Debbie Does Dallas* and get hit by a bus before I can return it. My widow gets a bill for two thousand bucks for some sleazy porn and—"

Rune said angrily, "That's *not* what he rented and I don't think you should joke."

The technician cleared his throat, kept an awkward grin on his face. He didn't apologize. He said, "Thing is, look at the TV. You know, him shooting it out? Maybe it's a coincidence but I'd say we better dust this tape pretty careful. Maybe the perp looked at it. And we do that, well, I'll tell you I wouldn't run it through *my* VCR with powder on it. This shit'll gum up anything."

Rune said, "You can't just take our tape."

She didn't care about Washington Square Video's inventory. No, what bothered her was that the cops were keeping the one thing that connected her to Robert Kelly. Stupid, she thought. But she wanted that tape.

"We can actually. Yeah."

"No, you can't. It's ours. And I want it."

The captain was irritated with her but Manelli, even if he too was pissed off, was trying to remain civil-servant polite. He said, "Why don't we go downstairs? You're not supposed to be here anyway."

Rune glanced one last time at Robert Kelly, then followed the detective into the hall, which was hot and filled with the smells of dust and mold and cooking food. They walked down the stairs.

Outside, leaning on an unmarked police car, Manelli said to her, "About the tape—we've gotta keep it. Sorry. Your boss wants to complain, have him or his lawyer call the corporation counsel. But we gotta. Might be evidence."

"Why? You think the killer watched the movie?" she asked.

The detective said, "He may have picked it up to see if it was worth taking."

"And then shot the TV because it wasn't?"

The detective said, "Maybe."

"That's crazy," Rune said.

"Murder's crazy."

She was remembering the pattern the blood made on Mr. Kelly's chest.

He asked, "Tell me true. How well did you know him?"

Rune didn't answer for a moment. She wiped her eyes and nose with the tail of her shirt-vest. "Not well. He was a customer is all."

"You couldn't tell us anything about him?"

Rune started to say, sure, but then realized that, no, she couldn't. Everything she thought she knew, which was a lot, she'd just made up: the wife who was dead of cancer, the children who'd moved away, a distinguished military career in the Pacific, a job in the garment district, a totally cool retirement party he still talked about ten years later. In the past few years he'd met a group of retirees in the East Village, getting to know them over the months at the A&P or Social Security or one of the shabby drugstores or coffee shops on Avenues A or B. Gradually—he'd have been shy about it—he would've suggested getting together for a game of bridge or a trip to Atlantic City to play the slots or saved their money to hear a rehearsal at the Met.

These were scenes she could picture perfectly. Scenes from movies she'd seen a dozen times.

Only none of it was true.

All she could tell this cop was that Kelly, Robert, deposit: cash, wore suits and ties even in retirement. He liked to laugh. He was polite. He had the courage to eat in restaurants by himself on holidays.

And he was a lot like her.

Rune said to the cop, "Nothing. I don't really know a thing."

The detective handed her one of his cards. "And you really didn't see anything?"

"No."

He accepted this. "All right. You think of something, call me. Sometimes that happens. A day or two goes by and people remember things."

When he'd turned away and started up the stairs she said, "Hey."

He paused, looked back.

"You get the asshole that did this, that would be a real good thing, you know?"

"That's why I do what I do." He continued up the stairs.

The Crime Scene cop passed him and walked outside, carrying his metal suitcase. Rune glanced at him, started to walk away, then turned back. He looked at her, then away as he continued to his station wagon.

She called to him, "Oh, one thing. For your information, Mr. Kelly didn't rent dirty movies. For some reason—don't ask me why—he liked movies about cops."

How big a problem was it?

Haarte considered this, walking quickly toward the subway.

The day was plenty cool—nothing like a muggy spring day around the Mississippi River when they'd gotten Gittleman—but he was sweating like crazy. He'd ditched the exterminator coveralls—they were toss-aways, standard procedure after a job—but he was still hot.

He reflected on what'd happened. Part of it was bad luck but he was also at fault. For one thing, he'd decided against hiring local backup because the vic wasn't being minded by the marshals or anybody else. So there was just Zane and him for both surveillance and shooting. Which had worked fine for the St. Louis hit. But here he should've known that some innocents might show up. New York was a big fucking city. More people, more bystanders.

Then, he decided, he'd sent Zane down the alley too early. He just wasn't thinking. So they hadn't had any warning about whoever that girl was who showed up and rang the buzzer, which happened just as Haarte was about to shoot. The vic had risen from his chair and seen Haarte. Haarte had shot him. The old guy had fallen on the remote control and the sound on the TV had gone way up. So Haarte had shot the TV set out too. Which made another loud noise and filled the apartment with a gassy, smoky smell.

Then the girl called on the intercom again. She

sounded concerned. And a moment later there was a call from *another* woman.

Grand Central Station, Jesus . . .

He knew they were suspicious and that they'd be coming upstairs to check on the vic at any minute.

So Haarte decided to split up. He'd told Zane to get back to Haarte's apartment. He'd go by surface transportation. It wasn't a moment too soon. As he climbed out the fire escape window on the east side of the building he'd heard the scream. Then Zane took off and Haarte jumped into the alley and disappeared.

When they'd talked ten minutes later Zane, to his dismay, told him there were witnesses. Two women. One of them had been hit by the Pontiac but the other jumped out of the way in time.

"ID you?" Haarte asked.

"Couldn't tell. I already changed the tags but I think we oughta get the fuck out of town for a while."

Haarte considered this. The broker in St. Louis wouldn't pay without some confirmation of the vic's death. And Haarte hadn't had time to take a Polaroid. He also didn't want to leave the witnesses alive.

"No," he'd told Zane. "We stay. Listen, we need that backup now. Find out who's in town."

"What kind of backup?" Zane asked.

"Somebody who can shoot."

"Hi, there."

Rune, leaning on the fence in front of Robert Kelly's building, turned. The woman she'd met in the entryway, the woman with the bag of cans, was standing unsteadily on the stoop, arms crossed, tears running down her face.

They'd just brought the old man's body out. Rune had started to leave, after Manelli returned to the apartment, but then she'd decided to stay. She wasn't sure why.

"Your name's Amanda?"

The woman wiped her face with a paper towel and nodded. "That's right. How you know?"

"The cops mentioned it. I'm Rune."

"Rune . . ." She spoke absently.

Other tenants had come downstairs, gossiped about the shooting, then returned to their rooms or headed up the street.

The two detectives left. Manelli said, "Good-bye." The captain hadn't even glanced at her.

Amanda cried some more.

Unable to stop herself, Rune cried too. Wiped her face with the tail of the shirt again.

"How you know him?" Amanda had an accent, Rune decided, that sounded like a female Bob Marley's. Low and sexy.

"From the video store. Washington Square Video. Where he rented movies."

Amanda looked at her like a VCR and renting movies were a luxury she couldn't even imagine.

Rune asked, "How'd *you* know him?"

"Neighbors. Met him when he move in, a month ago. But we got close real fast. What it was, about Robert, he *talk* to you. Nobody else here talk to you. He always ask about my kids, ask where I came from. You know . . . So hard to find somebody who just likes to listen."

Amen, Rune thought.

"He asked me a lot about me too. But he no say much about himself."

"Yeah, that's true. He never seemed to like to talk about the past."

"I no believe this happen. What do you think it was? Why somebody do this?"

Rune shrugged. "Drugs, I'll bet. Around here . . . What else?"

"I no understand why they kill him. He wasn't no threat. If they want to rob him they could take it and just let him be. Why kill?"

Murder's crazy . . .

"He so nice," Amanda continued, speaking softly. "So nice. When I have problems with the landlord, problems with INS, Mr. Kelly help me out. I only know him one month but he write letters for me. He real smart." More tears. "What'm I gonna do?"

Rune put her arm around the woman.

"He help me with my rent. The INS, they took my check. My paycheck. I working but they took my check. I applied for the card, you know. I was trying to do it right, I no cheat nobody or anything. But they wouldn't let me have any money. . . . But Mr. Kelly, he lend me money for the rent. What'm I gonna do now?"

"They going to send you back home?"

She shrugged.

"Where's that?" Rune asked. "Home?"

"I *come* from the Dominican Republic," Amanda said, then added defiantly, "but *this* is my home now. New York City is my home. . . ." She looked back at the building. "Why they kill somebody like him? There're so many bad people out there, so many people with bad hearts. Why they kill somebody like Robert?"

There was no answer for that, of course.

"I have to go," Rune said.

Amanda nodded, wiped her eyes with the shredding paper towel. "Thank you."

Rune asked, "For what?"

"Waiting till they take him away. To say good-bye. That was good of you. That was very good."

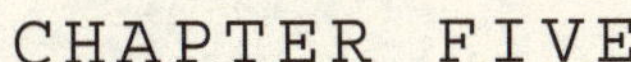

CHAPTER FIVE

Near quitting time, Tony came back to the store.

"So where the hell were you this afternoon?"

"I needed to clear my head," Rune told him.

Tony snickered. "That'd take more than one afternoon."

"Tony, no crap. *Por favor.*"

He dropped his backpack in front of the counter and dodged around a cardboard cutout of Sylvester Stallone, who brandished a large cardboard gun. He checked the receipts. "You should've argued with the cop. Christ, that tape . . . it's over a hundred bucks wholesale."

"I gave you the name of the cop to talk to, you want," she shot back. "It's not *my* job. You're the manager."

"Yeah, well, at least you should've come back after. Frankie Greek was here by himself. He gets overloaded when he's got to work by himself."

She said in a low voice, "He gets overloaded when he has to tie his shoes by himself."

Frankie, a scrawny aspiring rock star and high school dropout, had long, curly hair and reminded Rune of the poodle on the pink skirt she'd bought last week at Second-Hand Rose, a vintage clothing store on Broadway. He was in the back room at the moment.

"Well, where *were* you?" Tony persisted.

"Walking around," Rune said. "I didn't feel like coming back. I mean, he was dead. I saw him. Right in front of me."

"Whoa. You see the bullet holes and everything?"

"Oh, Jesus Christ. Hang it up, okay?"

"Are they like in the movies?"

She turned away, kept wiping the counter with Windex. Tony and Frankie both smoked. It made the glass filthy.

"Well, you shoulda called. I was worried."

"Worried? Like, I'm *sure,*" she said.

"Just call next time."

Rune had a feel for it now. He was backing down. No trips to unemployment this week. *Them's the breaks* . . . She felt like pushing so she pushed. "There won't *be* a next time. I don't do any more pickups, okay? That's a rule."

"Hey, we're all simpatico here, no? The Washington Square Video family." Tony glanced at Frankie as the skinny young man came out of the back room.

"Think I can fix that monitor," Frankie said.

"Yeah, well, that's not your priority. Locking up's your priority."

The large man slung his dirty red nylon backpack over his shoulder again and disappeared out the front door.

Frankie said, "Like, I heard you talking to Tony."

"And?"

"How come you didn't make up something? About

coming in late today? Like say your mother got sick or something?"

Rune said, "Why would I lie to *Tony*? You only lie to people who have power over you. . . . So what happened with the Palladium?"

Frankie was crestfallen. "We only got one pass and Eddie, like, won the toss. Man. It was Blondie too."

He glanced at a stack of porn tapes that had been returned and needed to be reshelved. One title seemed to interest him. He put it aside. He said, "That guy who was killed. He was that old guy you liked, right?"

"Yeah."

"I don't remember him too good. Was he cool?"

She leaned on the counter, playing with her bracelets. She looked outside. The city had these weird orange streetlamps. It was close to eleven P.M. but the light made the city look like afternoon during a partial eclipse. "Yeah, he was cool." She dug under the counter and found the bootleg tape she'd made for Kelly. Turned it over in her hands. "Also, he was kind of different."

"Like, what? Weird?"

"Not weird the way *you* mean."

"What, uhm, way do I mean?"

She didn't answer. A thought was in her mind. "But there was one thing weird about him. Not him personally. He was the nicest old guy you'd ever want to meet. Polite."

"So what was weird about him?"

"Well, he'd only been a member for a month."

"And?"

"He rented the same movie a lot."

"A lot?"

Rune typed on the keyboard of the little Kaypro portable computer on the counter. Then she read from the screen. "Eighteen times."

"Wow," Frankie said, "that's weird."

"*Manhattan Is My Beat,*" Rune said.

"Never heard of it. About a, like, reporter?"

"A cop. Walking a beat. One of those old-time cop movies from the forties. You know, all the men wearing those big drapey double-breasted suits and have their hair slicked back. Nobody really famous in it. Dana Mitchell, Charlotte Goodman, Ruby Dahl."

"Who're they?"

"You wouldn't know them. They're not part of the Brat Pack. Anyway, the movie just came out on tape a month ago. I'm not surprised nobody was in a hurry to release it. I watched it but it wasn't my style. I like the black and white though. I hate colorization. It's a political issue with me.

"Anyway, Mr. Kelly shows up the day after it's released. We had a poster up in the window. The distributor sent it. . . . Uh, there it is, in the back. . . ."

Frankie glanced. "Oh, yeah, I remember it."

Rune continued. "He comes in and wants to rent it. He wasn't a member so he asks about joining. Then—this *is* weirdness for you—he asks how he puts tapes in his TV. Can you believe it? He doesn't know about VCRs! So I tell him if he doesn't have a player he's got to get one and I tell him where Audio Exchange and Crazy Eddie's are. Well, he doesn't have much money, I can tell, cause he goes, 'Do you think they'll take a check? See, I just moved and it doesn't have my address on it. . . .' That kind of stuff. And I was thinking, yeah, right, the reason they won't take the check isn't the address, it's that there's no money in the account. So I tell him about this place on Canal where they have all kinds of used stuff and he can probably get a VCR for fifty bucks."

"Beta only, I'll bet." Frankie sneered.

"No, they've got VHS. And he leaves and I think

that's the last I'll see of him. But the next day he's back when the store opens and he says he found a player. And he joins and rents this movie he's so interested in. Turns out he's a real sweetheart, we bullshit some, talk movies. . . ."

"Yeah, your date," Frankie observed. "I remember him."

"And he's not flirting or anything. He's just talking. Takes the film home. Eddie picks it up the next day. Okay, couple days later, he calls a delivery in. Rents something I don't know what it is and what else? *Manhattan Is My Beat* again. This goes on for weeks."

Frankie nodded, his shaggy hair bobbing.

"Christ," Rune told him, "I feel so sorry for the guy—I picture him spending all his Social Security check on this stupid movie. I told him just to buy it. But you know Tony. How he marks up? He was charging almost two hundred. What a rip-off. So I tell Mr. Kelly I'm going to copy it for him."

"Man, Tony'd be super pissed, he finds out," Frankie said, lowering his voice as if the store were bugged.

"Yeah, whatever," Rune said. She pictured Mr. Kelly again. "You should've seen his eyes. I thought he was going to cry, he was so happy. Anyway, it was, like, noon or something and he asked if he could take me to lunch, you know, to thank me."

"So did you make the dupe for him?"

Rune's face fell. After a moment she said, "I did, yeah. But it was just a couple days ago. I never got the chance to give it to him. I wish I had. I wish he'd seen it once at least—the tape *I'd* made, I mean. He said he didn't have anything much to give me now but when he got rich, he'd remember me."

"Yeah, right, I've heard that before."

"I don't know. He said it in a funny way. Like, *when*

his ship came in. It was like . . . Hey, you know fairy stories?"

"Uhm . . . I don't know. You mean, like, Jack and the cornstalk?"

She rolled her eyes. "I was thinking about this one from Japan. About the fisherman Urashima."

"Like, who?" Frankie Greek's eyes were close together too. Like the detective in Mr. Kelly's apartment. Manelli.

"Urashima saved a turtle from some children who were stoning it. He helped it back to the ocean. Only it turned out to be a magic turtle and took him to the sea lord's palace under the ocean."

"How could he breathe underwater?"

"He just could."

"But—"

"Don't worry about it. He could breathe, okay? Anyway, the lord's daughter gave him money and pearls and jewels. Maybe everlasting youth too, I don't remember."

"Man, not too shabby," Frankie said. "Happily ever after."

Rune didn't say anything for a moment. "Not exactly. He blew it."

"What happened?" Frankie seemed marginally interested.

"One of the things the daughter gave him was a box he wasn't supposed to open."

"Why not?"

"Doesn't matter. But he *did* open it and, bang, got turned into an old man in about five seconds flat. See, fairy tales have rules too. You have to play by them. He didn't. You've gotta listen to magic turtles and wizards. So, that's what I was thinking of when Mr. Kelly said something about getting rich. That I did a good deed and he was going to give me a reward."

Frankie added, "Just don't open any magic boxes."

Rune looked up. "So, that's my story about Mr. Kelly. Is it totally bizarre, or what?"

"You ever ask him about it, why he rented it so often?"

"Sure. And you want to hear a sad answer? He said, 'That movie? It's the high-point of my life.' He wouldn't say anything else. I'll bet his wife and him saw it on their honeymoon. Or maybe he had a wild affair with some vampy woman the night it was released and they were in a hotel in Times Square with the premiere right outside their window."

"Like, what'd the cops say about him getting whacked? They have any idea why?"

"They don't know anything. They don't care."

Frankie flicked through the pages in a rock music magazine, undid one of his earrings, looked at it, put it into a third hole in his other ear. He said, "So, you've seen it, you think it's worth being the high-point of someone's life?"

"Depends on how low your life has been."

"Like, what's it about?" the young man asked. "This movie?"

"There's a bank robbery in the 1930s or '40s, okay? Somewhere down in Wall Street. The robbers're holed up with a hostage in the bank and this young cop—you know, in love with the girl next door's name is Mary, *that* kind of hero—goes into the bank to exchange himself for the hostage. Then he kills the robber. . . . And then what happens is the cop can't resist. See, he's in love and he wants to get married but he doesn't have enough money. So he takes the loot and sneaks it out of the bank. Then he buries it someplace. The cops find out about it and throw him off the force and arrest him and he goes to jail."

"That's all?"

"I think he gets out of jail and gets killed before he

digs up the money, only I got bored and didn't pay a lot of attention."

Frankie said, "Hey, here it is. Listen." He read from the video distributor catalogue. " '*Manhattan Is My Beat*. Nineteen forty-seven.' Oh, this is so bogus. Listen. 'A gripping drama of a young, idealistic policeman in New York City, torn between duty and greed.' "

Rune glanced at the clock. Quitting time. She locked the door. "All I know is, if I ever made a movie, I'd shoot anyone who called it a 'gripping drama.' "

Frankie said, "If I ever make a movie anybody can call it anything they want, as long as I, like, get to play on the sound track. Hey, it says here it's based on a true story. About a real bank robbery in Manhattan. Somebody got away with a million dollars. It says it was never recovered."

Really? Rune hadn't known that.

"It's late," she told Frankie. "Let's get out of here. I need to—"

A loud knock on the glass door startled them. A threesome stood outside—a man and woman, arm in arm, and another woman. In their twenties. The couple was in black. Jeans, T-shirts. She was taller than he was, with very short yellow-white hair and pale, caked makeup. Dark purple lips. The man wore high black boots. He was thin. He had a long face, handsome and angular. High cheekbones. They both had yellow Sony Walkman wires and earphones around their necks. Her cord disappeared into his pocket. The look was Downtown Chic and they displayed it like war paint.

The other woman was chubby, had spiky orange hair and she moved her head rhythmically—apparently to music that only she could hear (she *didn't* wear a Walkman headset). The cut and color of her hair reminded Rune of Woody Woodpecker's.

Another knock.

Frankie looked at the clock. "What do I say?"

"One word," Rune said. "The opposite of Open."

But then the young man in black touched the door like a curious alien and gave Rune a smile that said, *How can you do this to us?* He lifted his hands, pressed them together, praying, begging, then kissed his fingertips and looked directly into Rune's eyes.

Frankie called, "Like, we're closed."

Rune said, "Open it."

"What?"

"Open the door."

"But you said—"

"Open the door."

Frankie did.

The man outside said, "Just one tape, fair lady, just one. And then we'll depart from your life forever. . . ."

"Except to return it," Rune said.

"There's that, sure," he said. Walking into the store. "But tonight, we need some amusement. Oh, sorely."

Rune said to the blond woman, "When do you have to have him back to Bellevue?"

The woman shrugged.

The Woodpecker said nothing but walked through the racks of movies, studying them while her head rocked back and forth.

"Are you members?" Rune asked.

The blonde flashed a WSV card.

"Three minutes," Rune said. "You've got three minutes."

The man: "Such a small splinter of life, don't you think?"

"Two and three-quarters," Rune responded. "And counting."

Was this guy over the edge or not? Rune couldn't decide.

The blonde spoke. She asked Frankie, "What's good?"

"Like, I don't know, I'm new here."

"We're all new everywhere," the young man said meaningfully, looking at Rune. "All the time. Every three minutes, every two and a half minutes. David Bowie said that. You like him?"

"I *love* him," Rune said. "How'd he get two different-colored eyes?"

The man was looking at her own eyes. He didn't answer. Didn't matter; she forgot that she'd asked him a question.

Rune found her lipstick and carefully put it on. She brushed out her hair with her fingers. She decided she should be more coy. Looked at her watch. "Two minutes. Less now."

He asked her, "Want to go to a party?"

Rune looked into his eyes. Brown, swimming, paisley. She said, "Maybe. Where?"

"Your place, darling," he said.

Oh, *that* again.

But he caught the expression on her face and, suddenly sounding much more down to earth, said, "All of us, I mean. A party. Wine and Cheez-Its. Innocent. Swear."

Rune looked at Frankie. He shook his shaggy head. "My sister's gonna have her baby anytime. I gotta get home."

"Please?" Downtown Man asked.

Why not? Rune thought. Recalling that her last date had been when there was snow piled up in the gutters.

"One minute," the man said. "Our time is almost depleted." He was back in the ozone and was speaking to the blonde. She looked at the orange-haired friend and said, "We need a movie. Pick one."

"Me?" the Woodpecker asked.

"Hurry," the blonde whispered.

The man: "We have less than a minute until the floods mount, the earth will tremble. . . ."

"Do you always talk that way?" Rune asked.

He smiled.

The Woodpecker grabbed a movie from the shelf. "How about this one?"

"I can live with it," the blonde answered grudgingly.

Frankie checked them out.

The man said, "Poof. Time's up. Let's go."

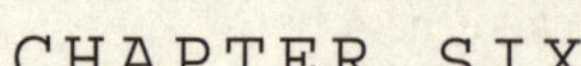

CHAPTER SIX

"This is an example of Stanford White's finest work," Rune told them.

Riding up in a freight elevator. A metallic grinding sound, chains clinking. The smell was of grease and mold and wet concrete. Floors under construction, floors dark and abandoned, fell slowly past them. The sound of dripping water. It was a building in the TriBeCa neighborhood—the triangle below Canal Street—dating back to the nineteenth century.

"Stanford White?" the blonde asked.

"The architect," Rune said.

The mysterious man said, "He died for love."

He *knew* that? Rune thought. Impressed. She added, "Murdered by a jealous lover on the top floor of the original Madison Square Garden."

The blonde shrugged as if love were *never* worth dying for.

The Woodpecker said, "Is this legal, living here?"

"But what, of course, is legal?" the man mused. "I mean *whose* sets of laws apply? There are layers upon layers of laws we have to contend with. Some valid, some not."

"What *are* you talking about?" Rune asked him.

He grinned and raised his eyebrows with ambiguous significance.

His name had turned out to be Richard, which disappointed Rune. Somebody this truly renegade should have been named Jean-Paul or Vladmir.

At the top floor the car stopped and they stepped out into a small room filled with boxes stenciled with block Korean letters, suitcases, a broken TV set, an olive-drab drum of civil defense drinking water. A dozen stacks of old beauty magazines. The Woodpecker strolled over to them and studied the covers. "Historical," she said. The only door was labeled "Toilet" in blotchy black ink.

"No windows, how can you stand it?" Richard asked. But Rune didn't answer and disappeared behind a wall of cartons. She climbed an ornate metal stairway, which was in the middle of the room. From the floor above she gave a shrill whistle. "Yo, follow me. . . . Hey, you imagine the trouble I have getting groceries up here? As if I buy groceries."

The trio stopped cold when they reached the next floor. They stood in a glass turret: a huge gazebo on top of the building, its sides rising like a crown. Ten stories below, the city spread around them. The Empire State Building, distant but massive, stern like an indifferent giant out of a Maxfield Parrish illustration. Beyond it, the elegant Chrysler Building. Southward, the city swept away toward the white pillars of the Trade towers. To the east, the frilly Woolworth Building, City Hall. Farther east was a blanket of lights—Brooklyn and Queens. Opposite, the soft darkness of Jersey. Through the glass of the domed ceiling they could see low clouds, glowing pinkish from the city lights.

"She's out—my roommate," Rune explained, looking around. "She's playing Russian roulette in a singles bar. If I don't find her back by this time, eating ice cream from the carton and watching sitcoms, that means she got lucky. Well, that's how *she* describes it."

Rune pulled off her jacket; it went on a hanger, which she hooked onto the armature of a bulbless floor lamp that held an ostrich-feather boa and a fake-zebra-skin sport coat. She unlaced her boots and set them on the floor next to two battered American Touristers. She opened one, looking over shirts and underwear, which she smoothed, adjusting away creases, refolding some of the wild-colored clothes, then took off her socks and put them into the other suitcase.

To Richard she said, "Dresser and dirty clothes hamper." Nodding at the suitcases.

"You rent this?" the Woodpecker asked.

"I just live here. I don't pay any rent."

"Why not?"

"Nobody's asked me to yet."

Richard asked, "How did you get it?"

Rune shrugged. "I found it. I moved in. Nobody else was here."

He said, "It becomes you."

"Being and becoming . . . ," Rune said, recalling something she'd overheard a couple of guys talking about in the video store a week or so ago.

He lifted his eyebrows. "Hey, you know Hegel?"

"Oh, sure," Rune said. "I love movies."

The circle of the floor was divided by a cinder-block wall, which she'd painted sky blue and dabbed with white for clouds. On Rune's side of the loft were four old trunks, a TV, a VCR, three futons piled on top of one another, a dozen pillows in the corner. Two bookcases, completely filled with books, mostly old ones. A half-size refrigerator.

"Where do you cook?" asked the Woodpecker.

"What does it mean, cook?" Rune replied in a thick Hungarian accent.

Richard said, "I feel something epiphanic about this place. Very watershed, you know." He looked in the refrigerator. A bag of half-melted ice cubes, two six-packs of beer, a shriveled apple. "It's not turned on."

"It doesn't work."

"What about utilities?"

Rune pointed to an orange extension cord snaking down the stairs. "Some of the construction guys working downstairs, they let me have electricity. Isn't that nice of them?"

The Woodpecker asked, "What if the owner finds out, couldn't he kick you out?"

"I'd find someplace else."

"You're a very existential person," Richard said.

And the blonde: "I want to start our party."

Rune shut the lights out, lit a dozen candles.

She heard the rasp of another match. The flare reflected in a dozen angled windows. The ripe raw smell of hash flowed through the room. The joint was passed around. Beer too.

The blonde said to the Woodpecker, "Play the movie, the one you picked out."

Rune and Richard sat back on the pillows, watched the blonde take the cassette from the Woodpecker and open the plastic container. Rune whispered to him, "Are you two like an entity or something?" Nodding at the blonde. Then she thought about it. "Or are you *three* an entity?"

Richard's paisley eyes followed the blonde as she crouched and turned on the VCR and television. He said, "I don't know the redhead. But the other one—I met her last year at the Sorbonne, I was writing a thesis on semiotic interpretations of textile designs."

Is this a joke?

"I was sitting outdoors on the Boulevard St. Germain, and saw her get out of a limousine. I was filled with an intense sense of pre-ordination."

"Like Calvinism," Rune said, remembering something she'd heard her mother, a good Presbyterian, say once. His head turned to her. Frowning, falling out of character, suddenly analytical. He said, "Oh, predestination? Well, that isn't really . . ." He nodded, as he considered something. Then smiled. "Oh, you mean, sort of damned if you do, damned if you don't. . . . That's pretty good. That's perceptive."

"I get off a good one once in a while." What the hell is going on? she wondered. Didn't matter, she supposed. He *seemed* impressed. Appearances count. Though she realized she still didn't have a clue about his relationship with the sullen blonde.

Rune was about to say something cool and giddy about *Casablanca*—about Rick and Ilsa in Paris—when Richard leaned over and kissed her on the mouth.

Whoa . . .

Rune backed off, eyeing the blonde, wondering if she was going to get into a catfight here. But the woman didn't notice—or didn't care. She was stepping back, handing the joint to the Woodpecker, who was adjusting the TV.

Is this crazy? Letting three strangers into my loft.

Sure, it is.

Then, on impulse, she kissed Richard back. Didn't back away until she felt the pressure of his hand on her breast. Then she sat back. "Let's just take it a little easy, okay? I've only known you for a half hour."

"But time is relative."

She kissed his cheek, an innocent peck. Destined

never to be a tall, sultry lover, Rune had flirtatious down cold.

"I'm feeling deprived," he pouted.

She started to give him another *Oh, please* glance but he meant the joint the Woodpecker was holding. "Hey, darling, to each according to his need." The woman inhaled long and gave it to him. He took a drag then passed it to Rune.

He said, "What we'll do is assume a Tantra yoga position."

Rune said, "Tantra yoga?"

"Isn't that the sex one?" the Woodpecker asked.

Rune gave Richard an exasperated grimace.

He said, "People think sex is the thing with Tantra yoga. Wrong. It's breathing. It teaches you how to breathe the right way."

Rune said, "I *know* how to breathe. I'm good at it. I've been doing it all my life."

"Shall we assume the position?"

She was about to hit him with a pillow, when he slipped into an awkward sitting position, three feet away from her, and started to breathe deeply. "Fully clothed," he said. "I meant to add that."

Rune said, "You look like you hurt yourself in a bad fall."

The TV screen flickered, the copyright notice came on.

"Sit next to me," he said. She hesitated. Then did. Their knees touched. She felt a spark of electricity but didn't move any closer.

"What do we do now?"

"Breathe deep and watch the show."

"Yeah," Rune called to the Woodpecker, "what's the movie you picked?"

The credits for *Lesbos Lovers* came on the screen. The blonde pulled the Woodpecker groggily toward her and covered her mouth with her own. Their arms wound around each other and their fingers began undoing buttons.

Rune whispered to Richard, "Oh, you meant *that* show?"

Richard shrugged. "Either one."

In the morning, when Rune woke up, Richard was making coffee on her hot plate.

She asked, "Where're your friends?" She was looking intently for something under the cushions. She surfaced with her Colgate and toothbrush.

He looked around. "Dunno."

"You find the john?"

"Downstairs. I liked the plastic dinosaurs. You did the decorating yourself, I assume."

Rune was examining him. Now he seemed out of place, wearing the black outfit—night clothes—in the bright, open-air loft.

He said, "What's your real name? It's not really Rune, is it?"

"Everybody asks me about my name."

"What do you tell them?" he asked. "The truth?"

"But what's the truth?" Rune smiled at him ambiguously.

Richard laughed. "But the fact you've got a fake name is very interesting. Philosophically, I mean. You know what Walker Percy says about naming? He doesn't mean like first names or family names but humans giving names to things. He says that naming is different from everything else in the universe. A wholly unique act. Think about that."

She did, for a moment, then said, "A year ago, I worked in a diner over on Ninth Avenue. I was Doris then. I think I only took the job to get the name tag they gave us. It said, 'Chelsea Diner. Hi! I'm Doris.' "

He nodded uncertainly. "Doris."

She said, "So, what do you do, Richard?"

"Stuff."

"Oh. I see," she said dubiously.

"Okay. I'm working on a novel." She knew he was a writer or artist. "What's it about?"

"I don't really talk about it much. I'm at a tricky part right now."

This was even better. A mystery man writing a mysterious novel. In the throes of creative angst.

"I write," she said.

"You do?"

"A diary." Rune pulled a thick, water- and ink-stained booklet off the shelf. A picture of a knight—cut from a magazine—was pasted on the cover. "My mother's kept a diary every day of her life. I've only been doing it for a few years. But I write down everything that's major in my life." She nodded at a dozen other booklets on the shelf.

"Everything?" he asked.

"Nearly."

"You going to write anything about me?" Richard asked. He was looking at the notebooks as if he wanted a peek.

"Maybe," Rune said, combing her hair out with her fingers.

He said, "And you . . . You want to be an actress, right?"

"Guess again. You're thinking of what's-her-name: Woody Woodpecker."

"Who?"

"Your friend last night. With the orange hair. The one who ran off with your girlfriend?"

"Whoa, not my girlfriend. She's not even close to bi. I made a pass at her once—"

"You?" Rune asked sarcastically.

"I met her last week at a party. We give good image."

"You—?"

He explained. "We look good together, being chic and making entrances. That's it. Not a meaningful relationship. I don't even know her name."

"Hard to introduce her to your parents in that case."

"That's not in the offing." He carried the coffee to her, set it on the floor next to the futon.

"What about the Sorbonne?" Rune asked.

"Pas de Sorbonne."

"I thought so."

"But I've been to France."

"Jean-Pierre" would be a good name for him too. Or "François." Yeah, he definitely looked like a "François."

"Richard" had to go.

Rune glanced out the window, dug under a futon, and found some sunglasses. She put them on.

"Feeling like a celebrity?" Richard asked, nodding at the fake Ray-Bans.

Suddenly the sun came over the building to the east and the entire room filled with intense raw sunlight.

"Ouch," he said, blinded.

"I maybe'll get curtains. But I can't afford them and my roommate won't help pay."

"You're not paying rent, why have a roommate?"

"Well, she pays *me* something. Anyway, having a roommate's like trial by fire. It toughens you is what it does."

"You don't seem tough to me."

"That's part of being tough—not *looking* tough. Anyway, I'll have to be out in a few months. The owner sold the building and I'm only staying here 'cause I told the contractor that I'm the mistress of the old owner and he dumped me so they're letting me stay until they start renovating this floor. So you going to ask me out on a date?"

"A date? I haven't heard that word for a long time. It sounds, I don't know, like Swahili. I'm not used to it."

True, she supposed. Really chic people don't ask other chic people out on dates. They just *go* places together. Still, there was a certain commitment involved in the concept. So she said, "Date, date, date. There. *Now* you're used to it. So you can ask me out."

"We just spent the night together—"

"On separate futons," she pointed out.

"—and you want a date?"

"I want a date."

"How about dinner?" he asked.

"That's good."

"Okay. I asked you on a date. We'll go out. You happy?"

"It's not a date yet. You have to tell me when. And I mean exactly. Not a month, not a week."

"I'll call you."

"Oh, *that*? Are you kidding? Are men genetically programmed to say those three little words? Gimme a break."

He looked around helplessly. "I don't have my Daytimer here."

He'd *call* her and he had a Daytimer. This was scary. Richard was rapidly losing his appeal.

"Never mind," she said cheerfully.

"Okay, how about tomorrow?" he asked. "I know I'm not doing anything tomorrow."

Not too eager now—watch it. "I guess."

"Where do you want to go?" he asked.

"You can come here. I'll cook."

"I thought you didn't cook."

She said, "I don't cook *well*. But I do cook. We'll save

the Four Seasons for a special occasion." She looked at her wrist. She wore two watches. They'd both stopped working. "What time do you have?"

"Eight."

"Shit, I have to go," Rune said, slipping off her T-shirt.

She could sense Richard watching her thin body, eyes sweeping up and down. She turned to him, wearing only her Bugs Bunny panties. "So, what are you staring at?" Put her hands on her hips.

And got him to blush.

Yes! Score one for me.

"Glad you don't shop at Frederick's of Hollywood," he said.

A good recovery. This boy had potential.

As she dressed, Richard asked, "What's the hurry? I didn't think your store opened until noon."

"Oh, I'm not going to work," she said. "I'm going to the police."

CHAPTER SEVEN

"Miss Rune," Detective Manelli said, "we *are* investigating the case."

She looked at his organized desk. Here—not standing in front of a corpse—he seemed like an insurance agent. The close-together eyes weren't so noticeable; they moved quickly, surveying her, and she decided he might be smarter than she'd thought. His first name was Virgil. She looked at the nameplate twice to make sure she'd read it right.

She nodded at the file open on his desk, the one he'd been reading. "But that's not his case. Mr. Kelly's, I mean."

He took a breath, let it out. "No, it's not."

"Which one is his?" she asked stridently. "How far down is it?" She gestured at the stack of folders.

The captain—the one she'd met in Mr. Kelly's apartment—breezed in. He glanced down with a splinter of recognition but didn't say anything to her.

"They want to hear today," he told Manelli. "About the tourist killing."

"They'll hear today," Manelli said wearily.

"You got anything?"

"No."

"The mayor. You know. The *Post*. The *Daily News*."

"I know."

The captain looked at Rune once again. He left the office.

"We're doing everything according to procedures," Manelli told her.

"Who's the tourist?"

"Somebody from Iowa. Knifed in Times Square. Don't start with me on that."

She said, "Just let me get this straight: You're no closer to finding Mr. Kelly's killer than you were yesterday."

On Manelli's desk, opening up like a mutant flower, was a piece of deli tissue around a mass of corn muffin. He broke off a chunk and ate it. "How 'bout you give us a day or two to make the collar?"

"The . . . ?"

"To arrest the killer."

"I just want to know what happened."

"In New York City, we've got to deal with almost fifteen hundred homicides a year."

"How many people are working on Mr. Kelly's case?"

"Me mostly. But there're other detectives checking things out. Look, Ms. Rune . . ."

"Just Rune."

"What exactly is your interest?"

"He was a nice man."

"The decedent?"

"What a gross word that is. Mr. *Kelly* was a nice man. I liked him. He didn't deserve to get killed."

The detective reached for his coffee, drank some, put it down. "Let me tell you the way it works."

"I know how it works. I've seen enough movies."

"Then you have no idea how it works. Homicide—"

"Why do you have to use such big fancy words? Decedent, homicide. A *man* was *murdered.* Maybe if you said he was *murdered,* you'd work harder to find who did it."

"Miss, murder is only one kind of homicide. Mr. Kelly could have been a victim of manslaughter, negligent homicide, suicide. . . ."

"Suicide?" Her eyebrows lifted in disbelief. "That's a really bad joke."

Manelli snapped back, "A lot of people stage their own deaths to look like murder. Kelly could've hired somebody to do it. For the insurance."

Oh. She hadn't thought of that. Then she asked, "Did he have an insurance policy?"

Manelli hesitated. Then he said, "No."

"I see."

He continued. "Can I finish?"

Rune shrugged.

"We'll interview everybody in the building and everybody hanging around on the streets around the time of the killing. We took down every license number of every car for three blocks around the apartment and we'll interview the owners. We're going through all of the deced—through Mr. Kelly's personal effects. We'll find out if he had any relatives nearby, if any friends have suddenly left town, since most perps—"

"Wait. Perpetrators, right?"

"Yeah. Since more of 'em are friends or relatives of, or at least *know,* the vic. That's the *victim.* Maybe, we're lucky, we'll get a description of a suspect that'll go something like *male Caucasian, six feet. Male black, five eight, wearing dark hat.* Really helpful, understand?" His eyes dropped to a notepad. "Then we'll take what ballistics told us about the gun"—he hesitated—"and check that out."

She jumped on this. "So what do you know about the gun?"

He was glancing at his muffin; it wouldn't rescue him.

"You know *something,*" Rune insisted. "I can see it. Something's weird, right? Come on! Tell me."

"It was a nine-millimeter, mounted with a rubber-baffled silencer. Commercial. Not home-made, like most sound suppressors are." He seemed not to want to tell her this but felt compelled to. "And the slugs . . . the bullets . . . they were Teflon coated."

"Teflon? Like with pots and pans?"

"Yeah. They go through some bulletproof vests. They're illegal."

Rune nodded. "That's weird?"

"You don't see bullets like that very often. Usually just professional killers use them. Just like only pros use commercial silencers."

"Keep going. About the investigation."

"Then sooner or later, while we're doing all that work, maybe in three or four months, we'll get a tip. Somebody got ripped off by a buddy whose cousin was at a party boasting he iced somebody in a drug robbery or something because he didn't like the way somebody looked at him. We'll bring in the suspect, we'll talk to him for hours and hours and hours and poke holes in his story until he confesses. That's the way it happens. The way it *always* happens. But you get the picture? It takes *time.* Nothing happens overnight."

"Not if you don't want it to," Rune said. And before he got mad she asked, "So you don't have *any* idea?"

Manelli sighed. "You want my gut feeling? Where he

lived, some kids from Alphabet City needed crack money and killed him for that."

"With fancy-schmancy bullets?"

"Found the gun, stole it from some OC soldier—organized crime—in Brooklyn. Happens."

Rune rolled her eyes. "And this kid who wanted money enough to kill for it shot the TV? And left the VCR? And, hey, did Mr. Kelly have any money on him?"

Manelli sighed again. Pulled a file from halfway down the stack on his desk, opened it. He read through it. "Walking-around money. Forty-two dollars. But the perp probably panicked when you showed up and ran off without taking anything."

"Was the room ransacked?"

"It didn't appear to be."

Rune said, "I want to look through it."

"The room?" The detective laughed. "No way. It's sealed. No one can go in." He studied her face. "Listen up. I've seen that look before. . . . You break in, it'll be trespassing. That's a crime. And I'd be more than happy to give your name to the prosecutor."

He broke off another piece of muffin, looked at it. Set it down on the paper. "What exactly do you want?" he asked. It wasn't a dismissal; he seemed just curious. His voice was formal and soft.

"Did you know he'd rented that movie that was in his VCR eighteen times in one month?"

"So?"

"Doesn't that seem odd?"

"I seen people jump off the Brooklyn Bridge because they think their cat's possessed by Satan. Nothing seems odd to me."

"But the movie he rented . . . get this. It was about a true crime. Some robbers stole a million dollars and the money was never found."

"When?" he asked, frowning. "I never heard about that."

"It was, like, fifty years ago."

Now Manelli got to roll his eyes.

She leaned forward, said enthusiastically, "But it's a mystery! Don't mysteries excite you?"

"No. *Solving* mysteries excites me."

"Well, this's one that oughta be solved."

"And it will be. In due time. I gotta get back to work."

"What about the other witness?" Rune asked. "Susan Edelman? The one who got hit by the car."

"She's still in the hospital."

"Has she told you anything?"

"We haven't interviewed her yet. Now, I really have to—"

Rune asked, "What'll happen with Mr. Kelly's body?"

"He doesn't seem to have any living relatives. His sister died a couple of years ago. There's a friend in the building? Amanda LeClerc? She put in a claim for permission to dispose of the body. We'll keep it in the M.E.'s office until that's approved. So. That's all I can tell you. Now, you don't mind, I have to get back to work."

Rune, feeling an odd mixture of anger and sorrow, stood and walked to the door. The detective said, "Miss?" She paused with her hand on the doorknob. "You saw what happened to Mr. Kelly. You saw what happened to Ms. Edelman. Whatever you feel, I understand. But don't try to help us out. That's a real bastard out there. This isn't the movies. People get hurt."

Rune said, "Just answer one question. Please, just one?"

Silence in the small office. From outside: the noise of computer printers, typewriters, voices from the offices around them. Rune asked, "What if Mr. Kelly was a rich banker? Would you still not give a shit?"

Manelli didn't move for a moment. Glanced at the

muffin. Didn't say anything. Rune thought: He thinks I'm a pain in the ass. He sort of likes me but I'm still a pain in the ass.

He said, "If he was from the Upper East Side? He was a partner in a big law firm? Then I wouldn't be handling the case. But if I was, the file'd still be seventh in my stack."

Rune nodded at his desk. "Take a look. It's on the top now."

CHAPTER EIGHT

She'd called Amanda LeClerc but the woman wasn't home to let her into Mr. Kelly's building.

So she had to do it the old-fashioned way. The way Detective Manelli unknowingly suggested.

Breaking and entering.

At the bodega up the street from Mr. Kelly's building she told the clerk, "Two boxes of diapers, please. Put them in two bags."

And paid twenty bucks for one pair of Playtex rubber gloves and two huge boxes of disposable diapers.

"*Muchos niños?*" the lady asked.

Rune took the bulgins bags and said, "*Sí.* The Pope, you know?"

The clerk, not much older than Rune, nodded sympathetically.

She walked out of the bodega toward Avenue B. It was already fiercely hot and a ripe, garbagey smell came from the streets. She passed an art gallery. In the window were wild canvases, violent red and black slashes of paint. She smelled steamed meat as she passed a Ukrainian restaurant. In front of a Korean deli was a sign: HOT FOOD $1.50/QTR LB.

Alphabetville . . .

At Kelly's building Rune climbed the concrete stairs to the lobby. Remembering the man's voice from the intercom. Who was it? She shivered as she stared at the webby speaker.

She tried Amanda once again but there was no answer, so she looked around. Outside there was only one person on the street, a handsome man in his thirties. A Pretty Boy, a thug, from a Martin Scorsese film. He wore a uniform of some kind—like the people who read gas and electric meters do. He sat across the street on a doorstep and read a tabloid newspaper. The headline was about the tourist who'd been knifed in Times Square. The case Detective Manelli was supposed to talk to the captain about. Rune turned back, set the bags down, opened one box of diapers, and stuffed two of the pads under her black T-shirt. She buttoned the white blouse over it. She looked about thirteen months pregnant.

Then she picked up the bags, crimped them awkwardly under her arms, and opened the huge leopard-skin purse, staring into the black hole with a scowl, dipping her hand into the stew of keys, pens, makeup, candy, Kleenex, a knife, old condom boxes, scraps of paper, letters, music cassettes, a can of cheese spread. For five minutes she kept at it. Then she heard the steps, someone coming down the stairs, a young man.

Rune looked up at him. Embarrassed, letting one of the bags of diapers slide to the ground.

Just be a klutz, she told herself; Lord knows you've had plenty of practice. She picked up one of the bags and accidentally on purpose dropped her purse on the ground.

"Need a hand?" the young man asked, unlocking the outer door and pushing it open for her.

Retrieving her purse, stuffing it under her arm. "My keys are in the bottom of this mess," she said. Then, thinking she should take the initiative, she frowned and said quickly: "Wait—you new here? I don't think I've seen you before."

"Uhm. About six months." He was defensive.

She pretended to relax. She walked past him. "Sorry, but you know how it is. New York, I mean."

"Yeah, I know."

"Thanks."

"Yeah." He disappeared down the first-floor hallway.

Rune climbed to the second floor. There was a red sign on the door to Mr. Kelly's apartment. DO NOT ENTER. CRIME SCENE. NYPD. The door was locked. Rune set the diapers in the incinerator room and returned to Mr. Kelly's door. She took a hammer and a large screwdriver from her purse. Eddie, from the store, who'd made her promise to forget he'd given her a lesson in burglary, had said the only problem would be the dead bolt. And if there was a Medeco and a metal door frame she could forget it. But if it was just the door tumbler and wood and if she didn't mind a little noise . . .

Rune put on the Playtex gloves—thinking about fingerprints. They were the smallest size she could find at the bodega but were still too big and flopped around on her hands. She tapped the screwdriver into the crack between the door and the jamb just about where the bolt was. Then looked up and down the hall and took the hammer in both hands. Drew it back like a baseball bat, remembering when she used to play tomboy softball in high school. She looked around again. The corridor was empty. She swung as hard as she could at the handle of the screwdriver.

And, just like at softball, she missed completely. The

gloves slipped and with the crack of a gunshot the hammer streaked past the screwdriver and slammed through the cheap paneling of the door.

"Shit."

Trying to pull the hammer out of the thin wood, she worked a large splintery piece toward her. It cracked and fell to the floor.

She drew back again, aiming at the screwdriver, but then she noticed that the hole she'd made was large enough to get her hand through. She reached in, found the door lock and the dead bolt, and got it open. Then pushed the door wide. She stepped inside and closed the door quickly.

And she froze.

Bastards!

A tornado had hit the place. The explosive clutter of disaster. Goddamn bastards, goddamn police! Every book was on the floor, every drawer open, the couch slashed apart. The boxes dumped out, clothing scattered. One bald spot in the mess: under Kelly's floor lamp, next to the chair with its dark, horrible stain and the small bullet holes with spiny brown tufts of upholstery stuffing sprouting outward. Whoever had ransacked the room had stood there—or even sat in the terrible chair!—under the light and examined everything, then thrown it aside.

Bastards.

Her first thought had been: The police did this? And she was ready to cab it right back to the police station and give Virgil Manelli hell, the narrow-eyed son of a bitch, but she remembered the detective's neat desk, his brisk haircut and trimmed mustache. And she decided that someone else had done it. A window was open and the fire escape was right outside the sill. Anybody could've broken in. Hell, *she* had.

But it wasn't druggies either: the VCR and clock radio were still here.

Who had it been? And what were they looking for?

For an hour, Rune browsed through the mountains of Mr. Kelly's life. She looked at everything—*almost* everything. Not the clothes. Even with the gloves on, they were too spooky to touch. But the rest she studied carefully: books, letters, the start of a diary—only three entries from years ago, revealing nothing except the weather and his sister's health—boxes of food the bold roaches were already looting, bills, receipts, photos, shoeboxes.

As she sifted carefully through everything, she learned a bit about Mr. Robert Kelly.

He'd been born in 1915 in Cape Girardeau, Missouri. He'd come to New York in 1935. Then moved to California. He'd volunteered for the Army Air Corps and served with the Ninth Air Force. A sergeant, supervising ordnance. In some of his letters (he'd used the words "Dearest Sister" or "Darling Mother," which made Rune cry) he'd written about the bombs that were loaded into the A-20 airplanes on their raids against occupied France and Germany. Sometimes he'd write his name in chalk on the 500-pounders. Proud that he was helping win the war.

She found pictures of him in performances in the USO for soldiers in someplace called East Anglia. He seemed to be a sad-faced stand-up comic.

After the war there seemed to be a five-year gap in his life. There was no record of what he'd done from 1945 until 1950.

In 1952 he'd married a woman in Los Angeles and had apparently begun a series of sales jobs. Insurance for a while, then some kind of machinery that had something to do with commercial printing. His wife had died ten years ago. They'd had no children, it seemed. He was close to his sister. He took early retirement. Somehow he'd ended up back here in the New York area.

Most of what she found was simply biographical. But there were several things that troubled her.

The first was a photograph of Mr. Kelly with his sister—their names were on the back—taken five years before. (He looked exactly the same as he had last week and she decided he was the sort that aged early, like her own father, and then seemed frozen in time in their later years.) What was odd about the picture was that it had been torn into pieces. Kelly himself hadn't done it, since one square had been lying on the dried bloodstain. It had been torn by the ransackers.

The other thing that caught her attention was an old newspaper clipping. A bookmark in a battered copy of a Daphne du Maurier novel. The clipping, from the *New York Journal American,* dated 1948, read, *Movie Tells True Story of Gotham Crime.* It was underlined and asterisks were in the margin.

Fans of the hit film Manhattan Is My Beat, *now showing on Forty-second Street, may recognize on the silver screen the true story of one of New York's finest. . . .*

Footsteps sounded outside the door. Rune looked up. They passed by but she thought they'd slowed. A chill of panic touched her spine and wouldn't leave. She remembered where she was, what she was doing. Remembered that Manelli had warned her not to come here.

Remembered that the killer was still at large.

Time to leave . . .

Rune slipped the clipping into her bag and stood. She looked at the door, then at the window, and decided the fire escape was the choice of pros. She walked to the window and flung the curtain aside.

Jesus my Lord!

She stumbled backward as the man on the fire escape, his face a foot away from her, screamed.

Not a gasp or shout but a gut-shaking scream. She'd scared the hell out of him. He'd been standing outside on the fire escape, peering cautiously through the window. Now he backed away slowly, nearly paralyzed with terror, it seemed, easing step by step up the peeling black-enameled metal. Then he turned and sprinted up toward the third floor.

She guessed he was in his late sixties. He was balding, with a face that was tough and pocked and gray. Not the kind of face that should be screaming.

Her heart was pounding from the shock of the surprise. Her legs felt rubbery. She stood up slowly and pushed her head out the window.

Squinting, she watched him—his fat belly taut above hammy pumping legs—as he climbed through the window directly above Kelly's apartment. She heard his footsteps walking heavily and quickly overhead. She heard a door slam.

Rune hesitated, then walked to the front door, knelt down, and looked out through the crack. Coming down the stairs: scuffed shoes, baggy fat-man's pants, and suit jacket tight around the arms. Then his tough, pocked face, under a brown hat.

Yes, it was him, the man from the fire escape. He walked very quietly. He didn't want to be heard.

He's leaving, thank you, God. . . .

His face was the color of cooked pork; sweat glistening on his forehead.

. . . thank you, thank you, thank—

Then he stopped and looked at the door to Mr. Kelly's apartment for a long while. No, it's okay. He thinks I've left. He won't try to come inside.

Thank . . .

The man stepped closer. No . . . It's all right, she

told herself again. He thinks that once he went upstairs I climbed out onto the fire escape and got away through the alley.

. . . *you.*

Another step, as cautious as Don Johnson closing in on a dozen drug dealers in *Miami Vice*. The man paused, a foot away.

Rune was afraid to lock the dead bolt or put the chain on; he'd hear her. She pressed her palms against the door, pushing as hard as she could. The man walked directly to it, then stopped, inches away. The thin wood—hell, she'd whacked right through it herself—was all that protected her. Rune's small muscles trembled as she pressed against the door.

Which is when the screwdriver slid out of her pocket. In horror, she watched it fall—as if it were in slow motion. It was a scene from a Brian DePalma movie. She grabbed at the tool, caught it, then fumbled it . . . *No!*

She reached down fast and managed to snag the screwdriver an inch above the oak slats of the floor.

Thank you . . .

Frozen in position, like the game of statue she played as a kid, Rune listened to the man's labored breathing. He hadn't heard anything.

He'd *have* to know she left. He'd *have* to!

She slipped the screwdriver back into her pocket, but as she did so, she brushed the claws of the hammer, which was hooked into the waistband of her pants. The tool fell straight to the floor, its head bouncing twice with echoing slams.

"No!" she shouted in a whisper. Planting her feet on the opposite wall, leaning hard into the door, Rune ducked her head, waiting for the fist that she knew would slam through the cheap wood, clawing for her hair, her eyes. She'd be dead. Just like Robert Kelly. It would only be a matter of minutes, seconds, and she would die.

But, no . . . He turned and ran down the stairs.

Finally Rune stood, staring at her shaking hands and remembering some movie she'd seen recently where the teenage hero had escaped from some killer and had stood frozen, gazing at his quivering hands; Rune had groaned at the cliché. But it wasn't a cliché at all. Her hands were trembling so badly she could hardly open the door. She peered out, hearing sounds of chatting voices and far-off TVs. Children's squeals.

Why had he run? she wondered. Who was he? A witness? The killer's accomplice?

The killer?

Rune—every muscle shaking—walked fast to the incinerator room, scooped up the diapers, and hurried down the stairs. Two women on the landing nodded at her, preoccupied with their conversation.

Rune started past them, head down. But then she paused and in an exasperated voice said, "People don't know how to behave anymore. They don't know a thing about it, do they?"

The women looked at her, smiling in polite curiosity.

"That guy a minute ago? He almost knocked me over."

"Me too," one woman said. Her gray hair was in pink curlers.

"Who is he?" Rune asked, breathing hard, leaning against the banister.

"That's Mr. Symington. In 3B. He crazy." The woman didn't elaborate.

So he lived here. Which meant he probably wasn't the killer. More likely a witness.

"Yeah," the woman's friend added, "move up there last month."

"What's his first name?"

"Victor, I think. Something like that. Never says hello or nothing."

"So what?" the curler woman said. "He's nobody you'd want to talk to anyway."

"I don't know," Rune said indignantly. "*I'd* have a couple things to tell him."

The curler woman pointed to the box of diapers. "Greatest invention ever was."

"After TV," her friend said.

Rune said, "Well, sure," and started down the stairs.

She ran into Amanda on the street corner.

"Look," the woman said. She'd been to Hallmark and had bought a fake silver picture frame. Inside she'd put a picture of her and Mr. Kelly. It was at Christmas and they were in front of a skinny pine tree decorated with a few lights and tinsel. There was still a smear of adhesive on the glass from the price tag.

"It's totally cool," Rune said, and started to cry once more.

"You have babies?" Amanda was looking at the diapers.

"Oh. Long story. You want them?"

A faint laugh. "Did that years and years ago."

Rune pitched them out. "I've got a question. What do you know about Victor Symington?"

"That guy live upstairs?"

"Yeah."

Amanda shrugged. "Not so much. He been in the building for maybe six weeks. A month. He never say hi, never say how you doing. I no like him so much. I mean, why not say good morning to people? What's so hard about that? You tell me what's so hard."

"You said Mr. Kelly never talked about his life much?"

"No, he didn't."

"Did he mention anything about a bank robbery? Or a movie called *Manhattan Is My Beat*?"

"You know, I think he say something about that movie. Yeah. A couple times. He was real happy he find it. But he never say anything about a bank robbery."

"Are you going to have a funeral for him? I talked to the police and they said you wanted to bury him."

The woman nodded. Rune thought: This is what you think of when somebody says a "handsome" woman. Amanda wasn't beautiful. But she was ageless and attractive. "He has no family," Amanda said. "I have a friend, he cuts grass at Forest Lawn. Maybe I can work something out with him to get Mr. Kelly buried there. That's a nice place. If I can stay here in the U.S., I mean. But I no think that going to happen."

Rune whispered to her, "Don't give up just yet."

"What?"

"I think Mr. Kelly was about to get a lot of money."

"Mr. Kelly?" Amanda laughed. "He never said anything about that to me."

"I can't say anything for certain. But I think I'm right. *And* I think this Symington knows something about it. If you see him, will you let me know? Don't say anything to him." She gave the woman the number of the video store. "Call me there."

"Sure, sure. I call you."

Rune watched the skepticism surface on her face.

"You don't believe me, do you?" she asked Amanda.

The woman shrugged. "Believe that Mr. Kelly was going to get some money?" She laughed again. "No, I no think so. But, hey, you find it, you let me know," she said. Looked at the picture once more. "You let me know."

Once upon a time . . .

Walking west toward Avenue A. Rune looked up and down the street for Symington. Gone.

The heat was bad. City heat, dense heat, wet heat. She didn't feel like hurrying but she also didn't want to get into a shouting match with Tony so she broke one of her personal rules and hurried to work.

Once upon a time, in a kingdom huge and powerful and filled with many wonders, there was a princess. A very small princess who no one took seriously. . . .

She continued along the sidewalk, feeling exhilarated. She'd met her first black knight—a pock-faced man in his sixties, wearing an ugly brown hat—and escaped from him without being broadsworded to death.

Oh, she was a beautiful princess though she was too short to be a model. A beautiful princess—and would be a lot more beautiful when her hair grew out. Then one day the princess became very sad because a terrible dragon killed a kind old man and stole his secret treasure. A secret treasure that he'd promised to give her part of and that'd also save the bacon of a friend of his who was getting hassled by the creeps at Immigration and Naturalization.

Third Avenue. Broadway. University Place.

So the beautiful princess herself set out to find the dragon. And she did and she slayed him, or slew *him, or at least bagged his ass so he'd have to hang around Attica for twenty-five to thirty years. She got the treasure of gold, which she split with the friend and they both netted a cool half million.*

Rune walked into the video store, watching Tony inhale the breath that would come out as "Where the fuck've you been?"

"Sorry." Rune held up her hands to pre-empt him. "It's been one of those mornings."

She stepped behind the counter and logged onto the register so fast that she didn't notice, across the street, the man she'd thought of as Pretty Boy, the one in the meter-reader jacket, slide into a booth in the coffee shop. He continued to watch her, just like he'd been watching her as he'd followed her from the building on Tenth Street where they'd hit the old man.

Rune grabbed a handful of tapes, started to reshelve them. Thinking:

And the princess lived happily ever after.

CHAPTER NINE

On the phone with Susan Edelman.

The pink-suited jogger, the one who'd been struck by the car in the alley beside Mr. Kelly's building, couldn't talk long. She was very groggy. "I'm being released, uhm . . . tomorrow. Can you . . . uhm, call me then?"

She gave Rune her phone number but it had only six digits, then tried again and couldn't remember the last four numbers.

Oh, she'll be a great witness, Rune thought sourly.

"I'll look it up in the phone book," Rune told her. "You listed?"

"Uhm, yeah."

"Feel better," Rune told her.

"I got hit by a car," Susan said, as if telling Rune for the first time what had happened.

Rune reshelved a few more tapes, then, as soon as

Tony left, she told Frankie she was going for coffee, then booked out of the store.

Outside, she looked around the streets of the city. Caught a glimpse of somebody who looked familiar—a young man with dark, curly hair—but she couldn't place him. His back was to her. Something familiar about the stance, his muscular build. Where'd she seen him?

Where?

But he stepped quickly into a deli, so she didn't think anything more about him. That was one thing about Greenwich Village. You were always running into people you knew. Everyone thought New York was a huge city but that wasn't true; it was a collection of small towns. A Yellow Cab cruised up the street and she flagged it down. She was in the New York Public Library in twenty minutes.

The books on general city history—there were hundreds—didn't help her much at all. The history of *crime* in New York . . . that was something else. One thing she learned was that in Manhattan there were more bank robberies per square mile than anywhere in the country—and most of them occurred on Friday. The traditional payday. So with that volume of heists, the Union Bank stickup didn't get much coverage. She found a few references to it. The only one that gave any details was in a book about the Mafia, which reported only that the Family probably wasn't involved.

The newspapers were better—though the robbery didn't get a lot of coverage because it hadn't occurred on a slow-news day. At the same time the hero cop was bargaining with the holdup man for the hostage's life, the rest of the world was following King Edward's abdication, which had filled all the city papers with features and sidebars. Rune couldn't help but read some of the articles; she decided it was the most romantic thing she'd ever heard. She studied the picture of Mrs. Simpson.

Would anybody give up a kingdom for me?

Would Richard?

She couldn't come up with a satisfactory answer to that question and turned back to the stories about the Union Bank robbery.

After the shootout was over: the robber was in the morgue and the million bucks was missing, though that didn't seem too important at first because the hostage was safe and Patrolman Samuel Davies was a hero. The only hiccup was that there was no satisfactory explanation as to how the robber passed the suitcase containing the money to his partner outside the bank before Davies started negotiating with him.

> An accomplice of the deceased robber, it is suspected, secreted himself outside the bank and, in a moment of confusion while Patrolman Davies was boldly approaching the bank, seized the ill-gotten loot and absconded.

A month later the question of what had happened to the money had been answered and the newspaper stories were very different.

> Hero Patrolman Indicted in Union Bank Theft—Boy Admits Hiding Cop's Loot in Mother's House—A "Shame and Disgrace," Says Commissioner.

Rune, sitting at the huge oak platform of a table, felt a queasy shiver for the cop. The story came out that he'd talked the robber into exchanging himself for the hostage, who fled from the bank. Then he'd convinced the thief to hand over his revolver.

What happened next was speculation: Davies claimed the robber had a change of mind and jumped him. There was a scuffle. The robber knocked down the cop and went for the gun. Davies tried to pull the pistol away from him. They fought. The gun went off. The robber was killed.

But a young shoeshine boy testified that he'd been hiding outside the bank, waiting for something to see, when a door above him opened and a man looked out. It was Davies, the cop.

> Yes, sir, I can identify him, sir. He looks just like that man right there, sir, only that day he was wearing a uniform.

He asked for the boy's address and then handed him a suitcase, told him to take it home.

> He says to me . . . he says that if I opened the bag, or I said anything about what happened, I'd go to reform school and get the tar beat out of me every day. I done what he said, sir.

Davies denied it all—murdering the robber, taking the money, breaking into the shoeshine boy's home in Brooklyn and stealing the suitcase, then hiding the loot somewhere. The policeman made a tearful defendant, the papers reported. But that didn't sway the jury. Davies got five to fifteen years. The Patrolmen's Benevolent Association claimed all along he was the victim of a frame-up and urged his parole. He served seven years of the sentence.

But controversy around Davies continued after his release. Only two days after he walked out the front door of Sing Sing in Ossining, New York, in 1942 he was tommy-gunned to death at the corner of Fifth Avenue and Ninth Street, in front of the gothic Fifth Avenue Hotel. No one knew who was behind the shooting, though it looked like a professional hit. The money was never recovered.

Nothing more about the crime appeared in the press until the tiny blurb about the movie *Manhattan Is My Beat*—the clipping Rune had found in Kelly's apartment.

A homeless man sat down next to her at the library table. She smelled foulness in the wake of the air around him. Like most derelicts, he managed to seem both harmless and scary at the same time. He whispered to himself, wrote on a piece of wrinkled paper in the tiniest handwriting she'd ever seen.

One of her watches seemed to be working. She glanced at it. Oh shit! It was after two. Her ten-minute break had stretched to longer than two hours. Tony could be back. She took a cab to the Village but, on impulse, had the cabbie stop at 24 Fifth Avenue, the site of the Fifth Avenue Hotel. She paced back and forth slowly, wondering where Samuel Davies was when he was gunned down—what he'd been doing, what went through his mind when he realized what was happening, if he'd seen the black gun muzzle pointed at him.

She walked in wide circles, weaving through the crowd, until a cop—a real-life cop, NYPD—who was leaning on a patrol car must have decided she was acting a little suspicious and started walking slowly in her direction. Rune looked at the menu taped in the window of the glitzy restaurant on the corner, frowned, and shook her head. She strolled toward University Place.

The cop lost interest.

Back at the store, Tony was waiting for her. He lectured her for a whole two minutes on promptness and she did her best to look contrite.

"What?" he grumbled. "Thought I'd be out all day, huh?"

Like you usually are? she thought. But said, "Sorry, sorry, sorry. Won't happen again. Cross my heart."

"I *know* it won't. This's your last chance. Late once more and you're outa here. I've got people lined up to get a job."

"Lined up?" She looked out the front door. "Where, Tony? Out back? In the alley?" She then realized she should be more contrite. "Sorry. Just a joke."

He glowered and handed her a pink While-You-Were-Out slip. "Another thing, this isn't message central. Now, go get coffee and make it up to me."

"You bet," she said cheerfully. He eyed her uncertainly.

The message was from Richard. It said, "Confirming our 'date.'" She liked the quotation marks. She folded the pink slip of paper and slipped it into her shirt pocket.

"Here," Tony grumbled. Handing her money for the coffee.

"Naw, that's okay," she said. "It's on me."

Perplexing the poor man no end.

"You're from Ohio?"

It was eight P.M. They were sitting in Rune's gazebo, listening to the Pachelbel Canon. Rune had eight different recordings of the piece. She'd liked it for years—even before it had caught on, the way *Greensleeves* and *Simple Gifts* had.

Richard continued. "I've never met anyone from Ohio."

She was wearing a black T-shirt, black stretch pants, and red-and-white-striped socks. She'd done this as a homage to Richard's costume the other night. He, however, was in baggy gray slacks, Keds, and a beige Texaco Service shirt with the name Ralph embroidered on the pocket.

This man is *pure* Downtown. I love him!

Rune sang, "'What's round on the ends and high in

the middle? It's O-Hi-O!' That's it. One more syllable and Rodgers and Hammerstein could've written a musical about it."

"Ohio," Richard said thoughtfully. "There must be something in that. Solid, dependable. Working-class. Sort of metaphoric. You were there and now you're"—he waved his hand around the loft—"here."

"It's a nice state," she said defensively.

"I don't mean anything bad. But why'd you come here and not Chicago or L.A.? A job?"

"No."

"I know. Boyfriend."

"Nope."

"You moved to Manhattan by yourself?"

"To go on a real quest, you *have* to go by yourself. Remember *Lord of the Rings*?"

"Sort of. Refresh my memory."

Sort of? How could he not remember the best book of all time?

"All the hobbits and everybody started out together, but in the end it was Frodo who got to the fiery pit to destroy the ring of power. All by his little-old lonesome."

"Okay," he said, nodding. Not sure what the connection was. "But why Manhattan?"

Rune explained. "I didn't spend a lot of time at home in the afternoons. After school, I mean. My dad was pretty sick and my mom'd send my sister and me out to play a lot. She got the dates and boyfriends. I got the books."

"Books?"

"I'd hang out at the Shaker Heights Library. There was this book of pictures of Manhattan. I read it once and just *knew* I had to come here." Then she asked, "Well, how 'bout *you*?"

"Because of what Rimbaud says about the city."

"Uhm." Wait. She'd *seen* the movie and hated it. She

didn't know *Rambo*'d been a book. She thought of the cardboard cutout in Washington Square Video—of Stallone with his muscles and that stupid headband. "Not sure."

"Remember his poem about Paris?"

Poem? "Not exactly."

"Rimband wrote that the city was death without tears, our diligent daughter and servant, a desperate love, and a petty crime howling in the mud of the street."

Rune was silent. Trying hard to figure Richard out. Downtown weird *and* smart. She'd never met anyone like him. She was watching his eyes, the way his long fingers went through a precise ritual of pulling a beer can out of the plastic loops that held the six-pack, tapping the disk of the top to settle the foam, then slowly popping it open. Watching his lean legs, long feet, the texture of his eyes. She had a feeling that the posturing was just a facade. But what was underneath it?

And why was *she* so drawn to him? Because there was something she couldn't quite figure out about him?

Because of the mystery?

Richard said, "You're avoiding my question. Why did you come here?"

"This is the Magic Kingdom."

"You're not addressing Rimbaud's metaphor."

Addressing? Why did he have to talk that way?

Rune asked, "You ever read the Oz books?"

" 'Follow the yellow brick road,' " he sang in a squeaky voice.

"That's the movie. But Frank Baum—he was the author—he wrote a whole series of them. In his magic kingdom of Oz, there were lots of lands. All of them are different. Some people are made out of china, some have heads like pumpkins. They ride around on sawhorses. That's just what New York is like. Every other city I've ever been in is like a discount store. You know—clean, cheap, convenient. But what, basically? Unsatisfying, that's what. They're *literal*. There's no magic to them. Come here." She took his hand and led him to the window. "What do you see?"

"The Con Ed Building."

"Where?"

"Right there."

"I don't see a building." Rune turned to him, her eyes wide. "I see a mountain of marble carved by three giants a thousand years ago. They used magic tools, I'll bet. Crystal hammers and chisels made out of gold and lapis. I think one of them, I forget his name, built this castle we're in right now. And those lights, you see them over there? All around us? They're lanterns on the horns of oxen with golden hides circling around the kingdom. And the rivers, you know where they came from? They were gouged out of the earth by the gods' toes when they were dancing. And then . . . and then there're these pits underground, huge ones. You ever heard the rumblings underneath us? They're worms crawling at fifty miles an hour. Sometimes they get tired of living in the dark and they turn into dragons and go shooting off into the sky." She grabbed his arm urgently. "Look, there's one now!"

Richard watched the 727 making a slow approach to LaGuardia. He stared at it for a long time.

Rune said, "You think I'm crazy, don't you? That I live in a fairy story?"

"That's not bad. Not necessarily."

"I collect them, you know."

"Fairy stories?"

Rune walked to her bookshelves. She ran her finger across the spines of maybe fifty books. Hans Christian Andersen, the Brothers Grimm, *Perrault's Fairy Tales,* the Quiller-Couch Old French stories, Cavendish's book on Arthur and three or four volumes of his *Man, Myth and*

Magic. She held up one. "An original edition of Lady Gregory's *Story of the Tuatha Dé Danann and of the Fianna of Ireland.*" Handed it to him.

"Is it valuable?" Richard flipped through the old book with his gorgeous fingers.

"To me it is."

"Happily ever after . . ." He scanned pages.

Rune said, "That's not the way fairy stories end. Not all of them." She took the book from him and began thumbing past pages slowly. She stopped. "Here's the story of Diarmuid. He was one of the Fianna, the warrior guards of ancient Ireland. Diarmuid let an ugly hag sleep in his lodge and she turned into a beautiful woman from the Side, that's the other side, capital S—the land of magic."

"That's sounds pretty happy to me."

"But that wasn't the end." She turned away and stared past her dim reflection at the city. "He lost her. They both had to be true to their natures—he couldn't live in the Side and she couldn't live on earth. He had to return to the land of mortals. He lost her and never found love again. But he always remembered how he much he'd loved her. Isn't that a sad story?"

She thought, for some reason, of Robert Kelly.

She thought of her father.

Tears pricked her eyes.

"You sure have a lot of stories," he said, eyes on the spines of her books.

"I love stories." She turned to him. Couldn't keep her eyes off him. He was aware of it and looked away. "You were like him, coming after me. The other night, all dressed in black. I thought of Diarmuid when I first saw you. Like a knight errant on a quest." She scrunched her face up. "Accompanied by two tacky wenches."

Richard laughed. Then added, "I *was* on a quest. For you." He kissed her. "You're my Holy Grail."

She closed her eyes, kissed him back. Then said suddenly, "Let's eat."

The cutting board in the shape of a pig was her kitchen table. She cut open a round loaf of rye bread, spread mayonnaise on both sides. She noticed him watching her. "Watch closely. I told you I could cook."

"That's cooking?"

"I think I can really cook. I just haven't done it much. I have a bunch of cookbooks." She pointed to the bookcases again. "My mother gave them to me when I left home. I think she wanted to give me a diaphragm but lost her nerve at the last minute, so she gave me Fannie Farmer and Craig Claiborne instead. I can't use them much. Most recipes you need a stove for."

She poured cold Chinese food from the carton onto the sliced loaf and cut it in half. The cold pork poured out the sides when she sawed the dull knife through the bread, and she scooped up the food with her hands and spread it back between the domes of rye.

"Okay," he said dubiously. "Well. That's interesting."

But when she handed him the sandwich he ate enthusiastically. For a skinny boy he had quite an appetite. He looked *so* French. He really *had* to be François.

"So," he asked, "you going with anybody?"

"Not at the moment."

Or for any moments in the last four months three weeks.

"Half my friends are getting married," he said. He went through his beer-can ritual again, his long fingers beating out a hesitant rhythm on the top of the can, then opening it and pouring the beer while he held the glass at an angle.

"Marriage, hmm," she said noncommittally.

Where was all *this* headed?

But he was on to a new subject. "So what're your goals?"

She took a big bite of rye bread. "To eat dinner, I guess."

"I mean your life goals."

Rune blinked and looked away from him. She believed she'd never asked herself that question. "I don't know. Eat dinner." She laughed. "Eat breakfast. Dance. Work. Hang out . . . Have adventures!"

He leaned forward and kissed her on the mouth. "You taste like Hunan mayonnaise. Let's make love." His arms encircled her.

"No." Rune drained her second beer.

"You sure?"

No . . .

Yes . . .

She felt herself pulled forward, toward him, and she wasn't sure whether he was actually pulling her or she was moving by herself. Like a Ouija board pointer. He rolled on top of her. They kissed for five minutes. Growing aroused, that warm water sensation flowing up her calves into her thighs.

No . . . yes . . . no.

But she was saved from the debate by a voice shouting, "Home!" A woman's head appeared up the stairway. "Zip it up!"

A woman in her late twenties, wearing a black minidress and red stockings, climbed up the stairs. High heels. Her hair was cut short in a 1950s style and teased up. The hair was black and purple.

So the roomie's date hadn't turned out the way she'd hoped.

Rune muttered, "Sandra, Richard, Richard, Sandra."

Sandra examined him. She said nothing to him but to Rune: "You did okay." Then turned toward her half of the room, unzipping her dress as she walked, revealing a thick white strap of bra.

Rune whispered. "She's a jewelry designer. Or that's

what she wants to do. Days, she's a paralegal. But her hobby is collecting men. She's slept with fifty-eight of them so far. She has the score written down. Of course she's only come twenty-two times so there's some debate on what she can count. There's no *Robert's Rules of Order* for this sort of thing."

"I suppose not."

Richard's eyes followed a vague reflection of Sandra in the window. She was on the far side of the cloud wall, stripping slowly. She knew she was being watched. The bra came off last.

Rune laughed and took his chin in her hand. Kissed him. "Darling, don't even think about it. That woman is a time bomb. You get into bed with her, it's like a group grope with a hundred people you don't know where they've been. Christ . . ." Rune's voice grew soft. "I worry about her. I don't like her but she's on some kind of weird suicide thing, you ask me. A guy looks at her, and bang, it's in the sack."

Richard said, "There're ways to be safe. . . ."

Rune shook her head. "I knew a guy, a friend used to work at one of the restaurants I tended bar at. I watched his boyfriend get sick and die. Then I saw my friend get sick and die. I was at the hospital. I saw the tubes, the monitors, the needles. The color of his skin. Everything. I saw his eyes. I was there when he died."

An image of Robert Kelly's face came back to her, sitting in the chair in his apartment.

An image of her father's face . . .

Richard was silent and Rune knew she'd committed *the* New York City crime: being too emotional. She cleaned up the remnants of dinner, kissed Richard's ear, and said, "Let's watch a movie."

"A movie? Why?"

"Because I have to catch a killer."

CHAPTER TEN

She'd already seen *Manhattan Is My Beat* once but watching it this time was different.

Not because she was on a quote date unquote with Richard, not because they were lying side by side in the loft, with hazy stars visible overhead through the peaks of glass.

But because when she'd watched it before, it had just been a movie that a nice, quirky old man had rented. Now it was the rabbit hole—a doorway to an adventure.

The film was hokey, sure. Filled with those classic images from that whole cumbersome era she'd told Frankie Greek about—the baggy suits, stiff hair, the formalities of the dialogue. The young cop, twirling his billy club, would say, "Well, now, Mrs. McGrath, how are the Mister's corns this morning?"

But she paid little attention to the period costumes and the words. Mostly what she noticed, watching it this time, was the grit. The film left a sandy uneasiness in her heart. Shadows everywhere, the contrasty black and white, the unanticipated violence. The shootings—where the robber winged one of the hero's fellow cops and a bystander, for instance, or the scene where the cop died in front of the hotel—were very disturbing, even though there was no Sam Peckinpah slow-motion blood splattering, no special effects. It was like that great old Alan Ladd movie *Shane*—unlike modern thrillers, there'd been only a half dozen gunshots in the entire film but they were loud and shocking and you felt each one of them in your gut.

Manhattan Is My Beat also seemed pretty G-rated. But Rune felt the studio pulling a fast one in its portrayal of the cop's virginal girlfriend, played by—what a name—Ruby Dahl. It was so clear to Rune that the poor thing was lusting. You'd never know it from her lines ("Oh, I can't explain my feelings, Roy. I just worry about you so. There's so much . . . evil out there.") But if her dresses and sweaters were high-necked, Ruby's bosom was sharp and beneath the tame dialogue you knew she had the hots for Roy. *She* was the character that got the long camera shot when the judge announced that her fiancé was going to prison. She was the one Rune cried for.

At two A.M. Sandra threw a shoe at them and Rune shut off the VCR and the TV.

"Not bad once," Richard said. "Why'd we have to sit through it twice?" He himself had given up his own quest for the evening and had kept his hands off her for the past several hours.

"Because I didn't take notes the first time." She rewound the tape, the bootleg copy she'd made for Robert Kelly. She looked at the scrawl of notes she'd written on the back of a flier for a health club.

Richard stretched and went into some weird yoga position, like a push-up with his pelvis pressed into the floor, his head back at a crazy angle, staring at the stars above them. "Okay, I slept through most of it the second time, I have to be honest. Were you joking about the killer?"

"The movie is why that customer I told you about is dead."

"He saw it *three* times. He couldn't take it anymore. He killed himself."

"Don't joke." She was whispering and he missed the flare in her voice.

She pulled her bag toward her and handed him the clipping she'd found in Kelly's apartment. He looked at it but put it down before he could have read more than a couple of paragraphs. He closed his eyes. She frowned and took the yellow, brittle paper.

"What it is," she explained, "the movie was a true story. There really *was* a cop in the thirties who stole some robbery money and hid it. He denied the whole thing and nobody ever found the million dollars. He got out of Sing Sing and got gunned down a few days later. And supposedly he never had a chance to collect the money. It's just the way it happened in the film."

Richard yawned.

Rune, on her knees, crouched like a geisha, holding the clipping. "I think what happened was Mr. Kelly bought an old book at a secondhand store on St. Marks. . . . You know the book vendors near Cooper Union? There was this clipping in it. He read it—I think he was interested in New York history—so he got a kick out of it but didn't think too much about it. Then what happens?"

"What?"

"Then," she said, "last month he's walking past Washington Square Video and sees the poster for the film. He rents it, he watches it. And he gets the bug. You know what I mean? The bug." She waited. Richard seemed to be listening. She said, "That feeling that gets to you when you know there's something out there. But you don't know what. But you *have* to find out what the mystery is."

"Like you. You're mysterious."

She felt a trill of pleasure. "That's what my name means, you know."

"Rune? I thought a rune was a letter."

"It is. But it also means 'mystery' in Celtic."

"And what does 'Doris' mean?"

"Anyway," she said, ignoring him, "I think Mr. Kelly and I were a lot alike. Sort of like you and me."

She let that sit between them for a minute, and when he didn't respond she wondered, And what's *your* mystery, François Jean-Paul Vladmir Richard?

After a moment he said, "I'm awake. I'm listening."

Rune continued. "What Mr. Kelly did was decide he was going to find the money."

"What money?"

"The money the cop took! That was never recovered."

"The million dollars? Come on, Rune, the robbery was when, fifty years ago?"

"Sure, maybe somebody found it. Maybe it got burned up. . . . You can always find excuses to give up on your quest before you start. Besides, quests aren't just about finding money or grails or jewels. They're about adventures! Mr. Kelly'd been alone for years. No family, not many friends, living by himself. This was his chance for an adventure. What was his life? Just sitting by the window all day and watching pigeons and cars. Here was a chance for a treasure hunt." She started bouncing up and down, remembering something. "He told me, listen to this, *listen*, when he took me out to lunch, he told me when his ship came in, he was going to do something nice for me. Well, what was the ship? It was a million dollars."

Richard said, "I'm tired. I have to work tomorrow."

"On your novel?"

He hesitated for a minute. And she didn't think he was being completely honest when he said, "That's right."

First date. Too early to push. She asked, "Are you going to put me in it? In your novel?"

"Maybe I will."

"Will you make me a little taller and grow my hair out?"

"No. I like you just the way you are."

As he rolled over on his side she reread the old newspaper clipping.

"Now, remember, in the movie, what the cop did with the money?"

The groggy answer: "He snuck outside the bank and gave it to a shoeshine boy, who took it home. The cop broke into the kid's house and stole it. I was awake for that part."

"And there was that totally melodramatic struggle, all that loud music, and the boy's mother fell down a flight of stairs," Rune pointed out. "That was big in old-time movies. Old ladies falling down flights of stairs. That, and angelic kids getting the dread unnamed disease guaranteed to make them waste away slowly." She thought back to the film. "Okay, in the newspaper stories there *was* a shoeshine boy. The cop—his real name was Samuel Davies, not Roy—gave the kid the money and said take it home or, basically, I'll beat the crap out of you. That was the last anybody every heard of the money in real life. But in the movie the cop gets it back from the kid and buries it in a cemetery someplace. Who came up with that idea? Hiding the money in a graveyard?"

"The writer, who else? He made it up." Richard's eyes were closed.

The writer . . . Interesting . . .

Then her attention returned to the TV. She turned the VCR on again and fast-forwarded it to the scene where Dana Mitchell, playing the dark-haired, square-jawed cop, buries the suitcase in a city cemetery.

She hit the freeze-frame button on the VCR and advanced the tape one frame at a time.

As the images shuffled slowly past, Rune said, out loud but mostly to herself, "The answer's here. It's here someplace. He watched it eighteen times, eighteen, eighteen, eighteen. . . ." Chanting the word. "Mr. Kelly gets a clue, he finds out something. And then he figures out where the money is. Or, okay, maybe . . . he can't get it himself, he's getting old. He had arthritis, a limp. He can't go digging around in cemeteries alone. He needs help. He tells somebody. A friend, an acquaintance. Somebody younger—who can help him. Mr. Kelly tells this guy everything and then, what's he do? He gets the money and kills Mr. Kelly. Maybe he was the guy in the green car. . . ."

"What green car?"

She hesitated. Another good social rule: On a first date don't tell the guy that a killer just tried to run you over at a murder scene.

"The police mentioned the killer was driving a green car."

Richard pointed out, "In which case it's gone. The killer left town with his million dollars. So what can you do?"

"Find him is what I can do. He killed a friend of mine. Anyway, part of that money's mine. And there's this friend of my friend in the building who's going to get deported if she doesn't get some money."

He said, "Why don't you just go to the police?"

"Police?" She laughed. "They don't care."

"Why else?" He was looking at her closely now.

"All right," she admitted. "Because they'd keep the

money. . . . I know it's out there. I mean, it could be. What you said before . . . about the writer making it up. He must've researched the real crime, wouldn't you think?"

"I'd guess," Richard responded.

"I mean, isn't that what you do for your novels? Research?"

"Yeah, sure. Research. A lot of research."

Rune mused, "Maybe he knows something. . . . 'Course he wrote the script fifty years ago. Think he's still alive?"

"Who knows?"

"How could I find out?"

He shrugged. "Why don't you ask somebody at the film school at NYU or the New School?"

It was a good idea. She kissed his ear. "See, you like quests as much as I do."

"I don't think so. But I also have a feeling I can't talk you out of this, can I?"

"Nup. You never give up on a quest. Until you succeed or you . . ." Her voice trailed off, seeing once again the pale skin of Robert Kelly dotted with his own blood, the green car speeding toward her, Susan Edelman flying into the brick wall. "Well, until you succeed. That's all there is to it."

She looked at Richard's face, his eyes closed, lips parted slightly. She tried to decide which she liked better, his looking dreamy—he was real good at dreamy—or the intense paisley eyes gazing intensely back at her. Dreamy, she concluded. He wasn't a warrior knight—not an Arthur or Cuchulain or Percival de Gales. No, he was more of a poet-knight. Or a philosopher-knight.

She heard his breath, steady, slow. How nice, she thought, to feel the warm weight of somebody next to you in sleep. She wanted so badly to lie beside him, feeling him against her whole body.

But instead of stretching out, she pulled off her Wicked Witch socks and aimed the remote control at the VCR, then watched the movie one more time until the scripty words *The End* splashed up on the screen.

CHAPTER ELEVEN

A karate flick was on the monitor.

Oriental men in black silk trousers sailed through the air, fists hissing like jet planes. Every time somebody got hit, it sounded like a cracking board.

One of the Chinese actors stepped toward a couple of rivals and spoke in a southern drawl. "Okay, you two, back outa here real slow and you won't get hurt."

Rune leaned back on the stool in front of the register at Washington Square Video. Squinted at the monitor. "Hey, you hear that? That is completely wild! He sounds just like John Wayne."

Tony held his blue deli coffee cup and cigarette in one hand and flipped through the *Post* with the other. He looked up at the screen critically. "And he's going to beat the shit out of those guys in ten seconds flat."

It took closer to sixty and while he was doing it Rune mused, "You think that's easy? Dubbing, I mean. You think I could get a job doing that?"

Tony asked, "Don't tease me, Rune. You quitting? . . . Or you mean when you get fired?"

Rune spun her bracelets. "They don't have to memorize their lines, do they? They just sit in a studio and read the script. That'd be so cool—it'd be like being an actress without having to get up in front of people and memorize things."

Frankie Greek was combing out his shaggy hair with a pick. He rubbed the mustache he'd started a month ago; it looked like a faint smudge of dirt. He stared at the TV screen. "Shit, look at that! He kicked four guys at once." He turned to Rune. "You know, I just found this out. A lot of music in movies, they do it afterward. They add it on."

"What, you thought they had a band on set?" Rune shut off the VCR. Tony looked at the TV. "Hey, what're you doing?"

"It stinks," she said.

"It doesn't stink. It's great."

"The acting's ridiculous, the costumes are silly, there's no story . . ."

Frankie Greek said, "That's what makes it so, like, you know . . ." The end of his sentence got away from him, as they often did. He prowled through the racks to find another film.

Rune looked over the store: the stained gray industrial carpet, the black strings—left over from promotional cards—hanging down from the air-conditioning, the faded red-and-green holiday tinsel that was stuck to the walls with yellowing glue. "I was at a video store on the Upper East Side and it was a lot classier than here."

Tony looked around. "What do you want? We're like the subway. We serve a valuable function. Nobody gives a shit we're classy, not classy."

Rune checked out two movies to a young man, one of the Daytime People, she called them. They'd rent movies during the day; they worked at night—actors, waiters, bartenders, writers. At first she'd envied them their alternative lifestyles but after she got to thinking about it—how they were always bleary-eyed or hung over and seemed dazed, smelled like they hadn't brushed their teeth—she decided aimlessness like that depressed her. People would be better off going on quests, she concluded.

She returned to her previous topic and said to Tony, "That place uptown? The video store? They had all these foreign films and ballets and plays. I'd never heard of most of them. I mean, it's like you go in there ask for *Predator Cop*, this alarm goes off and they throw you out."

Tony didn't look up from *Dear Abby*. "Got news, babe: *Predator Cop* makes us money. *Master-fucking-piece Theatre* doesn't."

"Wait, is that a real movie?" Frankie said. "*Master* . . . What?"

"Jesus Christ," Tony muttered.

Rune said, "I just think we could doll the place up some. Get new carpet. Oh, maybe we could have a wine-and-cheese night."

Frankie Greek said, "Hey, I could get the band to come down. We could play. Some Friday night. And, like, how's this? You could put a camera on us, put some monitors in the front window. So people, the ones outside'd notice us and they'd come in. Cool. How's that?"

"It sucks, that's how it is."

"Just an idea." Frankie Greek slipped a new cassette into the VCR.

"Another one?" Rune said, watching the credits.

"No, no. This is different," Frankie said. He showed Tony the cover.

"Now you're talking." Tony folded up the newspaper and concentrated on the screen. Patient as a priest with a novitiate, he said, "Rune, you know who that is? It's

Bruce Lee. We're talking classic. In a hundred years people'll still be watching this."

"I'm going to lunch," she said.

"You don't know what you're missing."

"Bye."

"Be back in twenty."

"Okay," she called. Adding, once she was outside, "I'll try."

Richard's idea about the film school was a good one. But she didn't actually need to go to the film department itself.

She stopped at the Eighth Street Deli, which did a big business selling overpriced sandwiches to rich NYU students and professors.

She paused on her way inside, looked around. This was the deli where that guy with the curly hair—the one she sorta recognized/sorta didn't—had ducked into yesterday. She wondered again if he'd been checking her out.

Thinking, You've got yourself *more* secret admirers? First Richard, now him. Never rains but . . .

Get real, she reminded herself, and walked up to the counterman, who said, "Next . . . oh, hi."

"Hey there, Rickie," Rune said.

He was working his way through school. He was an NYU junior, a film major, and he could have been Robert Redford's younger brother. When Rune first started working at WSV, she'd spent a ton of money and many hours here, talking to Rickie about films—and hoping he'd ask her out. They'd remained good friends even after Rickie introduced her to his live-in boyfriend.

She lifted the cello-wrapped apple pie for him to see, opened it, began eating. He handed her usual—coffee with milk, no sugar. They talked about movies for five minutes, while he made tall sandwiches out of roast beef and turkey and tongue. Rickie knew a lot of heavy-duty stuff about movies and even though he always said "film" or "cinema," never "movies," he didn't get obnoxious about it. She finished the pie and he refilled her coffee.

"Rickie," Rune asked, "you know anything about a film called *Manhattan Is My Beat*?"

"Never heard of it."

"Came out in the late forties."

He shook his head. Then she asked, "Is there like an old film museum at your school?"

"We've got a library. Not a museum. The public library's got that arts branch up at Lincoln Center. MOMA's probably got an archive but I don't think they let just anybody in."

"Thanks, love," she said.

"Hey, I don't make the rules. Start working on a grant proposal or get a letter from your grad school adviser and they'll let you in. But that's pretty heady stuff. Experimental films. Indies. What do you need to know?"

"I need to find the screenwriter."

"What studio made it?"

"Metropolitan."

He nodded. "Good old Metro. Why don't you just call 'em up and ask?"

"They're still around?"

"Oh, they're like everybody else nowadays, owned by some big entertainment conglomerate. But, yeah, they're still around."

"And somebody there'd know where the writer is now?"

"Be your best bet. Screen Writers Guild probably won't give out any information about members. Hell, I were you, I wouldn't even call; I'd just go pay 'em a visit."

Rune paid. He charged her a nickel for the pie. She

winked her thanks. Then said, "Can't afford to fly out to L.A."

"Take a subway, it's cheaper."

"You need a hell of a lot of transfers," Rune said.

"The Manhattan office, darling."

"Metro has an office here?"

"Sure. All the studios do. Oh, the East Coast office wants to rip the throat out of the West Coast office and vice versa but they're still part of the same company. They're that big building on Central Park West. You must've seen it."

"Oh, like I *ever* go uptown."

Awesome.

The corporate office building of the Entertainment Corporation of America, proud owner of Metropolitan Pictures.

Forty stories overlooking Central Park. A *single* company. Rune couldn't imagine having twenty stories of fellow workers above you and twenty stories below. (She tried to imagine forty stories of Washington Square Video, filled with Tonys and Eddies and Frankie Greeks. It was scary.)

She wondered if all the Metro employees ate together in a single cafeteria? Did they all go on a company picnic, taking over Central Park for the day?

Waiting for the guard to get off the phone, she also wondered if someone would see her and think she was an actress and maybe pull her onto a soundstage and throw a script into her hand. . . .

Though as she flipped through the company's annual report she realized that that probably wouldn't be happening because this wasn't the *filmmaking* part of the studio. The New York office of Metro did only financing, licensing, advertising, promotion, and public relations.

No casting or filming. But that was all right; her life was a little too busy just then for a career change that'd take her to Hollywood.

The guard handed her a pass and told her to take the express elevator to thirty-two.

"Express?" Rune said. Grinning. *Excellent!*

Her ears popped in the absolutely silent, carpeted elevator. In twenty seconds she was stepping off on the thirty-second floor, ignoring the receptionist and walking straight to the ceiling-to-floor window that offered an awesome view of Central Park, Harlem, the Bronx, Westchester, and the ends of the earth.

Rune was hypnotized.

"May I help you?" the receptionist asked three times before Rune turned around.

"If I worked here I'd never get any work done," Rune murmured.

"Then you wouldn't be working here very long."

Reluctantly she pried herself away from the window. "This is the view you'd have if you flew to work on a pterodactyl." The woman stared. Rune explained, "That's a flying dinosaur." Still silence. Try being adult, Rune warned herself. She smiled. "Hi. My name's Rune. I'm here to see Mr. Weinhoff."

The receptionist looked at a chart on a clipboard. "Follow me." She led her down a quiet corridor.

On the walls were posters of some of the studio's older movies. She paused to touch the crisp, wrinkled paper delicately. Farther down the hall were posters of newer films. The ads for movies hadn't changed much over the years. A sexy picture of the hero or heroine, the title, some really stupid line.

He was looking for peace, she was looking for escape. Together, they found the greatest adventure of their lives.

She'd seen the action movie *that* line referred to. And if the story had been their greatest adventure, well, then those characters'd been leading some totally bargain-basement lives.

Rune paused for one last aerial view of the Magic Kingdom, then followed the receptionist down a narrow hallway.

Betting herself that Mr. Weinhoff's would be one totally scandalous office. A corner one, looking north and west. With a bar and a couch. Maybe he'd be homesick for California so what he'd insisted they do to keep him happy was to put a lot of palm trees around the room. A marble desk. A leather couch. A bar, of course. Would he offer her a highball? What *was* a highball exactly?

They turned another corner.

She pictured Weinhoff fat and wearing a three-piece checkered suit, smoking cigars and talking like a baby to movie stars. What if Tom Cruise called while she was sitting in his office? Could she ask to say hello? Hell, yes, she'd ask. Or Robert Duvall! Sam Shepard? Oh, please, please, please . . .

They turned one more corner and stopped beside a battered Pepsi machine. The receptionist nodded. "There." She turned around.

"Where?" Rune asked, looking around. Confused.

The woman pointed to what Rune thought was a closet, and disappeared.

Rune stepped into the doorway, next to which a tiny sign said S. WEINHOFF.

The office, about ten feet by ten, had no windows. It wasn't even ten by ten really, because it was stacked around the perimeter with magazines and clippings and books and posters. The desk—chipped, cigarette-burned wood—was so cluttered and cheap that even the detective with the close-together eyes would've refused to work at it.

Weinhoff looked up from *Variety* and motioned her

in. "So, you're the student, what's the name again? I'm so bad with names."

"Rune."

"Nice name, I like it. Parents were hippies, right? Peace, Love, Sunshine, Aquarius. All that. Can you find a place to sit?"

Well, she got one thing right: he was fat. A ruddy nose and burst vessels in his huge cheeks. A great Santa Claus—if you could have a Jewish Santa. No checkered suit. No suit at all. Just a polyester shirt, white with brown stripes. A brown tie. Gray slacks.

Rune sat down.

"You want coffee? You're too young to drink coffee, you ask me. 'Course my granddaughter drinks coffee. She smokes too. God forbid that's all she does. I don't approve, but I sin, so how can I cast stones?"

"No, thanks."

"I'll get some, you don't mind." He stepped into the corridor and she saw him making instant coffee at a water dispenser.

So much for the highballs.

He sat back down at his desk and said to her, "So how'd you hear about me?"

"I called the public relations department here?" Her voice rose in a question. "See, I'm in this class—*The Roots of Film Noir,* it's called—and I'm writing this paper. I had some questions about a film and they said they had somebody on staff who'd been around for a while. . . ."

" 'Around for a while,' I like that. That's a euphemism is what that is."

"And here I am."

"Well, I'll tell you why they sent you to me. You want to know?"

"I—"

"I'll tell you. What I am is the unofficial studio historian at Metro. Meaning I've been here nearly forty years and if I were making real money or had anything to do with production they'd've fired my butt years ago. But I'm not and I don't so I'm not worth the trouble to boot me out. So I hang around here and answer questions from pretty young students. You don't mind, I say that?"

"Say it all you want."

"Good. Now the message said—do I believe it?—you've got some questions about *Manhattan Is My Beat*?"

"That's right."

"Well, that's interesting. You see a lot of students or reporters interested in Scorsese, Welles, Hitch. And you can always count on Fassbinder, Spielberg, Lucas, Coppola. Three, four years ago we got calls about Cimino. That *Heaven's Gate* thing. Oh, we got calls! But I don't think anybody's ever done anything about the director of *Manhattan Is My Beat.* Hal Reinhart. Anyway, I digress. What do you need to know?"

"The movie was true, wasn't it?"

Weinhoff's eyes crinkled. "*Nu,* that's the whole point. That's why it's such a big-deal movie. It wasn't shot on sets, it was based on a real crime, it didn't cast Gable, Tracy, Lana Turner, Bette Davis, Gary Cooper, or any of the other sure-draw stars. You understand? None of the actors that'd guarantee that a film, no matter it was a good film, it was a bad film, that a film *opened,* you know what I mean, *opened*?"

"Sure." Rune's pen sped across the pages of a notebook. She'd bought it a half hour before, had written *Film Noir 101* on the cover, then smeared the ink with her palm to age it, like a master forger. "It means people go to see it no matter what it's about."

"Right you are. Now, *Manhattan Is My Beat* was probably the first of the independents."

"Why don't you hear about it nowadays?"

"Because it was also the first of the *bad* independents. You've seen it?"

"Four times."

"What, you also tell your dentist to drill without novocaine? Well, if you saw it that many times, you know it didn't quite get away from the melodrama of the big studio crime stories of the thirties. The director, Reinhart, couldn't resist the shoeshine boy's mother falling downstairs, the high camera angles, the score hitting you over the head you should miss a plot twist. So other films got remembered better. But it was a big turning point for movies."

His enthusiasm was infectious. She found herself nodding excitedly.

"You ever see *Boomerang*? Elia Kazan. He shot it on location. Not the greatest story in the world for a crime flick—I mean, there's not much secret who did it. But the point isn't what the story was but *how* it was told. That was about a real crime too. It was a—whatta you call it?—evolutionary step up from the studio-lot productions Hollywood thought you had to do. *Manhattan Is My Beat* was of the same ilk.

"Oh, you gotta understand, the era had a lot to do with it too, I mean, shifting to movies like that. The War, it robbed the studios of people and materials. The big-production set pieces and epics—uh-uh, there was no way they could produce those. And it was damn good they did. You ask me—hey, who's asking me, right?—but I think movies like *Manhattan* helped move movies out of the world of plays and into their own world.

"*Boomerang. The House on 92nd Street.* Henry Hathaway did that. Oh, he was a gentleman, Henry was. Quiet, polite. He made that film, I guess, in forty-seven. *Manhattan Is My Beat* was in that movement. It's not a good film. But it's an important film."

"And they were *all* true, those films?" Rune asked.

"Well, they weren't documentaries. But, yeah, they

were accurate. Hathaway worked with the FBI to do *House*."

"So, then, if there was a scene in the movie, say the characters went someplace, then the real-life characters may have gone there?"

"Maybe."

"Did you know anyone who worked on *Manhattan*? I mean, know them personally?"

"Sure. Dana Mitchell."

"He played Roy, the cop."

"Right, right, right. Handsome man. We weren't close but we had dinner two, three times. Him and his second wife, I think it was. Charlotte Goodman we had signed here for a couple films in the fifties. I knew Hal of course. He was a contract director for us when studios still did that. He also did—"

"*West of Fort Laramie*. And *Bomber Patrol*."

"Hey, you know your films. Hal's still around, I haven't talked to him in twenty years, I guess."

"Is he in New York?"

"No, he's on the West Coast. Where, I have no idea. Dana and Charlotte are dead now. The exec producer on the project died about five years ago. Some of the other studio people may be alive but they aren't around here. This is no business for old men. I'm paraphrasing Yeats. You know your poetry? You studying poets in school?"

"Yeah, all of them, Yeats, Erica Jong, Stallone."

"Stallone?"

"Yeah, you know, *Rambo*."

"Your school teaches some strange things. But education, who understands it?"

Rune asked, "Isn't there anybody in New York who worked on the film?"

"Whoa, darling, the spirit is willing but the mind is weak." Weinhoff pulled out a film companion book. And looked up the movie. "Ah, here we go. Hey, here we go.

Manhattan Is My Beat, 1947. Oh, sure, Ruby Dahl, who could forget her? She played Roy's fiancée."

"And she lives in New York?"

"Ruby? Naw, she's gone. Same old story. Booze and pills. What a business we're in. What a business."

"What about the writer?"

Weinhoff turned back to the book. "Hey, here we go. Sure. Raoul Elliott. And if he was credited as the writer, then he really wrote it. All by himself. I know Raoul. He was an old-school screenwriter. None of this pro-wrestling for credits you see now." In a singsong voice Weinhoff said, " 'I polished sixty-seven pages of the tenth draft so I get the top credit in beer-belly extended typeface and that other hack only polished fifty-three pages so he gets his name in antleg condensed or no screen credit at all.' *Whine, whine, whine* . . . Naw, I know Raoul. If he got the credit he wrote the whole thing—first draft through the shooting script."

"Does he live in New York?"

"Ah, the poor man. He's got Alzheimer's. God forbid. He'd been in a home for actors and theatrical people for a while. But last year it got pretty bad; now he's in a nursing home out in Jersey."

"You know where?"

"Sure, but I don't think he'll tell you much of anything."

"I'd still like to talk to him."

Weinhoff wrote down the name and address for her. He shook his head. "Funny, you hear about students nowadays, they don't want to do this, they don't want to do that. You're—I pegged you right away, I don't mind saying—you're something else. Talking to an old yenta like me, going to all this trouble just for a school paper."

Rune stood up and shook the old man's hand. "Like, I think you get out of life what you put into it."

All right. I'm two hours late, she thought.

She wasn't just hurrying this time; she was sprinting. To get to work! This was something she'd never done that she could ever remember. Tony's voice echoing in her memory. *Back in twenty, back in twenty.*

Along Eighth Street. Past Fifth Avenue. To University Place. Dodging students and shoppers, running like a football player, like President Reagan in that old movie of his. The one without the monkey.

No big deal. Tony'll understand. I was on time this morning.

Them's the breaks.

He's not going to fire me for being a measly two hours late.

A hundred twenty minutes. The average running time for a film.

How could he possibly be upset? No way.

Rune pushed into the store and stopped cold. At the counter Tony was talking to the woman who was apparently her replacement, showing her how to use the cash register and credit card machine.

Oh, hell.

Tony looked up. "Hi, Rune, how you doin'? Oh, by the way, you're fired. Pack up your stuff and leave."

He was more cheerful than he'd been in months.

CHAPTER TWELVE

The woman, an attractive redhead in her twenties, looked uncertainly at Rune. Then at Tony.

Rune said, "Look, Tony, I'm really, really sorry. I got . . ."

You only lie to people who can control you.

But I don't want to get fired. I don't, I don't, I don't.

". . . I got stuck on the subway. Power failure. Or somebody on the tracks. It was disgusting. No lights, it was smelly, it was hot. And I—"

"Rune, I've had it. Frankie Greek's sister went into labor just after you left and he had to take her to the hospital. And I *know* she did, 'cause I called her ob-gyn to check."

"You did *what*?" Rune asked.

Tony shrugged. "He coulda been faking. What'd I know? But whatta you want me to do when *you* give me some half-assed excuse about the subway? Call the head of the MTA? Ask him if the E train got stuck at Thirty-fourth Street?"

"Please don't fire me."

"I had to work by myself for two fucking hours, Rune."

"Jesus, Tony, it's not like a hot dog stand at Giants Stadium at halftime. How many customers did you have?"

"That's not the point. I missed lunch."

"I'll be better. I really—"

"Time out," the redhead said, shutting them both up. She added, "I'm not taking the job."

"What?" Tony was looking at her.

"I can't take somebody else's job."

"You're not. I fired her before I hired you. It's just that she didn't know."

"Tony," Rune said. Hated that she was pleading but she couldn't help it. What would Richard think if he heard she got canned? He already thought she was totally irresponsible.

"I'd feel too guilty," the redhead explained.

Tony: "You said you needed a job."

"I do. But I'll find something else."

"No, no, doll," Tony said, "don't worry."

But then she said in a stony voice, "You fire her, I'm leaving too."

Tony closed his eyes momentarily. "Jesus Christ." He then leaned forward and glared at Rune. "Okay. Frankie's only going to be working half-days until his sister's back home. You can fill out his schedule. But if you miss any more shifts, without a *real* excuse, that'll be it."

"Thank you, thank you, thank you."

Tony then smiled at the woman, probably thinking he'd scored some points with her for his generosity. He didn't notice that her expression, as she looked back at him, was the way you squint at a roach just before you squoosh it.

"Rune," Tony said, "this is Stephanie. Isn't she pretty? Great hair, don't you think? Why don't you show our beautiful new employee the ropes? I'm going to the health club."

He sucked his gut in, slung his backpack over his shoulder, and pushed out the door.

Isn't she pretty, got great hair . . .

Rune stepped on the jealousy long enough to say to Stephanie, "Thanks. I don't know what to say. I can't really afford to get fired right now."

"Oh, I've been there." Stephanie glanced at the door as Tony disappeared down the street. "So *he's* really in a health club?"

"You bet he is," Rune whispered.

Then said, "Burger King," at the same time Stephanie said, "McDonald's?" They burst into laughter.

"You don't want to get the straight and gay adult mixed up when you're putting them back," Rune was explaining.

"Right. You don't." The woman *did* have incredible hair—long red-blond strands that tumbled over her shoulders the way hair seems to do only in shampoo commercials.

"What's your name again?" Rune now asked her. It started with an S. But she had a lot of problems with S names. Susan, Sally, Suzanne . . .

"Stephanie."

Right. Rune stored it away in her brain and continued with the training session. "See, we don't have covers on the porn so people have to rent them by the titles. With some it's easy. *Soldier Boys, Cowboy Rubdown, Muscle Truckers,* you know? But some, you can't tell. We had one guy rent *Big Blonds,* only it turns out that blondes with an

E on the end is girl blondes and *without* the E is boy blonds. Did you know that? I didn't. Anyway, he got boys with big dicks and he wanted girls with big boobs. He wasn't happy. Hey, your hair *is* totally radical. Is that your real color?"

"For now it is." Stephanie examined Rune's arm. "Love your bracelets."

"Yeah?" Rune shook her arm. They jingled.

Stephanie said, "Someone wanted me to do a porn movie once. In L.A. This guy said he was a UCLA film grad. Came right up to me in a coffee shop—I was hanging, reading *Variety*—and asked me if I wanted to do skin flick."

"No kidding," Rune said. Nobody'd ever asked her to do a porn film. She was wondering if she should feel insulted.

Stephanie paused, looking at a poster for *Gaslight*. "Ingrid Bergman. She was beautiful."

"Even with short hair," Rune said. "Like in *For Whom the Bell Tolls*." She ran her fingers over her head. Patted the strands down again. Thought about a wig. "The porn, did you do it?"

"Naw. Just didn't seem right."

"I'd be scared to death of, you know, catching something."

Stephanie shrugged. "Where'd you get them? The bracelets?"

"Everywhere. I'll be walking down the street and then there's this feeling I get and it's a bracelet calling me. Next store I come to, bang, there's one in the window."

Stephanie looked at her skeptically.

"It happens. I swear to God."

"Tony said you were slacking off."

"Every minute I spend not making his life easier is his definition of slacking off. What it is, this friend of mine got murdered. And I'm trying to find out what happened."

"No!"

"Yeah."

Stephanie said, "I got carjacked in Hollywood. I was in a Honda. You wouldn't think anybody'd kill somebody for a Honda. But I thought they were going to shoot me. I let 'em take it. They just drove off. Stopped at a stop sign and signaled to make a right turn. Like nothing'd happened. Doesn't it seem weird they'd kill you for a car? Or even just a few hundred dollars?"

Or for a *million* dollars, Rune thought. Seeing in her mind's eye Robert Kelly, lying back in his chair. The bullet holes in his chest. And the one in the TV.

Stephanie added, "I took a self-defense course after that. But that doesn't do you any good against a guy with a gun."

Rune pushed the sad thoughts from her mind and walked through the shelves, putting the tapes back, gesturing Stephanie after her.

"You'll learn stuff, working here. About human nature. That's why I took the job. Of course I don't exactly know what to do with the human nature I learn. But it's still fun to watch people. I'm a voyeur, I think."

"What can you learn about people in a video store?"

"How's a for-instance? There's this guy, cute, a stockbroker, always smelled like garlic but I flirted with him anyway. He rents all these Charles Bronson films, Chuck Norris, Schwarzenegger. Then he shows up here one night and he's got this yuppie trendoid girl hanging on him like he's a trapeze, okay? Suddenly no more *Commando*. All he wants are things like *The Seventh Seal* and Fellini and a lot of the recent Woody Allen—you know, not *Bananas* but the relationship stuff. And things you'd see on PBS, right? That lasts for a month, then Miss Culture goes bye-bye and it's back to *Death Wish 8* for a couple months. Then he comes in with some other girl all in leather and studs. I know what you're thinking but guess what she likes? Old musicals. Dorothy Lamour, Bing Crosby, Bob Hope, Fred and Ginger. That's all he rents for *two* months. Guy's going to develop a complex. I mean, you've gotta be yourself, right?"

Stephanie was brushing her hair.

Rune continued. "Like, speaking of adult films . . . Oh, don't call them dirty movies. Tony doesn't like that, and besides, it's a mega-business. We make forty percent of our gross on them even though they're only twelve percent of inventory. . . . Well, what I was saying was that now women rent almost as many as men. And they don't rent all that much straight . . . mostly it's gay male flicks."

"Yeah?" Stephanie's sullen eyes flashed with a splinter of interest then the lids lowered again. The brush went back into her purse. Rune decided Stephanie would be a Washington Square Video employee for thirty days max. She could get just as boring work in restaurants and the pay would be three times as good. "Why would women rent gay films?"

"Way I figure it," Rune said, "it's that the guys in gay films look a lot better than guys in straight films, you know, they're really hunks, cut. Work out, take care of themselves. Straight films, you see a lot of flab . . . I've heard."

Stephanie, glancing with boredom at the adult section, said, "Lesbians are out of luck, sounds like."

"Naw, naw, that's another good market. We've got, let's see, *Girls on Girls, Lesbos Lovers, Sappho Express* . . . But it's mostly men rent those. There're more girlfriends over in the West Village. Not so many here."

Rune walked back to the counter, fluffed her hair out with her fingers. Stephanie looked at it, said, "That's an interesting effect, with the colors. How did you do it?"

"I don't know. It just kind of happened." Trying to figure if her comment was a compliment. Rune didn't think so. *Interesting*. That's a bitch of a word. *Interesting*.

"You have any freaks come in?"

Rune said, "Depends on what you mean. There's a guy knows every line—even the TV and radio broadcasts—in *Night of the Living Dead*. Then this lawyer told me he and his wife rent *Casablanca* after they have sex. And I can look up in the computer and tell you that they must be having problems. There's this one guy, Mad Max, he's real creepy and always rents slasher films. Those stupid things like *Halloween* and *Friday the 13th, Part 85*, you know."

"Sexist bastards," Stephanie said, "that's who makes those films."

"But turns out he's a social worker for a big hospital uptown and volunteers for Meals on Wheels, things like that."

"Seriously?"

"I keep telling you . . . a video store is a great education."

Stephanie said, "You have a boyfriend?"

"I'm not sure," Rune said. She decided this was a pretty accurate statement.

"Is Rune your real name?"

"For now it is."

A queue formed—and Rune walked Stephanie through the check-out procedure.

"I can't believe this is your first day. You're a born clerk," Rune told her.

"Thanks loads," Stephanie drawled. "Don't tell Tony, but what I'm hoping is I'll meet some producers or casting agents here. I want to be an actress. Just a dry spell right now. I haven't auditioned for a month."

"What about all those casting calls in L.A.?"

"A casting call doesn't mean you get the part. L.A. is yucky. New York's the only place to be."

"I *knew* I liked you," Rune said, and rented *The Seven Samurai*, *Sleeping Beauty*, and *Lust Orgy* to a pleasant, balding businessman.

CHAPTER THIRTEEN

The rivers are moats, the buildings are parapets . . .

Wait, is that right? What exactly is a parapet?

Anyway . . .

The buildings are parapets. The stone, pitted and stained with age and cloudy water. Dripping. Slick stalactites and stalagmites. Dark windows with bars on the dungeons. We're riding down, down, down . . . The hooves of our horses muted by the cold brick. Down into the secret entrance that leads under the moat, out of the Magic Kingdom, out of the Side.

Richard guided the old Dodge into the Holland Tunnel and headed for New Jersey.

"Isn't it wild?" Rune asked. The orange lights flashed by, the gassy sweet smell of exhaust flowing into the car.

"What?"

"There is probably a hundred feet of water and yuck on top of us right now. That's really something."

He looked dubiously up at the yellowing ceiling of the tunnel, above which the Hudson River was flowing into New York Harbor.

"Something," he said uneasily.

It was *his* car, the Dodge they were in. This was pretty odd. Richard lived in Manhattan and he actually owned a car. Anybody who did that had to have a pretty conventional side to them after all. Paying taxes and parking and registration fees. This bothered her some but she wasn't really complaining. It turned out that the nursing home where the writer of *Manhattan Is My Beat* lived was forty miles from the city and she couldn't afford to rent wheels for this part of her quest.

"What's the matter?" she asked.

"Nothing."

And they drove through the rest of the claustrophobic yellow tunnel in silence. Rune was careful; when men got moody, it could be a real pisser. Put them with their buddies, let 'em get drunk and snap their jocks and throw footballs or lecture you about Buñuel or how airplane wings work and they were fine. But, holy St. Peter, something serious comes up—especially with a woman involved—and they go all to pieces.

But after twenty minutes, when they were out of the tunnel, Richard seemed to relax. He put his hand on her leg. More sparks. How the hell does that happen? she wondered.

Rune looked around as they headed for the Turnpike. "Gross." The intersections were filled with stoplight poles and wires and mesh fences and gas stations. She looked for her favorite service station logo—Pegasus—and didn't see one. That's what they needed, a winged horse to fly them over this mess.

"How did you get off work?" Richard asked her.

It was Sunday and she'd told him that she'd been scheduled to work.

"Eddie covered for me. I called him last night. That's a first for me—doing something responsible."

He laughed. But there wasn't a lot of humor in his voice.

Richard removed his hand and gripped the wheel. He turned southwest. The fields—flat, like huge brown lawns—were on either side of the highway. Beyond were marshes and factories and tall metal scaffolding and towers. Lots filled with trailers from semi trucks, all stacked up and stretching for hundreds of yards.

"It's like a battlefield," Rune said. "Like those things—what do you suppose they are, refineries or something?—are spaceships from Alpha Centauri."

Richard looked in the rearview mirror. He didn't say anything. He accelerated and passed a chunky garbage truck. Rune pulled an imaginary air horn and the driver gave her two blasts on his real one.

"Tell me about yourself," she said. "I don't know all the details."

He shrugged. "Not much to tell."

Ugh. Did he have to be such a *man*?

She tried a cheerful "Tell me anyway!"

"Okay." He grew slightly animated; the hipster from the other night had partially returned. "He was born in Scarsdale, the son of pleasant suburban parents, and raised to become a doctor, lawyer, or other member of the elite destined to grind down the working class. He had an uneventful boyhood, distinguished by chess club, Latin club, and a complete inability to do any kind of sport. Rock and roll saved his ass, though, and he grew to maturity in the Mudd Club and Studio 54."

"Cool! I loved them!"

"Then, for some unknown reason, Fordham decided to give him a degree in philosophy after four years of driving the good fathers there to distraction with his contrarian ways. After that he took the opportunity to see the world."

Rune said, "So you *did* go to Paris. I've always wanted to see it. Rick and Ilsa . . . *Casablanca*. And that hunchback guy in the big church. I felt so sorry for him. I—"

"Didn't exactly get to France," Richard admitted. Then slipped back into his third-person narrative. "What he did was get as far as England and found out that working your way around the world was a lot different from *vacationing* around the world. Being a punch press operator in London—if you can get to be a punch press operator at all—isn't any better than being one in Trenton, New Jersey. So, the young adventurer came back to New York to be a chic unemployed philosopher, going to clubs, playing with getting his M.A. and Ph.D., going to clubs, picking up blondes without names and brunettes with pseudonyms, going to clubs, working day jobs, getting tired of clubs, waiting to reach a moment of intersubjectivity with a woman. Working away."

"On his novel."

"Right. On his novel."

So far he seemed to be pretty much on her wavelength—despite the car and the moods. She was into fairy stories and he was into philosophy. Which *seemed* different but, when she thought about it, Rune decided they were both really the same—two fields that could stimulate your mind and that were totally useless in the real world.

Somebody like Richard—maybe him, maybe not—but somebody like him was the only sort of person she could be truly in love with, Rune believed.

"I know what's the matter," she said.

"Why do you think something's the matter?"

"I just do."

"Well," he said, "what? Tell me."

"Remember that story I told you?"

"Which one? You've told me a lot of stories."

"About Diarmuid? I feel like we're a fairy king and queen who've left the Side—you know, the magic land." She turned around. Gasped. "Oh, you've got to look at it! Turn around, Richard, *look*!"

"I'm driving."

"Don't worry—I'll describe it. There're a hundred towers and battlements and they're all made out of silver. The sun is falling on the spires. Glowing and stealing all that energy from the sun—how much energy do you think the sun has? Well, it's all going right into the Magic Kingdom through the tops of the battlements . . ." She had a sudden feeling of dread, as if she'd caught his mood. A premonition or something. After a moment she said, "I don't know, I don't think I should be doing this. I shouldn't've crossed the moat, shouldn't've left the Side. I feel funny. I almost feel like we shouldn't be doing this."

"Leaving the Side," he repeated absently. "Maybe that's it." And looked in the rearview mirror again.

He might have meant it, might have been sarcastic. She couldn't tell.

Rune turned around, hooked her seat belt again. Then they swept around a long curve in the expressway and the country arrived. Hills, forests, fields. A panoramic view west. She was about to point out a large cloud, shaped like a perfect white chalice, a towering Holy Grail, but Rune decided she'd better keep quiet. The car accelerated and they drove the rest of the way to Berkeley Heights, New Jersey, in silence.

"He hasn't had a visitor for a month," the nurse was saying to Rune.

They stood on a grassy hill beside the administration

building of the nursing home. Richard was in the cafeteria. He'd brought a book with him.

"That's too bad. I know it's good for the guests," the nurse continued. "People coming to see them."

"How is he?"

"Some days he's almost normal, some days he's not so good. Today, he's in fair shape."

"Who was the visitor last month?" Rune asked.

She said, "An Irish name, I think. An older gentleman."

"Kelly, maybe?"

"Could have been. Yes, I think so."

Rune's heart beat a bit faster.

Had he come to ask about a million dollars? she wondered.

Rune held up a rose in a clear cellophane tube. "I brought this. Is it okay if I give it to him?"

"He'll probably forget you gave it to him right away. But, yes, of course you can. I'll go get him. You wait here."

"They don't come to see me much. Last time was, let me see, let me see, let me see . . . No, they don't come. We have this party on Sundays, I think it is. And what they do is, it's real nice, what they do is put, when the weather's nice, put a tablecloth on the picnic benches, and we eat eggs and olives and Ritz crackers." He asked Rune, "It's almost fall now, isn't it?"

The nurse said, in a voice aimed at a three-year-old, "You know it's spring, Mr. Elliott."

Rune looked at the old man's face and arms. It seemed like he'd lost weight recently and the gray flesh hung on his arms and neck like thick cloth. She handed him the flower. He looked at it curiously, then set it on his lap. He asked, "You're . . ."

"Rune."

He smiled in a way that was so sincere it almost hurt. He said, "I know. Of course I know your name." To the nurse: "Where's Bips? Where'd that dog get to?"

Rune started to look around but the nurse shook her head and Rune understood that Bips had been in puppy heaven for years.

"He's just playing, Mr. Elliott," the nurse said. "He'll be back soon. He's safe, don't you worry." They were on a small rise of grass underneath a huge oak tree. The nurse set the brakes on his wheelchair and walked away, saying, "I'll be back in ten minutes."

Rune nodded.

Raoul Elliott reached up and took her hand. His was soft and very dry. He squeezed it once, then again. Then released it like a boy testing the waters with a girl at a dance. He said, "Bips. You couldn't believe what they do to him, these boys and girls. They poke at him with sticks if he gets too close to the fence. You'd think they'd be brought up better than that. What day is it?"

"Sunday," Rune answered.

"I know that. I mean the date."

"June fifteenth."

"I know that." Elliott nodded. He fixed a gaze on an elderly couple strolling down the path.

The grounds were trimmed and clean. Couples, elderly and mostly of the same sex, walked slowly up the paved paths. There were no stairs, curbs, steps, low plants; nothing to trip up old feet.

"I saw one of your movies, Mr. Elliott."

Flies buzzed in, then shot away on the warm breeze. Big thick white clouds sent their sharp-edged shadows across the grass. Elliott said, "My movies."

"I thought it was wonderful. *Manhattan Is My Beat.*"

His eyes crinkled with recognition. "I worked on that with . . . Ah, this memory of mine. Sometimes I think

I'm going loony. There were a couple of the boys. . . . Who were they? We'd have a ball. I ever tell you about Randy? No? Well, Randy was my age. A year or two older maybe. We were all from New York. Some'd been newspapermen, some were writing for the *Atlantic* or editing for Scribner's or Condé Nast. But we were all from New York. Oh, it was a different town in those days, a very different town. The studio liked that, they liked men from New York. Like Frank O'Hara. We were friends, Frank and I. We used to go to this bar near Rockefeller Center. It was called . . . Well, there were a lot we went to. In Hollywood too. We'd hang out in Hollywood."

"You worked on a newspaper?"

"Sure I did."

"Which one?"

There was a pause and his eyes darted. "Well, there were the usual ones, you know. It's all changed."

"Mr. Elliott, do you remember writing *Manhattan Is My Beat*?"

"Sure I do. That was a few years ago. Charlie gave it a good review. Frank said he liked it. He was a good boy. Henry too. They were all good boys. We said we didn't like reviews. We said, what we said was reviewers were so low, you shouldn't even ignore them." He laughed at that. Then his face grew somber. "But we did care, oh, yes, ma'am. But your father can tell you that. Where is he, is he around here?" The old head with its wave of dry hair swiveled.

"My father?"

"Isn't Bobby Kelly your father?"

Rune saw no point in breaking the news about Mr. Kelly's death to the old man. She said, "No. He's a friend."

"Well, where is he? He was just here."

"He stepped away for a few minutes."

"Where's Bips?"

"He's off playing."

"I worry about the traffic with him. He gets too excited when there's cars about. And these boys. They poke sticks at him. Girls too." He was aware of the flower again and touched it. "Did I thank you for this?"

She said, "You bet you did." Rune sat down on the grass beside the wheelchair, cross-legged. "Mr. Elliott, did you do your own research for the movie? For *Manhattan Is My Beat?*"

"Research? We had people do our research. The studio paid for it. Pretty girls. Pretty like you."

"And they researched the story that the movie was based on? The cop who stole the money from Union Bank?"

"They aren't there anymore, I'll bet you. They went on to Time-Life a lot of them. Or *Newsweek*. The studio paid better but it was a wild sort of life some of them didn't want. Is Hal doing okay now? And how's Dana? Handsome man he was."

"Fine, they're both fine. Did you find out anything about the cop who stole the money? The cop in real life, I mean?"

"Sure I did."

"What?"

Elliott was looking at his wrist, where his watch probably should have been. "I've lost it again. Do you know when we'll be leaving? It'll be good to get home again. Between you and I, I mean, between you and *me,* I don't like to travel. I can't say anything to them though. You understand. Do you know when we're leaving?"

"I don't know, Mr. Elliott. I sure don't . . . So what did you find out about the cop who stole the money?"

"Cop?"

"In *Manhattan Is My Beat?*"

"I wrote the story. I tried to write a good story.

There's nothing like that, you know. Isn't that the best thing in the world? A good story."

"It was a wonderful story, Mr. Elliott." She got up on her knees. "I especially liked the part where Roy hid the money. He was digging like a madman, remember? In the movie it was hidden in a cemetery. In real life did you ever have any idea where the cop who stole the money hid it?"

"The money?" He looked at her for a second with eyes that seemed to click with understanding. "All that money."

And Rune felt a low jolt in her stomach, a kick. She whispered, "What *about* the money?"

His eyes glazed over again and he said, "What they do here—they'll do it when the weather's nice—they put paper on the tables, like tablecloths and we have picnics here. They put nuts in little paper cups. They're pink and look like tiny upside-down ballet dresses. I don't know where the tables are. I hope they do that again soon. . . . Where's Bips?"

Rune sank back down on her haunches. She smiled. "He's playing, Mr. Elliott, I'll look out for him." They sat in silence for a moment and she asked, "What did Robert Kelly want when he came to visit you a month ago?"

His head nodded toward her and his eyes had a sudden lucidity that startled her.

"Who, Bobby? Why, he was asking me questions about that damn movie." The old face broke into a smile. "Just like you've been doing all afternoon."

Rune, leaning forward, studying his face, the lines and gnarls. "What exactly did you talk about, you and Bobby Kelly?"

"Your father, Bobby? Oh, the usual. I worked on *Manhattan* with some of the boys."

"I know you did. What did Bobby ask you about it?"

"Stuff."

"Stuff?" she asked cheerfully.

Elliott frowned. "Somebody else did too. Somebody else was asking me things."

Her heart pounded a little faster. "When was that, Mr. Elliott? Do you remember?"

"Last month. No, no, just the other day. Wait, I remember—it was today, little while ago." He focused on her. "It was a girl. Boyish. Looked a lot like you. Wait, maybe it *was* you."

He squinted.

Rune felt that he was on the verge of something. She didn't say anything for a moment. Like the times she and her father would go fishing in rural Ohio, playing the heavy catfish with the frail Sears rods. You could lose them in a wink if you weren't careful.

"Bobby Kelly," she tried again. "When he came to visit, what did he ask you about the movie?"

The eyes dropped and the lids pressed together. "The usual, you know. Are you his daughter?"

"Just a friend."

"Where is he now?"

"He's busy, he couldn't make it. He wanted me to say hello to you and tell you that he had a great time talking to you last month. You talked, he told me you talked all about . . . what was it again?"

"That place."

"What place?"

"That place in New York. The place I sent him. He'd been looking for it for a long time is what he told me."

Rune's heart thudded hard. She turned her head and looked directly into his milky eyes.

"He was happy when I sent him there. You should have seen his face when I told him about it. Oh, he was real happy. Where's Bips?"

"Just playing, Mr. Elliott. I'm looking after him. Where did you send Bobby Kelly?"

"He was real anxious to find it and I told him right off, I'm sure I did."

"Do you remember now?"

"Oh, one of those places . . . there are lots of them, you know."

Rune was leaning forward. *Please try to remember,* she thought. *Please, pleasepleaseplease* . . . Didn't say anything.

Silence. The old man shook his head. He sensed the importance of her questions and there was frustration in his eyes. "I can't remember. I'm sorry." He rubbed his fingers together. "Sometimes I think I'm going loony. Just loony. I'm feeling pretty tired. I could use a nap."

"That's okay, Mr. Elliott." She tasted her disappointment. But she smiled and patted his arm, then moved away quickly when she felt how thin it was. Thought of her father. "Hey, don't worry about it."

Rune stood up, walked behind him and took the white plastic handles of the chair. Undid the brakes. She started to wheel the chair toward the sidewalk. Elliott said suddenly, "The Hotel Florence. Five fourteen West Forty-fourth. At Tenth Avenue."

Rune froze. She dropped into a crouch next to him, her hand on the frail bone of his arm. "That's where you sent him?"

"I . . . I think so. It just came to me."

"That's wonderful, Mr. Elliott. Thank you so much." She leaned forward and kissed his cheek. He touched the spot and seemed to blush.

Richard appeared and stepped up toward them, starting to speak. Rune held up her hand to him. He stopped.

Raoul Elliott said, "I want to take a nap now. Where's Bips?"

"He's playing, Mr. Elliott. He'll be here soon."

Elliott looked around. "Miss, can I tell you something?"

"Sure."

"I lied."

Rune hesitated. Then said, "Go ahead. Tell me."

"Bips's a little shit. I've been trying to give him away for years. You know somebody who wants a dog?"

Rune laughed. "I sure don't. Sorry."

Elliott looked at the flower, curious again, started to pull off the cellophane wrapping; it defeated him and he set it back on his lap. Rune took the flower from him and opened it up. He held it lightly in his hands. He said, "You'll come back sometime, won't you? We have this party when it's spring. We can talk about movies. I'd like that."

Rune said, "I'd love to."

"You'll say hi to your father for me."

"Sure, I will."

The nurse was approaching. The old man's head sagged against the side of the wheelchair. He breathed slowly. His eyes were not quite completely closed but he was asleep. He started to snore very softly.

Rune looked at him, thinking again how much he resembled her father toward the end of his life. Cancer or AIDS or old age . . . death's packaging is all so similar.

The nurse nodded to her and took the chair, wheeled it down the path. The flower fell to the sidewalk. The nurse picked it up and set it on his lap again.

A dense shadow of a cloud that Rune thought looked just like a dragon rearing up on its sturdy hind legs passed over them. She turned to Richard. "Let's get out of here. Let's get back to the Side."

CHAPTER FOURTEEN

The Florence Hotel, near the Hudson River, was in Hell's Kitchen, west of Midtown.

Rune knew her New York history. At one point this had been one of the most dangerous areas in the city, the home of the Gophers and the Hudson Dusters, murderous gangs that made the Mafia look tame. Most of the dangerous elements had been urban-renewed away when the tunnel to New Jersey was built. But the dregs of some Irish and Latino gangs remained. It was, in short, not a neighborhood to be hanging out in alone at night.

Thanks tons, Richard, she thought.

He'd left her there after dropping her off in front of the Florence, a four-story flophouse with a scarred and peeling facade. She'd started to ask him again what the matter was but then some kind of radar kicked in and she decided it would be a bad move.

"Can't really hang around," he'd told her. "You'll be okay?"

"I'll be fine. Wonder Woman. That's me."

"Gotta meet some people tonight. Otherwise, I'd stay."

She hadn't asked who. Been dying to. But hadn't.

"No, that's fine. You go on."

"You sure?"

"Go on."

Some people . . .

She watched his car drive away. He gave her a formal wave. She hesitated only a moment before she stepped carefully around the bum who slept in front of the beer-can-filled flower box under the narrow front window. She pushed open the lobby door and stepped inside. The smells were of damp wallpaper, disinfectant, some vague, unpleasant animal scents. The sort of place that made you want to hold your breath.

The clerk looked up at her from behind a Plexiglas security barrier that distorted his features. A thin man, hair slicked back, wearing a dress shirt and rust-colored corduroy pants. The shirt had dark stains, the pants, light.

"Yeah?" he called.

"I'm a social worker from Brooklyn?" Rune said.

"You asking me?"

"I'm telling you who I am."

"Yeah, a social worker."

"I'm trying to find some information about a patient of mine, a man who stayed here for a month or so."

"Don't you call 'em clients?"

"What?"

"We get social workers here all the time. They don't have patients. They have clients."

"One of my clients," she corrected herself.

"You got a license?"

"A license? A driver's license? Look, I'm older than I—"

"No, a social work license."

A license?

"Oh, that. See, I was mugged last week when I was on assignment. In Bedford Stuyvesant. Visiting a client. They took my purse—my other purse, my good purse—and that had my license in it. I've applied for a new one but you know how long it takes to get a replacement?"

"Tell me."

"Worse than a passport. I'm talking *weeks*."

The man was grinning. "Where'd you go to social work school?"

"Harvard."

"No shit." The smile didn't leave his face. "If there's nothing else, I'm pretty busy." He picked up a *National Geographic* and flipped it open.

"Look, I have my job to do. I have to find out about this man. Robert Kelly."

The clerk glanced up from his magazine. He didn't say anything. But Rune, even through the scuffed plastic, could see caution in his eyes.

She continued. "I know he stayed here for a while. I think somebody named Raoul Elliott recommended that he come here."

"Raoul? Nobody's named Raoul."

Summoning patience, Rune asked, "Do you remember Mr. Kelly?"

He shrugged.

She continued. "Did he check anything here? A suitcase? Maybe a package in the safe?"

"Safe? We look like the kinda hotel's gotta safe?"

"It's important."

Again, the man didn't respond. Suddenly Rune understood. She'd seen enough movies. She lifted her purse slowly and opened it, reached in and took out five dollars. She slid it seductively toward him. Just like an actor in a movie she'd seen a month or so ago. Harrison Ford, she thought. Or Michael Douglas.

That actor'd gotten results; she got a laugh.

Rune gave the clerk another ten.

"Look, kid. The going rate's fifty for information. That's the way it is all over the city. It's like a union."

Fifty? Shit.

She handed him a twenty. "That's all I got."

He took the money. "I don't know nothing—"

"You bastard! I want my money back."

"—except one thing. About your *client* Kelly. This priest or minister, Father so-and-so, called, I don't know, a couple days ago. He said Kelly'd dropped off a suitcase for safekeeping. He couldn't get him at his apartment and had this as his only other number. This priest figured I might know where Kelly was. He didn't know what to do with the suitcase."

Yes! Rune thought. Remembering the scene in *Manhattan Is My Beat* where Roy buried the money in a cemetery next to a church!

"Excellent, that's great! You know where the church was? You have any idea?"

"I didn't write nothing down. But I think he said he was in Brooklyn."

"Brooklyn!" Rune's hands were up against the grimy Plexiglas. She leaned forward, bouncing on her toes. "This's awesome!"

The man slipped her money into his pocket. "Well, happy day." He opened the magazine again and began reading an article about penguins.

Outside, she found a pay phone and called Amanda LeClerc.

"Amanda, it's Rune. How are you?"

"Been better. Missing him, you know? Robert . . . Only knew him for a little while but I miss him more than some people I knew for years and years. I was thinking about it. And you know what I thought?"

"What's that?"

"That maybe because we weren't so young no more we got to be more closer faster. Sort of like there wasn't a lot of time ahead of us."

"I miss him too, Amanda," Rune said.

"Haven't heard nothing about Mr. Symington."

"He hasn't been back?"

"No. Nobody's seen him. I was asking around."

"Well, I've got good news." She told her about the church and the suitcase.

The woman didn't answer for a moment. "Rune, you really thinking there maybe's some money? They keep coming after me for the rent. I'm trying to find a job. But it's tough. Nobody hires old ladies like me."

"I think we're on the right track."

"Well, what do you want me to do?"

"Start calling churches in Brooklyn. See if Mr. Kelly left a suitcase there. You can go to the library and get a Brooklyn phone book. We've got one at the video store. I'll take A through L. You take M through Z."

"Z? Do any churches start with a Z?"

"I don't know. St. Zabar's?"

"Okay. I'ma start calling first thing in the morning."

Rune hung up. She looked around her. The sun was down now and in this part of the city the bleakness was wrenching. But what she felt was only partly the sorrow of the landscape; the rest was fear. She was vulnerable. Low buildings—a lot of them burned-out or in various stages of demolition—a few auto repair shops, an abandoned diner, a couple of parked cars. Nobody on the street who'd help her if she was attacked. A few kids in gang colors, sitting on steps, sharing a bottle of Colt .45 or a crack pipe. A hooker, a tall black woman on nose-bleed-high heels, leaned against a chain-link fence, arms crossed. Some bums shoring on grates or in doorways.

She felt very disoriented. She was back in Manhattan but she still felt that something separated her from her element, from the Side.

Starting down the street, eyes on the filthy pavement, keeping close to the curb—away from the alleys and the buildings, where muggers and rapists lurk.

Thinking back to *Lord of the Rings.* Thinking how quests always start off in springtime, with nice weather, good friends around to see you off, hearty food and drink in your pack. But they end up in Mordor—the bleakest of kingdoms, a place full of fire and death and pain.

It seemed to her that someone was following, though when she looked back she could see nothing but shadows.

She worked her way to Midtown and caught a subway. An hour later she was back home, in the loft. No note from Richard. And Sandra was out—a date on Sunday? Totally unfair! Nobody ever had a date on Sunday. Hell. She slipped *Manhattan Is My Beat* in the VCR and started it once more. The movie was halfway through before she realized that she'd been reciting the dialogue along with the actors. She'd memorized it perfectly.

Damn scary, she thought. But kept the film running till its end.

Haarte was angry.

It was Monday morning and he was sitting in his town house. Zane had just called and told him that the one witness, Susan Edelman, was about to be released from the hospital and that the other girl, the one with the weird name, was investigating the case harder than the NYPD.

Angry.

Which was a difficult emotion in this business. Haarte wasn't *allowed* to be angry when he'd been a cop. There was nothing he could *do* with his anger as a soldier and mercenary. And now—as a professional killer—he found anger to be a liability. A serious risk.

But he *was* mad. Oh, he was furious.

He was in his town house. Thinking about how messy this fucking job had become. Killing a man ought to be simplicity itself. He and Zane had gotten drunk a month ago, sitting in the bar in the Plaza hotel. They'd both grown maudlin and philosophical. Their job, they decided, was better than most because it was simple. And pure. As they poured down Lagavulin Scotch, Haarte had derided advertising execs and lawyers and salesmen. "They've got complicated, bullshit lives."

Zane had countered, "But that's reality. And reality's complicated."

And he'd answered, "If that's reality you can have it. I want simplicity."

What he meant was that there was a weird kind of ethics at work here. Haarte really believed this. Someone paid him money and he did the job. Or he couldn't do it. In which case he gave the money back or he tried again. Simplicity. Either someone was dead or not.

But this hit wasn't simple anymore. There were too many loose ends. Too many questions. Too many directions it might take. He was at risk, Zane was at risk. And of course the people who'd hired them were at risk too.

The man in St. Louis didn't know exactly what was going on but if he found out he'd be enraged.

And that made Haarte all the angrier.

He wanted to do something. Yet he couldn't decide what. There was the witness in the hospital. . . . There was the weird girl, the one in the video store. . . . He needed to snip some of those loose ends. But, as he sipped his morning espresso, he couldn't decide exactly how to handle it. There are many ways to stop people who're a risk to you. You can kill them, of course. Which is the most efficient way in some cases. And sometimes killing witnesses and meddlers makes the case so much more difficult to investigate that the police put the matter low on their list of priorities. But sometimes killing people does the opposite. It gets the press involved. It galvanizes cops to work even harder.

Killing's one way. But you can also hurt people. Scare them. It doesn't take much physical pain at all to put somebody out of commission for a long, long time. Lose a limb or your eyesight . . . Often they get the message and develop amnesia about what they saw or what they know. And the cops can't even get you for murder.

You can also hurt or kill someone *close* to the person you want to stop, their friends or lovers. This works *very* well, he'd found.

What to do?

Haarte stood up and stretched. He looked at his expensive watch. He walked into his kitchen to make another cup of espresso. The thick coffee made Zane agitated. But Haarte found it calmed him, cleared his head.

Sipping the powerful brew.

Thinking: What was supposed to be simple had become complicated.

Thinking: Time to do something about that.

There she was, up ahead.

Haarte had waited for her there, an alley, for a half hour.

Walking down the street in her own little world.

He wondered about her. Haarte often wondered about the people he killed. And he wondered what there was about him that could study people carefully and learn about them for the sole purpose of ending their lives. This fact or that fact, which somebody might find interesting or cute or charming, could in fact be the linchpin of the entire job. A simple fact. Shopping at this store, driving this route to work, fucking this secretary, fishing in this lake.

A half-block away she paused and looked in a storefront window. Clothes. Did women always stop and look at clothes? Haarte himself was a good dresser and liked clothes. But when he went shopping it was because a suit had worn out or a shirt had ripped, not because he wanted to amuse himself by looking at a bunch of cloth hanging on racks in a stuffy store.

But this was a fact about her that he noted. She liked to shop—window-shop at least—and it was going to work out for the best. Because farther up the street, a block away from the store she was examining, he noticed a construction site.

He crossed the street and jogged past her. She didn't notice him. He looked over the site. The contractor had rigged a scaffolding around a five-story building that was about to be demolished. There were workmen in the building but they were on the other block and couldn't even see this street. Haarte walked underneath the scaffold and stepped into the open doorway. He looked at the jungle of wires and beams inside the chill, open area of what had been the lobby. The floor was littered with glass, conduit, nails, beer cans.

Not great but it would do.

He glanced up the street and saw the girl disappear into the clothing store.

Good.

He pulled latex gloves out of his pocket and found a piece of rope, cut a 20-foot length with the razor knife he always kept with him. Then he went to work with the rope and several lengths of pipe. Five minutes later, he was finished. He returned to the entryway of the building and hid in the shadows.

Long to wait? he wondered.

But, no, it turned out. Only four minutes.

Strolling down the street, happy with her new purchase, whatever it was, the girl was paying no attention to anything except the spring morning as she strolled along the sidewalk.

Twenty feet away, fifteen, ten . . .

She started under the scaffolding and when she was directly opposite him he said, "Oh, hey, miss!"

She stopped, gasped in fright. Took a deep breath. "Like, you scared me," she said angrily.

"Just wanted to say. Be careful where you're walking. It's dangerous 'round here."

He said nothing else. She squinted, wondering if she'd seen him before. Then she looked from his face to the rope he held in his hand. Her eyes followed the rope out the doorway along the sidewalk. To the Lally column she stood beside.

And she realized what was about to happen. "No! Please!"

But he did. Haarte yanked the rope hard, pulling the column out from underneath the first layer of scaffolding. He'd loosened the other columns and removed the wood blocks from under them. The one that the rope was tied to was the only column supporting the tons of steel and two-by-eights that rose for twenty feet above the girl.

As she cried in fear her hands went up, fingers splayed. But it was just an automatic gesture, pure animal reflex—as if she could ward off the terrible weight that now came crashing down on her. The commotion was so loud that Haarte never even heard her scream as the wood and metal—like huge spears—tumbled over her, sending huge clouds of dust into the air.

In ten seconds, the settling was over. Haarte ran to

the column and undid the rope. He tossed it into a Dumpster. Then he pulled off the latex gloves and left the construction site, careful to avoid the spreading pool of blood migrating outward from the mound of debris in the center of the sidewalk.

■

The man stood at the top of the stairs, turning three hundred sixty degrees around the girl's loft.

Any notes? Any diaries? Any witnesses?

He was wearing a jacket with a name stitched on it, *Hank.* Below the name he himself had stenciled *Dept. of Public Works. Meter Reading Service.*

The Meter Man turned back to the loft. Walked along the bookshelves, pulled out several books, and flipped through them.

There had to be something here. She'd looked like a scavenger. The sort who doesn't throw anything away. And, fuck, it looked like she hadn't.

He got to work: Looking through all the books, papers, all the shit. Stuffed animals, scraps of notes, diaries . . . Shit, she wasn't the least bit organized. This was gonna take forever. His urge was to fling everything around the room, rip open the suitcases, cut open mattresses. But he didn't. He worked slowly, methodically. This was against his nature. If you're in a hurry, do it slowly. Somebody told him that and he always remembered it. One of the guys he worked for, a guy now dead—dead not because he got careless but dead because they were in a business where you sometimes got dead and that was all there was to it.

You're in a hurry, do it slowly.

Carefully looking through the cushions, boxes, bookcases.

A box stuffed into the futon was labeled MAGIC CRYSTALS. Inside were pieces of quartz. "Magic." He whispered the word as if he'd never said it before, as if it were Japanese.

Jesus. I'm in outer fucking space.

He found a cassette labeled *Manhattan Is My Beat* and picked it up, set it down.

Then: footsteps.

Shit. Who the hell was *this*?

Giggling. A woman's voice: "Not here, come on. No, wait!"

He reached into his pocket and wrapped his hand around his pistol.

A twentyish woman, in a white bra and dress bunched around her waist, stopped at the top of the stairs. She looked at him. He looked at her tits.

"Who the fuck are you?" she demanded. Pulling the cloth halfheartedly up to her chest.

"Who're *you*?" he asked.

The way he asked it she said, "Sandra," immediately.

"You're her roommate?"

"Rune? Yeah, I guess."

He laughed. "You *guess*? How long you known her?"

"Not, you know, long."

He took in this information carefully, noted her body language. If she was dangerous, innocent. If she'd ever killed anyone. "How long is 'you know long'?"

"Huh?"

"How the fuck long've you known her?"

"A couple of months is all. What the hell're you doing here?"

A man, late twenties, blond, jockish, came up the stairs. He squinted, then stepped up beside Sandra.

The Meter Man ignored him.

She said, "Like, what're you doing here?"

He finished looking through the bookcase. Jesus, he didn't want to have to flip through every book. There must've been five hundred of them.

"Hey," the blond man called, "the lady asked you a question."

Sounded like a line from a really bad movie. The Meter Man loved movies. He lived alone and spent every Saturday afternoon at the Quadriplex near him.

He squinted. "What was it? The question?"

"What're you doing here?" she asked uneasily.

He pointed to his chest. "I read meters."

"You can't just come in here," the young man said. Sandra tried to shush him—not concerned so much about the words themselves as the attitude. But the boy waved her off. "You can't enter without permission. It's trespassing. That's actionable."

"Oh. Actionable. What's that mean?"

"That she can sue your ass."

"Oh. Actionable. Well, we had reports of a leak."

"Yeah, what leak?" Sandra asked. "Who reported it?"

The Meter Man grinned at her, looked at her chest again. Nice tits. And she wasn't ugly. Just needed some color and to get rid of that punky makeup. And why a white bra like old ladies wear? He shrugged. "I dunno. Somebody downstairs complained."

"Well, I don't see a leak," she said. "So why don't you leave?"

"You haven't had any water damage lately?"

"Why's a meter reader interested in repairs and leaks?" From Sandra's horny companion.

The Meter Man glanced out the window. It really was one fucking incredible view. He looked back. "When there's a leak you can tell by looking at the meter. That makes sense, don'tcha think?"

"Were you looking through Rune's stuff?"

"Naw, I was looking for the meter."

Sandra said, "Well, it's not up here. So why don't you leave?"

"Why don't you say please?"

The blond jock did it just like Redford or Steve McQueen or Stallone would've. He stepped in front of Sandra. Crossed his arms in his Polo shirt and said, "The lady wants you to leave."

Professional or not? The meter man debated. *That* side gave in, the way it usually did. He said, "If she's a lady why's she fucking an asshole like you?"

The blond smiled, shaking his head, stepping forward. Tensing the muscles that came from the magic of Nautilus machines. "You're outa here."

It turned out not to be that much fun and the Meter Man decided it hadn't been worth the unprofessional part. Oh, mixing it up with a guy who knew what he was doing . . . that would've been one thing. Going a few rounds. Really getting a chance to trade knuckles. But this fucking yuppie . . . Christ.

They did a little scuffling, a little push-pull. Saying that stuff you said in street fights "Why, you motherfucker . . ." That sort of thing.

Then the Meter Man got bored and decided he couldn't risk being there any longer, and who knew who this pair had called. He broke free and got Blondie once in the solar plexus, then once in the jaw.

Zap, that was it. Two silent punches. The guy went to his knees. More nauseated than hurt, which is what gut punches do. Probably the first fight the guy had been in ever.

Shit, he's going to—

The guy puked all over the floor.

"Jesus, Andy," Sandra said. "That's gross."

Meter Man helped Andy to his feet. Eased him down on the bed.

Okay, enough fun, he thought. Time to get professional again. He said to Sandra, "Here's the deal—I'm from a collection agency. Your friend owes a couple thousand on her credit card and she's been dodging us for a year. We're tired of it."

"That sounds like Rune, sure. Look, I don't know where she is. I haven't heard—"

He held up his hand. "You fucking tell anybody you saw me here, I'll do the same thing to you." He nodded at the young man, who lay on his back, moaning, his arm over his eyes.

Sandra shook her head. "I won't say anything."

As he walked out, Sandra said, "You fight good." She let the dress slip, revealing her breasts again. The Meter Man tugged the dress back up, smiled, said, "Tell your boyfriend he should always keep his left up. He's a defense kinda guy."

CHAPTER FIFTEEN

"Ms. Rune?"

She turned, paused, as she was walking through the door of Washington Square Video.

Rune, however, wasn't looking at the man who'd stopped her. It was the badge and the ID card in the battered wallet that got her attention. He was a U.S. marshal.

Neat, she thought before she decided she ought to be nervous.

"My name's Dixon."

He looked just like what a casting director would pick for a federal agent. Tall and craggy. He had a faint Queens accent. She thought about Detective Virgil Manelli and how he'd worn a suit. This guy was wearing jeans and sneakers, a black baseball jacket: bridge-and-tunnel clothes—meaning: from the outer boroughs. He wouldn't get into Area, her favorite after-hours club, wearing this kind of outfit. Trimmed brown hair. He looked like a contractor.

"It's just Rune. Not Ms."

He put the badge away and she caught a glimpse of a huge gun on his hip.

Awesome . . . That's a Schwarzenegger gun, she thought. Man, that would shoot through trucks.

Then remembered she should be nervous again.

He squinted, then gave a faint smile. "You don't remember me."

She shook her head. Let the door swing shut.

"I saw you the other day—in the apartment on Tenth Street. I was part of the homicide team."

"In Mr. Kelly's apartment?"

"Right."

She nodded. Thinking back to that terrible morning. But she didn't remember anything except Manelli's close-together eyes.

The shot-out TV.

Mr. Kelly's face.

The blood on his chest.

Dixon looked at a notebook, put it back in his pocket. He asked, "Have you been in touch with a Susan Edelman recently?"

"Susan . . . Oh, the other witness." The yuppie with the designer jogging outfit. "I called her yesterday, the day before. She was still in the hospital."

"I see. Can I ask why you called her?"

Because somebody's got to find the killer, and the cops couldn't care less. But she told Dixon, "Just to see how she's doing. Why?"

Dixon paused for a moment. She didn't like the way he was looking at her face. Assessing her. He said, "Ms. Edelman was killed an hour ago."

"What?" she gasped. "No!"

"I'm afraid so."

"What happened?"

Dixon continued. "She was walking past a construction site. A scaffolding collapsed. It might have been an accident but, of course, we don't think so."

"Oh, no . . ."

"Has anyone threatened you? Or have you noticed anything suspicious since the killing on Tenth Street?"

"No." She looked down for a moment, uneasy, then back to the marshal.

Dixon examined her face closely. His expression gave away nothing. He said, "For your sake, for a lot of people's sake, I need you to tell me what your involvement with this whole thing is."

"There's no—"

"This's real serious, miss. It might've seemed like a game at first. But it isn't. Now, I can have you put into protective custody and we'll sort it out later. . . . I really don't think you'd like to spend a week in Women's Detention? Now, what's the story?"

There was something about his voice that sounded as if he was really concerned. Sure, he was threatening her in a way but that just seemed to be his style. It probably went with the job. And she felt that he was really worried that she might end up like Kelly or Susan Edelman.

So she told him a few things. About the movie, the stolen bank loot, about the connection between Mr. Kelly and the robbery. Nothing about Symington. Nothing about churches or suitcases. Nothing about Amanda LeClerc.

Dixon nodded slowly and she couldn't tell what he was thinking. The only thing that seemed to interest him was the old robbery.

Why'd he lift his eyebrow at that? she wondered.

Dixon asked, "Where do you live?"

She gave him the address.

"Phone number?"

"No phone. You can call here, the video store, leave a message."

Dixon thought for a moment. "I don't think you're in danger."

"I didn't see anything, I really didn't. Just this green car. That's all I remember. No faces, no license plates. There's no *reason* to kill me."

This seemed to amuse him. "Well, that's not really the issue, miss. The reason you're not dead is that somebody doesn't want you dead. Not yet. If they did, you'd be gone. If I were you, though, I'd forget about this bank robbery money. Maybe that's what was behind Mr. Kelly's shooting. You're probably safe for now but if you keep poking around . . . who knows what could happen?"

"I was just—"

Suddenly his face softened and he smiled. "You're a pretty woman. You're smart. You're tough, I can see that. I just wouldn't want anything to happen to you."

Rune said, "Thanks. I'll keep that in mind." Though she was really only thinking two things: That Dixon wasn't wearing a wedding ring. And that he was a hell of a lot cuter than she'd thought at first.

"What was that all about? Did that guy have a *badge*?" Stephanie sounded breathless.

Rune walked behind the counter at Washington Square Video, joining Stephanie at the register. She answered, "He was a U.S. marshal. . . ." Then she shook her head. "The other witness—to Mr. Kelly's murder?—she was killed."

"No!"

"It might've been an accident. Maybe not." Rune stared at the monitor. There was no movie in the VCR and she was looking at silent snow. "Probably not," she whispered.

"Are you, uhm, safe?" Stephanie asked.

"He thinks so."

"Thinks?"

"But there's one thing funny."

"What?"

"He was a U.S. marshal?"

"You said that."

"Why would he be involved in a murder of somebody in the East Village?"

"What do you mean?"

Rune was thinking. "I saw this movie on Dillinger. You know John Dillinger?"

"Not personally."

"Ha. He robbed banks. Which is, like, a federal offense—so it wasn't the *city* cops who were after him. It was the G-men."

"G-men?"

"Federal agents. You know, *government* men. Like the FBI. Like U.S. Marshals."

"Oh, wait, you're not thinking he's investigating that bank robbery you were telling me about. The one fifty years ago?"

Rune shrugged. "He didn't say anything but it's kind of a coincidence, don't you think? He seemed real interested when I said something to him about it."

Stephanie turned back to *Variety*. "Little far-fetched."

But what's far-fetched in the whole scheme of things—as Richard might have asked.

Rune found the Brooklyn Yellow Pages. She opened it to Churches. Seemed funny you could find escort services, Roto-Rooter companies, and churches in the same directory.

She flipped through the pages. Man, there were a lot of pages.

She started to make calls.

A half hour later Stephanie asked Rune, "You think I'll get the part?"

"What part?" Rune asked absently, phone tucked between her ear and her shoulder. She was on hold. (It also seemed weird to call a church and be put on hold.)

"Didn't I tell you? I'm auditioning next week. It's only a commercial. But still . . . They pay great. I've *got* to get it. It's totally important."

Rune stiffened suddenly as the minister came on the line.

"Hello?"

"Reverend, Father, sir . . . I'm trying to find some information about my grandfather? Robert Kelly? About seventy. Do you know if he spent any time at your parish?"

"Robert Kelly? No, miss, I sure don't."

"Okay, Father. Thank you. Oh, and have a nice day." She set the receiver in the cradle, pushed aside the Yellow Pages, and asked Stephanie, "Do you say that to priests?"

"What?"

" 'Have a nice day?' I mean, shouldn't you say something more meaningful? More spiritual?"

"Say whatever you want." Stephanie put *Variety* away, began reshelving cassettes in the stacks. She said, "If I don't get the job I'll just die. It's a whole commercial. Thirty seconds. I'd play a young wife with PMS and I can't enjoy my anniversary dinner until I take some pills."

"What pills?"

"I don't know. 'Cramp-Away.' "

"What?"

"Well, something *like* that. Then I take them and my husband and I waltz off happily. I get to wear a long white dress. That's so disgusting when they do that, wear white in menstrual commercials. I'm also worried 'cause I can't waltz. Dancing isn't exactly my strong suit. And I can't—just between you and me—I can't sing too good either. It's a real pain in the ass getting jobs when you can't sing and dance."

"You've got a great body and great hair."

And you're tall, Goddammit.

Flipping through more pages, ignoring the synagogues and mosques. "Amanda's calling too. . . . I feel sorry for her. Poor woman. Imagine—her friend's killed *and* they're kicking her out of the country."

"By the way, I don't think they're all parishes," Stephanie said.

"You think I was pissing them off by calling them parishes?" Rune was frowning.

"I think they get pissed when you worship Satan and cast spells. I don't think they care what you call their churches. I'm just telling you for your own, you know, edification."

Rune picked up the phone and then put it down again. She glanced at the door as a thin young woman, dark-complected, entered. The woman had a proper pageboy cut and was wearing a navy-blue suit, carrying a heavy, law- or accounting-firm briefcase in one hand. Rune swiftly sized her up, whispered to Stephanie, "A dollar says it's Richard Gere."

Stephanie waited until the woman moved to the comedy section and pulled *The Sting* off the shelf before reaching into her pocket and slipping four quarters onto the countertop. Rune put a dollar bill next to them. Stephanie murmured, "Think you're getting to be hot shit, huh? You can spot 'em?"

"I can spot 'em," Rune said.

The woman wandered around the aisles, not sensing Rune and Stephanie watching her while they pretended to work. She came up to the counter and set the

Newman-Redford movie on the rubber change mat beside the cash register. "I'll take that." She handed Rune her membership card. Stephanie, smiling, reached for the money. The woman hesitated and then said, "Oh, maybe I'll get another one too." Stepping away to the drama section.

She set *Power* next to *The Sting*. Richard Gere's bedroom eyes gazed out from the cover. Stephanie pushed the two dollars toward Rune and rang up the rental. The woman snagged the cassettes and left the store.

"How'd you know?" Stephanie asked Rune.

"Look." She typed in the woman's membership number into the computer and called up a history of all the movies she'd rented.

"That's cheating."

"Don't bet if you don't know the odds."

"I don't know, Rune," Stephanie said. "You think Mr. Kelly was into hidden treasure or something, but look, here's this woman rents Richard Gere films ten times in six months. That's just as weird as Kelly."

Rune shook her head. "Naw, you know why she does that? She's having an affair with him. You know the way it is now, sex is dangerous. You have to take matters into your own hands. So to speak. Makes sense to me."

"Funny, you seem like more of a risk-taker—tracking down hidden treasure and murderers. But you won't go to bed with a guy."

"I'll sleep with somebody. I just want to make sure it's the right somebody."

" 'Right'?" Stephanie snorted. "You *do* like your impossible quests, don't you."

Rune slipped the bootleg *Manhattan Is My Beat* into the VCR. A few minutes later she mused, "Wasn't she beautiful?" On the screen Ruby Dahl, with the bobbed blond hair, was walking hand in hand with Dana Mitchell, playing her fiancé, Roy, the cop. The Brooklyn Bridge loomed in the background. It was before the robbery. Roy had been called in by his captain and told what a good job he was doing. But the young patrolman was worrying because he was broke. He had to support his sick mother. He didn't know when he and Ruby'd be able to get married. Maybe he'd leave the force—go to work for a steel company.

"But you're so good at what you do, Roy, darling. I would think they'd want you to be commissioner. Why, if I were in charge that's what I'd make you."

Handsome Dana Mitchell walked beside her solemnly. He told her she was a swell gal. He told her what a lucky stiff he was. The camera backed away from them and the two people became insignificant dots in a shadowy black-and-white city.

Rune glanced down at the countertop. "Ohmygod!"

"What?" Stephanie asked, alarmed.

"It's a phone message."

"So?"

"Where's Frankie? Dammit. I'm going to kick his butt. . . ."

"What?"

"He took the message but he just left it here under these receipts." She held it up. "Look, look! It's from Richard. I haven't heard from him since yesterday. He dropped me off on the West Side." Rune grimaced. "Kissed me on the cheek good-bye."

"Ouch. A cheek-kiss only?"

"Yeah. And after he'd seen me topless."

Stephanie shook her head. "That's not good."

"Tell me about it."

The message read:

Rune—Richard asked you over for dinner tomorrow, at seven, hes cooking. He has a surprise for you and he also said why the hell don't you get a phone. Ha ha but he was kidding

"Yes! I thought he'd given up on me after we went to the nursing home on Sunday."

"Nursing home? Rune, you gotta pick more romantic places for dates."

"Oh, I'm going to! I've got this totally excellent junkyard I go to—"

"No, no, no."

"It's really neat." She fluffed her hair out again. "What should I wear? I have this polka-dot tank top I just got at Second-Hand Rose. And this tiger-skin skirt that's about eight inches wide . . . What?"

"Tiger skin?"

"Oh, like, it's not *real*. . . . If you're into rain forests and stuff like that. I mean, it was made in New Jersey—"

"Rune, the problem isn't endangered species."

"Well, what *is* the problem?"

Stephanie was examining her closely. "Are those glow-in-the-dark earrings?"

"I got them last Halloween," she said defensively, touching the skulls. "Why are you looking at me that way?"

"You like fairy stories, right?"

"Sure."

"You remember Cinderella?"

"Oh, it's the *best*. Did you know in the real story, the Brothers Grimm story, the mother cut the ugly sisters' heels off with a knife so their feet would fit into the—"

"Rune." Stephanie said it patiently.

"What?"

"Let's think about the Disney version for a minute."

Rune looked at her cautiously. "Okay."

"You remember it?"

"Yeah."

Stephanie walked around Rune slowly, examining her. "You understand what I'm getting at?"

"Oh . . . a makeover?"

Stephanie smiled. "Don't take it personal. But I think you need a fairy godmother."

CHAPTER SIXTEEN

Rune wanted slinky.

Stephanie reluctantly indulged her but the expedition to stores that specialized in svelte was a failure. Rune spent a half hour in tiny, hot changing rooms trying on long black dresses and playing with her hair, trying to look like Audrey Hepburn, trying to look slinky. But then the word *frumpy* crept into her mind and, even though she could strip and look at her flat stomach and thin legs and pretty face, once she thought *frump*, that killed it. No long dresses today.

"You win," she muttered to Stephanie.

"Thank you" was the abrupt reply. "Now let's get to work."

They walked south, out of the Village.

"Richard likes long and slinky," Rune explained.

"Of course he does," Stephanie replied. "He's a man. He probably likes red and black bustiers and garters too." But she went on to explain patiently that a woman should never buy clothes for a man. She should buy clothes for herself, which will in turn make the man respect and desire her more.

"You think?"

"I *know*."

"Radical," Rune said.

Stephanie rolled her eyes and said, "We'll go for European."

"Richard's very French-looking. I'd like to get him to change his name."

"To what?"

"It *was* François. Now I'm leaning toward Jean-Paul."

"What does he think about that?"

"Haven't told him. I'm going to wait a few weeks."

"Wise."

SoHo, the former warehouse and manufacturing district adjoining Greenwich Village, was just becoming chic. The area used to be a bastion of artists-in-residence—working painters and sculptors, who were the only people who could legally live in the neighborhood under the city zoning code. But while the city granted permits only to certified artists, it did nothing about controlling the cost of the huge lofts, and as the galleries and wine bars and boutiques moved into the commercial buildings, the residential prices skyrocketed into the hundreds of thousands. . . . It was funny how many lawyers and bankers suddenly found they had talent to paint and sculpt.

They passed one clothing store, painted stark white inside. Rune stopped abruptly and gazed at a black silk blouse.

"Love it."

"So do I," Stephanie agreed.

"Can we get it?"

"No."

"Why not? What's wrong with it?"

"See that tag? That's not the order number. That's the price."

"Four hundred and fifty dollars!"

"Come on, follow me. I know a little Spanish place up the street."

They turned off West Broadway onto Spring and walked into a store that Rune loved immediately because a large white bird sitting on a perch by the door said, "Hello, sucker," to them when they entered.

Rune looked around. She said, "I'm game. But it's not funky. It's not New Wave."

"It's not supposed to be."

After twenty minutes of careful assembly, Stephanie examined Rune with approval and only then allowed her to look in a mirror.

"Awesome," Rune whispered. "You're a magician."

The maroon skirt *was* long though it was more billowy than slinky. On top she wore a low-cut black T-shirt and over that a lacy see-through blouse. Stephanie picked out some dangly earrings in orange plastic.

"It's not the old me but it's definitely a *sort of* me."

"I think you're evolving," Stephanie told her.

As the clerk wrapped up the clothes Rune said, "You know the story of the little red hen?"

"Was it on *Sesame Street*?"

"I don't think so. She was the one who was baking bread, and nobody helped her, except this one animal. I forget what it was. Duck, rabbit. Who knows? Anyway, when the bread was done all the other animals came to the hen and said they wanted some. But she said, 'Haul ass, creeps.' And she only shared it with the one that helped her. Well, when I find the bank money I'm going to share it with you."

"Me?"

"You believe me. Richard doesn't. The police don't."

Stephanie didn't say anything. They stepped outside

and returned to West Broadway. "You don't have to do that, Rune," she said finally.

"But I want to. Maybe you can quit the stupid video store and audition full-time."

"Really . . ."

"No." The Hungarian accent was back. "Don't argue with peasant woman. Very pigheaded . . . Oh, wait." Rune glanced at a store across the street. "Richard said he's got a surprise for me. I want to get him something."

They ran across Broadway, dodging traffic. Rune stopped, caught her breath, looked in the window. "What do men like?" she asked.

Stephanie said, "Themselves." And they walked inside.

The store seemed futuristic but it may actually have been antique, Rune reasoned, since it reminded her of how her mother described the sixties—gaudy and filled with weird glowing lights and spaceships and planets and a confusion of incense smells: musk, patchouli, rose, sandalwood.

Rune looked at a black-lit poster of a ship sailing in the sky and said, "Highly retro."

Stephanie looked around, bored.

In the display cases: geodes, crystals, stones, opals, silver and gold, magic wands of quartz wrapped with silver wire, headdresses, meteorites, NASA memorabilia, electronic music tapes, optical illusions. Colored lights broken apart by spinning prisms crawled up and down the walls.

"It's going to make me epileptic," Stephanie groused.

"This is the most radical store ever, don't you think? Isn't it fantastic?" Rune picked up two dinosaurs and made them dance.

"The jewelry's nice." Stephanie was leaning over a counter.

"What do you think he'd like?"

"This stuff is too expensive. A rip-off."

Rune spun a kaleidoscope. "He's not really into toys, I don't think."

The clerk, a thin black man with a round, handsome face framed by Rastafarian dreadlocks, said to Rune in a deep musical voice, "What you see in there?"

"Nirvana. Look." She handed the heavy tube to him.

He played along, peering inside. "Ah, nirvana, there she is. Special today on kaleidoscopes that show you enlightenment. Half price."

Rune shook her head. "Doesn't seem right you should pay for enlightenment."

"This is New York," he said. "Whatchu want?"

Stephanie said, "I'm hungry."

Then Rune saw the bracelets. In a huge glass pyramid, a dozen silver bracelets. She walked to the end of the counter, staring at them, her mouth slightly open. Exhaling an *Oh*.

"You like them, do you?" the clerk asked.

"Can I see that one, there?"

Rune took the thin bracelet, held it up to her face. Turned it over and over. The silver grew thicker and thinner and the ends were like two hands clasped together.

The Rastafarian grinned. "She look nice. She look nice on your arm but . . ."

" 'She'?" Stephanie asked.

The clerk was studying Rune's face. "Mebbe you thinkin' 'bout givin' her away to someone. Mebbe you thinkin' that?" He held the bracelet in his long, sensuous fingers, studied it carefully. Rune thought of Richard's hands slowly opening a beer can. The clerk looked up. "To some man friend of yours."

Rune didn't pay attention to his words. "How did you know that?" Stephanie asked him.

He grinned, silent. Then said, "He's a nice man, I think."

Stephanie looked at him uneasily. "How did you *know*?"

And Rune, who wasn't surprised at all by the clerk's words, said, "I'll take it."

"It's too expensive."

The Rastafarian frowned. "Hey, I offer you satori, I offer you love, and you say that be too expensive?"

"Bargain with him," Stephanie commanded.

Rune said, "Wrap it for a present."

The Rastafarian hesitated. "You sure?"

"Sure I'm sure. Why?"

"Oh, jus' this bracelet, she be important in your life, I got this feelin'. Be very important." He fingered the metal hoop. "Don't be too fast to give her away. No, no, don't be too fast to do that."

"Can we eat now?" Stephanie asked. "I'm hungry."

As they walked to the door the clerk called to Rune, "You hear me?"

Rune turned. Looked into his eyes. "I hear you."

" 'I'll go in, sir,' "

Rune handed Stephanie a hot dog she'd bought from the vendor in front of Trinity Church downtown, near Wall Street. She continued speaking. " 'I'll go in, sir' is what Roy the cop—Dana Mitchell—says to his captain. They're all standing around the front of the bank with their bullhorns and guns. 'I'll go in, sir.' And it's a big surprise because he's just a beat cop and a young guy. Nobody'd been paying any attention to him. But he's the one who volunteers to rescue the hostage."

Rune took her own hot dog from the man. They sat

down beside the wrought-iron fence in front of the cemetery. Thousands of people were walking past on Broadway, some disappearing down Wall Street into the curving, solemn griminess of the buildings.

Stephanie ate thoughtfully, looking at the hot dog uncertainly after each bite.

"Then Roy goes, 'Let me try it, sir. I can talk him out. I know I can.' "

"Uh-huh." Stephanie was gazing straight ahead; the hordes of passing crowds were mesmerizing.

"So the lieutenant goes, 'All right, officer, if you want to go, I won't stop you.' "

Rune threw out her half-eaten hot dog. Stood up. " 'But it's dangerous.' " She sounded as melodramatic as the character in the film itself. "That was another cop, a friend of his, said that. And Dana—remember that dreamy kind of look he had?—Dana says, 'I'm not letting anyone get killed on *my* beat.' His jaw was all firm and he pulled his hat straight and handed his nightstick to his friend then walked across the street and climbed in the side window." Rune started pacing. "Come on, let's go. I want to see the real bank."

Stephanie glanced at the last inch of hot dog, then pitched it into a garbage can. She wiped her hands and mouth with a thin napkin.

They descended into Wall Street. A white luminescence shone through the milky clouds, but the Street, with its narrow, packed rows of dark office buildings, was gloomy.

Rune said, "They shot the movie at the old Union Bank Building itself—that's were the actual robbery took place. The bank went bust years ago and the building was sold. It's been a bunch of things since then. Last year some company bought it and made a restaurant out of the ground floor."

Stephanie said, "Can we get some coffee there? I need some coffee."

Rune was excited, walking ahead of her, then slowing and falling back into step. "Isn't this too much? Walking the same streets the actors did forty years ago? Maybe Dana Mitchell stopped right here and put his foot up on that fire hydrant to tie his shoe."

"Maybe."

"Oh, look!" Rune gripped her arm. "There, the corner! That's where the robber fired a shot as the cops were closing in after the alarm went off. It's a great scene." She ran toward the corner, dodged past a young woman in a pink suit, and pressed back against the marble as if she were under fire. "Stephanie! Get down! Get under cover!"

"You're crazy," Stephanie said, walking slowly to the wall.

Rune reached forward. "You want to get shot? Get down!"

She pulled Stephanie, laughing, into a crouch. Several passersby had heard her. They looked around, cautious. Stephanie, pretending she didn't know Rune, whispered, "You're out of your mind!" Looking at the crowd, speaking louder: "She's out of her mind."

Rune's eyes were bright. "Can you imagine it? The bank's around the corner. And . . . . Listen!" A jackhammer sounded in the distance. "A machine gun! The robber's got a machine gun, an old tommy gun. He's blasting away at us. Okay, it's right around the corner and he's got a hostage and a million dollars. I've got to save him!"

Stephanie laughed and tugged at Rune's arm. Playing along now. "No, no don't go, it's too dangerous."

Rune adjusted an invisible hat, eased her shoulders back. "Nobody gets killed on my beat." And turned the corner.

Just in time to see a bulldozer shovel what had been

one of the floors of the Union Bank Building into a huge Dumpster.

"No . . ." Rune stopped in the middle of the congested sidewalk. Several businesspeople bumped into her before she stepped back. "Oh, no." Her hand went to her mouth.

The demolition company had taken down most of the building already. Only part of one wall remained. The stubby dozer was shoveling up masses of shattered stone and wood and metal.

Rune said, "How could they do it?"

"What?"

"They tore it down. It's gone."

Rune stepped away from Stephanie, her eyes on the men who worked the clanking jackhammers. They stood on the edge of the remaining wall, forty feet up, and dug apart the masonry at their feet. She glanced up the street, then walked slowly across it, to the plywood barricade that shut out pedestrians from the demolition site.

She couldn't look through the peepholes cut by the workers; they were at a six-footer's level. So she walked into the site itself through the open chain-link gate. A huge ramp of earth led down to the foundation where the truck holding the Dumpster idled. There was a resounding crash as the tons of rubble dropped into the steel vessel.

Stephanie caught up with her. "Hey, I don't think we're supposed to be here."

"I feel weird," Rune told her.

"Why?"

"They just destroyed the whole place. And it was so . . . familiar. I knew it so well from the movie and now it's gone. How could they do it?"

Below them, a second bulldozer lifted a huge steel-mesh blanket and set it on top of a piece of exposed rock. There was a painful hoot of a steam whistle above their heads. The bulldozer backed away. Then two whistles. A minute later the explosives were detonated. A jarring slam under their feet. Smoke. The metal blanket shifted a few feet. Three whistle blasts—the all-clear—sounded.

Rune blinked. Tears formed. "It's not the way it should be."

She stooped and picked up a bit of broken marble from the bank's facade—pinkish and gray, the colors of a trout, smooth on one side. She looked at it for a long time, then put it in her pocket.

"It's not the way it should be at all," she repeated.

"Let's go," Stephanie urged.

The bulldozer lifted the mesh away and began to dig out mouthfuls of the shattered rock.

CHAPTER SEVENTEEN

She'd wrapped it up, the bracelet.

But then walking up to Third Avenue—past the discount clothing stores, the Hallmark shop, the delis—she'd decided the wrapping paper was too feminine. It had a viney pattern that wasn't anything sissier than you'd see in the old *Arabian Nights* illustrations. But Richard might think they were flowers.

So halfway to his apartment she slipped her hand, with its newly polished nails—pink, not green or blue, for a change—into her bag and tore off the paper and ribbon.

Then, waiting for the light on Twenty-third Street, Rune started to worry about the box. Giving him something in a box, something supposed to be, what was the word?, spontaneous, seemed too formal. Men got scared, you gave them something that was too premeditated.

Goddamn men.

The nails went to work again and opened the box,

which joined the crumpled Arabian paper in the bottom of the leopard-skin purse. She held the bracelet up in the light.

Wait. Was it too feminine?

Did it matter? He was a *philosopher* knight, remember, not the kind killing peasants with a broadsword. Anyway there *definitely* was something androgynous about him—like Hermaphroditus. And now that she thought about it, Rune decided that was one of the reasons they were so compatible. The male-female, yin-yang was in flux for both of them.

She put the bracelet in her pocket.

See, what it is, I was buying one for me—remember I told you I love bracelets, so what I did was I saw this one, and it looked too masculine for me and I thought, well, it just occurred to me you might . . .

Rune stopped for the light. She was in front of an Indian store, sitar music and the smell of incense flooded out into the street. The light changed.

See, I got this special deal at a jewelry store I go to. Two for one. Yeah, no shit. Amazing. And I thought: who do I know who'd like a bracelet? And, guess what? You won . . .

Crossing the street.

Then she saw his apartment building a block ahead. She tried to be objective. But was still disappointed. It was a boxish high-rise, squatting in a nest of boxish high-rises, a little bit of suburbia in Manhattan. She couldn't picture her black-clad knight living among tiny widows and salesmen and nurses and med students from NYU.

Oh, well . . . She continued along the sidewalk and stopped outside his building.

Hey, Richard, would you like a bracelet? If not, no big deal, I could give it to my mother, sister, roommate . . . But if you'd like it . . . It's a pretty radical design, don'tcha think?—take a look at it.

Rune stepped away from the building and looked at her reflection in the window.

Oh, a bracelet? Rune, it's fantastic! Put it on me. I'll never take it off.

She polished the silver on her sleeve then dropped it into her pocket again.

Oh, a bracelet. Well, the thing is, I never wear them. . . .

Well, the thing is my girlfriend gave me a bracelet just like this the day she killed herself. . . .

Well, the thing is I'm allergic to silver. . . .

Goddamn men.

Seeing him, with that dark hair and the long French face, that crazy electricity hit her again. She knew her voice was going to shake, and she thought, goddammit, get this under control.

What's best? Flirty, surprised? Seductive? She opted for a neutral "Hi." She stood in his doorway. Neither of them moved.

He gave her one of those scary we're-just-friends looks. He almost seemed surprised to see her. "Rune, hey, how you doing?"

"Great, good. . . . You?"

Hey, how you doing?

"Okay." He nodded and she saw he was definitely uncomfortable. Though he kept the smile on his face. There were major explosions in her. Wanting to vaporize away, wanting to ease her arms around him and never leave. Mostly she wondered what the hell was wrong.

Silence, as an elderly lady with a jutting, sour mouth walked her cairn terrier past, glancing disdainfully at them. Richard said, "So how's the video business?" He looked her up and down. Didn't say a word about the new outfit. Glanced at the earrings. Didn't say anything about them either.

"Good. Okay."

"Well, why don't you come on in."

She followed him inside.

Wait, she thought, looking him over. What's going on? He was wearing a baby-blue button-down shirt, tan chino slacks, and Top-Siders. Ohmygod, Top-Siders! Nothing black, nothing chic. He looked like a yuppie from the Upper East Side.

Then she glanced around his apartment. She couldn't figure it—that somebody who wore black leather and tapped the tops of his beer cans with such elegant fingers could live in a place with white Conran furniture, rock and roll posters on the wall, and a metal sea gull statue.

A copper sea gull?

"Just let me check on something."

He disappeared into the kitchen. Whatever he was cooking smelled great. None of her girlfriends could get that kind of smell out of a kitchen. Lord knew, *she* never had.

She was examining his bookshelves. Mostly technical books about things she didn't understand. College paperbacks. Stacks of the *New York Times* and the *Atlantic Monthly*.

He came back into the room. Stood with his arms crossed. "So." Skittish now.

"Uh-huh. So." She couldn't think of anything to say for a moment. Then she blurted out, "I thought, maybe, after dinner, you might want to go for a ride. I found a great place. It's in Queens, a junkyard. I know the owner. He lets me in. It's really radical, like a huge dinosaur graveyard. You can sit up on some of the wrecks—it's not gross dirty, you know, like garbage—and watch the sunset over the city. It's really wild. It's your mega junkyard. . . . Okay, Richard, come on. Tell me what I did to fuck up tonight."

"The thing is—"

"Hi," came the woman's voice from the door.

Rune turned to see a tall woman with long, blond hair walk through the open door. The woman was wearing a gray pin-striped suit and black pumps. She gave Rune a friendly glance, then walked up to Richard and hugged him.

"Rune, this is Karen."

"Uhm, hi," Rune said. Then to Richard, "Your message? About dinner?"

Karen lifted a perfect eyebrow knowingly, took a bottle of wine out of a paper bag, and disappeared tactfully into the kitchen.

"Actually," Richard said delicately, "that was supposed to be Thursday."

"Wait. The message said tomorrow. And the date on it was yesterday."

He shrugged. "I told the guy I talked to—Frankie somebody—I told him Thursday."

She nodded. "And he thought *today* was Thursday. Goddamn heavy metal. It's destroyed his brain cells . . . Shit, shit, shit."

Yo, Fairy Godmother! Yo! Wave your magic wand and get me the hell out of here.

"Listen, you want to stay? Have some wine?"

That'd be a pretty picture, she thought. The three of us sipping wine while he's waiting for me to leave so he can put the Tantra moves on too-tall Karen.

"No, think I'll go."

"Sure. I'll walk you to the elevator."

Oh, don't argue *too* hard now.

Richard continued. "Oh, wait, let me get you what I have for you."

"My surprise?"

"Right. I think you'll like it."

"So, Rune, how do you know Richard?" Karen was calling from the kitchen.

Yeah. He picked me up the other night and's been trying to fuck me ever since.

"Met in a video store. We talk about movies some."

"I *love* movies," Karen called. "Maybe we could all go sometime.

"Maybe."

Richard appeared from his bedroom. He was carrying a white envelope.

That's my present?

"Be right back," he said to Karen.

"This sauce is *so* good," she called from the kitchen. She stuck her pert head into the doorway. "Nice meeting you. Oh, love the earrings!"

As they walked to the elevator Richard said, "Karen's a friend. We work together."

Rune wondered: How does somebody work *with* you when you write novels?

They got four doors down the corridor before he said, "This's a little awkward but she and I *really* are just friends."

"We *are* going out, aren't we? You and me, I mean."

"Sure, we're going out. I mean, we aren't going out all the time though, right? We *can* have other friends."

"Sure. That's the way it has to work."

"Right."

I am absolutely going to murder Frankie Greek. . . .

He pushed the down button.

Aren't *we* in a hurry.

"Oh, here." He thrust the envelope at her.

She opened it. Inside was an application to the New School, over on Fifth Avenue.

A joke. It had to be a joke.

"I've got a buddy works for admissions," Richard explained. "He told me they're starting this new program. Retail management. You don't even need to get a degree. You get a certificate."

She felt sick. "Wait. You're giving me career counseling?"

"Rune, you're so smart, you've got so much energy, you're so creative. . . . I'm worried about you wasting your life."

She stared, numb, at the paper in her hand.

Richard said, "You could work your way up in the video store business. Become a manager. Then maybe you could buy a store. Or even a chain. You could really be on a hell of a vertical track."

She laughed bitterly. "But . . . that's not *me*, Richard. I'm not a vertical-track kind of person. Look, I've worked in that diner I told you about, in a bike repair shop, a deli, a shoe store. I've sold jewelry on the street, done paste-ups and mechanicals for a magazine, sold men's colognes at Macy's, and worked in a film lab. And that's just in the couple years I've been here. Before I die I'm going to do a lot more than that. I'm not going to devote my life to being manager of a video store. Or any other one thing."

"Don't you want a career?"

She felt utterly betrayed. More so than if she'd found Karen and Richard in bed, an event that was probably only minutes away.

When she didn't answer he said, "You should think about it."

Rune said, "Sometimes I get this idea I should go to school. Get a degree. Law school, maybe business school like my sister. Something. But then, you know what happens? I have this image. Of myself in ten years at a cocktail party. And somebody asks me what I do. And—this is the scary part—I have an answer for them." She smiled at him.

"Which is . . . ?"

He didn't get it. "*That's* the point. It doesn't matter; the scary part is that I *have* an answer. I say, 'I'm a lawyer, an accountant, a hoosey-whatsis maker.' Bang, there I am. Defined in one or two words. That scares the hell out of me."

"Why're you so afraid of reality?"

"My life is real. It's just not, apparently, *your* kind of reality."

He said harshly, "No, it's *not* real. Look at this game of yours . . ."

"What game?"

"Find-the-hidden-treasure."

"What's wrong with that?"

"Do you understand that a man was killed? Did it ever occur to you that it wasn't a game to Robert Kelly? That you could get hurt? Or a friend of yours could get hurt? That *ever* occur to you?"

"It'll work out. You just need to believe . . ."

She gasped as he took her angrily by the shoulders and led her to a window at the end of the hallway. Pointed outside. Beneath them was a mass of highways and rail sidings and rusting equipment—huge turbines and metal parts. Beyond that was a small factory, surrounded by standing yellowish water. Mud. Filth.

"What's that?" he asked.

She shook her head. Not understanding.

"What *is* it?" His voice rose.

"What do you mean?" Her voice crackled.

"It's a factory, Rune. There's shit and pollution. It makes a living for people and they pay taxes and give money to charity and buy sneakers for their children. Who grow up to be lawyers or teachers or musicians or people who work in other factories. It's nothing more than that. It's not a spaceship, it's not a castle, it's not an entrance to the underworld. It's a *factory*."

She was completely still.

"I like you a lot, Rune. But going with you is like living in some movie."

She wiped her nose. The cars below whined past. "What's wrong with movies? I love movies."

"Nothing. As long as you remember they aren't real. You're going to find out I'm not a knight and that, okay, maybe there was some bank robbery money—which I think is the craziest frigging thing I've ever heard—but that it's spent or stolen or lost somewhere years ago and you'll never find it. And here you are pissing your life away in a video store, jumping from fantasy to fantasy, waiting for something you don't even know what it is."

"If that's your reality you can keep it," she snapped, wiping her nose.

"Fairy stories aren't going to get you by in life."

"I told you they don't all have happy endings!"

"But even if they don't, Rune, you close the book, you put it on your shelf and you go on with your life. They. Aren't. Real. And if you live your life like you're in one you're going to get hurt. Or somebody around you's going to get hurt."

"So why're you the expert on reality? You write novels."

He sighed, looked away from her. "I don't write novels. I was trying to impress you. I don't even *read* novels. I write audiovisual scripts for companies. 'Hello, I'm John Jones, your CEO, welcome to Sales-Fest '88. . . .' It's not weird. It's not fun. But it pays the bills."

"But you . . . you're just like me. The clubs, the dancing, the magic . . . we like the same things."

"It's an act, Rune. Just like it is for everybody who lives that way. Except for you. Nobody can sustain your kind of weirdness. When you're frivolous, when you're *irresponsible*, you miss trains and buses and dinner dates. You—"

"But," she interrupted, "there'll *always* be a next train." She wiped her eyes and saw the mascara had run. Shit. She must look pathetic. She said softly, "You lied to me."

The elevator arrived. She pulled away from him and stepped into the car.

"Rune . . ."

They stood three feet away, she inside, he out. It seemed to take forever before the doors started to close. As they slowly did she thought that Diarmuid, or any knight, wouldn't let her get away like this. He'd push in after her, shove the doors aside, hold her.

Tell her they could work out these differences.

But Richard just turned and walked down the corridor.

"There'll always be another train," she whispered as the doors closed.

" 'Your stepsisters keep you in tatters like this? No, no, no, dear, that will never do. How can you be the fairest one at the ball in these rags? Now, let me see what I can do. Yes, oh, my, that should be just right. . . .'

"And closing her eyes, she waved her magic wand three times. There appeared as if from thin air a gown of silk and lace, stitched with golden and silver thread. And for her feet . . ."

Rune recited this from memory as she walked along University Place. She paused, crumpled up the New School application, and three-pointed it into a trash basket.

She glanced at herself in a mirror hanging in a wig shop. The lipstick was fine and the blusher on the cheekbones was fun to do and easy. Thank you, Stephanie. The eyes had been okay—at least before the tears'd turned her into a raccoon.

Rune took another sip of Miller—from her third can—wrapped in a paper bag. She'd bought a six-pack at a deli up the street but had somehow managed to drop three cans within the past two blocks.

A couple holding hands walked past.

Rune couldn't help staring at them. They didn't notice. They were in love.

" 'Oh, dear,' Cinderella's fairy godmother said, 'coachmen. What's the good of turning a pumpkin into a coach if you have no coachmen to drive you? Ah-ha, mice . . .' "

Rune turned back to the mirror, teased her hair with her fingers, and stepped back to look at the results.

She thought: I don't look like Cinderella at all. I look like a short whore.

Her shoulders sagged and she dug into her bag. Found a Kleenex and scrubbed the rest of the makeup off her face, combed her hair back into place.

She pulled off the orange earrings, which Karen the girls' basketball champ had loved so much, and dropped them into her purse.

What was wrong? Why was it so hard to get men interested in her?

She considered everything.

I'm not tall and blond, true.

I'm not beautiful. But I'm not dog-ugly either.

Maybe she was a lesbian.

Rune considered this.

It seemed possible. And it explained a lot. Like why she got hit on by men but never proposed to—they could sense her orientation probably. (Not that she wanted to get married necessarily—but she *did* want the chance to say, "Lemme think about it.")

No, she just wasn't the sort men went for. That was

probably all part of it, maybe the way the Gods made you the way you were. They might make you short and cute, a little like Audrey Hepburn, but not enough to make men—real men, chivalrous men, Cary Grant men, knights errant—fall for you. The Gods are just letting you down easy. Saying: if they'd meant you to have somebody like Richard, they'd have made you four inches taller and a thirty-six C, or B at least, and given you blond hair.

But being gay . . . this was something to think about. Could she deal with it? It'd be hard to own up to but maybe she'd have to admit it. Some things you can't run from.

Admitting it, she felt relief flood through her. It explained why she was reluctant to sleep with a man right away—she probably didn't really *like* sex with men. And if Richard turned her on like an electric current it was probably just because of what she'd realized before—that there was something feminine about him. Sure, that made sense.

Telling Mother would be hard.

Maybe she should get a crew cut.

Maybe she should become a nun.

Maybe she should kill herself.

At the corner of Eighth Street, rather than turn toward the subway to get a train to the loft, she turned the other way, to return to the video store.

She knew what she wanted to do.

Get a movie. Maybe *It Happened One Night.* As long as I'm going to cry anyway, why not get a movie to go along with it? Ice cream, beer, and a movie. Can't lose with that combination.

How about *Gone With the Wind*?

How about *Lesbos Lovers*?

Ten minutes later she pushed inside Washington Square Video. Frankie Greek was behind the counter and he was looking totally sheepish.

Well, he damn well ought to. Fucking up when he took that message from Richard . . . She was going to give him hell. But, as she looked at him playing nervously with the VCR remote, it seemed there was something else on his mind. He *was* nervous but it wasn't because of her.

"Hello, Rune."

"What is it, Frankie? Your sister okay?"

"Yes, she's fine," he recited. "She had a baby."

"I know. You told us. What's the matter?"

"How are you tonight? Doing okay, I hope. Doing good." A wanna-be rock musician talking like Mister Rogers? Something was really wrong here. "What's with you?"

"Nothing, Rune. I heard it was kind of cold out there tonight." It was like he was in a bad skit on *Saturday Night Live.*

"Cold. What the hell are you—"

"Rune?" a man's deep voice asked.

She turned. Oh, it was that U.S. marshal. Dixon, she remembered.

"Hi," he said.

"Hey, Marshal Dixon."

He laughed. "You make it sound like a sheriff in a bad western. Call me Phillip."

She looked at Frankie, paler than Mick Jagger in February. "I saw his badge," Frankie said.

"He arrests people who screw up phone messages," Rune muttered.

"Huh?"

"Never mind."

"How you doing?" Dixon asked, smiling. Then he

frowned, looked at her face. "There's a little . . ." He pointed at her cheek.

She grabbed a paper towel and scrubbed away at a bit of eye makeup.

"That's got it," Dixon said. "Hey, love the outfit."

"Really?"

His eyes swept over it—and, sure enough, she felt a bit of that electric sizzle again. Not as high-voltage as with Richard, but still . . .

"I never do drugs," Frankie Greek said.

Dixon looked at him curiously.

"Some musicians do. I mean, you hear about it. But I never have. Some of my songs are about drugs. But that's, like, just something to write songs about. I stay away from them."

"Well, good for you."

Rune gave him an exasperated look then said to the marshal, "Anything more on the case?"

"Naw." Then he seemed to think he shouldn't be talking quite so blue-collar and added, "No. No evidence in the Edelman death." He shrugged. "No prints at the scene. No witnesses. You haven't seen anything odd lately? Been followed?"

"No."

Dixon nodded. Looked at some videos. Picked one up. Put it down.

"So," he said.

Two "so's" from two different men in one night. Rune wondered what this one meant.

"Could I talk to you?" he asked, motioning her to the front of the store.

"Sure."

They stood by the window, next to a distracting cardboard cutout of Michael J. Fox.

"Just thought you'd like to know. I checked out that case you told me about. The Union Bank heist?"

"You did?"

He shook his head. "I didn't find anything. Technically, it's still open but nobody's been on the case since the fifties. They only keep murder cases open indefinitely. I tried to find the file but it looks like it was pitched out ten, twenty years ago."

"I thought maybe *you* were investigating it."

"The robbery? Me?" Dixon laughed again. He had a nice smile. Richard, she was thinking, had that mysteriousness about him. Something going on under the surface—you couldn't quite believe his smile. Dixon's seemed totally genuine.

He took off his baseball cap, rubbed his hair in a boyish way, put the hat back on.

She said, "I mean, it was kind of a coincidence you were asking about Mr. Kelly and everything."

"Bank robbery'd be the FBI, not the Marshals. I'm involved only 'cause the killer used the kind of bullets a lot of hit men use. We check stuff like that out."

"Teflon," Rune said.

"Oh, you know about that?"

"The police told me. But if you don't care about the robbery then why'd you look up the case?"

He shrugged, looked away. "I dunno. Seemed important to you."

A little tingle. Nothing as high-voltage as with Richard. But it *was* something. Besides, Richard, who she thought she was in love with, had just been giving her crap about her life, while this guy, almost a stranger, had gone to the trouble to help her with her quest.

Little red hen . . .

She gave him a coy look, a Scarlett O'Hara look. "That's the only reason you came all the way down here? To tell me about a fifty-year-old case?"

He shrugged, avoided her eyes. "I stopped by your place and you weren't there and I called here and they said sometimes you just hang out and talk about movies with people." He said this as if he'd practiced it. Like a shy boy rehearsing his lines to ask a girl out on a date. Embarrassed. He crossed his arms.

"So you took the chance I'd be here?"

"Right." After a moment he said, "And I'll bet you want to know why."

"Yeah," she said. "I do."

"Well." He swallowed. How could somebody with such a big gun be so nervous? He continued. "I guess I wanted to ask you out. I mean, if you don't want to, forget it, but—"

"Rune," Frankie called, "phone!"

"Wait right there," Rune told Dixon, then added emphatically, "Don't go away."

"Sure. Sure. I won't go anywhere."

She picked up the phone. It was Amanda LeClerc. "Rune, I thought you want to know," the woman said quickly, her accent more pronounced because of her excitement. "Victor Symington's daughter, she over here. I mean, right now. You want to see her?"

Rune glanced at Dixon, who was looking at video boxes. He glanced at the X-rated section, blushed, and looked away quickly.

Rune, debating furious—what should she do?

A man who wanted to ask her out versus the quest.

This was totally unfair.

"Rune?" Amanda said. "I don't think she going to stay too long."

Eyes on Dixon.

Eyes on the Brooklyn Yellow Pages.

Oh, shit.

Into the phone she blurted out, "I'll be right over."

CHAPTER EIGHTEEN

"You had the baby?"

Rune looked up from the building directory, so thick with graffiti she couldn't find the number of Amanda LeClerc's apartment.

Her surprised eyes rested on the surprised face of the young man who'd let her into the apartment building two days before—when she'd been extremely pregnant. Now, she let him open the door for her again and she walked inside.

"I did, thanks," Rune said. "Courtney Madonna Brittany. Six pounds, four ounces."

"Congratulations," he said. He couldn't help but stare down at her belly. "You, uh, feeling okay?"

"Feeling great," Rune assured him. "I just ran out for a minute and forgot my keys."

"Where's your little girl?" he asked.

When you lie, lie with confidence. "She's upstairs. Watching TV."

"Watching TV?"

"Well, she's with her father and *he's* watching TV. They both like sitcoms. . . . Say, which apartment is Amanda LeClerc in again?"

"Oh, Amanda? On the second floor?"

"Yeah."

"I think 2F."

"Right, right, right." Rune started up the stairs two at a time.

"Don't you think you should take it a little easy?"

"Peasant stock," she called back cheerily.

On the second-floor landing she noticed that there was a piece of plywood over the hole in Mr. Kelly's door. There was also a large padlock on it. The police tape had been replaced. She walked past it.

It'd been hard to turn down Phillip Dixon (*he*, unlike Richard, was somebody who had no problem with either the word or the concept of "date").

"Rain check?" he'd asked.

"You bet. Hey, you like junkyards?" she'd asked him on her way out the door of the video store.

He hadn't missed a beat. "Love 'em."

Rune now knocked on Amanda's door and the woman called, "Who's there?"

"Me, Rune."

The door opened. "Good. She's upstairs. I talk her inta staying to see you. Didn't want to but she is."

"Has she heard anything from her father?"

"I don't know. I didn't ask her. I just said you were looking for him and it was important."

"What apartment is he in again?"

"Three B."

Rune remembered that Symington lived directly above Mr. Kelly.

Rune climbed the stairs. Amanda's and Mr. Kelly's floor had smelled like onions; this one smelled like bacon. She paused in the hallway. The door to 3B was six inches open.

Rune eased forward, seeing first the hem of a skirt, then two thin legs in dark stockings. They were crossed in a way that suggested confidence. Rune started to knock but then just pushed the door open all the way. The woman on the bed turned to her. She was looking through a stack of papers.

She had high cheekbones, a face glossy with makeup, frosted hair forced into place with a ton of spray. She looks like my mother, Rune thought, and guessed she was in her early forties. The woman wore a plaid suit and she smoked a long, dark brown cigarette. She gazed at Rune then said, "That woman downstairs . . . she said somebody was looking for my father. Is that you?"

"Yes."

The woman turned away slowly, stubbed out the cigarette, pressing it into an ashtray. It died with a faint crushing sound. She looked Rune up and down. "My, they're getting younger and younger."

"Like, excuse me?"

"How old are you?"

"Twenty. What's that got to do with anything? I just want to ask you a few—"

"What did he promise you? A car? He did that a lot. He was *always* giving away cars. Or saying he would. Porsches, Mercedes, Cadillacs. Of course then there'd be problems with the dealer. Or the registration. Or something."

"Cars? I don't even—"

"And then it came down to money. But that's life, isn't it? He'd promise a thousand and end up giving them a couple of hundred."

"What are you talking about?" Rune asked.

Another examination. The woman got as far as Rune's striped stockings and clunky red shoes before her face revealed her dismay. She shook her head. "You couldn't . . . forgive me, but you couldn't've charged all that much. What *was* your price? For the night?"

"You think I'm a hooker?"

"My father called them girlfriends. He actually brought one to Thanksgiving dinner once. At my house! In Westchester. Lynda with a y. You can imagine *that* scene. With my husband and children?"

"I don't even know your father."

The woman frowned, wondering if Rune might be telling the truth. "Maybe there's some misunderstanding here."

"I'll say there is."

"You're not . . ."

"No," Rune said. "I'm not."

A faint laugh. "I'm sorry . . ." The woman extended her hand. "My name's Emily Richter."

"I'm Rune." She reluctantly shook it.

"First name?"

"And last."

"Actress?"

"Sometimes."

"So, Rune, you really don't know my father?"

"No."

"And you're not here for any money?"

Not exactly, she thought. She shook her head.

Emily continued. "What do you want to see me about?"

"Do you know where he is?"

"That's what I'm trying to find out. He just vanished."

"I know he did."

Emily examined Rune's face carefully. The woman had probing eyes and Rune looked away. Emily said, "And I have a feeling you know *why*."

"Maybe."

"Which is?"

"I think he witnessed a murder."

"That man who was killed in the building?" Emily asked. "I heard about that. It was downstairs, wasn't it?"

"Right."

"And you think Father saw it happen?"

Rune walked farther into the apartment. She sat down on a cheap dining room chair. She glanced around the place. It was very different from Mr. Kelly's. She couldn't figure out why at first. Then she realized. This was like a hotel room, furnished by one phone call to a store that sold everything: pictures, furniture, carpet. A lot of light wood and metallic colors and laminate. Coordinated. Suburban tack.

What did it remind her of? Ohmygod, Richard's place . . .

Emily lit another cigarette.

Rune glanced into the kitchen. She saw enough food to last through a siege. Like her mother's pantry, she thought. With its provisions of flour, yellowing boxes of raisins and oatmeal and cornstarch. The colored cans. Green, Del Monte. Red, Campbell's. Only here, the difference was that everything was new. Just like the furniture.

Emily's voice was softer as she said, "I didn't mean to suggest anything. What I said before. Ever since our mother died, Father's been, well, a little unstable. He's had a series of young friends. At least he waited until she died to turn adolescent again." She shook her head. "But a murder . . . So maybe he's in danger." The cigarette paused halfway to her mouth, then lowered.

Rune told her, "I guess he's okay. I mean, I don't know that he isn't. He sure didn't hang around for very long after the man downstairs was killed."

"What happened?"

Rune told her about Robert Kelly's death.

"Why do you think my father saw it happen?"

"What it was, I came back here to pick up something after Mr. Kelly was killed. And I was in the apartment downstairs—"

"How did you know him, this Mr. Kelly?"

"He was a customer at the store where I work. We were sorta friends. Anyway, I saw your father. And he saw me in the apartment. He was terrified. That was weird—*me* scaring anybody." She laughed. "But the way I figure it, the day Mr. Kelly was killed your father was hanging out on his fire escape. He saw the killer come out of the apartment after he killed Mr. Kelly. I think your father got a look at the killer."

Emily shook her head. "But why would he run, just seeing you?"

"I don't know. Maybe he couldn't see me too clearly and thought I was the killer who'd come back to destroy some evidence or something."

Emily was looking down at the fake Oriental carpet. "But the police haven't called me"—she nodded again—"which must mean you haven't told them about him."

"No."

"Why not?"

Rune's eyes drifted away. "The thing is, I don't like police."

Emily watched her carefully for a moment more. Then said probingly, "But that's not exactly *the* thing, is it? There's something else."

Rune looked away. Trying to be cool and poised. It wasn't taking.

"Well, all I know is that I'm worried about my father," Emily said. "He can be exasperating at times but I still love him. I want to find him. And it sounds like you do too. Why won't you tell me?"

Then, from somewhere, Rune managed to find an adult gaze. She slapped it on her face and gave Emily a woman-to-woman smile. "I have this feeling you're not telling me everything either."

The woman hesitated. She inhaled and blew a fat stream of smoke away from them. "Maybe I'm not."

"I'll show you mine if you . . ."

Emily didn't want to smile. But she did. "Okay, the truth?" She looked around the apartment. "I've never been here before. This is the first time. I haven't been in *any* of his apartments for the past year. . . . Isn't that an awful thing to say?"

Rune said nothing. Emily sighed. She was looking much *less* adult than she had. "We had a fight. Last summer. A bad one."

There was silence.

Then she smiled at Rune. A bleak lifting of her mouth. Trying to make light. The smile faded. "He ran away from home. Isn't that silly?"

"Your father ran away from home? Like, that's radical."

Emily asked, "Are your parents still alive?"

"My mother is. She's in Ohio. My father died a few years ago."

"Did you get along with them when you were at home?"

"Pretty good, I guess. My mom is a sweetheart. My dad . . . I was sort of his favorite. But don't tell my sister I said that. He was really, really cool."

Emily looked at her with a cocked head. "You're lucky. My father and I fought a lot. We always have. Even when I was young. I'd have a boyfriend and Dad wouldn't like him. He wasn't from the right kind of family, he didn't make enough money, he was Jewish, he was Catholic . . . I fought back some but he was my father and fathers have authority. But then I grew up and after my mother died a few years ago, something odd happened. The roles switched. *He* became the child. He'd retired, didn't have much money. I'd married a businessman and I was rich. He needed a place to stay and he moved in with us.

"But I didn't do it right. Suddenly *I* had the power, *I* could dictate. Just the opposite of the way it was when I lived at home. I handled it badly. Last summer we were arguing and I said some terrible things. I didn't mean them, I really didn't. They weren't even true. I thought Dad'd just fight back or ignore them. Well, he didn't. What he did was he took some things and disappeared." Her voice quaked.

Emily fell silent. She held her cigarette in an unsteady hand. "I've been trying to find him ever since. He stayed at the Y for a while, he stayed at a hotel in Queens. He had an apartment in the West Village. I don't know when he moved here. I've been calling people he knows—some of his old co-workers, his doctors—trying to find him. Finally a receptionist at his doctor's office broke down and gave me this address."

Emily smoothed her skirt. It was a long skirt, expensive silk. Slinky was the only way to describe it, Rune decided. "Now I've missed him again," Emily told her.

"Didn't you just call and apologize?"

"I tried a few months ago. But he hung up on me."

"Why don't you just give it time? Maybe he'll calm down. He's not that old, is he? In his sixties."

A look at the carpet again. "The thing is, he's sick. He doesn't have much longer. That's why the doctor's receptionist agreed to tell me where he was. He has cancer. Terminal."

Rune thought of her father. And now she recognized Symington's gray face, the sweaty skin.

She thought too: He'd better not die before she herself had a chance to find him and ask him about Mr. Kelly and the stolen money. Feeling guilty. But thinking it anyway.

"So what is it *you're* not telling *me*?" The adult Emily had returned. "Time to show me *yours*."

"I'm not sure he's just a witness," Rune said.

"What do you mean?"

"Okay, if you really want to know. I think your father might be the murderer."

CHAPTER NINETEEN

"Impossible."

Rune said, "I think Mr. Kelly found some money and your father found out about it. I think your father stole the money and killed him."

Emily was shaking her head. "Never. Dad'd never hurt anybody."

Once again Rune thought of Symington's face—how terrified he'd seemed. "Well, maybe he had a partner who killed him."

Emily started to shake her head. But then she paused.

"What?" Rune asked. "Tell me."

"Dad wouldn't kill anybody. I *know* that."

"But . . . ? I see something in your face. Keep talking." A good adult line to say. Right out of a Cary Grant movie, she believed. The sort Audrey Hepburn had said a million times.

"But," the woman said slowly, "the last time I talked to him I asked if he needed money and he said—he was really angry—but he said that he was about to get more money than I could imagine and he'd never take another damn penny from me or Hank ever again."

"He said that?" Rune asked excitedly.

Emily nodded.

"We've got to find him," Rune said.

"Will you turn him in to the police?" Emily asked.

Rune was going to say no. But she stopped herself.

You only lie to people who can control you.

"I don't know. I think I believe he didn't kill Mr. Kelly. I want to talk to him first. But where is he? How can we find him?"

Emily said, "If I knew I wouldn't be here now."

"Is there anything there?" Rune nodded toward the mail Emily had been looking through.

"No, it's mostly just Dear Occupant. . . . The only lead I've got is the name of his bank. I tried calling them to see if they had an address but they wouldn't talk to me."

Rune was thinking about another movie she'd seen a few years ago. Who was in it? De Niro? Harvey Keitel? The actor—a private eye—had bluffed his way into a bank and gotten information.

Maybe it was Sean Connery.

"Look, you don't understand . . . The man is dying! For God's sake, give me his address. Here's his account number."

"Sir, I can't. It's against policy."

"Hell with your policy. A man's life *is at stake."*

"You have the account number?" she asked Emily.

"No."

"Well, how about the branch?"

"I've got that."

"That should be all we need."

"I don't think they'll give you any information."

"You'd be surprised. I can be extremely persuasive."

Rune wiped her eyes—thinking how Stephanie, the only real actress she knew—would do it.

"I'm sorry. But it's really, really important."

The young man was a vice president of the bank but he looked young enough to be a clerk at a McDonald's, what with that wimp mustache and baby-smooth cheeks.

It was the next morning, nine-thirty, and the branch had just opened. The lobby surrounding them was deserted.

The vice president seemed uncomfortable with this young woman sitting in front of his desk, crying. He scanned his desktop helplessly then looked back at Rune. "He's not getting his bank statements? Any of them?"

"None. He's very upset. Grandfather's such a tense man. I'm sure that was the reason for the stroke. He's very . . . what's the word? You know."

"Fastidious?" the young man offered. "Meticulous?"

"That's it. And when he realized he's not getting the statements, Jesus, he really had a fit."

"What's his account number?"

Rune was digging in her purse. One minute. Two. She heard Muzak pumping through the glossy white marble lobby. She stared into the pit of her purse. "I can't seem to find it. Anyway, we probably couldn't read it. He tried to write it down for me but he can't control his right hand too well and that frustrates him, and I didn't want to upset him unnecessarily."

"I can't do anything without his account—"

"His face was all red and his eyes were bulging. I thought he was going to burst a—"

"What's his name?" the man asked quickly. The mustache got an anemic swipe and he leaned toward his computer.

"Vic Symington. Well, Victor."

He typed. The young man frowned. He typed some more, his fingers flying across the keys. He read, frowned again. "I don't understand. You mean that your grandfather wants another copy of his *final* statement?"

"Final statement? He's moved, see, and the statement hasn't come to his new address. What do you have listed as the new address?"

"We've got a problem, miss." The hamburger-slinging vice president looked up.

Rune felt herself start to sweat, her stomach churning. She'd blown it now. He was probably pushing one of those secret buttons that alerts the guards. Shit. She asked, "Problem?"

"Someone closed out your grandfather's account two days ago. If he thinks he's still got money in this bank, something's wrong."

"How could he have gotten here to close his account? The poor man can't even eat by himself."

"He didn't do it in person. It says 'POA' next to the withdrawal. He issued a power of attorney and the attorney-in-fact closed the account."

"Mother! She didn't!" Rune's hands went to her face. "She's always said that she'd rob Grandfather blind. How could she've done it?" Rune was sobbing again, dry tears pouring into her hands. "Tell me! You have to! Was it Mother? I have to know."

"I'm sorry, miss, it's against our policy to give out information on customers witout written permission."

Oh, this sounded familiar. Remembering the movie.

She leaned forward. "To hell with your policy. A man's *life* is at stake."

"His life?" the vice president asked placidly, sitting back. "Why?"

"Well, because . . ." (In the De Niro or Keitel or Connery movie the bank officer had just caved.)

"Because why?" the man asked. He wasn't really suspicious. He was just curious.

"The stroke. If Mother stole his money . . . It could be the end for him. Another stroke, a heart attack. I'm *really* worried about him."

The young man sighed. Another mustache swipe. Another sigh. He looked at the computer screen. "The check was drawn to Ralph Stein, Esquire. He's a lawyer. . . ."

"Oh, thank God," Rune exclaimed. "That's Grandfather's lawyer. S-t-i-n-e, right?"

"E-i-n."

"Oh, sure. We call him Uncle Ralph. He's a sweetheart." Rune stood up. "Here in Manhattan, right?"

"Citicorp Building."

"That's the one."

The vice president, tapping computer keys like a travel agent, said, "But does your grandfather think he still has an account here?"

Rune walked toward the exit. "The poor man, he's really like a child, you know?"

The man placed his fingers together. They were pudgy fingers and Rune imagined that he would leave good fat fingerprints on whatever he touched, just like a clumsy felon. His nails were dirty too.

The office where they sat was large, yellow-painted, filled with boxes and dusty legal books. A dead plant sat in the greasy window. Diplomas from schools she'd never heard of hung on one wall, next to a clock.

It was two in the afternoon—it had taken her this long to track down Attorney Stein. She had to be at work at four but there was still plenty of time. Don't panic, she told herself.

The lawyer looked at her with a cool gaze. *Neutral*

was the word that came to mind. He seemed to be the sort of man who wanted to find some weakness about you and notice it and let you know he noticed it even though he'd never mention it.

He wore a suit that fit very closely, and monogrammed cuffs that protruded. The sausages of fingers pressed together.

"How do you know Victor?" His voice was soft and neutral and that surprised her because she expected lawyers would ask questions with gruff voices, sneery and mean.

Rune swallowed and realized suddenly she couldn't be Symington's granddaughter. Stein might have done the man's will; he'd know all the relatives by heart. Then she remembered who his daughter, Emily, thought she was at first. She smiled and said, "I'm a *friend*." Putting special emphasis on the word.

He nodded. Neutrally. "From where?"

"We used to live near each other. The East Village. I'd come and visit him sometimes."

"Ah. And how did you know about me?"

"He mentioned you. He said good things about you."

"So, you'd *visit* him." The lawyer looked her up and down with a whisper of lechery on his face.

"Once a week. Sometimes twice. For an old guy he was pretty . . . well, energetic. So can you tell me where he is?" Rune asked.

"No."

She swallowed again and was mad that this man was making her swallow and be nervous. Sometimes it was so hard to be adult. She cleared her throat and sat forward. "Why not?"

The lawyer shrugged. "Client confidentiality. Why do you want to see him?"

"He left in such a hurry. I wanted to talk to him is all

and I didn't get a chance to. One day he was on Tenth Street and the next he was gone."

"How old are you?"

"Isn't that some kind of crime to ask how old someone is?"

"I'm not discriminating against you on the basis of your age. I just want to know how old you are."

Rune said, "Twenty. How old are you?"

"I assume you don't really want to *talk* to him. Do you? I assume your relationship or whatever you want to call it wasn't based on talking. Now—"

"Five hundred," she blurted out. "He owed me five hundred."

"For one night?" Stein looked her up and down again.

"For one *hour,*" Rune said.

"One hour," he responded.

"I'm very good."

"Not that good," the lawyer said. "One client of mine paid four thousand for two hours."

Four thousand? What'd that involve? She thought of several best-selling tapes at Washington Square Video: *Mistress Q* and *House of Pain.*

Sick world out there.

The lawyer's neutral voice asked, "And if I were to give you that five hundred dollars, would you forget about Mr. Symington? Would you forget that he left in a hurry? Would you forget everything about him?"

"No," Rune said abruptly. The man blinked. Got a rise out of him there. She tried on her adult persona again. "But I will for two thousand."

Which got an even bigger rise and he actually gave her a smile. It was—naturally—neutral but it was a smile nonetheless. He said, "Fifteen hundred."

"Deal." She started to extend her hand to shake but apparently this wasn't done in matters of this sort.

He pulled a pad toward him. "Where should I send the check?"

"Here." Rune held her hand forward, palm out.

Another smile. Irritated, less neutral this time. She was supposed to be stupid and intimidated. But here she was, staring back into his eyes, looking, more or less, adult. Finally he rose. "I'll just be a minute. Payable to cash, I assume?"

"That'll work."

He walked silently out of the office, buttoning his jacket as he left. He was gone longer than Rune thought he'd be—thinking he'd just tell his secretary to cut a check—but no, he was gone for a full five minutes.

Which was more than enough time for Rune to lean forward and flip through Stein's Rolodex and find Victor Symington's card. The address had been crossed out several times and a new one written in.

In Brooklyn. The address was in Brooklyn. She recited it several times softly out loud. Closed her eyes. She tested herself and found she'd memorized it. She flipped the Rolodex back to where it had been.

Rune fell back into her slouch in the chair and looked at the lawyer's wall, wondering if there were some special kinds of frames you were supposed to use for diplomas. Mr. Go-to-School-and-Lead-a-Productive-Life Richard didn't have *any* goddamn diplomas on *his* ugly beige suburban walls.

Phillip Dixon, the U.S. marshal, hadn't even gone to college, she bet. He seemed perfectly happy. But before she could play her game of making up an elaborate life for him, starting with his partner being tragically gunned and dying in his amrs, Lawyer Stein returned.

He had an envelope and a sheet of paper. Handed her both. She scanned the document quickly but it was full of *whereases* and words like *indemnity* and *waiver*. She gave up after the first paragraph.

"That's a receipt for the money. You agree that if you don't keep your bargain we can sue you for all this money back plus costs and attorney's fees, and . . ."

Rune was staring at the check.

". . . punitive damages."

What*ever.*

Rune signed the paper, put the check in her bag.

"So Mr. Symington doesn't exist, right?"

"Mr. who?"

CHAPTER TWENTY

"So how was the date?" Stephanie asked.

"With Richard?" Rune responded.

"Who else?" the redhead replied.

Rune considered the question for a moment. Then asked. "You ever see *Rodan*?"

They were at the counter of Washington Square Video.

"You mean his sculpture?"

Who? This was like Stallone's poetry. "No, I mean the flying dinosaur that destroyed Tokyo. Or maybe New York. Or someplace. A movie from the fifties."

"Missed that."

"Anyway, *that* was my date. A disaster. Not even a Spielberg disaster movie. A B-movie disaster."

She told Stephanie about Karen.

"Shit. That's bad. Other-woman stuff. Hard to get around them."

Them's the breaks . . .

Rune said, "Here." She reached into her purse and handed Steph the orange earrings.

"No," the woman protested. "You keep them."

"Nope. I'm off high fashion. Listen, do me a favor, please?"

"What?"

"I've got to go to Brooklyn. Can you work for me?"

"I guess. But won't Tony be pissed?"

"Just tell him . . . I don't know. I had to go someplace. To visit Frankie's sister in the hospital."

"She's home. With the baby."

"Well, I went to see her at home."

"Tony'd call and check."

Rune nodded. "You're right. Just make up something. I don't care."

"What're you gonna do in Brooklyn?"

"The money. I've got a lead to the money."

"Not that stolen bank money?"

"Yep. And don't forget the story of the Little Red Hen."

Stephanie smiled. "I'm not quitting my day job just yet."

"Probably a good idea." Rune slung her leopard-skin purse over her shoulder and headed out the door. "But keep the faith. I'm getting close."

Ten minutes later she was en route to Brooklyn. In search of Victor Symington.

On the subway, the riders were silent, subdued. One woman whispered to herself. A young couple had their precious new TV on the seat next to them, bundled in thick string, a receipt from a Crazy Eddie store taped to the box. A Latino man stood leaning forward, staring absently at the MTA map; he didn't seem to care much where he was headed. Almost everyone in the car, bathed in green fluorescence, was slumped and sullen as the car lurched into the last station in Manhattan before the descent beneath the East River.

Uneasy again.

Leaving the Side, leaving *her* territory.

Just before the doors eased shut, a man walked stiffly onto the train. He was white but had a dark yellowish tan. She couldn't guess his age. The car wasn't full but he sat directly across from Rune. He was wearing dusty clothes. Coming home from a construction job or hard day labor, tired, spent. He was very thin and she wondered if he was sick. He fell asleep immediately and Rune couldn't help but stare at him. His head bobbed and swayed, eyes closed, his head rolled. Keeping his blind focus on Rune.

She thought: He's Death.

She felt it deep inside her. With a chill. Death, Hades, a Horseman of the Apocalypse. The dark angel who'd fluttered into her father's hospital room to take him away. The spirit who wrapped his ghostly arms around Mr. Kelly and held him helpless in the musty armchair while someone fired those terrible bullets into his chest.

The lights flickered as the train switched tracks and then slowed as it rolled into one station. Then they were on their way again. Five minutes later the train lurched and they stopped again. The doors rumbled open. Waking him up. As his eyes opened he was staring directly into Rune's. She shuddered and sat back but couldn't look away. He glanced out the window, stood up quickly. "Shit, missed my stop. Missed my stop." He walked out of the car.

And because she kept staring at him shuffling along the platform as the train pulled out, Rune saw the man who'd been following her.

As her gaze eased to the right she glanced into the car

behind her. And saw the young man, compact, Italian-looking.

She blinked, not sure why she remembered him, and then recalled that she'd seen somebody who looked a lot like him someplace else. The loft? No, in the East Village, near Mr. Kelly's apartment . . .

Outside Mr. Kelly's apartment the day she'd broken in. Yes, that was it! And it was the same guy who'd ducked into the deli when she'd been on the street in front of Washington Square Video.

Pretty Boy, wearing the utility jacket. Sitting on the doorstep, smoking and reading the *Post.*

Or was it?

It *looked* like him. But she wasn't sure. No Con Ed jackets today.

The man wasn't looking her way, didn't even seem to know she was there. Reading a book or magazine, engrossed in it.

No, it couldn't be him.

Paranoid, that's what she was. Seeing the man with the yellow eyes, seeing Death, had made her paranoid.

It was just life in a city of madmen, dirty screeching subways, fifteen hundred homicides a year, a thousand police detectives with close-together eyes. U.S. marshals who like to flirt.

Paranoia. What else could it be?

Hell, she thought, get real: it could be because of a million dollars.

It could be because of a murder.

That's what else it could be.

The lights went out again as the train clattered through another switch. She leapt up, heart pounding, ready to run, sure that Pretty Boy'd come pushing through the door and strangle her.

But when the lights came back on the man was gone,

was probably standing in a cluster of people by the door, about to get off at the next stop.

See, just paranoia.

She sat down and breathed deeply to calm herself. When the crowd got off he wasn't in the car any longer.

Two stops later, at Bay Ridge, Rune slipped out of the car, looking around. No sign of any Pretty-Boy meter readers. She pushed through the turnstile, climbed to the sidewalk.

Glancing up and down the street, trying to orient herself.

And saw him. Walking out of the other subway exit a half-block away. Looking around—trying to find *her*. Jesus . . .

He *had* been following her.

She looked away, trying to stay calm. Don't let him know you spotted him. He pushed roughly through crowds of exiting passengers and passersby, aiming in her direction.

Trying to look nonchalant, strolling along the street, pretending to gaze at what was displayed in store windows but actually hoping to see the reflection of an approaching taxi. Pretty Boy was getting closer. He must've shoved somebody out of the way: she heard a macho exchange of "fuck you, no, fuck *you*." Any minute he'd start sprinting toward her. Any minute he'd pull out the gun and shoot her dead with those Teflon bullets.

Then, reflected in a drugstore window, she saw a bright yellow cab cruising down the street. Rune spun around, leapt in front of a pregnant woman, and flung the door open before the driver even had a chance to stop.

In a thick Middle-Eastern accent the driver cried, "What the hell you doing?"

"Drive!"

The cabbie was shaking his head. "No, uh-uh,

no. . . ." He pointed to the off-duty lights on the top of the yellow Chevy.

"Yes," she shouted. "Drive, drive, drive!"

Rune saw that Pretty Boy'd stopped, surprised, not sure what to do. He stood, cigarette in his hand, then began taking cautious steps forward toward them, maybe worried that the scene at the cab would attract some cops.

Then he must have decided it didn't matter. He started to run toward her.

Rune begged the driver, "Please! Only a few blocks!" She gave him an address on Fort Hamilton Parkway.

"No, no, uh-uh."

"Twenty dollars."

"Twenty? No, uh-uh."

She looked behind her. Pretty Boy was only a few doors away, hand inside his jacket.

"Thirty? Please, please, please?"

He debated. "Well, okay, thirty."

"Drive, drive, drive!" shouted Rune.

"Why you in a hurry?" the driver asked.

"Forty fucking dollars. Drive!"

"Forty?" The driver floored the accelerator and the car spun away, leaving a cloud of blue-white tire smoke between the Chevy and Pretty Boy.

Rune sat huddled down in the vinyl, stained rear seat. "Goddammit," she whispered bitterly as her heart slowed. She wiped sweat from her palms.

Who was he? Symington's accomplice? Probably. She'd bet he was the one who'd killed Mr. Kelly. The triggerman—as the cops in *Manhattan Is My Beat* had called the thug who'd machine-gunned down Roy in front of the hotel on Fifth Avenue.

And, from the look in his dark eyes, she could tell he intended to kill *her* too.

Time for the police? she wondered. Call Manelli. Call

Phillip Dixon . . . It made sense. It was the *only* thing that made sense at this point.

But then there was the matter of the million dollars . . . She thought of Amanda. Thought of her own perilous career. Thought of how she'd like to pull up in front of Richard and Karen in a stretch limo.

And decided: No police. Not yet.

A few minutes later the cab stopped in front of a light-green-and-brick two-story row house.

The driver said, "That's forty dollars. And don't worry about no tip."

She stood on the sidewalk, hidden behind some anemic evergreens, looking at the row house that was, according to his lawyer's Rolodex, Victor Symington's current residence. A pink flamingo stood on one wire leg on the front lawn. A brown Christmas wreath lay next to a croquet mallet beside the stairs. An iron jockey with black features painted Caucasian held a ring for hitching a horse.

"Let's do it," she muttered to herself. Not much time. Pretty Boy would be looking for a pay phone just then to call Symington and tell him that he couldn't stop her and that she was on her way there. It wouldn't be long before Pretty Boy himself'd show up.

She thought she could handle Symington by himself. But with his strong-arm partner, probably a hothead, there'd be trouble.

She rang the doorbell. She had her story ready and it was a good one, she thought. Rune would tell him that she knew what he and Pretty Boy had done and that she'd given a letter to *her* lawyer, explaining everything and mentioning their names. If anything happened to her, she'd tell him, the letter would be sent to the police.

Only one flaw. Symington wasn't home. Goddammit. She hadn't counted on that.

She banged on the door with her fist.

No answer. She turned the knob. It was bolted shut.

Glancing up and down the street. No Pretty Boy yet. She clumped down the gray-painted stairs and walked around to the back door. She passed a quorum of the Seven Dwarfs, in plaster, planted along the side of the building, then found the gate in a cheap mesh fence around the backyard.

At the back door Rune pressed her face against the glass, hands shrouding out the light. It was dark inside. She couldn't see much of anything.

Part of her said Pretty Boy could be there at any minute.

The other part of her broke out a small windowpane with her elbow. She reached in and opened the door. She tossed the broken glass into the backyard, which was overgrown with thick bright grass. She stepped inside.

She walked through to the living room. "Like, minimal," she muttered. In the bedroom were one bed, a dresser, a floor lamp. The kitchen had one table and two chairs. Two glasses sat on the retro Formica counter, spattered like a Jackson Pollock painting. A few chipped dishes and silverware. In the living room was a single folding chair. Nothing else.

Rune paused in front of the bathroom. There was a stained glass window in the door. "Oooo, classy poddy," she muttered. Somebody's initials on the door. "W.C." The guy who built the house, she guessed.

She looked through the closets—all of them except the one in the bedroom, which was fastened with a big, new glistening lock. Under the squeaky bed were two suitcases. Heavy, battered leather ones. She pulled them out, starting to sweat in the heat of the close, stale apartment. She stood up and tried to open a window. It was nailed shut. Why? she wondered.

She went back to the suitcases and opened the first one. Clothes. Old, frayed at the cuffs and collar points. The browns going light, the whites going yellow. She closed it and slid it back. In the second suitcase: a razor, an old double-edged Gillette, a tube of shave cream like toothpaste; a Swiss Army knife; keys; a small metal container of cuff links; nail scissors, toothbrush.

She dug down through the layers.

And found a small, battered brown accordion folder with a rubber band around it. It was very heavy. She opened it. She found a letter—from Weissman, Burkow, Stein & Rubin, P.C.—describing how his savings, about fifty-five thousand, had been transferred to an account in the Cayman Islands. A plane ticket, one-way coach, to Georgetown on Grand Cayman. The flight was leaving day after tomorrow.

Next to it, she found his passport. She'd never seen one before. It was old and limp and stained. There were dozens of official-looking stamps in the back.

She didn't even look at the name until she was about to put it back.

Wait. Who the hell was Vincent Spinello?

Oh, shit! At Stein's law firm, when she'd looked through the lawyer's Rolodex, she'd been so nervous she'd misread the name. She'd seen *Vincent Spinello* and thought *Victor Symington.* Oh, Christ, she'd gotten it all wrong. And she'd even broken the poor man's window!

All a waste. She couldn't believe it. The danger, the risk, Pretty Boy . . . all a waste.

"Goddamn," she whispered harshly.

Only, wait . . . The letter.

She opened the letter again. It *was* addressed to Symington and at *this* address. So what was he doing with Vincent Spinello's passport?

But as she looked at the passport again, the condensed, grim little picture, there was no doubt. *Spinello* was the man she'd seen at Robert Kelly's apartment. Who was he?

She dug to the bottom of the folder and found out. What made it so heavy was something that was wrapped in a piece of newspaper—a pistol. With it was a small box of cheap cardboard, flecked brown-green. The box, too, was heavy. On the side was printing in what she thought was German. She could make out only one word. *Teflon.*

Oh, God . . .

Symington—or Spinello—was the man who'd killed Robert Kelly. He and Pretty Boy *had* found the Union Bank robbery money. They'd stolen it and killed him! And the loot was in the closet!

Rune dropped to her knees and looked at the padlock on the closet. Leaned close, squinting. Pulled it, rattled the solid lock.

Then she froze. At the sound of a door opening then closing.

Was it the front or the back door? She couldn't tell. But she knew one thing. It was either Pretty Boy or Symington. And she knew something else: they both wanted her dead.

Rune gave one last tug at the closet door. It didn't move a millimeter.

Footsteps inside now. Nearby. If he finds me here, he'll kill me! She stuffed the accordion envelope into her bag and slung it over her shoulder.

A creak of floorboards

No, no . . .

She thought they were in the front of the apartment. In the living room, which wasn't visible from where she was. She could probably get out the back without being seen. She glanced into the corridor fast, then ducked back into the bedroom. Yep, it was empty.

Rune took a breath and ran from the bedroom.

She slammed right into Victor Symington's chest.

He gasped in terror, stepped back, the ugly hat falling from his head. In reflex he lunged out and slugged her hard in the stomach, doubling her over. "Oh, God," she wheezed. A huge pain shot through her chest and jaw. Rune tried to scream but her voice was only a whisper. She dropped to the floor, unable to breathe.

Symington, furious, grabbed her by the hair and spun her around. Dropped to his knees. His hands smelled of garlic and tobacco. He began to search her roughly.

"Are you with them?" he gasped. "Who the fuck are you?"

She couldn't answer.

"You are, aren't you? You're working for them!" He lifted his fist. Rune lifted an arm over her face.

"Who?" she managed to ask.

He asked, "How did you . . ."

He stopped speaking. Struggling to catch her breath, Rune looked up. Symington was staring at the doorway. Someone stood there. Pretty Boy? Rune blinked, rolled to her knees.

No . . . Thank you, thank you, thank you . . . It was his daughter, Emily.

Rune was so grateful to see the woman that it wasn't until a second later that she wondered: How'd Emily find the place? Had she *followed* me here?

Wait, something is wrong.

Symington let go of Rune, backed up.

Emily said, "How did we find you, you were going to ask? Haarte has some good contacts."

Haart? Rune wondered. "Who's Heart?" she asked.

"Oh, no, it's Haarte?" Symington whispered. Then he nodded hopelessly. "I should've guessed."

"What's going on?" Rune demanded.

Symington was looking at Emily with an imploring expression on his face. "Please . . ."

Emily didn't respond.

He continued. "Would it do any good to say I have a lot of money?"

"The money!" Rune said. "He killed Mr. Kelly and stole his money!"

Both Symington and Emily ignored her.

"Is there *anything* I can do?" Symington pleaded.

"No," Emily said. And took a pistol from her pocket. She shot him in the chest.

CHAPTER TWENTY-ONE

The way he fell is what saved Rune.

The gun was small but the impact knocked Symington backward and he slammed into the pole of the floor lamp, which fell against the bathroom door, sending a shower of glass into the hallway.

Emily danced out of the way of the splinters, which gave Rune a chance to sprint into the bedroom. But the woman recovered fast. She fired the gun again and Rune heard a terrible stereo sound of noises: the blasts of the gun behind her, the crash of the bullets slamming into the plaster wall inches from her head.

Then—with another punch of breathtaking pain—she dove through the bedroom window.

Hands covering her face, shards of glass flying around her, trailing the window shade, she rolled onto more sad evergreens and dropped onto the grass, coming to rest against one of the plaster dwarfs. Panting, she lay on the lawn. The smell of dirt and damp grass enveloped her. She could hear birds squabbling in the trees overhead.

And then the air around her exploded. A dwarf's face disintegrated into white splinters and dust. On the street, fifty feet away, Rune caught a glimpse of a man with shotgun. She couldn't see his face but she knew it was Pretty Boy—Heart probably, the one Symington mentioned. Or Heart's partner. He and Emily were working together. . . . She didn't know who they were exactly or why they wanted to kill Symington but she didn't pause to consider those questions. She rolled under another plant, then scrabbled to her feet. Clutching her purse, she sprinted into the backyard. Then clambered over the chain-link fence.

And then she ran.

Behind her, from Symington's yard, came a shout. A second shotgun blast. She heard the hiss of something over her head. It missed and she turned, down an alley. Kept running.

Running until her vision blurred. Running until her chest ignited and she couldn't breathe another ounce of air.

Finally, miles away it seemed, Rune stopped, gasping. She doubled over. Sure she was going to be sick. But she spit into the grass a few times and remained motionless until the nausea and pain went away. She trotted another block but pulled up with a cramp in her side. She slipped into another backyard—behind a house with boarded-up windows. She crawled into a nest of grass between a smiling Bambi and another set of the Seven Dwarfs, then lay her head on her purse, thinking she'd rest for ten, fifteen minutes.

When she opened her eyes a huge garbage truck was making its mournful, behemoth sounds five feet away from her. And it was dawn.

They'd be watching for her.

Maybe at the Midtown Tunnel, maybe at a subway stop. Emily and Pretty Boy. And not just them. A dozen others. She saw them *all* now—Them with a capital T. Walking down the streets of Brooklyn on this clear, cool spring morning. Faces glancing at her, knowing that she was a witness. Knowing that she and her friends were about to die—to be laid out like Robert Kelly, like Victor Symington.

They were all after her.

She was hitching her way back to Manhattan, back to the Side. She'd thumbed a ride with a delivery van, the driver a wild-eyed Puerto Rican with a wispy goatee who swore at the traffic with incredible passion and made it to the Brooklyn Bridge, a drive that should have taken three-fourths of an hour at this time of day, in fifteen minutes.

He apologized profusely that he couldn't take her into Manhattan itself.

And then she ran once more.

Over the wooden walkway of the Brooklyn Bridge, back into the city, which was just starting to come to life. Traffic hissed beneath her; the muted horns of the taxis sounded like animals lowing. She paused halfway across to rest, leaning against the railing. The young professionals walked past—wearing running shoes with their suits and dresses—on their way to Wall Street from Brooklyn Heights.

What the hell had she been thinking of?

Quests? Adventures?

Knights and wizards and damsels?

No, she thought bitterly. *These* were the people who lived in the Magic Kingdom: lawyers and secretaries and accountants and deliverymen. It wasn't a magic place at all; it was just a big, teeming city filled with good people and bad people.

That's all. Just a city. Just people.

It's a factory, Rune. There's shit and pollution. It makes a living for people and they pay taxes and give money to charity and buy sneakers for their children. Who grow up to be lawyers or teachers or musicians or people who work in other factories. It's nothing more than that.

Once over the bridge she walked north toward the courthouses, past City Hall, staring up at the twisty gothic building—the north face made of cheap stone, not marble, because no one ever thought the city would spread north of the Wall Street district. Then into Chinatown and up through SoHo to Washington Square Park.

Which, even this early, was a zoo. A medieval carnival. Jugglers, unicyclists, skateboard acrobats, kids slamming on guitars so cheap they were just rhythm instruments. She sat down on a bench, ignoring a tall Senegalese selling knockoff Rolexes, ignoring a beefy white teenager chanting, "*Hash, hash, sens, sens, smoke it up, sens.*" Women in designer jogging outfits rolled their expensive buggies of infant lawyers-to-be past dealers and stoned-out vets. It was Greenwich Village.

Rune sat for an hour. Once, some vague resolve coalesced in her and she stood up. But it vanished swiftly and she sat down again, closed her eyes, and let the hot sun fall on her face.

Who *were* they? Emily? Pretty Boy?

Where was the money?

She fell asleep again—until a Frisbee skimmed her head and startled her awake. She looked around, in panic, struggling to remember where she was, how she'd gotten there. She asked a woman the time. Noon. It seemed that a dozen people were staring at her suspiciously. She stood and walked quickly through the grass, north through the white, stone arch, a miniature Arc de Triomphe.

They were old films, both of them.

One was *She Wore a Yellow Ribbon,* the John Wayne cavalry flick. It was playing now. Rune didn't notice what the other one was. Maybe *The Searcher* or *Red River*. *Yellow Ribbon* was showing when she sat down. The seats in the old theater on Twelfth Street were stiff—thin padding under crushed fabric upholstery. There were only fifteen or so people in the revival house, which didn't surprise her—the only time this place had ever been crowded was on Saturday night and when they were showing selections from the New York Erotic Film Festival.

Watching the screen.

She knew the old John Ford-directed western cold. She'd seen it six times. But today, it seemed to her to be just a series of disjointed images. Salty old Victor McLaglen, the distinguished graying Wayne, the intensified hues of the forty-year-old Technicolor film, the shoulder-punching innocent humor of the blue-bloused horse soldiers . . .

But today the movie made no sense to her. It was disconnected images of men and women walking around on a huge rectangle of white screen, fifty feet in front of her. They spoke funny words, they wore odd clothing, they played into staged climaxes. It was all choreographed and it was all fake.

Her anger built. Anger at the two dimensions of the film. The falsity, the illusion. She felt betrayed. Not only by Emily Symington or whoever she was, not only by what had happened in Brooklyn, but by something else. Something more fundamental about how she lived her life, about how the things she believed in had turned on her.

She stood and left the theater. Outside, she bought a pair of thick-rimmed dark glasses from a street vendor and put them on. She turned the corner and walked down University Place to Washington Square Video.

Tony fired her, of course.

His words weren't cute or sarcastic or obnoxious like she'd thought he'd be. He just glanced up and said, "You missed two shifts and you didn't call. You're fired. This time for real."

But she didn't pay him much attention. She was staring at the newspaper on the counter, lying in front of Tony.

The headline: *Mafia Witness Hit.*

Which didn't get her attention as quickly as the photo did: a grainy flashlit shot of Victor Symington's town house in Brooklyn, the six surviving dwarfs, the shattered window. Rune grabbed the paper.

"Hey," Tony snapped. "I'm reading that." One look at her eyes, though, and he stopped protesting.

> A convicted syndicate money launderer who had been a key witness in a series of Racketeering Influenced Corrupt Organizations (RICO) trials of midwest crime leaders earlier this year was shot to death yesterday in a gangland-style hit in Brooklyn.
>
> Vincent Spinello, 70, was killed by gunshots to the chest. A witness, who asked not to be identified, reported that a young woman with short hair fled from the scene and is a primary suspect in the case.
>
> Another witness in the same series of cases,

Arnold Gittleman, was murdered, along with two U.S. marshals, in a St. Louis hotel last month.

The paper crumpled in her hands. Me! she thought. That's me, the young woman with short hair.

She *used* me! Emily. The bitch used me. She knew all along where Symington was and got me out there to make it look like *I* killed him.

And, hell, my fingerprints're all over the place!

Primary suspect . . .

Tony snatched the newspaper away from her. "You can pick up your check on Monday."

"Please, Tony," she said. "I need money now. Can't I get cash?"

"No fucking way."

"I've got to get out of town."

"Monday," he said. Returned to his paper.

"Look, I've got a check for fifteen hundred bucks. Give me a thousand and I'll sign it over to you."

"Yeah, like *you've* got a check that's going to clear. I'm sure."

"Tony! It's payable to cash. From a law firm."

"Out."

Frankie Greek stuck his head out of the storeroom and said, "Hey, Rune, like, you got a couple calls. This cop, Manelli. And that U.S. marshal guy. Dixon. Oh, and Stephanie too."

Tony barked, "But don't call 'em from here. Use the pay phone outside."

Stephanie! Rune thought. If they'd been following me, they've seen me with her.

Oh, Jesus Mary, she's in danger too.

She ran back to the counter and swept the phone off the cradle. Tony started to say something but then seemed to decide that it wasn't worth fighting the battle; after all, he'd won the war. He turned on his worn heel and retreated to the other counter, carrying the newspaper.

Stephanie's groggy voice finally answered.

"Rune! Where've you been? You missed work last night. Tony's really pissed—"

"Steph, listen to me." Her voice was raw. "They murdered that man I was trying to find, Symington, they're trying to make it look like I did it."

"What?"

"And they tried to kill me!"

"Who?"

"I don't know. They work for the Mafia or something. I think they might've seen you too."

"Rune, are you making this up? Is this one of your fantasies?"

"No! I'm serious."

Several customers glanced at her. She felt a shiver of fear. She cupped her hand over the receiver and lowered her voice. "Look on the front page of the *Post*. The story's there."

"You have to call the police."

"I *can't*. My fingerprints're all over the house where Symington got killed. I'm a suspect."

"Jesus, Rune. What a mess."

"I'm going back to Ohio."

"When? Now?"

"As soon as I can get some money. Tony won't pay me."

"Prick," Stephanie spat out. "I can lend you some."

"I can give you a check for fifteen hundred."

"Are you serious?"

"Yeah, it's payable to cash. You can have it. But, listen, you have to come with me!"

"Come with you?" Stephanie asked. "Where?"

"To Ohio."

"No way. I've got an audition next week."

"Stephanie . . ."

"I'll get you a couple of hundred. I'll stop at the bank. Where'll you be?"

"How 'bout Union Square Park? The subway entrance, southeast side."

"Okay. Good. A half hour."

"Is it safe?" Stephanie asked cautiously.

"Pretty safe."

A pause. "I don't want to get beat up or anything. I bruise real easy. And I can't be bruised for my audition."

As she stepped into the street, Rune heard the man's voice right beside her.

"You're a hard person to find."

Panicked, Rune spun around.

Richard was leaning on a parking meter. The yuppie in him had been exorcized; Mr. Downtown was back. He wore boots, black jeans, and a black T-shirt. He also wore a gold hoop in his ear. She noticed that it was a clip-on. He looked tired.

"You have," he continued, "as FDR said, a passion for anonymity. I called you at the store a couple of times. I was worried about you."

"I haven't been in for a while."

"There was this party last night. I thought you might want to go."

"You didn't ask . . . what's her name? Cathy the Amazon?"

"Karen." He held on to the parking meter and spiraled around it slowly. "We've only had dinner that once. Don't worry about her. We're not going out."

"That's your business. I don't care."

"Don't act so possessive."

"How can I be acting possessive if I tell you I don't care what you do with Cathy/Karen?"

"What's wrong?" He was frowning. Following her eyes to the short, dark-complected man with curly hair standing two doors away. His back was to them.

Rune inhaled with a frightened hiss. The man turned and walked past them. It wasn't Pretty Boy.

She turned back to Richard, trying to focus on him, though what she was seeing was the stupid grin of the plaster statue of Dopey or Sneezy as it disintegrated under the shotgun blast. The gun had been astonishingly loud. Sounded more like a bomb going off.

Richard took her by the shoulders. "Rune, aren't you listening to me? What's wrong?"

She backed away, eyes narrowing slowly. "Leave me alone."

"What?"

"Stay *away* from me. Do you want to get hurt? I'm poison. Stay away."

"What are you talking about?" He reached out and took her hand.

"No, no!" she shouted. The tears started. She hesitated, then hugged him. "Get away from me! Forget about me! Forget you ever met me!"

She turned and ran through the crowds of Greenwich Village toward Union Square.

■

Waiting under the art-deco steel entrance to the subway, Rune slouched against the cool tile.

She absently watched a crane, a lopsided T-shaped structure rising above an enormous new housing project on Union Square. It's just a crane, she told herself. That's all it was. Not a tool of the gods, not a huge skeleton of a magic animal. What she saw was just a construction crane. Moving slowly, under the control of a faceless union worker, lifting steel reinforcing rods for workmen in dusty jeans and jackets to install.

Magic . . . hell.

She thought again about calling Manelli or Dixon.

But why should they believe her? There was probably an all-points bulletin out on her already, just like there'd been for Roy the cop after he'd stolen the loot in *Manhattan Is My Beat.* At least she'd had the foresight to get rid of some of the evidence: When she'd stopped by her loft to pick up the check, she'd realized she still had Spinello's accordion envelope and thrown it into the trash. If the cops found her with *that,* it'd be a sure conviction.

No, she'd leave town, leave the Side, leave the Magic Kingdom. Go back home. Get a job. Go to school.

Well, it was damn well about time.

Time to grow up. Forget quests . . .

She saw Stephanie, her reddish hair glowing in the afternoon sun as she walked through the park. They waved at each other. It seemed ridiculously innocent, Rune thought, as if they were girlfriends meeting for drinks after work to complain about bosses and men and mothers.

Rune looked around, saw no one suspicious—well, no one *more* suspicious than you'd normally see in Union Square Park—then joined Stephanie.

"You're hurt." The woman glanced at her forehead, where Rune had been cut by a piece of glass or plaster.

"It's okay."

"What happened?"

Rune told her.

"God! You have to go to the police. You can talk to them. Tell them what happened."

"Yeah, right. They can place me at two different crime scenes. I'm the number one suspect."

"But won't the cops find you in Ohio?"

She gave a faint smile. "They might—if they knew my real name. Which they don't."

Stephanie smiled back. "True. Oh, here." She handed

Rune a wad of bills. "It's about three hundred. That enough?"

Rune hugged her. "I don't know what to say." She gave Stephanie the check.

"No, no, this is too much."

"Little Red Hen, remember? I just need enough to get home on. You keep the rest. Tony'll probably fire you too. Just for helping me."

"Come on," Stephanie told her. "I'll help you pack and take you to the airport." They started down into the subway. "You think it's safe to go back to your loft?"

"Emily and Pretty Boy don't know about it. Manelli and that U.S. marshal do, but we can sneak in through the construction site. Nobody'll see us. We can—"

A chill like ice down her back. She gasped.

Ten feet away Pretty Boy stepped out from behind a pillar, holding a black pistol. "Don't fucking move," he muttered to Rune.

Anger on his face, he moved forward toward Rune, not paying any attention to Stephanie. Apparently he didn't even think they were together.

Rune froze. But Stephanie didn't.

She stepped past him fast, which caught him completely off guard. Screaming "Rape, rape!" she shoved her palm, fingers stiff and splayed, into his face. His head snapped back and he staggered against the wall, blood pouring from his nose.

"Fuck," he cried.

Her self-defense class . . .

Stephanie stepped toward him again. It looked like she was going to kick him this time.

But Pretty Boy was good too; he knew what he was doing. He didn't try to fight back. He leapt to the side about three steps, out of range, wiped the blood from his mouth and started to raise the pistol toward her.

Then the arm closed around his neck.

A passenger—a huge black man—had heard Stephanie's cry and had come up behind their attacker and locked his muscular arm around Pretty Boy's throat. Choking, he dropped the gun and grabbed the man's forearm, trying futilely to break the grip.

The big man behind him seemed to be enjoying the whole thing. He said cheerfully to Pretty Boy, "H'okay, asshole, leave th'ladies 'lone. You hear me?"

They ran.

Stephanie in the lead.

She *must* have belonged to a health club—she was moving like a greyhound. If Pretty Boy was there, Rune figured, Emily must be nearby too. Besides, the token seller would've called the cops by then; Rune wanted to get as far away from the station as possible.

Gasping, running. Following Stephanie as best she could.

They were two blocks from the subway when it happened.

At Thirteenth and Broadway a taxi jumped a red light just before it changed.

Which was the exact moment Stephanie ran into the intersection between two double-parked trucks.

She didn't have a chance . . .

All she could do was roll onto the hood to keep from getting crushed under the wheels. The driver hit the brakes, which gave a low, wild scream, but still the cab hit her hard. Some part of her body—her face, Rune thought in despair—slammed into the windshield, which turned white with fractures. Stephanie cartwheeled onto the concrete, a swirl of floral cloth and red hair and white flesh.

"No!" Rune screamed.

Two women ran up and started tending to her. Rune

dropped to her knees beside them. She hardly heard the litany of the cabdriver: "She ran through light, it wasn't my fault, it wasn't my fault."

Rune cradled Stephanie's bloody head in her arms.

"You'll be okay," she whispered. "You'll be okay. You'll be okay."

But Stephanie couldn't hear.

CHAPTER TWENTY-TWO

Rune stood by the window of the hospital, looking out onto the park.

It was an old city park on First Avenue. More rocks and dirt than grass, most of the boulders painted with graffiti, tinted red and purple. They seemed to be oozing from the underbelly of the city itself like exposed organs.

She turned away.

A doctor walked by, not looking at her. None of them had looked at her—the doctors, the orderlies, the nurses, the candy stripers. She'd given up waiting for a kindly old man in a white jacket to come into the hallway, put his arm around her, and say, "About your friend, don't you worry, she'll be fine."

The way they do in movies.

But movies're fake.

Richard's words echoed: *They. Aren't. Real.*

No one had stopped to talk to her. If she wanted any information she had to ask the nurses. Again.

And she'd get the same look she'd gotten two dozen times before.

No news. We'll let you know.

She looked out the window once more. Watching for Pretty Boy. Thinking maybe he'd gotten away from the man in the subway and escaped from the cops. Followed the ambulance here.

Paranoia again.

But it's not paranoia if they're really after you.

Hoping that Stephanie had hurt Pretty Boy really bad when she'd hit him. A character in one of her fairy stories, a friendly witch, had told someone never to hope for harm to someone else. Hope for all the good you want but never wish harm on anyone. Because, the witch said, harm's like a wasp in a jar. Once you release it you never know who it's going to sting.

But now Rune hoped Stephanie had hurt the bastard real bad.

She wandered up to the nurses' station.

An older woman with a snake of a stethoscope around her neck finally looked up. "Oh. We just heard about your friend."

"What? Tell me!"

"They just took her to Radiology for more scans. She's still unconscious."

"*That's* what you were going to tell me? That you don't know anything?"

"I thought you'd want to know. She'll be back in ICU in forty minutes, an hour. Depending."

Useless, Rune thought.

"I'll be back. If she wakes up, tell her I'll be back."

Oh, please, Pan and Isis and Persephone, let her live.

Rune stood by the East River, watching the tugs sail upstream. The Circle Line tour boat too. A barge, three or four cabin cruisers. The water was ugly and ripe-smelling. The traffic from the FDR Drive rushed past with a moist, tearing sound, which set her on edge. It sounded like bandages being removed.

Just an adventure. That's all I wanted. An adventure.

Lancelot searching for the Grail. Psyche for her lost lover Eros. Like in the books, in the movies. And Rune would be the hero. She'd find Mr. Kelly's killer, she'd find the million dollars. She'd save Amanda and would live happily ever after with Richard.

O God of heavenly powers, who by the might of thy command, drivest away from men's bodies all sickness and infirmity, be present in thy goodness . . .

These were the words she'd said so often during the last week of her father's life that she'd memorized them without trying to.

Her father, a young man. A handsome man. Who played with Rune and her sister all the time, taught them to ride bicycles, who read them stories, who took them to plays as readily as to ball games. A man who always had time to talk to them, listen to their problems.

No, fairy stories didn't always have happy endings. But they always had endings that were just. People died and lost their fortunes in them because they were dishonest or careless or greedy. There was no justice in her father's death though. He'd lived a good life and he'd still died badly, slow and messy, in the Shaker Heights Garden Hospice.

No justice in Mr. Kelly's death.

No justice in Stephanie's getting hurt. None if she died.

Please . . .

Speaking out loud now. "With this thy servant Stephanie that her weakness may be banished and her strength recalled."

Her voice fell to a whisper and then she stopped praying.

Staring at the ugly river in front of her, Rune took off her silver bracelets one by one and tossed them into the water. They disappeared without any sound that she could hear and she took that as a good sign that the gods who oversaw this wonderful and terrible city were happy with her sacrifice.

Though when she got to last bracelet, the one that she'd bought for Richard, she paused, looking at the silver hands clasped together. She heard his voice again.

You're going to find out I'm not a knight and that, okay, maybe there was some bank robbery money—which I think is the craziest frigging thing I've ever heard—but that it's spent or stolen or lost somewhere years ago and you'll never find it . . .

She gripped the bracelet firmly, ready to throw it after the others. But then decided, no, she'd save this one—as a reminder to herself. About how adventures can get friends and family hurt and killed. How quests work only in books and in movies.

And here you are pissing your life away in a video store, jumping from fantasy to fantasy, waiting for something you don't even know what it is.

She slipped the last bracelet back on her wrist and slowly returned to the hospital.

Upstairs, the nurses had changed shifts and no one could find Stephanie. Rune had a terrible moment of panic as one nurse looked at a sheet of paper and found a black space where there should have been a list of patients from Adult Emergency Services who'd gone to Radiology. She felt her hands trembling. Then the nurse found an entry that said Stephanie was still upstairs.

"I'll let you know," the nurse promised.

Rune stood at the window for a long time again, then heard a voice asking for her.

She turned. Froze. The doctor was very young and he had a mournful expression on his face. It seemed that he hadn't slept in a week. Rune wondered if he'd ever told anyone before that a patient had died. Her breath came fast. She gripped the bracelet maniacally.

"You're a friend of the woman hit by the cab?" he asked.

Rune nodded.

He said, "She's transitioned from a deteriorating status."

Rune stared at him. He stared back, waiting for a response.

Finally he tried again. "She's in a stable situation."

"I—" She shook her head, his words not making sense to her.

"She'll be okay," the doctor said.

Rune started to cry.

He continued. "She has a concussion. But there isn't much blood loss. Some bad contusions."

"What's a contusion?"

"A bruise."

"Oh," Rune said softly.

Stephanie, who didn't want to get bruised for her audition.

She asked him, "Is she awake?"

"No. She won't be for a while."

"Thank you, doctor." She hugged him hard. He endured this for a moment then retreated wearily back through the swinging doors.

At the nurses' station Rune asked for a piece of paper and a pen.

Rune wrote:

Steph:
I'm leaving. Thanks for everything. Don't come near me, don't try to contact me. I'll only get you hurt again. Love,

R.

She handed the note to the nurse. "Please give this to her when she wakes up. Oh, and please tell her I'm sorry."

Running again.

Looking behind her, as often as she looked forward. Past garbage cans, litter on the street, puddles. Past the fake, gaudy gold of the Puck Building in SoHo, surrounded by the sour smell of the fringe of the Lower East Side. Running, running. Rune felt the trickle of sweat down her back and sides, the pain in her feet as they slammed on the concrete through the thin soles of her cheap boots.

Air flooded into her lungs and stung her chest.

A block from her loft Rune pressed against the side of a building and looked behind her. No one was following. It was just a peaceful, shabby street. She checked out the street in front of her loft: No police cars, even unmarked ones. Familiar shadows, familiar trash, the same broken-down blue van that had been there for days, plastered with parking tickets. She waited until her pounding heart calmed.

If Emily and Pretty Boy found out about her place, would they come here? Probably not. They'd know the police would be staking it out. Besides, they were probably gone themselves. She'd been the fall guy they needed; their job was done. They'd probably left town.

Which is what I'm going to do. Right now.

Round on the ends and hi in the middle, it's O-Hi-O.

Rune walked around the block then snuck through

the plywood fence of the construction site. Workers in hard hats came and went.

She walked past them quickly, into her building. She started up in the freight elevator, smelling the grease and paint and solvents. She was already sick—from exhaustion and fear—and the scents turned her stomach even more.

The elevator clanked to a stop at the top floor. She unhooked the chain guard and stepped out. No sounds from the loft upstairs. But there was a chance somebody was there. She called, "Rune? It's me. Are you home?" No response. "It's your friend Jennifer. Rune!"

Nothing.

Then up the stairs, slowly, peering out of the opening in the floor. The empty loft stretched out around her. She raced to her side of the loft, grabbed one of the old suitcases she used for a dresser, opened it. She walked around the room, trying to decide what to take.

No clothes. No jewelry—she didn't own much other than her bracelets. She picked some pictures of her family and the friends she'd met in New York. And her books—twenty or so of them, the ones she'd never be able to replace. She considered the videos—Disney, mostly. But she could get new copies of those.

Rune noticed the tape of *Manhattan Is My Beat.* She picked it up and flung it angrily across the room. It crashed into a table, shattering several glasses. The cassette itself broke apart too.

She found a pen and paper. She wrote:

> Sandra, it's been radical rooming with you. I've got the chance to go to England for a couple years. So if anyone comes looking for me, you can tell them that's were I am. I'm not sure where but I think I'll be somewhere near London or Edinborow. Hope your jewelry makes it big, your

designs are really super and if you ever sell it in London I'll buy some. Good lox, Rune.

She folded the paper, left it on Sandra's pillow, and picked up the heavy suitcase.

Which is when she heard the footsteps.

They were on the floor below.

Whoever it was hadn't come up via the elevator. They'd snuck up the stairs. So they wouldn't be heard.

The only exit was the stairway—the one the intruder was now coming up. She heard cautious feet, gritty.

She looked across the loft to her side of the room—at her suitcase and leopard-skin bag.

No time to get a weapon. No time for anything.

Nowhere to run.

She looked around her glass house.

Nowhere to hide.

CHAPTER TWENTY-THREE

He took the stairs one at a time, slowly, slowly.

Pausing, listening.

And struggling to control his anger. Which throbbed like the pain in his face—from when that fucking redhead had nailed him in the subway. Listening above him and listening below. He was out of his uniform now—he'd ditched the meter reader's jacket a while ago, before he trailed the little short-haired bitch to Brooklyn—and downstairs some of the construction guys had given him some shit about just walking into the building. He'd just kept walking, giving them a fuck-you look and not even bothering to make up a cover story.

So, listening for somebody laying in wait for him upstairs, listening for somebody following.

But he heard no footsteps, no breathing, no guns being racked.

Pausing at the top of the stairs, head down.

Okay . . . go!

Walking fast into the loft, eyes taking in places he could go for cover.

Only he didn't have to worry. She wasn't there.

Shit. He'd been sure she'd come back. If only to get her stuff before she took off. Pointing the gun in front of him, he made a circuit of the loft. She'd been there—there was a suitcase half filled. There was that God-ugly purse of hers. But no sign of the bitch.

Maybe—

Then he heard it.

A click and a grind.

The elevator! He ran to the stairs, thinking she'd snuck out behind him. But, no, the cage was empty. It was going down. So, she *was* coming home. He'd gotten there before her.

He ducked behind a half-height wall of cinder block, out of view of the stairway, and waited for her to come to him.

Rune was exactly eight feet away from Pretty Boy, standing in the steady stream of wind outside the loft, a hundred feet above the sidewalk.

Her boots perched on a thin ridge of metal that jutted out six inches from the lower edge of the building's facade. Most of her body was below the glass windows, and if she ducked, Pretty Boy couldn't see her.

Only she was compelled to look.

Because she'd heard the elevator start down. Somebody was coming up!

And Pretty Boy was going to kill them.

Her hands quivered, her legs were weak, as if her muscles were melting. The wind was cold up there, the smells different. Raw. She looked down again, at the cobblestone patches of the street coming through the asphalt. She closed her eyes and pressed her face against her arm for comfort.

Cobblestones—the final scene in *Manhattan Is My Beat.* Ruby Dahl, walking slowly down the wet street, crying for her tormented fiancé gunned down in Greenwich Village.

Roy, Roy, I would have loved you even if you were poor!

Rune looked back into the loft and saw Pretty Boy shift slightly, then cock his ear toward the doorway.

Who was coming up in the elevator? Sandra? Some of the construction guys?

Please, let it be the police—Manelli or Dixon. Coming to arrest her for the shooting in Brooklyn. They had guns. They'd at least have a chance against the killer.

Suddenly, Pretty Boy crouched and held the gun's muzzle up, his right index finger on the trigger. He looked around him, turning his head as though listening.

Whoever was there was calling out some words. Yes, she could vaguely hear a voice, "Rune? Rune? Are you here?" It was a man.

Richard ran up the stairs, shouting something.

No, no, no! she cried silently. Oh, not him. Please, don't hurt him!

She closed her eyes and tried to send him a message of danger. But when she looked again she saw that he'd walked farther into the loft. "Rune?"

Pretty Boy couldn't see him from the other side of the wall. But he was following Richard's steps with the gun. Rune saw him cock it with his long thumb and point it to the spot where Richard was about to appear.

Oh, no . . .

There was nothing else to do. She couldn't let anybody else get hurt because of her. She raised her right fist above the glass. She'd break the window, scream for Richard to run. Pretty Boy would panic and spin around, shoot her. But Richard might just have enough time to leap down the stairs and escape.

Okay, now! Do it.

But just as she started to bring her fist down on the window, Richard paused. He'd seen the note—the note she'd written to Sandra. He picked it up and read it. Then shook his head. He looked around the loft one more time and then started down the stairs.

Pretty Boy peeked out from behind the wall, slipped his gun into his belt. He stood.

Thank you, thank you . . .

Rune lowered her right arm and held on to the ledge again. Pretty Boy searched the loft again, looking for her, then started down the stairs. Rune's fingertips were numb, though her arm muscles ached and her legs were on fire with pain. But she stayed where she was until below her she saw Pretty Boy jog out of the building and disappear east.

She edged to the small access door and crawled inside. She lay on her bed for five minutes until the quivering in her muscles stopped.

Then she picked up the suitcase and purse and left the loft. Not even thinking to say good-bye to her castle in the sky.

On the streets of TriBeCa she paused.

Looking around.

There were construction workers, there were businessmen and businesswomen, there were messengers.

She'd thought Pretty Boy and Emily were gone, wouldn't bother with her. But she'd been wrong there. And that meant they might have other partners. Was it any one of these people?

Several faces glanced at her, and their expressions were dark and suspicious. She shrank back into an alley, hid behind a Dumpster. She'd wait until it was night—just hide there—then hike up to the bus station.

Then she saw a bum coming up the alley. Only he didn't look *quite* like a bum to her. He was dirty like a homeless man and he wore shabby clothes. But his eyes seemed too quick. They seemed dangerous. He looked up and saw her. Paused for just an instant too long. Lowered his head again and continued up the alley.

Ignoring her. But really trying too hard to ignore her.

He was one of them too!

Go, girl. Go! She slung her purse over her shoulder, grabbed the heavy suitcase, and bolted from behind the Dumpster.

The bum saw her, debated a moment, then started running too. Directly behind her.

Rune couldn't run fast, not with the suitcase. She struggled into Franklin Street and paused, gasping, trying to figure which way to go. The bum was getting closer.

Then a man's voice: "Rune!"

She spun around, heart hammering.

"Rune, over here!"

It was Phillip Dixon, the U.S. marshal. He was waving toward her. She started toward him instinctively, then stopped, remembering that he was one of the people who wanted to arrest her.

What should she do?

She was in the middle of the street—thirty feet from the subway. She heard a rumbling underground—a train was approaching. She could vault the turnstile and be on her way uptown in fifteen seconds.

Thirty feet from the bum, running toward her, anger on his face.

Thirty feet from Dixon.

"Rune!" the marshal called. "Come on. It's not safe here. They're around here somewhere. The killers."

"No! You're going to arrest me!"

"I know you didn't kill Symington," Dixon said.

But what else was he going to say? And after the cuffs were on, it'd be: *You have the right to remain silent* . . .

The bum was closer, staring at her with dark, cold eyes.

The train was almost in the station. *Run for it! Now!*

"I want to help you," Dixon shouted. "I've been worried about you." He started across the street but stopped when she turned away from him, started toward the subway.

He held up his hands. "Please! They're after you, Rune. We know what happened. They set you up! They hadn't figured on you getting away in Brooklyn. But we *know* you didn't do it. You were just at the wrong place at the wrong time."

Choose, she told herself. *Now!*

She started across the street tentatively toward Dixon. The bum was closer now, slowing.

"Please, Rune," the marshal said.

Beneath her feet, through the grating, the train eased into the station, brakes squealing.

Choose!

Come on, you've gotta trust *somebody*. . . .

She bolted toward Dixon, ran to his side. He put his arm around her. "It's okay," he said. "You'll be all right."

She blurted out, "There's a man after me. In the alley." And saw a car pulling up at the curb beside them.

The bum turned the corner. He stopped cold as Dixon drew that huge black gun of his.

"Shit," the bum said, holding up his hands. "Hey, man, I'm sorry. I just wanted her purse. No big deal. I'm just going to—"

Dixon fired once. The bullet slammed into the bum's chest. He flew backward.

"Jesus!" Rune cried. "What'd you do that for?"

"He saw my face," Phillip said matter-of-factly, lifting the suitcase and purse away from Rune.

From the car that had just driven up, a woman's voice said to Dixon, "Come on, Haarte, you're standing right out here in broad daylight. There could be cops any minute. Let's go!"

Rune stared at the woman; it was Emily. And the car she was driving was the green Pontiac that had tried to run her and the other witness down at Mr. Kelly's apartment.

Wrong place, wrong time . . .

Phillip—or Haarte—opened the back door of the Pontiac. He shoved Rune inside, tossed her purse and suitcase into the trunk. Haarte got into the backseat with Rune.

"Where to?" Emily asked.

"Better make it my place," he answered calmly. "It's the one with the basement. Quieter, you know."

CHAPTER TWENTY-FOUR

Lost in a forest.

Hansel and Gretel.

Rune stared at the ceiling and wondered what time it was.

Thinking how fast she'd lost track of the hours.

Just like she'd lost track of her life over the past few days.

It reminded her of the time she was a little girl, visiting some relatives with her parents in rural Ohio. She'd wandered away from a picnic in a small state forest. Strolling for hours through the park, thinking she knew where she was going, where her family's picnic bench was. A little confused maybe but, with a child's confidence and preoccupation, never even considering that she was lost. Never knowing that hours had passed and she was miles away from her frantic family.

Now she *knew* how lost she was. And she knew, too, how impossible it was to get home again.

Welcome to reality, Richard would've told her.

The room was tiny. A storeroom in the cellar. It had only one window, a small one she couldn't possibly reach, barred with twisty bars of wrought iron. Part of the concrete floor was missing. The dirt beneath was overturned. When Haarte had shoved her into the room she'd noticed *that* right away: the dug-up dirt. She told herself it was just because he was doing some work down there. Replacing pipes, putting in a new concrete floor.

But she knew it was a grave.

Rune lay on her back and looked at the cold streetlight coming through the unreachable window.

Back-street light.

Light to die by.

There was a sudden metallic snap, and she jumped.

A shuffle of feet outside the door.

A second lock clicked and the door opened. Haarte stood in the doorway. He was cautious. He looked around the room, maybe to see if she'd rigged any traps or found any weapons. Then, satisfied, he nodded for her to follow. Tears of fear pricked in her eyes but she wouldn't let them fall.

He led her up some rickety stairs.

Emily's attention was on her. She was amused, studying Rune like a real estate agent appraising an apartment. When Rune hesitated outside the doorway Haarte pushed her in. Emily didn't seem to like that but she didn't say anything.

No one spoke. Rune felt the tension in the air. Like the scene inside the bank in *Manhattan Is My Beat* where the cop is staring down the robber. His hand is out, not moving, saying over and over, "Give me the pistol, son. Give it to me." The lighting shadowy and stark, the camera moving in close on the muzzle of the .38.

Would the robber shoot or wouldn't he? You wanted to scream from the tension.

Haarte pushed Rune into a cheap dining-room chair, stared down at her. She whimpered, feeling not the least bit adult.

But then, from somewhere in her mind, an image came. An illustration from one of her fantasy books. Diarmuid. Then another: King Arthur.

She ripped his hand off her shoulder. "Don't touch me," she snarled.

He blinked.

Rune waited a moment, staring into his eyes, then walked slowly to the chair. She adjusted it so she was facing Emily and sat down, then said in a sly, tough, Joan Rivers voice, "Can we talk?"

Emily blinked then laughed. "Just what we had in mind."

Haarte pulled up a chair and sat down too.

Rune kept spinning the sole bracelet on her wrist, slipping it on and off. Trying to be tough, looking as hip and cynical as she could. The silver ring spun. She looked down and saw the hands clasped together. She tried not to think about Richard.

Emily said, "We need to know who you told about Spinello and about me."

Rune snapped, "You killed Robert Kelly. Why?"

Emily looked at Haarte. He said, "You could say that it was his fault."

"What?"

"He moved into the wrong apartment," Emily said. "We felt bad. I mean, it looks bad for us. To make a mistake like that. Felt bad for him, too, of course."

Rune exhaled in shock. "He was just . . . You killed him by mistake?"

Haarte continued. "After Spinello testified in the St. Louis RICO cases in January, the U.S. Marshals moved him to New York. Witness protection. They gave him a new identity—Victor Symington—and put him in a place uptown but, well, you saw he was pretty paranoid. He didn't stay where they'd set him up and got the apartment down in the Village. He moved into Apartment 2B. But then he heard there was a bigger apartment available on the third floor. So he moved upstairs. Your friend Kelly moved into Spinello's place."

"The information we had from the people hiring us," Emily said, "was that the hit lived in 2B."

"And, I mean, what can we say?" Haarte reflected. "I checked the directory down in the lobby, but it was so covered up with graffiti, I couldn't read a fucking thing. Besides, Kelly and Spinello looked a lot alike."

"They didn't look a *thing* alike!" Rune spat out.

"Well, they did to me. Hey, accidents happen."

Rune asked, "Then you came back and tore up his place just for the fun of it?"

Haarte looked insulted. "Of course not. We heard on the news that this Robert Kelly guy'd been killed. That wasn't the hit's new name. So we started to think we'd hit the wrong man. I mean, *you* interrupted me during the job. We didn't have time to verify it. I checked out the place later and found a picture of Kelly with his sister, letters. They looked legit."

Rune remembered the torn picture. Haarte had probably lost his temper when he'd realized his mistake then ripped up the photo in anger.

He continued. "Witness relocation doesn't do *that* thorough a job, faking old family pictures. So I figured we'd fucked up. We had to make it right."

Make it *right*? Rune thought.

"When you came to the store," Rune said, "when you pretended to be that U.S. marshal, Dixon, you said you were part of the homicide team at Mr. Kelly's apartment."

"Fuck, of *course* I wasn't there." Haarte laughed. "That's the trick to lying. Make the person you're lying to your partner in the lie. I suggested I was there and you just assumed I was."

Rune remembered Mr. Kelly's apartment, looking through his books, finding the clipping, the heat and the stuffiness of the apartment. The horrible bloodstained chair. The torn photo.

Rune closed her eyes. She left overwhelmed with hopelessness. Her big adventure—it was all because of a mistake. There was no stolen bank loot. Robert Kelly was just a bystander—a weird old man who happened to like a bad movie.

"So, honey, we need to know," Emily said impatiently, "who'd you tell about me?"

"Nobody."

"Boyfriends? Girlfriends? You've had plenty of time to talk to people after you ran out of our little party at Spinello's house in Brooklyn."

"You knew where Spinello was all along?" Rune asked. "And you were just using me?"

"Of course," Emily said, "I just had to lead you there, through the bank and the lawyer, so there'd be a trail the police could find. The cops'd see that you were tracking him down, then they'd find him and your body—we were going to make it look like he shot you after you shot him. They'd have their perp. End of investigation. The police're like everybody else. They prefer the least work possible. Once they've found *a* killer they stop looking for anybody else. On to other cases. You know. So, come on: Who'd you tell?"

"Why would I say anything to anybody?"

"Oh, come on," Haarte said. "You see somebody killed right in front of you and you don't tell the police?"

"How could I? My fingerprints were all over Spinello's apartment. I *knew* I was a suspect. I figured out what you were doing."

"No, you didn't," Haarte said. "You're not that smart."

Rune remained silent. At least one thing was good, Rune thought. They don't know about Stephanie.

Suddenly Haarte leapt up from the chair, grabbed Rune's hair, and jerked her head back so far she couldn't breathe. She was choking. His face was close to hers. "See, you think it's better to live. No matter what I do to you. But it isn't. The only way we could let you live—and we aren't really inclined to kill you—but the only way we'd *let* you live is if we make it so that you can't tell anybody about us. Pick us out of a lineup, say."

He moved a finger slowly down toward her eye. She closed the lid and a moment later felt increasing pain as he pressed hard on her eyeball.

"No!"

His fingers lifted off her face. "There's a *lot* we could do to you." His hand massaged the back of her neck. "We could make you a vegetable." He touched her breasts. "Or a boy." Between her legs. "Or . . ."

He released her hair so quickly that she screamed. Emily looked on without emotion.

Rune caught her breath. "Please let me go. I won't say anything."

"It's demeaning to beg," Emily said.

"I'll give you the million dollars," she said.

"What million?" Haarte asked. "From that old movie? That's bullshit."

"Oh," Emily said, laughing, "your secret treasure?"

"I will. I found it!"

Haarte asked cynically, "You did?"

"Sure. Where do you think I've been for the past twenty-four hours? After what happened in Brooklyn, you think I'm going to hang around town? Why didn't I just leave yesterday as soon as you killed Spinello? I didn't leave because I had a lead to the money."

Haarte considered this. Rune thought he was genuinely intrigued. Rune, hands together, was kneading her one remaining silver bracelet. "It's true, I promise."

He shook his head. "No, doesn't make sense."

"Mr. Kelly *did* have the money. I found it. It's in a locker at the bus station."

"That sounds like a scene out of a movie," Emily said slowly.

"Whatever it sounds like, it's true."

They were both sort of believing her now. Rune could tell.

Rune fiddled with the bracelet again. "A million dollars!"

Haarte said to Emily, "It's old money. How hard to move?"

"Not that hard," she said. "They're always finding old bills. Banks have to take 'em. And the good news is even if they took the serial numbers years ago, nobody's gonna have the records anymore."

"You know anybody who could take 'em?"

"A couple guys. We could probably get seventy, eighty points on the dollar."

But then Haarte shook his head again. "No, it's crazy."

"A million dollars," Rune repeated. "Aren't you getting tired of killing people for a living?"

There was a pause. Haarte and Emily avoided each other's eyes.

The room was sepia, gloomy, lit by two dim lamps. Rune looked out the window. Outside, it was very dark, with only that one cold streetlight nearby. She played nervously with her bracelet, squeezing it.

Haarte and Emily whispered to each other, their heads down. Emily finally nodded and looked up. "Okay, here's the deal. You give us the names of everyone you've told about me and hand over the money, we'll let you live. You don't tell us, I'll let Haarte here take you downstairs and do whatever he wants."

Rune thought for a moment. "What will you do with them? Whoever I told?"

Haarte said, "Nothing. As long as there are no police after us. But if there are then we might have to hurt them."

Rune squeezed the bracelet again several times. Hard. It snapped in half.

She looked up. "You're lying."

"Honey—" Emily began.

That's the trick to lying. Make the person you're lying to your partner in the lie.

"But that's all right," Rune said matter-of-factly. "Because I was too." And leapt out of the chair.

CHAPTER TWENTY-FIVE

Emily laughed.

Because Rune might have run toward the front door of the town house or the rear. Or tried for a window. But she didn't do either. Instead, she rolled toward a small door in the living room.

"Rune," Emily said patiently, "what do you think you're doing? That's a closet."

And a locked one, at that, Rune learned, tugging on the glass knob.

Haarte looked at Emily. He shook his head at Rune's stupidity. There was no way out. She'd boxed herself in. Rune glanced back at them and saw with relief that they didn't have a clue what she really had in mind.

Until Rune jumped for the electric outlet she'd had her eye on for five minutes.

"No!" Emily shouted to Haarte. "She's going to—"

Rune pushed the two ends of the broken bracelet into the socket.

This bracelet, mon, she be important in your life, very important. Don't be too fast to give her away. . . .

There was a fierce white flash and a loud crack. Pure stinging fire poured through her thumb and finger. The lights throughout the town house went out as the fuse popped from the short circuit. She smelled the scorched-meat scent of the burn on her finger and thumb.

Instantly, ignoring the pain, she was on her feet and running. Emily and Haarte, blinded by the flash, were groping toward the doorway. Rune, who'd had her eyes closed when the spark arced, was already thirty feet ahead of them, running cautiously, crouched, toward the front door, her useless right arm cradled in her left hand.

She missed the two steps down, from the hallway to the entry foyer, and fell heavily forward. Her right arm shot out in front of her instinctively, and she felt the searing pain as the burned hand broke her fall. She couldn't stop the grunt of pain.

"There—she's over there," Emily called. "I'll get her."

Rune climbed to her feet, hearing the woman's high heels clattering after her. She couldn't see Haarte anywhere. Maybe he was down in the basement, changing the fuse.

Rune leapt toward the front door, chilled by panic from the thought of Emily, undoubtedly armed, moving close behind her.

She reached for the top latch on the door. Then stopped, stepped slowly, stepped back against the wall. No! Christ no!

There was a man outside. She couldn't see clearly through the lacy curtains but she knew it had to be Pretty Boy. Haarte's and Emily's partner. The halo of curly hair caught pale light from the street. He seemed to be looking in the window, wondering why the lights had gone off inside.

Rune turned and started toward the back of the house.

Slowly, listening for Emily's heels and Haarte's footsteps.

But there was no sound at all. Had they fled? Rune turned the corner and froze. There, only four or five feet away, was Emily, who inched forward, feeling her way along the wall, holding a gun. She'd kicked off her shoes, was silently barefoot.

Rune pressed against the wall. The woman's head turned, squinting into the gloom. Probably hearing Rune's shallow breathing. She had a vague image of the woman's silhouette lifting the gun. Pointing it toward Rune.

She'll hear my heart beating! She *has* to hear that.

And that it may please thee to preserve all who are in danger by reason of their labor.

The silenced gun fired with a loud clicking *pop*. There was a fierce slap as the bullet hit the plaster a foot away from Rune's head.

We beseech thee to hear us, good Lord.

Another shot, closer.

Rune struggled with all her will to remain silent.

Emily turned toward the front door. Rune's groping fingers grabbed the closest thing she could find—a heavy vase on a pedestal. She raised it and flung it hard toward the woman. It was a solid hit. Emily cried out in a high wail and fell to her knees. The gun disappeared into the shadows. The vase thudded, unbroken, onto the parquet.

"I can't find the fuses!" Haarte's voice shouted from very near. "Where the hell is she?"

"Help me!" Emily called.

Haarte walked forward. "I can't see a fucking thing."

Rune dodged out of his way.

"There!" Emily called. "Beside you!"

"What—" Haarte began, and Rune sprinted down the hallway, heading toward where the back door should be.

Yes! There it was. She could see it. And it didn't look like anybody was outside.

She heard Haarte's voice in the front of the house, calling to Emily.

And Rune knew then that it was going to be all right; she could escape. They were nowhere near her and Rune had to spring only twenty feet or so to get to the back door. She slammed the hallway door shut, wedged a chair under the knob, and kept running.

Haarte got to the door in a few seconds and tried to open it but it was tightly blocked.

Rune could see dim light coming through the lace curtains on the back door.

Nothing could stop her now. She'd get outside, into the alley, run like hell. Call 911 from the first phone she found.

Haarte slammed into the door and pushed it open slightly, but the chair still held.

Fifteen feet. Ten.

Another slam.

"Go around, through the kitchen," Haarte called to Emily.

But their voices were a world away. Rune was at the door. She was safe.

She undid the chain. Turned the latch and then the knob. She swung the door wide and stepped out onto the back porch.

And stopped cold.

Oh, no . . .

No more than two feet away from her was Pretty Boy. He was startled but not so startled he didn't lift his pistol like a quick-draw gunslinger and point it directly at her face.

No, no, no . . .

She leaned back against the doorjamb. Tears streaming down her face. Arms limp, shaking her head. Oh, no . . . It's over. It's over.

But then something odd happened, the sort of thing that happened in the Side, in the magic realm. Rune seemed to go out of her body. She felt as if she died and rose away into the air. Actually wondering—did he shoot me? Am I dead?

Floating away. Completely numb. Sailing up into the air.

And from there, from a cloud hovering over the Side, she looked down and saw:

Pretty Boy putting his arm around her and leading her away from the open back door of the town house, handing her off to another man behind him, a man in a blue jacket that said U.S. MARSHAL on the back, and from there to another man wearing what looked like a bulletproof vest printed with the letters "NYPD." Passed along again until finally at the end of the line was Detective Manelli, with his close-together eyes, with his funny first name.

Virgil Manelli.

The detective held a finger to his lips to keep Rune quiet, then led her away from the house. She looked back at the line of men clustered around the door. Big men with stony faces, wearing suits of thick blue armor and carrying stubby machine guns.

On the sidewalk, Manelli handed her off one last time—to two medics, who put her on a cot and began hovering over her, pouring ice water on her burnt hand and then wrapping it with bandages.

Rune paid no attention. She kept her eyes on the men around the back door. Then Pretty Boy said into a microphone on his collar, "Subject is clear. Move in, move in, move in!"

Everyone on the stairs, all the knights, charged

into the building, shouting, "Police, police, federal agents . . ." Flashlights illuminated the interior of the town house.

Rune heard a funny sound. Laughter. She looked at the attendant. But he wasn't laughing. His partner wasn't either. She realized that the sound was coming from her.

Delicately, one of the medics asked, "What's so funny?"

But she didn't answer. Because from inside the town house came the sound of gunshots. Then calls of "Medic, medic!"

And the men in the ambulance left her while they ran toward the back door with their bags in hand, their stethoscopes flapping around their necks.

CHAPTER TWENTY-SIX

She huddled away from him. From Pretty Boy.

"I want to see something. Some identification."

They were sitting in the back of a new-smelling Ford. Government issue. Manelli stood outside.

The NYPD detective rubbed his mustache and said, "He's legit."

"I want to *see* something!" Rune snapped.

Pretty Boy offered her his badge and an ID card.

She looked at the card three times before she actually read everything. His name was Salvatore Pistone.

"Call me Sal. Everybody does."

"You're, like, an FBI agent."

"You just insulted me. I'm a U.S. marshal." He was smiling. But his eyes were oddly cold.

"That's what Haarte said."

"Yeah, I found his fake badge and ID. He's used that identity before. Frosts me how often people don't fucking bother to read ID cards. You had, you woulda seen his was fake."

The medic stopped by the car. "Soak that hand in Betadine solution tonight before you go to bed. Tomorrow see your doctor. You know what Betadine is?"

She had no idea. She nodded yes.

Then, to Manelli, the man said, "Guy's dead."

Sal scoffed. "I shot him three times in the head. What the fuck else would he be?"

"Yeah, well. It's confirmed."

"Who?" Rune asked. "Haarte?"

Sal said, "Yeah. Haarte."

"The woman, she'll be okay?" Manelli asked.

"Hell of a bruise on her back. Don't have a clue how she got that—"

Rune remembered the vase. Wish she'd aimed for Emily's head.

"—but aside from that she'll be fine. The bitch'll *definitely* see the inside of a courtroom."

Manelli straightened up. "All right, miss, I'm handing you over to the feds. It's their case now. You shoulda listened to me and stayed out—"

"I—"

He held up a finger to his lips, shushing her again. "You shoulda listened." He walked off to his own car. He glanced at her with his close-together eyes but they were expressionless. He got inside, started the engine, and drove off.

Other cars were leaving. More of the nondescript sedans, some city blue-and-white police cars. And the small Emergency Service Unit trucks. The ESU men and women, like soldiers after a battle, were taking off their vests and loading the guns back into their car trunks or the compartments of the trucks.

"Who was he?"

"Samuel Haarte," Sal replied. "Professional hit man."

"I'm so confused."

She watched Sal's face. She decided there was something a little crazy about him. Indoctrinated. Like with the Moonies. She had this love/hate thing with Detective Manelli but she liked him. Sal scared her.

"She killed Victor Symington," Rune told him. "Emily did."

"So she was going by the name Emily. Any last name?"

"Richter."

"Haarte usually worked with somebody named Zane. I always thought it was a guy. But it must be her. One fucking tough woman."

Sal dug around in the back of the car, found a thermos, and sat back. He poured some coffee into the lid and offered it to her. "Black. Sweet." She took it and sipped the coffee. It was so strong it made her shiver.

Sal drank directly from the thermos. "Symington—I mean Spinello—he'd be alive if he hadn't panicked. He shouldn't've took off."

"What happened?" Rune asked.

He explained. "I'm with the Witness Protection Program. You know, giving federal witnesses new identities. Spinello and another witness—"

"That guy in St. Louis I read about?"

"Right. Arnold Gittleman. Spinello and Gittleman testified against some syndicate guys in the Midwest."

"But if they already testified, why kill them?"

Sal laughed coldly at her naiveté. "It's called revenge, sweetheart. To send the message that nobody else better talk. Anyway, Spinello took off—he didn't trust us to keep his ass safe and moved down to the Village on his own. Never told his handler about it. I was part of the team in the hotel in St. Louis guarding Gittleman." His cold eyes grew sad for a splinter of a second. Not an emotion he was used to, it seemed. "I went out to get some sandwiches and beer and those assholes got Gittleman and my partners."

"I'm sorry."

He shrugged off the sympathy. "So I went undercover to nail the pricks." Sal looked at the house. "And we sure as shit did. Looks like they were the only ones too. We waited as long as we could here in case somebody else showed up. But nobody did."

"What do you mean, you waited as long as you could?"

He shrugged. "We've been cooling our heels outside here for five fucking hours."

"Five hours!" she shouted. Then it became clear. "I *led* you here! I was bait."

Sal considered this. "Basically. Yeah."

"You son of a bitch! How long've you been following me?"

"You know that old blue van in front of your loft? With all the tickets?"

"That was yours?" she asked, dumbfounded.

"Sure."

"What'd you come up in my loft for? Earlier today?"

He frowned. "Actually, at that point, we figured you were dead. I was checking it out to see if your body was up there."

"Jesus Maria . . ." She nodded to the door. Ripped into him with a sarcastic "I hope when I escaped just now I didn't totally screw up your plans."

"Naw," Sal said, sipping more coffee. "It was good it worked out the way it did. They *might've* used you as a hostage. It was—whatta you say?—convenient you got away when you did."

"Convenient?" Rune spat. "You used me. Just like Emily did. You followed me to Brooklyn to find out where Symington was. And you followed me here to catch them!"

Now Sal grew angry too. "Listen. For a week, I thought you *might've* been one of the hit team. Think about it. We have a city police report that you were on the scene just after the Kelly killing. Then, when I'm staking out the site of the hit—that tenement on Tenth Street—you go in. Then Spinello runs outside and vanishes, like you scared the crap out of him. And then we had more reports that somebody who fits your description,—except is about nine months pregnant—has broken into Kelly's apartment and ransacked the hell out of it."

"That wasn't me," Rune protested. "It was them."

"But you *did* break in."

"The door was practically open."

"Hey, I'm not after any B and E count. I'm just telling you why I didn't walk up to you and introduce myself. Shit. And when we figured out you were an innocent and I tried talking to you, your friend the redhead just about breaks my nose and some fucking bodybuilder closes my throat up."

"How were we supposed to know?"

"Anyway, yeah, they found your prints all over Spinello's safe house in Brooklyn. But we checked you out pretty good and you didn't seem like the sort that Haarte or Zane'd hire. I talked to Manelli about you and we decided you were pretty much who you seemed to be. Just a kid in over her head."

"I'm not a kid."

"Yeah, I wouldn't take points on that one. What the hell were you doing in this mess in the first place?"

Rune told him about Mr. Kelly and the money and the movie.

"A million dollars?" Sal laughed. "Gimme a break. Stick with lotto. Or numbers. Better odds, sweetheart." He nodded. "But, yeah, that's what Manelli was thinking—that Kelly's death was a mistake. Well, whatever . . . That woman's going down. It's the prosecutor's game now. Good thing we've got a star witness."

"Who?" Rune asked. Then, when he just gave her a wry look, she said, "Hey, forget it. No way. They'll send another Haarte after me."

"Hey, not to worry," Sal said, finishing the coffee. "The Witness Relocation Program, remember? You'll get a whole new identity. You can be anybody you want. You can even make up your own name."

Sal frowned: he must have been wondering why she was laughing.

"Well, what do you think?" Rune called.

She sat sidesaddle, five feet off the ground, on a huge armature that rose phallic and rusty from a complicated tangle of industrial machinery scrap. They were surrounded by piles of pitted chrome and girders, wire, wrecks of trucks, and turbines and gears.

Richard walked around the corner. "Fantastic."

The junkyard was off Seventieth, in commercial Queens. But it was oddly quiet. They looked west, at the huge slash of orange brilliance behind Manhattan, as the sun eased through strips of dark cloud.

"You come here much?" he asked.

"Only for the sunsets."

The light hit the twisted metal and seemed to make the different shades of rust vibrate. A thousand oil drums became beautiful. Spindles of twisted iron became filaments of light and coils of BX cable were glowing snakes. Rune said, "Come on up!"

She was wearing the Spanish outfit once more. Richard climbed up next to her and they walked along the armature to a platform.

They had a magnificent view of the city.

On the platform was an old picnic basket. A bottle of champagne too.

"Warm," Rune apologized, cradling the bottle. "But it looks classy."

When they'd snuck through the fence a half hour ago, Richard had gazed at the Dobermans uneasily and stood paralyzed when one sniffed his crotch. But Rune knew them well and scratched their smooth heads. They wagged their stubby tails, sniffing at the cold macaroni-and-cheese sandwiches Rune had packed in the basket before prancing away on their springy legs.

Rune and Richard ate until dusk. Then she lit a kerosene lantern. She lay back, using the picnic basket as a pillow.

"I got another application to the New School," she told him. "I kind of threw out the one you gave me."

"You going to apply? For real?"

After a moment she asked, "I guess I'd have to take classes, wouldn't I?"

"It's an important part of going to school."

"That's what I figured. I'm not sure I'm going to do it though. I have to tell you." She snuck a furtive glimpse at his face. "See, this guy at the video store, Frankie Greek, remember him? Anyway, his sister just had a baby and she was a window designer and it turns out I can take her job while she's on leave. Only have to work half-days. Leave me free to do other stuff."

"What kind of stuff?"

"You know, stuff stuff."

"Rune."

"Oh, it'd be a radical job. Very artistic. In SoHo. Discounts for clothes. Slinky dresses. Lingerie."

"You're hopeless, you know that."

"Well, to be totally honest, I already took the job and threw out the other application too." She stared at the two or three stars whose light was bright enough to penetrate the city haze. "I had to do it, Richard. I *had* to. I was worried that if I got a degree or anything I'd get to be, like, too literal."

"We couldn't have that, could we?"

Then the stars were blocked out completely, as Richard leaned over her, bringing his mouth down slowly on hers. She lifted her head to meet him. They kissed for a long while, Rune astonished that she could be aroused by someone wearing a button-down shirt and Brooks Brothers slacks.

Very slow, it was all very slow.

Though not like slow motion in a film. More like vignettes, frame by frame, the way you'd hit a VCR pause button over and over again to watch a favorite scene.

The way she'd watched *Manhattan Is My Beat.*

Freeze-frame: The cloth of his collar. His smooth neck. His paisley eyes. The white bandage on her hand.

Freeze-frame: His mouth.

"We going to be safe?" he whispered.

"Sure," Rune whispered. She reached into the pocket of her skirt and handed him the small, crinkly square of plastic.

"Actually," he said, "I meant because we're twenty feet in the air."

"Don't worry," Rune whispered. "I'll hold you real tight. I won't let you fall."

Freeze-frame: She wrapped her arms around him.

CHAPTER TWENTY-SEVEN

"I don't howl."

In the loft Sandra was putting explosive red polish on her toenails. She continued sourly. "That was the deal. Remember? I don't howl when I'm in bed with a guy and you clean up after yourself."

She nodded at the mess Rune had made when she was frantically packing. "I have somebody over, I'm quiet as a mouse. *He* howls, there's nothing I can do about it. But me, I ask you, am I quiet, or what?"

"You're quiet." Rune bent over and picked up clothes, swept up the broken glass.

"Do I howl?"

"You don't howl."

"So where were you last night?" Sandra asked.

"We went to a junkyard."

"Brother, that boy's got a way to go." Sandra glanced up from her artistic nails, examined Rune critically. "You look happy. Got lucky, huh?"

"Didn't your mother teach you not to pry?"

"No, my mother's the one who taught me *how* to pry. So, you get lucky?"

Rune ignored her and repacked her clothes, put the books back on the shelf.

She paused. On the floor beside the bookcase was the shattered cassette of *Manhattan Is My Beat*. Rune picked it up. The loops of opaque tape hung out of the broken plastic reels. She looked at it for a moment. She was thinking of Robert Kelly. Of the movie. About the million dollars of bank loot that was never really there—never there for *her* to find anyway.

She tossed the cassette into the trash bin. Then glanced at Sandra's side of the loft. She picked up the good-bye note she'd written to her roommate. It was unopened. "Don't you read your mail?" she asked.

The woman glanced at it. "Whatsit? A love note?"

"From me."

"What's it say?"

"Nothing." Rune threw it out too. Then she flopped down on her pillows, staring into the blue-and-white sky. She remembered the clouds in New Jersey floating over the trimmed grounds of the nursing home as she crouched next to Raoul Elliott's wheelchair. They'd seemed like dragons and giants then, the clouds. She stared at them for a long time now. After the horror of the last few days she expected them to look merely like clouds. But, no, they still seemed like dragons and giants.

The more things change, the more they stay the same.

An expression of her father's.

She thought about the old screenwriter, Raoul Elliott. Next week she'd go out and visit him again. Bring him another flower. And maybe a book. She could read to him. Stories are the best, he'd said. Rune agreed with him there.

Five minutes later Sandra said, "Shit. I forget. Some

geek from that place you work, or used to work, the video store? Looked like a heavy-metal wanna-be."

"Frankie?"

"I don't know. Maybe. He came by with a couple of messages." She read a slip of paper. "One was from this Amanda LeClerc. He said he couldn't understand her too good. She's, like, foreign and he was saying if they come to this country why don't they learn to speak-a the language."

"The point, Sandra?"

"So this Amanda person, she called and said she'd heard from this priest or minister or somebody in Brooklyn. . . ." Sandra, juggling the nail polish, smoothed the wrinkled note.

Rune sat up.

A minister?

Sandra was struggling to read. "Like, I'm really not programmed to be a message center, you know. Yeah, okay. I got it. She said she talked to this minister and he's got this suitcase. It was somebody's named Robert Kelly's."

A *suitcase*?

"And he doesn't know what to do with it, the minister. But he said it's, like, very important."

Rune screamed, "Yes!" She rolled on her back, and her legs, straight up in the air, kicked back and forth.

"Whoa, take a pill or something." Sandra handed her the message.

She read it. St. Xavier's Church on Atlantic Avenue. Brooklyn.

"Oh, and here's the other one." She found another slip in her purse.

It was from Stephanie. She was out of the hospital and feeling a lot better. She'd stop by later.

"All right!" Rune cried.

"I'm glad *somebody's* happy." Sandra added, "I'm depressed. Not that anybody cares." She continued to paint her nails carefully.

"I've got to call Richard. We're taking a trip."

"Where?"

"Brooklyn!"

"Old folks homes, junkyards . . . Why am I not surprised? Hey, don't hug me! Watch the polish!"

Rune got Richard at home.

This was weird. It was the afternoon. What was he doing home?

She realized that he hadn't told her exactly *where* he wrote his boring meet-your-CEO scripts.

Rune was on the street, calling from the pay phone. "Hey, how come you're home? I thought you worked for a company. With what's her name? Too-tall Karen?"

He laughed again. "I do mostly freelance. I'm sort of an independent contractor."

"We need to go to Brooklyn. A church on Atlantic Avenue. Can you drive?"

He said, "You're home now?"

"I'm in my office."

"Office?" he asked.

"My exterior office."

"Oh." He laughed. "A pay phone."

"So, can we go?"

"What's going on in Brooklyn?"

She told him about the minister's message, then added, "I just called him—the priest Amanda found. I sort of told him a white lie."

"Which was?"

"That I'm Robert Kelly's granddaughter."

"That's not a white lie. It's a full-fledged lie. Especially to a man of the cloth. You oughta be ashamed.

Anyway, I thought you were going to forget about the money."

"I did. Forgot completely. It was *him* called me." She persisted. Said that Mr. Kelly'd been living in a home attached to the church until he found an apartment. And that he'd left a suitcase with the minister for safekeeping. He didn't want to carry it around until he was settled. It was—are you listening? He said it was too valuable to him to just carry around the streets of the city."

Another pause.

"It's too crazy," Richard said.

She added, "And get this. I asked him if there was a cemetery nearby—like in the movie *Manhattan Is My Beat*. See, Dana Mitchell, the cop, buries the money in a new grave. And there is!"

"Is what?"

"A cemetery. Next to the church. Don't you see? Mr. Elliott told Mr. Kelly about the church and Mr. Kelly went there and dug up the money."

"Okay," he said dubiously. Then he asked, "You're at your loft?"

"Will be in five minutes."

He said seductively, "You going to be by yourself?"

"Sandra's there."

"Bummer. Can't you send her out to buy something?"

"How 'bout we go to Brooklyn now. Then we'll think about some privacy."

"I'm on my way."

Rune reached the stop of the stairs in her loft and stopped.

"Stephanie!"

The redhead smiled wanly. She sat in Rune's half of the loft, on a pile of pillows. She was pale—paler than usual—and she wore a scarf that partially covered a bruise on her neck. There was also large bandage on her temple and an eggplant-colored mark on her cheek.

"Ohmygod," Rune blurted out, examining her. "You *do* bruise, don't you?" She hugged the woman carefully. "You look, well. . . ."

"I look awful. You can say it."

"Not for somebody who got run over by a cab."

"Hey, there's a compliment for you."

There was dense silence for a moment. "I don't know what to say, Steph." Rune was nervous and she did busywork, straightening up clothes. "I got you involved in this whole thing. I almost got you killed. And it was so stupid—we were running from a federal marshal."

"A what?" Stephanie gave a laugh.

"That guy in the subway, the one you hit—I thought he was working for *them*. But it turned out he was a U.S. marshal. Isn't that radical? Just like the Texas Rangers."

She told Stephanie about Haarte and Emily.

"I heard something about it on the news, in the hospital," Stephanie said. "A shooting at this town house. I never guessed you were involved."

Rune's eyes were excited again. "Oh, oh, and talk about adventures . . . . They want me to be the star witness."

"Isn't that scary?"

"Sure. But I don't care. I want that bitch to go away for a long time. They killed Mr. Kelly. And they tried to kill me—and you too."

"Well, I'm pretty sure there'll be plenty of cops to look out for you."

Rune wandered to the bookcase, replaced some of the books she'd packed to take home. "I called the video store. They told me you quit."

"That Tony," Stephanie said, "what an asshole. I couldn't deal with him—not the way he treated you."

Rune grinned coyly. "So, you want a hundred thousand dollars?"

"What?"

Rune told her about the minister. "Little Red Hen, remember? You believed in me. If there really is any money, you'll get some of it."

Stephanie laughed. "You think there is?"

"I'm not sure. But you know me."

"Optimist," Stephanie supplied.

"You got it. I—"

Plop.

Rune cocked her head. She heard the sound again. A drip. Soft. *Plop.*

She glanced at where it was coming from—Sandra's side of the apartment.

"You don't really have to give me anything, Rune."

"I know I don't *have* to. But I want to."

Plop, plop.

Damn! Sandra'd spilled her nail polish. There was a big red stain on the floor.

"Jesus, Sandra!"

Rune turned the corner and stopped. There was her roommate in her thick white bra and black panty hose, eyes staring at the apex of the glass ceiling. She lay on her futon. The bullet hole in her chest was a tiny dark dot. The stain wasn't nail polish. It was the blood that was trickling down her arm and onto the floor.

Stephanie stood up and pointed the gun at Rune. She said, "Come on back over here, love. Let's have a little talk."

CHAPTER TWENTY-EIGHT

"You're Haarte's partner," Rune whispered.

She nodded. "My name's Lucy Zane," the woman said coldly. "Haarte and I worked together for three years. He was the best partner I ever had. And he's dead. Thanks to you."

"Then who's Emily?"

"Just backup. We use her sometimes for jobs on the East Coast."

Rune, sitting down on the cushions, shaking her head. Everything floating in front of her—a big soup. Richard, the money, Pretty Boy, Emily, and Haarte. Robert Kelly. She felt the slamming of her heart in her chest as the hopelessness arose again. And she lowered her face into her hands. Whispering: "Oh, no, oh, no."

She was too numb for tears. Not even looking up, she said, "But your job at the video store? How'd you get the job?"

"How do you think? I fucked Tony."

"I hope it was disgusting," Rune spat out.

"Was. But it didn't last long. A minute or two."

"But you were my friend. . . . You helped me get the clothes. . . . Why? Why'd you do that?"

"I got close to you so we could set you up. Haarte and I killed two U.S. marshals in St. Louis. That put a lot of heat on us. And we fucked up the Spinello hit in the Village. So we needed a fall guy. Well, fall *girl*. You got elected. Almost worked too."

"Too bad the cab had good brakes," Rune said coldly.

"We're lucky sometimes. Even people like me."

Rune shook with anger and fear.

Stephanie continued. "I heard from Emily. The judge denied her bail request. But she said to say hello. She hopes you and I'd have a nice visit. And I think we will. Now, there's one thing I've got to know. Did you tell the cops or marshals anything about me?"

A click and a grind sounded behind them. Rune's eyes flashed for a second.

Richard.

Stephanie glanced at the sound, then turned back to Rune.

"Tell me," she said. "And I'll let you go."

"Bullshit." Rune scrabbled away into the cushions as if they'd protect her from the black gun.

"I'll let you go," the woman said. "I promise."

"I'm the only witness. How can you let me go? You *have* to kill me." She looked at the clouds outside the loft, the dragons, the giants, the trolls, marching past, miles high, not caring a bit for what was going on down on earth.

The grinding started again. The elevator was coming up.

"You must've told them about me after the accident. Did the marshal I hit in the subway think I was part of them? Did you tell them my name?"

"It's not real."

"No, but I've used it before. I can be traced through it."

Chains, clinking chains. And the grind of metal on metal. Another loud click, a scrape.

"Who's coming to visit, Rune?"

"I don't know."

Stephanie glanced at the stairway. Then back at Rune. She said, "So, what do you have in your hand."

Rune couldn't believe that the woman had seen her. Oh, she was good. She was very good.

"Show me," Stephanie persisted.

Rune hesitated, then held up her hand and slowly opened the bandaged fingers. "The piece of stone. From the Union Bank Building. My souvenir. The one I picked up when you were with me that day down in Wall Street."

"Now, what were you going to do with it?"

"Throw it at you," Rune responded. "Smash your goddamn face."

"Why don't you just toss it over there." Lucy Zane held the silenced gun very steadily on Rune's chest.

Rune pitched the stone away.

Just as Richard climbed the stairs and said, "Hi."

He froze, seeing the gun in Stephanie's hand. "What is this?"

Stephanie waved him in. "Okay. Just stand there." She backed up so that she could keep them both covered. She held the gun out straight. It was small and its black metal gleamed in the sunlight. The short cylinder of the silencer was dark too.

Her voice now had an edge to it. "I don't have much time. Who'd you tell about me, Rune? And what did you tell them? I want to know. And I mean now."

"Let him go."

Richard said, "What the hell is this? Are you two joking?"

Stephanie's left hand went out toward him. Palm up. The nails were done in careful purple-pink. "Shut up, asshole. Just shut up." To Rune: "*What* did you tell them?"

"God," Richard whispered, looking at Rune.

Rune sank back into the cushions, put her hands over her eyes, sobbing. "No, no . . . I don't give a shit about you or Emily or anybody. I won't testify. I'll tell them it wasn't Emily or you. Mr. Kelly's dead! Spinello's dead! Just leave us alone."

Stephanie said patiently, "Maybe I'll consider that. You have to understand, Rune. I like you. I really do. You're . . . charming. And I was really touched you were going to give me some of that ridiculous money. That almost choked me up. But you have to tell me. This's just business."

"All right . . . I didn't tell anybody anything about you."

"I don't believe you."

"It's true! All I did was write about you in my diary. I mentioned you and Emily." She sat back, hand in her lap, small, defeated. "I thought you were my friend. I described you and wrote how nice you were to help me buy some clothes."

If this choked her up too, Stephanie's expression didn't show it.

"Where is it?" the woman asked. "The diary. Let me have it and I'll let you go. Both of you."

"Promise?"

"I promise."

Rune debated then walked to her suitcase, rummaged through it. "I can't find it." She looked up, frowning. "I thought I packed it." She opened her leopard-skin bag, looked through that too. "I don't know. I . . . oh, there it is. On the bookcase. The second shelf."

Stephanie eased over to the bookcase. Touched a notebook. "This one?"

"No, the one next to it. On its side."

Stephanie pulled the book off the shelf and flipped it open. "Where do you mention—"

An explosion. The first bullet broke a huge chunk out of the blue-sky wall and sent fragments of cinder block raining through the room.

The second shattered a panel of glass in the ceiling.

The third tore apart a dozen books, which pitched through the air like shot birds.

The fourth caught Stephanie squarely in the chest as she was turning, shocked, mouth open, toward Rune.

There may even have been a fifth shot. And a sixth. Rune wasn't sure. She had no idea how many times she pulled the trigger of the gun—the one that Rune had pulled from the accordion folder she'd thrown away earlier—tossed into the trash can beside her bed.

All Rune saw was the smoke and dust and paper flecks and clouds and blue sky of concrete and broken glass flying through the loft around Stephanie—beautiful, pale Stephanie, who spiraled to the floor.

And all Rune heard was a huge ringing roar from the gun. Which, after a few seconds, as Richard scrambled from the floor and started toward her, was replaced by an animal's mad screaming she didn't even know was coming from her.

CHAPTER TWENTY-NINE

Head bowed at the altar, Rune was motionless.

Kneeling. She'd thought she could remember all the words. But they wouldn't come to her and all she could do was repeat over and over again, in a mumbling whisper, "We yield thee praise and thanksgiving for our deliverance from those great and apparent dangers wherewith we were compassed."

After a moment she stood and walked slowly up the aisle toward the back of the sanctuary.

Still whispering, she said to the man wearing black minister's robes, "This is a totally radical church, Reverend."

"Thank you, Miss Kelly."

At the door, she turned and curtsied awkwardly toward the altar. The minister of St. Xavier's glanced at her curiously. Maybe curtsying—which Rune had just seen a character do in some old Mafia movie—was only for Catholics. But so what? she decided. Stephanie was right about one thing: short of devil worship and animal sacrifices, ministers and priests probably aren't all that sensitive about technicalities.

They left the sanctuary.

"Your grandfather didn't mention any children when he stayed with us in our residence. He said his only relative was his sister but she'd died a few years ago."

"Really?" she asked.

"But then," the minister continued, "he didn't talk much about himself. He was a bit mysterious in some ways."

Mysterious . . .

"Yep," she said after a moment. "That was Grandfather. We used to say that about him. 'Wasn't Grandfather quiet.' All of us would say it."

"All of you? I thought you said there were just two of you. You and your sister."

"Oh, well, I mean all the kids in the neighborhood. He was like a grandfather to them too."

Watch it, Rune told herself. It's a minister you're lying to. And a minister with a good memory.

She followed the man through the rectory building. Filled with dark wood, wrought iron. The small yellow lights added a lot of churchy atmosphere to the place, though maybe they used small-wattage bulbs just to save money. It was very . . . well, *religious* here. Rune tried to remember a good movie she'd seen about religion and couldn't think of one. They tended not to have happy endings.

They walked into a large dormitory, newer than the church, though the architecture was the same—stained glass, arches, flowery carvings. She looked around. It was some kind of residence hall for senior citizens. Rune glanced into a room as they passed. Two beds, yellow walls, mismatched dressers. Lots of pictures on the walls. Homier than you'd think. There were two elderly men inside the room. As she paused, looking in, one of the men stood up and said, " 'I am a very foolish fond old man, fourscore and upward, not an hour more or less, and, to deal plainly, I fear I am not in my perfect mind.' "

"I'll say you're not in perfect mind," his friend chided. "You've got it all wrong."

"Oh, you think you can do better?"

"Listen to this."

His voice faded as Rune and the minister continued down the corridor.

"How long was Grandfather here?" Rune asked.

"Only four, five weeks. He needed a place to stay until he found an apartment. A friend sent him here."

"Raoul Elliott?" Rune's heart thudded harder.

"Yes. You know Mr. Elliott?"

"We've met once."

So, Elliott had been confused. He hadn't sent Mr. Kelly to the Florence Hotel but here—to the church. Maybe Mr. Kelly was staying in the Florence when he visited the screenwriter and the poor man's mind just confused them.

"Wonderful man," the priest continued. "Oh, he's been very generous to us here at the church. And not only materially . . . He served on our board too. Until he got sick. A shame what's happened to him, isn't it? That Alzheimer's." The minister shook his head then continued. "But we have so few rooms, Robert didn't want to monopolize one—he wanted to make it available for somebody less fortunate. So he moved into the Hotel Florence for a while. He left the suitcase here, said he'd pick it up when he moved into a safer place. He was worried about break-ins. He said the bag was too important to risk getting stolen."

Rune nodded nonchalantly. Thinking: *One million dollars.*

She followed him to a storage room. The minister

unlocked the door with keys on a janitor's self-winding coil. Rune asked, "Did Grandfather spend much time in the church itself?"

The minister disappeared into the storage room. Rune heard the sound of boxes sliding along the floor. He called, "No. Not much."

"How about the grounds? The cemetery? Did he spend much time there?"

"The cemetery? I don't know. He might have."

Rune was thinking of the scene in *Manhattan Is My Beat* where the cop, his life ruined, was lying in his prison cell, dreaming about reclaiming his stolen million dollars, buried in a cemetery. She remembered the close-up of the actor's eyes as he wakened and realized that it had just been a dream—the blackness of the dirt he'd been digging up with his fingers becoming the shadows of the bars across his hands as he woke.

The minister emerged with a suitcase. He set it on the floor. "Here you go."

Rune asked. "You want me to sign a receipt or anything?"

"I don't think that'll be necessary, no."

Rune picked it up. It was as heavy as an old leather suitcase containing a million dollars ought to be. She listed against the weight. The minister smiled and took the case from her. He lifted it easily and motioned her toward the side door. She walked ahead of him.

He said, "Your grandfather told me to be careful with this. He said it had his whole life in it."

Rune glanced at the suitcase. Her palms were moist. "Funny what people consider their whole life, isn't it?"

"I feel sorry for people who can carry their homes around with them. That's one of the reasons the church has this residence home. You really feel God at work here."

They walked to his small office. He bent over the

cluttered desk and sorted through a thick stack of envelopes. He said. "I wished Robert had stayed longer. I liked him a lot. But then, he was independent. He wanted to live on his own."

Rune decided that she was going to give the church some money. Fifty thousand, she decided. Then, on a whim, upped the ante to a hundred Gs.

He handed her a thick envelope addressed to "Mr. Bobby Kelly."

"Oh, I forgot to mention . . . this came for him care of the church a day or so ago. Before I got around to forwarding it, I heard that he'd been killed."

Rune stuffed it under her arm.

Outside, he set the suitcase on the sidewalk for her. "Again, my sympathies to your family. If there's anything I can do for you, please call me."

"Thank you, Reverend," she said. Thinking: You just earned yourself two hundred thousand.

Little Red Hen . . .

Rune picked up the suitcase, walked to the car.

Richard eyed the bag curiously. She handed it to him, then patted the hood of his Dodge. He lifted the bag and rested it on the car. They were on a quiet side street but heavy traffic swept past at the corner. Superstitiously they both refused to look at the scuffed leather bag. They gazed at the single-story shops—a rug dealer, a hardware store, a pizza place, a deli. The trees. The traffic. The sky.

Neither touched the suitcase, neither said anything.

Like knights who think they've found the Grail and aren't sure they want to.

Because it would mean the end of their quest.

The end of the story. Time to close the book, to go to bed and wake up for work the next morning.

Richard broke the silence. "I didn't even think there'd *be* a suitcase."

Rune stared at the patterns of the stains on the

leather. The elastic bands from a dozen old airline claim checks looped through the handles. "I had some moments myself," she admitted. She touched the latches. Then stepped back. "I can't do it."

Richard took over. "It's probably locked." He pressed the buttons. They clicked open.

"Wheel . . . of . . . Fortune," Rune said.

Richard lifted the lid.

Magazines.

The Holy Grail was magazines and newspapers.

All from the 1940s. *Time, Newsweek, Collier's*. Rune grabbed several, shuffled through them. No bills fluttered out.

"A million ain't going to be hidden inside of *Time,*" Richard pointed out.

"His whole life?" Rune whispered. "Mr. Kelly told the minister his whole life was in here." She dug to the bottom. "Maybe he put the money into shares of Standard Oil or something. Maybe there's a stock certificate."

But, no, all the suitcase contained was newspapers and magazines.

When she'd gone over every inch of it, pulled up the cloth lining, felt along the moldy seams, her shoulders slumped and she shook her head. "Why?" she mused. "What'd he keep these for?"

Richard was flipping through several of them. He was frowning. "Weird. They're all from about the same time. June 1947."

The laughter startled her, it was so abrupt. She looked at Richard, who was shaking his head.

"What?"

He couldn't stop laughing.

"What is it?"

Finally he caught his breath. His eyes were squinting as he read a thumbed-down page. "Oh, Rune . . . Oh, no . . ."

She grabbed the magazine. An article was circled in blue ink. She read the paragraph Richard pointed at.

> Excellent in his role is young Robert Kelly, hailing from the Midwest, who had no intention of acting in films until director Hal Reinhart spotted him in a crowd and offered him a part. Playing Dana Mitchell's younger brother, who tries unsuccessfully to talk the tormented cop into turning in the ill-gotten loot, Kelly displays striking talent for a man whose only experience onstage has been a handful of USO shows during the War. Moviegoers will be watching this young man carefully to see if he will be the next member of the great Hollywood dream: the unknown catapulted to stardom.

They looked through the rest of the magazines. In each one, *Manhattan Is My Beat* was reviewed and, in each, Robert Kelly was mentioned at least several times. Most gave him kind reviews and forecast a long career for him.

Rune, too, laughed. She closed the suitcase and leaned against the car. "So *that's* what he meant by his whole life. He told me the movie was the high point of his life. He must never have gotten any other parts."

Stuffed in one of the magazines was a copy of a letter written to Mr. Kelly from the Screen Actors Guild. It was dated five years before.

She read it out loud. " 'Dear Mr. Kelly: Thank you for your letter of last month. As a contract player, you would indeed be entitled to residual payments for your performance in the film *Manhattan Is My Beat*. However, we understand from the studio, which is the current owner of the copyright to the film, that there are no plans for its release on videotape at this time. If and when the film is released, you will be entitled to your residuals as per the contract.' "

Rune put the letter back. "When he told me he was going to be rich—when his ship came in—*that's* what he meant. It had nothing to do with the bank robbery money."

"Poor guy," Richard said. "He'd probably be getting a check for a couple hundred bucks." He looked up and pointed behind her. "Look."

The sign on the dormitory read ST. XAVIER'S HOME FOR ACTORS AND ACTRESSES. "That's what he was doing here. It had nothing to do with the money. Kelly just needed a place to stay."

Richard pitched the suitcase into the backseat. "What do you want to do with them?"

She shrugged. "I'll give them to Amanda. I think they'd mean something to her. I'll make a copy of the best review for me. Put it up on my wall."

They climbed into the car. Richard said, "It would have corrupted you, you know."

"What?"

"The money. Just like the cop in *Manhattan Is My Beat*. You know the expression, 'Power tends to corrupt, absolute power corrupts absolutely'?"

Of *course* I've never heard of it, she thought. But told him, "Oh, sure. Wasn't that another one of Stallone's?"

He looked at her blankly for a moment then said, "Well, translated to capitalistic terms, the same truth holds. The absoluteness of that much money would have affected your core values."

Mr. Weird was back—though this time in Gap camouflage.

Rune thought about it for a minute. "No way. Aladdin didn't get corrupted."

"The guy with the lamp? You trying to make a rational argument by citing a fairy tale?"

She said, "Yeah, I am."

"Well, what about Aladdin?"

"He wished for wealth and a beautiful princess to be his bride, and the genie gave him all that. But people don't know the end of the story. Eventually he became the sultan's heir and finally got to be sultan himself."

"And it was Watergate. He got turned into a camel."

"Nope. He was a popular and fair leader. Oh, and radically rich."

"So fairy tales may not *always* have happy endings," he said like a professor, "but sometimes they do."

"Just like life."

Richard seemed to be trying to think about arguing but couldn't come up with anything. He shrugged. "Just like life," he conceded.

As they drove through the streets of Brooklyn, Rune slouched in the seat, put her feet on the dash. "So that's why he rented the film so often. It was his big moment of glory."

"That's pretty bizarre," Richard said.

"I don't think so," she told him. "A lot of people don't even have a big moment. And if they do, it probably doesn't get put out on video. I'll tell you—if *I* got a part in a movie, I'd dupe a freeze-frame of me and put it up on my wall."

He punched her playfully on the arm.

"What?"

"Well, you saw the film, what, ten times? Didn't you see his name on the credits?"

"He had just a bit part. He wasn't in the above-the-title credits."

"The what?"

"That's what they call the opening credits. And the copy we watched was the bootleg. I didn't bother to copy the cast credits at the end when I made it."

"Speaking of names, are you ever going to tell me your real name?"

"Ludmilla."

"You're kidding."

Rune didn't say anything.

"You *are* kidding," he said warily.

"I'm just trying to think up a good name for somebody who'd do window displays in SoHo. I think Yvonne would be good. What do you think?"

"It's as good as anything."

She looked at the bulky envelope the minister had given her. The return address was the Bon Aire Nursing Home in Berkeley Heights, New Jersey.

"What's that?"

"Something Mr. Elliott sent to Mr. Kelly at the church."

She opened the envelope. Inside was a letter taped to another thick envelope, on which was printed in old, uneven type: *Manhattan Is My Beat,* Draft Script, 5/6/46.

"Oh, look. A souvenir!"

Rune read the letter out loud. " 'Dear Mr. Kelly. You don't remember me, I'm sure. I'm the nurse on the floor where Mr. Raoul Elliott's room is. He asked me to write to you and asked if you could forward the package I'm enclosing here to the young girl who came to visit him the other day. He was a little confused as to who she was—maybe she is your daughter or probably your granddaughter—but if you could forward it, we'd be most appreciative.

" 'Mr. Elliot has mentioned several times how nice it was for her to come visit and talk about movies, and I can tell you her visit had a very good effect on him. He put the flower she brought him by his bedside and a couple times he even remembered who gave it to him, which is pretty good for him. Yesterday he got this from his storage locker and asked me to send it to her. Thank her for making him happy. All best wishes, Joan Gilford, R.N.' "

Richard, driving through commercial Brooklyn, said, "What a great old guy. That was sweet."

Rune said, "I think I'm going to cry."

She tore open the envelope.

Richard stopped for a red light. "You know, maybe you can sell it. I heard that an original draft of somebody's play—Noël Coward, I think—went for four or five thousand at Sotheby's. What do you think this one'd be worth?"

The light changed and the car pulled forward. Rune didn't answer right away but after a moment said, "So far it's up to two hundred and thirty thousand."

"What?" he asked, smiling uncertainly.

"And counting."

Richard glanced over at Rune then skidded the car to a stop.

In Rune's lap were bundles of money. Stacks of wrapped bills. They were larger than modern Federal Reserve notes. The ink was darker, the seals on the front were in midnight-blue ink. The paper wrappers around the stacks were stenciled with *$10,000* in a scripty old-time typeface. Also printed on them was *Union Bank of New York.*

"Thirty-three, thirty-four . . . Let's see. Thirty-eight. Times ten thousand is three hundred and eighty thousand dollars. Is that right? I'm *so* bad with math."

"Christ," Richard whispered.

Cars honked behind them. He glanced in the rear-view mirror, then pulled to the curb, parked in front of a Carvel ice cream store.

"I don't understand . . . what . . . ?"

Rune didn't answer. She ran her hand over the money, replaying the great scene in *Manhattan Is My Beat* where Dana Mitchell is inside the bank and opens the suitcase of money—the camera cutting between his face and the stacks of bills, which had been lit to glow like a hoard of jewels.

"Raoul Elliott," she answered. "When he was researching the film he must have found where the loot was hidden. Maybe it *was* buried there. . . ." She nodded back toward the church. "So he donated a bunch back to the church and they built the home for actors. The minister said he'd been very generous to them. Raoul kept the rest and retired."

Two tough-looking kids in T-shirts and jeans walked by and glanced in the car. Richard looked at them then reached over Rune, locked the door, rolled up the windows.

"Hey," she protested, "what're you doing? It's hot out."

"You're in the middle of Brooklyn with four hundred thousand dollars in your lap and you're just going to sit there?"

"No, as a matter of fact"—she nodded toward the Carvel store—"I was going to get an ice cream cone. You want one?"

Richard sighed. "How 'bout if we get a safe deposit box?"

"But we're right here."

"A bank first?" he asked. "Please?"

She ran her hand over the money again. Picked up one bundle. It was heavy. "After, can we get an ice cream?"

"Tons of ice cream. Sprinkles too, you want."

"Yeah, I want."

He started the car. Rune leaned back in the seat. She was laughing. Looking at him, coy and sly.

He said, "You're looking full of the devil. What's so funny?"

"You know the story of the Little Red Hen?"

"No, I don't. How 'bout if you tell it to me?"

Richard turned the old car onto the Brooklyn Bridge and pointed the hood toward the turrets and battlements of Manhattan, fiery in the afternoon sun. Rune said, "It goes like this . . ."